NONE

SO

BLIND

Other Books in the Series

Do or Die
Once Upon a Time
Mist Walker
Fifth Son
Honour Among Men
Dream Chasers
This Thing of Darkness
Beautiful Lie the Dead
The Whisper of Legends

BARBARA FRADKIN

NONE SO BLIND

AN INSPECTOR GREEN MYSTERY

DUNDURN
TORONTO

Editor: Dominic Farrell
Design: Jennifer Gallinger
Cover image: © bizoo_n/iStock
Cover design by Jesse Hooper
Printer: Webcom

Library and Archives Canada Cataloguing in Publication

Fradkin, Barbara Fraser, 1947-, author
        None so blind / Barbara Fradkin.

(An Inspector Green mystery)
Issued in print and electronic formats.
ISBN 978-1-4597-2140-1 (pbk.).--ISBN 978-1-4597-2141-8 (pdf).--
ISBN 978-1-4597-2142-5 (epub)

I. Title. II. Series: Fradkin, Barbara Fraser, 1947- . Inspector Green mystery.

PS8561.R233N65 2014   C813'.6   C2013-908370-7   C2013-908371-5

1   2   3   4   5   18   ·17   16   15   14

We acknowledge the support of the Canada Council for the Arts and the Ontario Arts Council for our publishing program. We also acknowledge the financial support of the Government of Canada through the Canada Book Fund and Livres Canada Books, and the Government of Ontario through the Ontario Book Publishing Tax Credit and the Ontario Media Development Corporation.

Care has been taken to trace the ownership of copyright material used in this book. The author and the publisher welcome any information enabling them to rectify any references or credits in subsequent editions.

                                                                J. Kirk Howard, President

Printed and bound in Canada.

Visit us at
Dundurn.com | @dundurnpress | Facebook.com/dundurnpress | Pinterest.com/dundurnpress

Dundurn
3 Church Street, Suite 500
Toronto, Ontario, Canada
M5E 1M2

CHAPTER ONE

The letter lay in the middle of his new desk amid the jumble of the day's mail. It had no return address but Inspector Michael Green recognized the handwriting right away. Jagged and harsh, as if every pen stroke were the thrust of a sword. The address on the envelope was always the same:

Michael Green
474 Elgin St.
Ottawa, Ontario
K2P 2J6

No mention of Green's rank or the Ottawa Police Service headquartered at that address. At first, Green had assumed the man was hoping the letters would slip past the prison's Visits and Correspondence staff unnoticed, but over the years he'd come to see the exclusion of his rank as a subtle sign of contempt. Green had no doubt the man had kept scrupulous track of his progress through the ranks and knew every major investigation he'd headed up in the past twenty years.

Green's gut tightened as the memories flooded back. He'd hoped the letter campaign was over. After a silence of more than two years, he'd thought the man had finally capitulated and moved on. Despite his facility with computers, he'd always written the letters by hand, as if the vitriol contained in them demanded a more intimate touch.

At first Green had read them carefully, hoping for a change of heart, a confession, or even a reluctant acceptance of some sort, but none materialized. In the early years, Green had even phoned the prison psychiatrist and the chaplain, concerned for the man's relentless despair, but to no avail. Recently, he'd just skimmed the letters and added them to the pile in the man's file.

He picked up the cheap white business envelope warily. Usually the letters were stuffed with pages of meticulous counter-argument refuting the Crown's case against him. But this time the envelope was surprisingly thin. One sheet at most. A change in tactics, perhaps? Or was he finally running out of words?

Green debated not opening it this time, but in the end, curiosity, along with a perverse sense of kinship he had developed with the man over the years, won out. He slid his finger under the tightly glued flap, slipped out a single sheet of white paper and unfolded it.

Two words, printed in large block letters — once again a departure for the man who usually wrote with an elaborate cursive hand — followed by three exclamation points and underlined three times. Precision in all things, even now.

HE WINS!!!

Green knew immediately who "he" was. No need for explanation or context, only the puzzling question of how? And why now? The knot in his stomach tightened. Despite his best efforts, the man had gotten to him again. In all his twenty years of homicide investigations, no killer had haunted him more than this one. Green had two untenable choices — to dismiss the letter as just one more taunt from a damaged, embittered man ...

Or to find out what he meant.

Green excavated his calendar from the clutter on his desk. It was only mid-morning, but he had his new office to sort out and a dreary budget report to draft. Worse, his computer calendar was blinking a reminder from his brand new boss at CID, Superintendent Inge Neufeld, who wanted a thorough briefing on all personnel, policies, and procedures under her command. The three dreaded p's of his administrative duties.

Green had broken out the champagne a year earlier when his former boss, Barbara Devine, had finally snagged her much coveted transfer to East Division, the next rung on her ladder toward chiefdom. Green had even enjoyed the revolving series of acting superintendents who replaced her, for none had been around long enough to meddle. Despite Inge Neufeld's permanent status, Green had expected her to be no different, at least in the short term. A Calgary native who had climbed the ranks, first in the Calgary Police Service and later in the Manitoba RCMP, Neufeld was an outsider with no knowledge of Ottawa, its unique police culture, or the many competing law enforcement players in the National Capital Region. Green had hoped that learning curve would keep her out of his hair for a while.

But after less than a week on the job, Inge Neufeld was already meddling, and with this request, she was signalling her intention to dot every *i* and cross every *t*. "Just what I need," Green grumbled as he hunted for a spare half hour in which to meet with her.

He'd hoped to make an early getaway that day. Fresh snow had been falling since early morning and at least ten more centimetres were forecast before the January storm finally blew east toward the Maritimes. By rush hour, traffic would be snarled in snowdrifts, and after a day cooped up with their daughter, his wife's patience would be fraying. Aviva was tiny for five months, but she already had the willpower of an Olympian and the lungs of an opera star. Sharon could barely take her eye off her without the little girl finding some trouble, and at forty-one, Sharon was finding it hard to keep up. Many of the other domestic chores, including cooking, were left to Green's dubious skills, and if he was late getting home, the entire household might starve.

Irritated, Green pencilled in "super" in his late afternoon slot. Then he scribbled *James Rosten file* on a yellow Post-it Note, slapped it on the letter, and tossed it in his outbox. At that moment, a tall, muscular figure filled his doorway. Staff Sergeant Brian Sullivan tapped on the doorframe and entered without waiting for an answer. There was no trace of a smile on his broad, freckled face.

"Got a minute?"

Green was about to mutter about Neufeld but Sullivan's expression stopped him. The two men had been friends for twenty-five years and Green knew every worry line on his face. There was a new one he didn't recognize. Sullivan was the best NCO he'd ever worked with, head of the Major Crimes Squad, and used to handling gang executions and grisly domestic murders with equal calm. If Sullivan was worried, it had to be something more personal.

Sullivan had recently shed fifty pounds and was in training for next year's marathon, but less than eighteen months ago the job had nearly killed him. Praying it wasn't a new crisis with his health, Green gestured him inside. Sullivan paused and cast a dubious eye around the room. After twenty years as a detective and six as an inspector, Green had finally graduated to an office larger than a utility closet, with enough space for more than one guest at a time. At the moment, however, every surface was buried under boxes, binders, and books. Beneath the chaos, it was still a windowless cube painted dreary institutional beige. "Think of it as taupe," Sharon had said, but taupe lent it an elegance it did not deserve. At least beige was a kinder word than some that came to mind.

Sullivan shifted a box of procedure manuals to the floor and pulled the chair close.

"What's up?" Green asked.

Sullivan studied the desk, as if searching for a way to begin. His eyes lit on the letter in Green's outbox and his brows arched. "Rosten?"

Green nodded. "I was hoping I'd heard the last of him."

"What does he say?"

"A cryptic riddle. *He wins.* I assume I'm supposed to ask who and why. His new strategy to draw me out."

Sullivan frowned. "Hmm," was all he said.

"I know who, of course. Rosten's been fixated on the stepfather all along."

Sullivan hadn't been Green's partner during the original case, but in the years since, he had listened to Green relive it many times. He knew what the case had cost him in terms of sleepless nights and self-doubt. "The investigation was rock solid. You know that, Mike. The guy's just slinging mud every which way, hoping some of it will stick anywhere but him."

"But it's just such an *idée fixe*. That's what bothers me. Even his counsellors and the chaplain could never shake it. Reverend Goodfellow once told me he thought Rosten actually believed it."

Green thought back over the Jackie Carmichael case. It had begun as a Missing Persons involving a Carleton University student, his first real assignment as a newly minted junior detective barely out of training camp. For a week he had probed doggedly into her life, interviewing family, friends, and witnesses, including Rosten, before her half-buried body was discovered in a remote forest outside the city.

The discovery had been heartbreaking. During that first week, Green had formed bonds with her family and suspicions as to her killer, and so when the Ontario Provincial Police parachuted a team of investigators in from Toronto to take over the case, those close to her continued to seek him out to share their raw pain and outrage. The horror of the case haunted his nights. Young, idealistic, and impassioned, he had ignored every order and article of police protocol to continue working on the case.

In the years since, as the letters from Rosten kept coming, he'd asked himself a thousand times whether that horror had coloured his judgment. Made him see only what he wanted to see.

"Cops and chaplains aren't mind readers, Mike," Sullivan said, "not even that old fox Archie Goodfellow. We can't see inside a guy's head. A really smart psychopath can fool even the best of us, and Rosten was smart. He's been messing with your head for years."

Green fished the letter out of his outbox and handed it across the desk. "So this is his next game?"

Sullivan studied the page. Slowly he shook his head. "More like a commentary. That's what I came to tell you. Just heard on the locker-room grapevine that the stepfather died last week."

Green's eyes widened. "Murdered?"

Sullivan shook his head. "Heart attack shovelling snow. At least that was the ER doc's diagnosis."

"Any chance it was not?"

Sullivan's lips twitched into a smile. "You think James Rosten reached out from his prison cell and cast some kind of voodoo spell?"

Green didn't laugh. He retrieved the note and studied the words. "So that's what Rosten thinks? Now that Lucas Carmichael is dead, he will never be brought to justice?"

Sullivan nodded. "And James Rosten will never be cleared."

Green arrived at the Carmichael home almost half an hour late. Traffic on the eastbound Queensway had been excruciatingly slow. Yesterday's snowfall had been ploughed from the roads, but it lingered in slushy ridges along the edges, splattering the cars and slicking the roads. Rush-hour traffic out to the sprawling suburb of Orleans was bad in the best weather, but with slippery roads and poor visibility added to the mix, the freeway became immobilized.

The village of Navan was tucked into the middle of dairy-farm country south of Orleans. When Green had last visited, it still had much of its original flavour as a trading hub for farm produce and supplies, but now it was just the rural fringe of sprawling suburbia. Century-old farm houses and tiny wartime bungalows like the Carmichael's sat side by side with modern brick super-houses. Green barely recognized the place.

This was a courtesy call. Green knew he owed it to Marilyn Carmichael as well as to her remaining children, but he was dreading it. In his years as a Major Crimes investigator, he had learned to cope with the callous brutality of killers and the tragedy of lost lives, but the anguish of the survivors still haunted him, especially when the loss of an offspring was involved.

When he first met Marilyn Carmichael, she'd been like a tiger possessed, eyes flaming and teeth bared as she whipped the investigators on, insisting first that her missing daughter was alive but in danger, and later that her death must not go unanswered. It was only once the trial began, and the relentless spotlight of the media and police shone full-strength on her family and on her daughter's last hours, that she began to fold in on herself, rebuffing sympathy and shrivelling in defeat.

In the years since, Green had come to understand the pattern. Survivors needed a reason to go on, a cause to embrace, a purpose for their unbearable loss. Sometimes they founded campaigns, set up scholarships, or embarked on pilgrimages of memory. Almost always they threw themselves into the case, becoming the most relentless of investigators and prosecutors. As Jackie's case stretched into months, Green had kept in constant communication with Marilyn, updating, explaining, reassuring, and often just listening. He had watched helplessly as her passion slowly gave way to the empty ache of loss.

The past ten years had slipped by without contact, however, and now he hardly recognized her when she opened the door. Her once glossy auburn hair was completely white, plastered thin and lifeless against her scalp. Her eyes were bruised with grief, and her petite frame was lost inside a bulky knit sweater. He knew she wasn't yet sixty-five, but she looked ninety. Her eyes lit at the sight of him, however, and for an astonished moment he thought she was going to give him a hug.

Instead, she ducked her head, flustered, and backed away to lead him inside. "Any trouble remembering where the house was?"

He wasn't about to tell her of his battles with the Queensway or his GPS, which had been adamant that her little backcountry road was on the opposite side of the village.

"I had a good map," he said.

She shot him a very small smile. "You'd need one. Google and GPS don't have any idea. That's actually a blessing when you're trying to avoid people."

Green knew the family had considered selling the house shortly after the murder, uncertain they'd be able to live in the house that still echoed with their daughter's carefree chatter. Where neighbours gossiped behind half-drawn curtains and shook their heads in pity. But in the end, the memories themselves bound them to it. This remote wartime bungalow, tiny and squat behind its screen of overgrown spruce, was still suffused with the scents and sounds of their girl.

"Everything's a bit worn out, but then so are we." Marilyn had stopped in the centre of the dark living room as if embarrassed. Heavy drapes hung over the bay window and an assortment of brocade chairs and loveseats were crammed into the boxy space. Green remembered the chairs from twenty years ago, as if time had stopped for the Carmichaels at that time.

Marilyn gestured to one of them. "I'll make tea. I thought on a day like this, you'd appreciate the warmth. I even remember you take it with lemon."

Despite her forty years in Canada, her speech still retained the lilt of Yorkshire, and at first she'd insisted that any tea worth drinking needed two tablespoons of milk in the bottom of the cup. She had even tried to teach him and his partner how to make a proper pot. A woman who relied on ritual and bustle to keep the waves of panic at bay.

Recognizing this, Green accepted and followed her toward the kitchen. The walls were lined with her water-colour paintings — sunny flowers, lacy pines, and rocky bluffs — now sapped of life in the dingy hall light. One, depicting the ruins of an old limestone farmhouse long reclaimed by purple wildflowers, had once hung with pride over the fireplace but was now relegated to the darkest corner. *A metaphor for her life*, he thought.

The kitchen, too, was narrower and shabbier than he remembered, the once-white sink mottled with stains. "I'm sorry about Lucas, Marilyn," he ventured. "Are the kids home?"

Her lips tightened. "They're coming. That's why we're holding off on the memorial service until next month. So Gordon can arrange to get here from France, and Julia ..."

Her hesitation matched his own. "How is Julia?"

Marilyn busied herself spooning loose tea into a cracked china teapot covered in roses. "She has a new job in Costa Rica now. She's not one to stay in touch, you know, but I think she's finally doing okay."

"Will she come home too?"

"I don't know. It was harder on her, you know, losing her younger sister, and she never really — well, she wasn't that fond of Luke, to be honest."

Green refrained from comment. "Not fond" was a massive understatement. Julia had been moody and changeable when her sister died, and although she accused everyone close to her of failing Jackie in some way, she was especially hard on Lucas. Before Jackie's body was found, Julia had been convinced she'd run away to escape Luke and his drinking, and thus put herself in harm's way. She had barely spoken to him for over a year, and had moved out to sleep on a friend's basement couch throughout the trial. Marilyn had always made excuses for her, but Green had wanted to strangle the girl, for it was as if Marilyn had lost two daughters at once. Now, once again, as a woman in her forties, the daughter was putting her own needs first.

Marilyn handed him a plate of shortbread. Her eyes locked his in a silent warning: *Don't say a word.*

He didn't. She smiled. "You haven't changed a bit. You still don't look a day over thirty."

When Green was a rookie officer, he had regarded his freckles, sandy hair, and slight build as a hindrance, but over the years he'd learned to appreciate the value of being nondescript. And underestimated. Even now, only a few wisps of silver at his temples hinted at his age. "Work's given me a few grey hairs."

"So you're an inspector now. La-dee-dah."

He laughed. "All I had to do was live long enough."

"Oh, I doubt that. Rosten may have been your start, but you've done well for yourself since. Do you still enjoy it?"

"Not the paperwork or the office politics, but ..." He searched for words to describe what he enjoyed about his job and was surprised when none came to mind. He remembered himself as Marilyn had known him; not as a senior mandarin, drawing up budgets and shuffling personnel around, but down in the muck of the streets, railing simultaneously against injustice and villainy and against the strictures and bureaucracy of his job.

"But you like being the boss?" she asked, with a knowing twinkle in her eye.

He grinned. "It comes in handy. But I miss the real policing."

The kettle whistled. As she poured water into the teapot, she nodded to his left hand. "You've a new woman in your life, I see."

"I do. And two more children, plus a dog. You wouldn't recognize me."

She laughed, but her joy was fleeting. The remark had reminded them both of her own loss. She handed him his tea and led the way to the living room.

"In a way, I suppose he's at peace now," she said, choosing a hard-backed chair facing the window. "He never was during his life. Not for the past twenty years."

As he searched in vain for a worthy platitude, she peered at him through the gloom. After a pause, she rose to draw the drapes back a few inches, allowing bleached winter sun to leak into the room. She stood squinting out at the snow, her face hidden.

"We tried to move on, you know. I was never a quitter and I know Jackie would not have wanted that. Of course, at first there was all that horrid suspicion, but even after Rosten's conviction, there were those who still thought ... Luke never really escaped the cloud, did he? And that dreadful man himself, throwing up every roadblock, every argument. Even warning me to keep a watch out for Julia with Luke." She broke off. Took a deep breath. Shook her head sharply and turned back to him.

"I'm sorry, Mike. It's been difficult watching Luke fade away over all these years. At first he tried to keep working at the shop, but once they started cutting back his hours ... the shop was all he had to hold on to, really. Jacqueline had been his favourite. Well, she would be, wouldn't she? She was a sunny girl, never difficult like Julia. Never gave us a moment's worry. But it's no use dwelling on that. It was nice of you to drop by, Mike. Not too many people have. I guess they find it awkward, and to be honest, we've kept to ourselves. Easier that way. Normal chit-chat is such a struggle."

She returned to her chair and picked up her cup. "Will you be coming to the memorial?"

He hadn't intended to. He hadn't meant to re-enter this family's life after all these years. But he found himself nodding.

CHAPTER TWO

Green had hoped to be inconspicuous when he slipped into the cramped interior of the church and perched on an unforgiving wooden pew at the back. Outside, the tiny church had a quaint neo-Gothic charm, with a classic Ottawa Valley limestone façade and an elaborate bell tower that soared into the pallid sky. Inside, he felt trapped between stained-glass portraits of Mary at the rear and Jesus's Last Supper directly ahead. He could almost feel their steely stares.

He felt like an imposter. Up at the front, a handful of mourners were scattered across the pews, heads bent together in whispers. Green couldn't put names to most of them but assumed they were friends and neighbours, for he recalled that Lucas had no family and Marilyn had none on this side of the ocean. The pulpit was as yet unoccupied, but an organist sat at the side playing doleful hymns.

Green recognized Marilyn's bowed white head in the front pew. She was deep in whispered conversation with a thin man wearing a fedora and long purple scarf. Green has last seen Gordon Carmichael as a pudgy, downy-cheeked student, heading off to Paris ostensibly to study music, but really to put as many miles as possible between himself and the pain at home. Paris had clearly left its bohemian mark. In profile he resembled a large lizard, with bulbous eyes and a chin that disappeared behind the folds of the scarf. Deep in conversation, neither he nor his mother noticed Green's arrival.

The same could not be said for the woman on the other side of Marilyn. She was lounging in the pew, her gaze taking in the room. When it fell on Green, her face brightened. She reached his side in half a dozen stiletto strides.

"I was wondering if you'd come."

The years had taken away the lush schoolgirl curves, but Julia Carmichael was still an attractive woman — platinum blonde now with sparkling blue eyes and a deep golden tan. Her smile was teasing, but he was relieved to note it no longer stirred him.

"Hello, Julia. I'm sorry for your loss."

Her smiled faded and she grimaced. "I'm not."

"I suppose not. It's been a long time since you saw him."

"Twenty years." She sat down beside him and ran a finger over the polished wood. "Life's treated you well. New wife, I hear. Congratulations."

"Thanks. I hope life has treated you well too." He knew it sounded stiff. He didn't look at her, pretending instead to study the few incoming guests. "I'm glad you came, like me, for your mother's sake."

A small frown pinched her brow. "Luke was a useless, self-pitying drunk, but what I thought of him isn't important. Mum is one of those 'for better or for worse' types, and she would never hear a word against him."

"She and Luke have been through a lot. You all have. She'll need your support."

"Oh, I wouldn't worry." She looked away, her tone hardening. "She'll just erect another shrine, dust off her British stoicism, and carry on."

Still the same old changeable Julia, he thought, as he searched for a safe topic of conversation. When he was a young detective, barely older than her, she seemed to enjoy confounding him. Playful and passionate, but as unpredictable as a summer storm.

But just as abruptly as the storm clouds blew in, they abated. She sighed and leaned in toward him. "I'm sorry. Being back here after all this time has brought out the bitch in me. I thought I'd conquered her but sometimes she storms the barricades. All this gives me the willies...." She gestured to the crucifix and the stained-glass windows. "Churches, funerals, meaningless religious babble. I guess I'm just worrying about Mum. I have no idea what she's going to do now that she has no ..."

She looked up as a hush settled on the church. At the front, the minister had entered and was speaking to Marilyn with head bent and hands clasped piously over hers. "No one to fuss over but herself," she finished.

Green eyed her thoughtfully. Perhaps she'd matured in the last twenty years after all. "Will you be staying? At least for a while?"

"I can't be away from my job that long. I just started a new one as a hostess at a resort, and this is the busy

21

season. But I've invited Mum to come visit me in Costa Rica when she's up to it." She cast him a playful smile. "You should come down too. Bring your wife and family."

The organ pounded out some final chords and silence descended on the small crowd that barely filled the first three rows. The minister took his place at the pulpit and Green steeled himself for clichés of death and resurrection.

"Here we go," Julia muttered, putting words to his thoughts. Her brusque manner returned and she shifted down the bench, but made no move to return to her mother's side.

The minister, and the service, were mercifully brief. After the second hymn, played with gusto by the organ but sung by only a few straggling voices in the group, Marilyn rose to speak. She was dressed as Green had always remembered her, in the tailored navy suit that she'd worn every day at the trial. It hung around her frame now, faded and threadbare at the cuffs, and the chancel seemed to swallow her up as she stood on tiptoe to reach the mic.

She looked out over the scattering of upturned faces, squared her shoulders, and cast her voice out over the room as if it were filled with a thousand friends. "Thirty-five years ago last month," she began, "a stranger came by my house to pick up a load of laundry for his aunt. It was snowing like the Dickens and I offered him a cup of tea. I was fairly new to Canada back then and too naive to realize that a glass of whisky would have gone down better, but in any case, I had none on offer. He accepted with delight. I don't know what he thought. I must have been a sight, a single mum raising three small children in a basement flat you could barely swing a cat in, and I hadn't entertained a man in my house in years. My only common room was given over to laundry. Piles and piles of it, some wanting washing, some ironing, some mending. He had to move the ironing board just so he could sit down, and the whole place was as hot as a Turkish bath.

"But he stayed for three hours to help me fold sheets and feed the children. Porridge, if I recall. The next time he brought us all pizza and stayed for dinner; and when the spring came, he borrowed his aunt's car and took us all to a sugar bush in Quebec. That night, when he asked me to marry him, I never hesitated. I still wouldn't. He wasn't perfect — what man is? He had his moods and he wasn't much for talking, but I wish you could have known the man he used to be. Always ready with a hand to help out, a joke to make you smile, and a heart big enough to take in me and my children without a moment's pause. When my Jackie died — no, when *our* Jackie died — it ripped that heart right out of him."

Her voice quavered and she reached out to grip the edge of the podium. Even from the back of the hall, Green could see her limbs trembling. She wet her lips and plunged on. "We were all the family Luke had. His parents died when he was a teenager, so he came from Cape Breton to stay with his aunt. She was a spinster who did the right thing by him, but truth be told, she viewed him as unpaid help at best and a nuisance at worst.

"God must have seen the need we had for each other when he brought us together. Those joyful memories are all that sustained us during our more recent trials, and I draw some comfort from the fact that his passing was quick and painless for him, and that now, wherever their souls reside, he and Jackie are together."

Beside Green, Julia muttered. He shot her a quick glance, but her gaze was fixed on the ground. She did not look up when Marilyn walked over to the photo of Lucas, kissed her fingertips and brushed them over the glass.

"Good night, sweet Luke, and flights of angels sing thee to thy rest."

After the service, Green was hoping to pass on his condolences and slip away before the reception, pleading the demands of work. He waited dutifully as Marilyn made her way up the church aisle, stopping to smile her gratitude to people along the way. As soon as she spotted him, her smile vanished. She clutched at his hands like a survivor lost at sea.

"I need to talk to you."

"Why don't I phone you tomorrow?"

She shook her head and glanced at Julia, who was still standing beside him. Uncharacteristically, she raised her arms to hug him and pressed her lips to his ear. "Please, stay for the reception."

Reflexively, he held her for an instant, feeling her bird-like frame in his arms and her heart hammering against her chest. Catching Julia's raised eyebrow, he extricated himself gently and searched Marilyn's face. But it was a smiling mask again as she turned her attention to the next guest. Soon Green found himself alone in the church, watching as Julia and her mother filed out through the wooden doors.

Frustration battled curiosity as he walked outside. Fat, lazy snowflakes floated down, melting on the slick tarmac but already gathering in soggy piles along the verges where a scattering of cars was parked. At the station, he had a calendar packed with dreaded committee meetings, but the prospect of spending an hour making small talk with strangers in the church hall had even less allure. Resolutely, he turned to track down Marilyn, hoping she could find a moment for him now.

In the plain white hall behind the church, the small gathering hovered around a banquet table spread with sandwiches and squares. Urns of coffee and tea sat on a side table. Green's stomach contracted, for in his trek out to the country he had neglected to have lunch, but one glance at the small, crustless egg sandwiches dissuaded him.

He found Marilyn in the corner, talking intently with her children. Gordon was slouched against the wall, his fedora tilted and his eyebrow cocked with boredom, but Julia's arms were crossed in annoyance. Green strode up, catching Julia's impatient tone as he drew close.

"You should just bulldoze the whole place."

"But there are memories —"

"There are memories everywhere, Mum!"

"Marilyn —" Green began.

She turned. The exasperation in her eyes died instantly. "Oh good! You're still here! A lovely service, don't you think?" She linked her arm through his and led him out of earshot. "I know people feel awkward, but everyone's been so kind."

"Marilyn, is there something —?"

"He wrote to Julia."

Green stopped so abruptly that she stumbled. "Who?" Although he knew.

"That man. That horrid James Rosten!" Her eyes filled and her chin quivered. "He had the nerve to contact Julia. Not me, mind you, but poor Julia!"

"What did he say?"

"Some nonsense about how he knew the truth and he hoped she had some peace now."

Green's jaw tightened. Bastard! Rosten knew Julia was the vulnerable link in the family, and he'd gone straight for it. He glanced at Julia, who was pretending to talk to Gordon but was, in fact, watching their exchange obliquely. Wariness hooded her eyes.

"I'm sorry," he said. "How did she take it?"

"Oh, she didn't see it. Thank God! The letter came to the house and I intercepted it."

"When?"

"Yesterday." She hugged her thin arms to her chest. "He didn't waste any time, did he?"

"Have there been any other letters?"

"Not yet, but I'll keep a sharp eye out certainly. Not that he's likely to write me or Gordon; we're hardly his type."

"May I see the letter?"

She shook her head. "I burned it. I shouldn't have, I realize now, but I was so furious. Mike, he reached out from prison and came right into our home! I didn't know he even remembered where we live! We're unlisted now. For pity's sake, we've spent twenty years trying to escape the past and the press!"

He felt an angry knot in his chest. It had been bad enough when the man directed his obsession at Green, but if he was now turning his sights on the victim's family and on the surviving sister, he had gone way over the line. The letter should never have made it past prison security.

"I'll alert the prison, Marilyn. We'll stop him, I promise. It won't happen again."

Her pallid face tilted up, her eyes locked on his. "And if it does?"

"Then keep the letter and call me immediately. I'll lay charges."

But it damn well won't come to that, he was thinking as he calculated how long it would take to drive to the penitentiary and whether the snow would prevent his going that day.

Warkworth Penitentiary was a brutal grey scar seared into the gently rolling farmland of Northumberland County, about three hours' drive southwest of Ottawa along country highways slick with salt. Green arrived at noon, having been forced to delay his visit for almost a week, not only to untangle the red tape of the Correctional Service of Canada but also to convince his new boss it was part of his job. Managing Neufeld, he realized, was going to require even more finesse than previous bosses.

Although Green had had several discussions with security and medical staff at the penitentiary since Rosten was transferred there ten years earlier, he hadn't visited in years and was dismayed but not surprised by the tightened security. Warkworth had been conceived fifty years ago as a model of hope and rehabilitation, but its recent troubles with riots, lockdowns, and over-crowding reflected the harsher reality.

As he approached the first exterior gate, the looming twenty-foot perimeter fence with its barbed-wire cap was a stark reminder that, although this was a medium-security facility, it housed over six hundred violent criminals, 40 percent of them lifers. Despite the dire talk of stress among correctional officers, Green was relieved to find the guards at the gate cheerful and jocular as they waved him through. Outbuildings were scattered across sprawling lawns, and in the distance he glimpsed the grassy playgrounds and picnic areas designed to simulate normal family life.

Inside, it was still a place of steel, concrete, menace, and despair.

It took him nearly fifteen minutes to proceed through security, despite being allowed to bypass the straggling line of civilian visitors waiting to see their family and friends on the inside. Finally he was ushered into a small, windowless interview room.

In the week since Marilyn had told him of the letter, his anger had cooled to a slow simmer. The warden had expressed suitable outrage and had promised to investigate how a letter addressed to a victim's family could have slipped through their scrutiny. Likely a momentary lapse due to overcrowding and overwork.

While Green waited for James Rosten to be summoned from his cell, he wondered what to expect. He hadn't seen Rosten since his trial, but he knew he'd been severely injured in an assault by fellow inmates at Kingston Penitentiary ten years earlier. His face had been sliced and his spine damaged.

Green remembered him as a driven young man who'd fought for his freedom with every ounce of his considerable brains and energy. Yet, over the years, his letters had become increasingly bitter and desperate, no longer focused on freedom but on revenge. Twenty years of lost life, not to mention his injuries, had surely aged him. Green steeled himself for a shrivelled, hard shell of a man.

Despite that effort, he was not prepared when the automatic door glided open and James Rosten wheeled himself in. With slow, laborious turns he manoeuvred his wheelchair through the narrow space around the table and came to a final stop so close that his toes nearly touched Green's.

James Rosten was a study in grey. Grey hair, grey skin, grey lifeless eyes. His skin hung in crepe folds on his shrunken frame. A pale, glistening scar ran from his temple to his jaw, twisting his face into a parody of mirth. His hands were bony, his cheekbones sharp and angular, and his eyes now so deep-set they seemed to retreat inside his skull. Green searched them for a glimmer of the passion and fight he'd once displayed, but only defeat gazed back at him. Green felt the last vestiges of his anger slide away. He extended his hand across the corner of the table toward the man, whose hands were encased in fingerless gloves to provide better grip on the wheels.

Rosten, however, merely stared at his extended hand, resolutely still. "Can't say it's a pleasure, Inspector. What do you want?"

"How have you been, James?"

"Just hunky dory. I love it here, as well you know. So richly deserved."

In the silence, Green could hear the wheeze of Rosten's breath in his lungs. He relinquished his plans for subtlety. "James … You have to let it go. It's over. Your appeals are done; there is nothing further to be served by pointing fingers. It's time to think about what's next. For everyone, including you."

"Ah yes. The boundless, limitless possibilities of my future. Reinstatement at the university, reunion with my wife, a warm, fuzzy rapprochement with my kids. I'm a grandfather, by the way. Did you know that? Of course, I only learned that by reading the birth announcements online."

"Plenty of people have to start over."

"People who have paid their dues, who deserve what they got." He pressed his eyes shut. "Oh, fuck it. It doesn't matter. *I* don't matter. But at least now the family is safe from that monster. Julia is safe. Although I suppose …" He opened his eyes again and gave a twisted smile. "I keep forgetting she's over forty now. Hardly Lucas Carmichael's type. But does she have children?"

Green felt a chill. He had no intention of giving this man any new fuel to feed his fantasies. He had no idea whether Julia had ever married or had children, but it was safest to shake his head.

"Good. Gordon?"

"Neither Gordon nor Julia live in the country."

"How wise of them. But now they're safe." He shut his eyes again and drew in a weary breath. "Finally."

"Yes they are." Green leaned forward. "Time to let it go. Time to let *them* go."

Rosten kept his eyes shut. His frail body twitched. He breathed in. Out. Slowly he nodded. "You're right, time to let it all go. I've done what I could, to no avail, for myself or for them. I won't bother them anymore, if that's what you came about."

Green sensed a true change in the man. A final laying down of the sword he had brandished for so long. Once the battle barricades were gone, Green felt the pull of a question he had never dared broach before.

"James? Why are you so convinced it was Lucas Carmichael?"

Rosten's face grew rigid and his eyes flew open. Angry and accusatory, the James Rosten of old. "I sent you all those fucking letters! Didn't you read them?"

How should I answer that? Green thought. He had read them, at least at first, but had tried to dismiss them as self-serving rants. After all, he'd rarely met a con who didn't protest his innocence and blame even the most unlikely of suspects. Instead, he didn't answer, but merely waited.

Finally the belligerence in Rosten's face faded. He edged his chair even further forward, so that his knees touched Green's. He stared squarely into Green's eyes. "I have one big advantage over you; I know I didn't do it. So I looked around to see who could have. I remembered seeing a car like Lucas's near the cottage that day, and Julia's behaviour toward him got me thinking. This wasn't a random, serial killer–style attack by a stranger in the street. This person *knew* her. He knew she took my course, knew I was giving her private tutoring." He faltered only briefly over the phrase. "Maybe he'd even seen her in my car. This person had access to her papers, knew I had a cottage near Arnprior, and knew that dumping her body there would point suspicion toward me. So I asked myself, who would know all this? It's a classic stepfather scenario — man befriends single mother in order to have access to her children."

It was, of course, a scenario that the OPP detectives had investigated at the time, even after charging Rosten. "But Jackie was not a child. She was twenty years old, not the usual prey for a pedophile."

"But she had been a child when Carmichael came on the scene. You know yourself that abuse goes on for years in these cases. Maybe it had ended but she was threatening to blow the whistle on him."

Another theory they had all considered early in the investigation. Considered and rejected. Green thought back over the details. Julia had made some dark hints but balked at specifics, and Green had thought them more likely the product of Julia's fanciful imagination. Jackie had never exhibited any of the classic signs of an incest victim. No drug use or wild behaviour, no anxiety or depression, no hint of sexual problems. She had never breathed a word to teachers, counsellors, or friends. Everyone, including her boyfriend at the time, had described her as a happy, well-adjusted young woman.

"The facts simply didn't point that way, James," he said. "Even if you buy the idea that her body was dumped there to implicate you, it's still a leap to Lucas Carmichael. Would he even know you were tutoring her? Do twenty-year-old kids tell their parents everything that's going on in school?" *Certainly not mine*, he thought, but wisely kept his personal life to himself. "It's much more likely Jackie would tell a friend or her boyfriend. In fact, at one time I remember *he* was your chief suspect."

Rosten flicked his hand dismissively. "That was before I saw the hapless fellow on the stand and heard the whole of the Crown's case. Then I realized that although you were a tunnel-visioned, cocky young buck, you were right about one thing; this was a mature, cold-blooded set-up, not the work of a jilted college kid. The boyfriend would have panicked and botched it, at best tried to make it look like a serial killer copycat. Where would he have gotten the vehicle to transport her body? How would he have known, on the spur of the moment, where my cottage was, so that he could conveniently plant the body in the woods nearby? You saw Erik Lazlo during the trial. A penniless country boy savouring his first rush of big-city freedom. He was a silly, shallow boy, more enamoured with marijuana and music than with romantic commitment. He wasn't serious enough about her to carry out a crime of passion."

"But if he found out she was sleeping with you —"

Rosten rolled his eyes. "That tired old crap? If you had proof of that, you'd have trotted it out in the trial. I've admitted I tutored her. I gave her a lift to her residence one evening. Unwise, certainly, especially in light of how that hair on the upholstery crucified me, but hardly criminal."

"So you say. But Erik Lazlo may have thought —"

Rosten shook his head. "I didn't sense they had a grand passion. I've had that, Inspector, whether you believe me or not. With my ex-wife. I know the signs. Jackie and Erik had known each other a long time; they were friends long before they were lovers. Remember, he was Gordon's friend first; in fact he dated Julia too. Jackie was just the kid sister." He paused, caught up in the memories.

Green waited, filling the silence with his own memories of Erik Lazlo, a wiry, good-looking young man who shared Gordon's passion for dirt bikes, bush parties, and punk music, thrust by his parents into an engineering program for which he had no interest and even less talent. Certainly no match for the bright, ambitious Jackie. Beyond his looks, he could not have held her attention for long.

Rosten was right. Erik Lazlo was addicted to the next thrill. He liked fast music and faster bikes. He was not the type to brood or obsess about what had been lost.

Gradually Green became aware of Rosten's eyes on him. "You still believe I'm guilty, don't you?"

"What I believe doesn't matter. It's done. You've done your time —"

Rosten slammed the table. "It matters to me! You've built a nice career for yourself on the back of this case, but my life is ruined! Over! By God, at the end of it all, it would be nice to hear you admit you made a mistake."

Green pushed his chair back and started to edge around the wheelchair. "A word of advice …"

"From you? Hah!"

Green sat back down again. "Listen, you arrogant jackass, you still have a chance to salvage something. Fuck the past, fuck the injustices you think you've suffered, fuck —" He jerked his hand up to silence Rosten's protest. "Fuck the lost years. You're hurting no one but yourself by hanging on to this bitterness. Guys can turn over the page, even after twenty years inside. You're only fifty years old. You might have thirty or forty years left. You're smart and educated. Make a place for yourself!"

"In here? And in this?"

"Wheelchairs are not the barrier they once were. And next time you're up for parole —"

"I'll never get parole. They want to hear me confess my sins."

Green knew his flash of temper had been excessive, born as much of guilt as of anger. He forced himself to put his hand on the man's arm, feeling the thin ropes of muscle through the coarse fabric of his shirt. Rosten flinched beneath his touch but didn't pull away. "They're only words, James. And they might be worth it. To get you outside again."

"I've got no place to go."

"Talk to Archie Goodfellow. There are halfway houses. Agencies."

"Right. Ready to welcome the confessed schoolgirl murderer with open arms."

Green said nothing. He knew it was a hell of a millstone, but he'd also seen people rise above much worse. Above unimaginable loss.

"And what would I do?" James added.

"That's a question only you can answer. What do you want to do with the thirty years ahead? Rot in here, consumed with a bitterness and anger that everyone else has forgotten? Or get out there and see what use you can be."

CHAPTER THREE

Green could have phoned Marilyn right away, but a vague unease held him back. At the funeral she had almost spat out Rosten's name and Green could feel her suppressed fury. Lucas's death and Rosten's letter had torn the scab off the old wound, exposing it raw and bleeding to the open air. More than talk, she needed time to heal.

After two weeks of inner debate and doubt, however, he found himself back on the road to Navan, hoping his message would ultimately bring her peace. The day was crisp and clear, but the March sun held no warmth as it glared off the snowy fields. Parked in Marilyn's drive behind her ancient Honda was an unfamiliar pickup with stacks of folded cardboard boxes in the back.

Green skidded to a stop inches from its bumper and picked a path through the icy ruts to the front door. From inside came the warbling strains of "Yesterday" by The Beatles, sung with more gusto than accuracy. He tapped on the front door and the singing stopped abruptly. After an apparent eternity, he heard shuffling in the front hall and the door cracked open. Marilyn peered out, blinking with apprehension in the dazzling sunlight. Her face flushed deep red as she pulled the door wide.

"Oh my, but you gave me a fright! I'm sorry you had to hear that. I don't generally inflict my singing on my worst enemy, let alone my very dear friends."

He stepped into the narrow hallway and was hit by a wave of hot, stale air, redolent with chocolate and gin. Since it was barely noon, he suppressed a twinge of worry. It was not his business; the woman was entitled to use whatever crutch she needed to get through these first few months. He remembered his own father, who had retreated behind a silence so impenetrable after the death of Green's mother that Green had been powerless to breach the walls. In Sid Green's case, too, the scars of a previous unbearable loss had been ripped open again. The terrors of the Holocaust, the loss of his first wife and two infant children … All had come flooding back. No one had the right to judge how a survivor gets through the day.

Instead Green merely smiled. "We'll try a duet next time. Drive both our friends and enemies away."

She laughed and pushed wisps of white hair from her face. Her cheeks were still red and her eyes shone a little too brightly, but Green detected an inner peace in her expression. A softening of the brittle edges he had seen at the funeral. Perhaps she had even put a little weight on her frail frame.

"You're looking well," he said. "The kids still here?"

She tried for a light-hearted shrug. "What are they going to do here? Get in my hair? Make more work for me with all that cooking and washing up? They have no friends out here anymore, and truth be told, not many left in Ottawa either. When the trial ended, they both couldn't wait to get away. Start fresh. Can't blame them, can you? They were young and they had their own paths to make. I myself left my parents to come over here when I was just nineteen, and I never looked back. I went home to Leeds for their funerals but that was it. It's nature's way, isn't it?"

Green thought of his own daughter, Hannah, who swirled in and out of his life, leaving an ache in her wake and a delicious thrill at each return. He nodded. "You're right, of course. But I was wondering about that truck in the drive."

"Goodness, where are my manners? Come in! I'll put the kettle on."

As he followed her inside, he scanned the stuffy little house with a cop's practised eye. One could tell a great deal about a person by analyzing her surroundings. Despite the gin and her slightly manic air, Marilyn's house was well kept. The furniture was clear, the dishes washed, the tables dusted. There were no telltale glasses or bottles littered about.

"I'm doing okay," she said, as if she had read his mind. She stood at the kitchen tap, filling the kettle. "I know you're worried about me. But … I need to make a new life. Get out of the house, get involved in things. There's a marvellous group of women in the village and they've been after me to join their book club and their walking club. The Navan Streetwalkers, they call themselves. Isn't that a hoot?"

She plugged the kettle in and fetched two cups from the drainboard. "I'd never got involved before because I had Luke and, well, my focus was him. He wasn't one for going out, and toward the end, I didn't like to leave him just to go out with the girls. But now I'm free to —" She broke off and looked up at him with glistening eyes. "That sounds dreadful. I didn't mean ..."

"I know what you meant. I've seen a lot of people coping with grief, Marilyn. You're doing better than most."

"I've had practice. One foot in front of the other, I always say. There are so many things waiting to be done. I haven't read a book in years! Luke liked the telly. And I thought I'd try my hand at painting again. There's a marvellous arts and crafts fair here in the spring if I can still paint a decent tree." She laughed and rolled her eyes. "The truck is my friend Laura's. She's going to help me clear out Luke's things. For a man who barely had two pennies to rub together, he accumulated masses of stuff. Besides his clothes, there are his sports and wood-working magazines, catalogues, and oh! The basement! I haven't even begun that. That was his private space, and his workshop is full of tools and half-finished projects. I don't think he finished half the things he started! Birdhouses, jewellery boxes, and dollhouse furniture for the girls ... I'll have to sort it out and figure out what to toss and what to donate. I was thinking of a yard sale in the spring with some of the things I don't need. I could bring in some money and get rid of a lot of clutter in one fell swoop."

She paused to catch her breath and to pour water into the teapot. Once the tray was loaded, she picked it up and headed for the living room.

A question danced at the corner of his mind, unapproachable. The last time he'd checked, the Carmichaels had not yet parted with a single memento of Jackie's life. They had preserved her small bedroom as a memorial, complete with her linen on the bed, her college texts on the desk, and her Blue Rodeo and Sarah McLachlan posters on the walls. From the living room, Green could just see the closed bedroom door at the far end of the hall, leaving him to wonder if it remained untouched to this day.

An ordeal far greater than clearing out Lucas's workshop.

Instead, he followed her lead. "It will be good to give the place a new look. Fresh paint, new furniture."

"You won't recognize the place." She set the tea on the table and sank onto the loveseat, caressing the rough, worn brocade. "Luke loved this old sofa, always said it knew just where to give and where to fight back. He said it would be like throwing out an old friend. But it's past done its job now. In fact, maybe this weary little house has done its job."

Green, who had been fighting a broken coil in the chair seat opposite, looked up sharply. "You're thinking of selling?"

"Yes, maybe. I've had a real estate agent through it already, just to see what he thinks I could get. I was pleasantly surprised. The house itself is worth very little, he said, but the land might appeal to a developer. Who knew when we bought this little patch of forest in the back of beyond that the city would be lapping at our toes one day, and all this rock and maple bush might be in demand for houses. 'All the beauty of the country — at an affordable price, within twenty minutes' drive of the city,' the real estate agent said." She grinned at him with a twinkle in her eye. "Twenty minutes in the dead of night perhaps, as long as you boys in blue don't catch them streaking along the deserted Queensway."

"How much property do you have?"

"Eight acres." She shook her head as she poured the tea, remembering to place a sliver of lemon on his saucer. "I hate to see it overrun with bulldozers and cement, but the money ... well, I could certainly use it. Not that I've breathed a word to the children yet. They're eager enough to get their hands on the money. I told them I'm making friends and it's my home, which is true."

"Don't rush into anything, Marilyn. Take your time. Whatever you do, don't let a real estate agent talk you into putting it on the market until you're absolutely certain. And I ... I have some ideas I'd like to check out first."

"Why? You fancy moving out here?"

He laughed. "No, not me. You know me and the country. My city lawn is already a challenge."

She eyed him keenly over the rim of her raised teacup. "Oh, all right then, be mysterious. What did you come all the way out here for then? Certainly not to hear my singing."

"I came to reassure you about James Rosten. I paid him a visit. He won't be writing any more letters to you, or to Julia."

"Oh!" She set her cup down hastily and clasped her hands together. "Thank you." She breathed deeply as if wrestling back memories. "I suppose I should ask how he is."

"You don't have to do anything. You owe him nothing."

"I know. How is he?"

"Still in a wheelchair but quite mobile. He's working in the prison school, keeping to himself but out of trouble. In short, a model prisoner. Just one small flaw; he won't face up to his past. At least that keeps him behind bars."

Green was silent a half second too long. She jerked her head up. "It will keep him behind bars, won't it?"

"Probably. He is scheduled for a routine parole review in a couple of months, and it's possible, depending on what he says —"

"He wouldn't be sent to a halfway house around here, surely!"

He held up a placating hand as he saw her indignation gathering steam. "No. But it won't come to that. He will almost certainly say the wrong thing."

"Holy Jumpin', Sue! The place looks like it died and went to house hell twenty years ago!"

Detective Sue Peters stepped out into the soggy leaves and melting snow and eyed the bungalow at the end of the lane. Bob was right; it was a sorry sight. Way too small for the four kids she hoped to have; boxy and toad-like, with grimy peepholes for windows and a cracked cement porch that listed with age. Even the brick was ugly. Not the rich red of premium heritage brick, but the grey, second-class brick of the working class.

She and fellow detective Bob Gibbs had spent most of their days off since their honeymoon searching for the perfect house. Having grown up on a farm, Sue longed for wide-open fields, bridle paths, and a swimming hole for those hot summer nights. But Bob had never known a yard bigger than a postage stamp. He couldn't imagine living deep in the country, and, besides, as Major Crimes detectives, they couldn't afford an hour-long commute to headquarters in case of emergencies or overtime. The Village of Navan seemed like the perfect compromise.

When Inspector Green had mentioned the hilltop country house overlooking eight acres of rolling fields and woodland, Sue had pictured whispering trees, sun-lit meadows, and a gingerbread cabin by the creek, not this plain little box. The house had been built during the Second World War, when no one had the luxury or the supplies for style. It stood now, seventy years later, over-run by lilac and juniper, its legacy built not on elegant lawn parties and ladies' teas, but on sweat and struggle and simple dreams.

Sue loved it instantly.

"But we'd have to tear the place down," Bob said, struggling to extricate his beanpole frame from her little Echo. "Start from scratch."

"Not necessarily," Sue shouted over her shoulder as she squelched through the mud toward the house. Bare canes of climbing roses clung to the brick, promising a beautiful display in the summer, and spring crocuses were already poking their tips through the decaying leaves. "It's as solid as a tank. It's real brick all the way around, not a phony façade. It just needs a second storey. Imagine the view we'd get over that valley." She tilted her head up to the towering pines and maples that ringed the house. "And these trees! They must be as old as the house. Probably planted by the original owners. Oh, Bob, just think what we could do with all this land! A pond, a horse stable ..."

Bob headed across the yard to the shed, which he pried open with a screech. "It's full of junk," he called out. "It's going to be a real job just to clear it all out. Most of these tools probably haven't worked in twenty years."

Three sharp blasts of a horn startled them. Bob whirled around just as an aging Honda CR-V slewed into the lane. It jerked to a stop beside their car and a middle-aged woman climbed out. She was wearing a windbreaker that was much too large for her and her white hair stood out in all directions.

"What are you doing?" she cried.

Bob was frozen, with that deer-in-the-headlights look that Sue knew all too well. She stepped back into the drive. Aware that her pink-and-green neon ski jacket did not exactly scream *cop*, she tried for her most formal tone. "Mrs. Carmichael? Sorry to startle you. I'm Sue Peters and this is my husband, Bob Gibbs.

We're detectives, we work under Inspector Green. He told us ..." Her voice faded under the woman's scowl. "Maybe we jumped the gun. He mentioned you wanted to sell, and we've been looking for the perfect place for months."

The woman's glare softened marginally at the mention of the inspector. Sue walked closer, trying to disguise her limp. On damp days, or under stress, the old injuries still ached. The doctors said they always would.

"Well, he didn't tell me," Mrs. Carmichael said, slamming her car door and crossing her arms. "I wish he had. I would have told him not to rush out looking for buyers just yet."

"Well, he didn't really —" Sue broke off. The inspector had not actually said the house was on the market yet, but Sue had wanted an advance peek. What could be the harm in scouting the place out? The land and the location were the key elements anyway. "We figured it would be nice to save us all the real estate fees."

"B-but we don't mean to intrude, ma'am. We — we should have called." Bob, already hustling down the lane, shot Sue an I-told-you-so glance. It had been her idea to drive out to Navan unannounced. But she had been so excited by the possibility they might have finally found their house that she brushed aside all his concerns.

Mrs. Carmichael merely stared at them stonily, making no move toward the house. "I'm not selling," she said. "I toyed briefly with the idea and I did mention it to Inspector Green, but I've changed my mind."

"Well, we're not in a rush," Sue said, careful to avoid Bob's eye. He'd been listening to her increasingly frustrated rants for months. "We've been looking so long, if it's a few more months till —"

"I'm not selling, period."

Sue cast a longing look at the sorry little house, with its overgrown roses and magnificent view. She felt a tug of kinship. "If we've come at a bad time …"

"No."

Belatedly, Bob came to life. "Thank you for your honesty, Mrs. Carmichael. Sue, let's check out that other place."

"What other place?"

He gave her another look. The time-for-a-sock-in-it-Sue look. In the ten months since their wedding, she had become much better at reading him. Just because he stammered and became all flustered under stress, it didn't mean he was a pushover. In his own quiet way, Bob could be as immovable as a tank. A trait she would have to learn to manage. But not now. Not with the outraged homeowner about to erupt.

Marilyn Carmichael softened as they retreated toward their car. "I'm sorry. It's a bad time at the moment. The place is a mess. I'm still sorting through things and I can't think beyond that." She pressed her hand to her mouth as if she were struggling for control.

As Bob babbled apologies, Sue climbed into the car, puzzled. Green had said the woman was anxious to sell, anxious to move on. Grief takes many forms and travels many paths, as Sue knew only too well. The road to recovery from a catastrophic loss was not smooth or straight. It was full of setbacks, shocks, and disappointments.

As they bumped back down the muddy lane toward the main road, she looked back at the little house, where Marilyn still stood in the drive, her arms crossed and her body rigid. Watching them.

"You shouldn't have told them!"

Green was surprised by the vehemence in Marilyn's voice when he phoned to apologize. Meeting Gibbs and Peters in the cafeteria that morning, he'd found them strangely evasive. Since Gibbs usually became red and tongue-tied in his presence, Green would have given it little thought if bulldozer Peters hadn't had difficulty meeting his eyes.

A simple question had elicited a mumbled confession from Gibbs that their impromptu visit to Navan had not gone well. Not well, Peters burst out. The woman had refused to let them in the door and had virtually kicked them off the property.

Twenty years ago, Green had met this ferocious side of Marilyn Carmichael. When her emotions were fired up, she was a formidable force, but Green was surprised that a simple visit to the house, no matter how unexpected, would have roused her to the point of rudeness. She might be feisty, but her British courtesy was deeply ingrained.

That emotion was all the more puzzling because barely two weeks earlier she had been looking ahead to the sale of her house and the chance to start afresh. Now she seemed back in the mire.

On the phone now, he tried for a reassuring tone. "I'm sorry, Marilyn. You're right. I was trying to be helpful." He didn't add that although he had told the newlyweds about the house, he'd stopped short of suggesting a visit, particularly unannounced. He should have known Peters would seize the opportunity and charge ahead under full steam.

"It was an invasion of my privacy."

He was chastened for a moment as he finally grasped the subtext. The Carmichaels had endured twenty years of prying eyes and invasive questions, both from media and community. Their life had been laid bare and dissected. If Marilyn had become hardened and less forgiving, she could hardly be blamed. The sight of a strange car in her drive must have flooded her with old fears.

Nonetheless, he sensed another emotion lingering beneath the surface of her indignation. "Marilyn, is there something —"

"I've decided not to sell, that's all."

"Fair enough." He trod carefully. "As you said, you have friends there now. The book club and the arts fair …"

His voice trailed off when she left him dangling awkwardly in silence. Mumbling reassurances into the empty air, he hung up and sat looking at the phone. Worry piqued him. Marilyn sounded brittle and on the edge again. On his last visit, she had appeared to be looking forward to her new life, so he had been lulled into complacency. But Marilyn could act with the best.

She could hide her deepest pain. Living with her broken husband and navigating the complex feelings of her children, she had had plenty of practice.

And then there was the gin …

"I've seen her crash before, when the trial was over," he said to Sharon later that evening. He had waited until she had a rare moment of peace, nursing their daughter who had fallen asleep at her breast on the living room sofa. He had lit a fire and placed a cup of herbal tea at her elbow. Modo, their hundred-pound rescued mutt, was in her favourite spot, stretched beneath Sharon's feet. Snoring gently.

Sharon hadn't been part of his life back then. He had been on his own, his first wife having stormed out of his life in the middle of the case, taking their infant daughter with her. Ashley had been in way over her head as the young wife of a brand new detective. While Green waded hip-deep in human depravity and despair, she had been overwhelmed and self-absorbed, leaving Green without the support and safe haven he hadn't even known he needed.

Until Sharon. Now she was sprawled amid pillows, with her head resting on his shoulder and her tiny feet propped on the coffee table. Her diminutive frame had more curves now and her rich dark curls were shot through with silver, but she still stirred him. Although her eyes were shut, he knew she was listening, and he felt a twinge of guilt for burdening her. But no one had better insight into the contortions of the human mind than Sharon. No one listened better, and no one knew him better.

She nodded drowsily. "The trial was probably her only reason for getting up in the morning. Once the killer was convicted, her work was done."

He took a sip of wine, his mind replaying the memories. "Not quite. The jury took four days to reach a verdict. Arguments must have been fierce, because they finally brought down a compromise verdict of second-degree murder. The Crown was going for first."

"That wouldn't be punishment enough for her," Sharon said. It was a statement, not a question. Opening her eyes, she ran her finger down her daughter's plump, pink cheek.

For a moment he found it difficult to speak. His inexpertly laid fire sputtered and he disentangled himself to prod it back to life. "The jury split over the notion of premeditation. The Crown argued that Rosten had strangled her in the course of a sexual assault gone wrong. Murder committed in the course of another crime is automatically first degree. But the evidence for sexual assault was pretty flimsy. The post-mortem found signs of sexual activity, but no lacerations or semen. It was enough for the defence to drive a small wedge of reasonable doubt into that argument."

"Evidence of sexual activity wasn't enough?"

"A condom was used. Rapists don't usually bother with such niceties."

"They might if they're a biology professor familiar with DNA."

"The Crown tried that argument. But she had a boy-friend too. Marilyn was furious. 'How can they say it wasn't rape,' she said. 'Jackie was half naked! Her hands were bound and a gag stuffed into her mouth! And how can they say it wasn't premeditated? She was way out in the country on a remote logging road that wasn't even on the map. She wouldn't even have known that road existed, and in any case she had no car. He drove her there! If that doesn't show planning, what the hell does it take?'

"I kept trying to explain how the law and juries' minds worked. A first-degree conviction carries a man-datory twenty-five to life sentence, which is almost as brutal and final as an acquittal. Second-degree allows the hope of parole at the discretion of the judge."

"So he gets to walk free some day, while her daughter never does."

"More or less. The judge gave him eligibility after fifteen years, which is pretty stiff, although almost the whole world wanted at least twenty. We'd just had a high-profile sex killer get off on a technicality because his previous rape history was excluded. So the public was in a lynching mood. But the judge was afraid of giv-ing the defence more grounds for appeal."

"Was that likely?"

"Oh yes, and they took every goddamn ground they could get. The case was largely circumstantial. The vic-tim was last seen walking across campus with Rosten. One of her long hairs was found on the passenger head-rest of his car. A car matching his was spotted in the vicinity the afternoon of her disappearance. The dirt in its tire treads was consistent with the dirt in the woodlot where she was killed. Rosten had dirt on the knees of his jeans and a small cut on his forehead. But there was no tissue under her fingernails and no evidence she'd fought her assailant before being bound and gagged, and as Rosten's lawyer pointed out, the dirt could have come from his cottage near by."

"So the mother hit a brick wall."

"The whole thing finally wore her down. She hung on through all the appeals and motions, which dragged on for years. But I don't think she had a restful night's sleep or ate a full meal for years, and by the end she was a wraith. When she was finally admitted to hospital in complete collapse, every organ in her body had rebelled. For a few days, even her survival was in doubt."

Green fell silent, reliving those days sitting in the ICU waiting room during his off-duty hours, fending off Julia's anxiety and Lucas's drunken tears. Gordon was already overseas and not inclined to return home for his mother's latest drama. *Call me if she dies* seemed to be his message.

Green knew he should have seen the collapse coming. Marilyn had been fighting Rosten and the justice system with the fanaticism of someone running for her life. As indeed she was. Running from her own loss and impotence, from the image of her daughter's last terrified moments on that remote logging road. But he had been young and as yet unbowed by the emotional cost of his job. Mentally, he had long ago shoved Jackie

Carmichael's death into the closet and moved on to other cases.

The fire crackled in the silence. He felt Sharon's hand on his, her gentle squeeze.

"If you're worried, honey, go see her," she said.

"She may see that as an intrusion," he said. "She clearly didn't want to talk."

"Then don't go visit her. Just worry."

He turned his head to look at her. Her deep brown eyes were sympathetic, but a little smile twitched the corners of her lips. As a psychiatric nurse, no one cut through crap better than Sharon.

He breathed deeply. Chuckled. "Put that way …"

"The worst that happens is she runs you off her property. A moment of humiliation is a small price to pay for peace of mind."

"I've been run off worse places," he replied. The baby cooed and snuggled more deeply into the crook of Sharon's arm. Aviva was nearly eight months old now and a crawling speed demon most of the day, but they both cherished these rare moments when she was still an infant in arms.

He leaned over to plant two kisses on the women he loved. "Thank you," he whispered. "Do you want me to put her to bed?"

"That would be lovely. And on the way back, can you bring me an itty bitty glass of something stronger than tea?"

CHAPTER FOUR

$\mathbf{F}$acing yet a third drive out to Navan in as many months, Green used the Internet to discover a back-country route that circumvented the infuriating traffic of the Queensway, which alternated between parking lot and NASCAR racetrack. The route did not end up being any faster, but he arrived with his pulse and blood pressure below incipient coronary levels. The farm country was just awakening to spring. Fields still wallowed in mud, and leaf buds gave the merest dusting of green to the skeletal grey trees. The cows were out in the pasture, however, nibbling the dried grass and basking in the April sun.

Marilyn's SUV was in the drive, which was now a muddy swamp, but her friend's pickup was gone. To avoid outright rejection, Green had not called ahead, but he had chosen the late afternoon when she was most likely to have tea. He hoped she'd be ready to relax.

The house was quiet and still, the curtains drawn. Just as he was approaching the front door, however, a scream shattered the silence. Alarm shot through him as he pounded on the door. No answer. He knocked again, shouting. Tried the handle and shoved his weight against the door. It gave way, bouncing off the wall with a crash, and he blinked to adjust to the gloom.

Before he could move, Marilyn came running up the basement stairs. Dirt smudged her face and her clothes looked as if they'd been dragged from the bottom of the basement closet. She stared at him, her blue eyes leeched of colour by grief and lack of sleep. Gin fumes wafted around her.

"Good God, Marilyn," he exclaimed, reaching instinctively to steady her. "What happened?"

"Nothing."

"But you screamed."

"I — I stubbed my toe."

"It sounded like ..."

"That's all!" For an instant she clutched his hand before pulling back with an impatient shake of her head. "Why did you come?"

"Because I was worried. You're having a rough time."

"I'm mourning my husband! Can't I do that in peace?"

"Let's get some tea." He eased past her gently and headed toward the hall.

"No! Don't come in."

It was too late. He stood at the entrance to the living room, gawking. Boxes were everywhere, their contents spilling out onto the floor. Old clothes, old magazines, toiletries, and cleaning supplies were packed willy-nilly. Other clothes were stuffed into garbage bags or piled in a loose jumble in the hall.

Mail lay scattered on the coffee table, some of the letters unopened. Green stole a surreptitious peek, wondering whether she had received another letter from Rosten. The smell of stale food, mildew, and booze hung in the air. Marilyn glared at him, tears of shame glinting in her eyes. She clenched her fists. "Oh, why did you have to come? Damn it, Mike, leave me be!"

He turned in a slow circle, searching for the right words as he surveyed the chaos. "You need help with this, Marilyn. This is too much work for anyone alone. Are you eating? Sleeping?"

She still hovered in the hall, as if the room repulsed her. "I have … pills. Luke's pills. I do get some sleep. I just — I just … I'm doing it one day at a time."

Green reached down to pile some clothes back into the box nearest him. "Look, I'm off for the week-end. Why don't I help you —"

"Please don't touch that."

He looked at the jacket in his hand. It was an old plaid work jacket, smudged with paint. "At least let me bring a couple of my officers out here and we'll help you clear this out."

"No!" She clutched the doorframe and whipped her head back and forth. Pink blotched her pale cheeks. "This is my job. My house. I don't want strangers pawing through Luke's possessions. Throwing them out like he doesn't exist anymore."

"Okay, I get that." Green set the jacket down again gently. In his work he'd seen grief take many paths. Jackie Carmichael's room had been left untouched throughout the trial, as if she had just stepped out to go to class. And for three years after his mother's death, his own father had been unable to move a single item of hers, including her nightgown.

Now he turned toward the kitchen. "Let's make tea. We can have it outside on your patio. The spring sun is out."

She seemed to relax marginally when he left the living room. The ritual of preparing tea also soothed her, so that by the time she carried the tray outside, her step was steadier and her eyes clear.

There was a small stone patio outside the kitchen door, on which sat a glass table and two plastic chairs, all covered with dead leaves and winter grime. Piled in the corner outside the door were more boxes, and Green noticed another jumble in the fire pit by the shed.

Without bothering to wipe the table, Marilyn placed the tray down and sank into a chair. "I'm sorry, Mike. I didn't mean to be rude. This …" she nodded toward the boxes, "is difficult but it has to be done."

"What about your friend? Wasn't she going to help?"

"I don't want …" She took a deep breath to refocus. "This is private."

"But —"

"And I'm not selling the house, so it doesn't matter how long it takes."

"What about your fresh start?"

"I was premature. I'm sorry your two officers came out here for nothing. But there are too many memories here. Too much of Luke and Jackie in every nook and cranny." She broke off. Her hands clutched her teacup and her jaw quivered.

He tried for a lighter tone. "How's the streetwalking book club?"

"I put all that off for now. Too much else on my plate at the moment."

Green's gaze drifted to the jumble of boxes by the door, the decaying remnants of last year's garden, the leaves waiting to be raked, and the tangled rose canes to be pruned.

The mound of garbage waiting to be burned.

It looked overwhelming, even for him. This frail, worn-out widow was in no shape to tackle it alone. Yet she had almost panicked at the offer of help. What had caused her abrupt reversal? And that scream? Was it simply the next twist in her mourning, or had something else happened? Something to do with her selfish, uncaring children?

Or perhaps with James Rosten?

Green knew Archie Goodfellow was a busy man, who spent much of his day not cloistered in a musty church but on his motorcycle visiting prisons and group homes. He had a chaplaincy office in Belleville, but rarely lighted long enough to check his mail, let alone respond to phone messages. Bypassing the chaplaincy office, Green called his cellphone and left a message, hoping the man would find a spare moment sometime that week.

He was pleasantly surprised when Goodfellow returned his call less than an hour later. In the background, Green could hear the soft rumble of engines and the sibilant hiss of tires on wet pavement. Archie was on the move.

"Speak of the devil!" Goodfellow boomed in his deep, honeyed voice long since perfected to waken the sinners in the farthest pews of cavernous church halls. "I've been meaning to call you. Good work, Inspector. Whatever you told James Rosten — and I don't need to know, although curiosity may be the death of me — he's turned a corner. He has a mandatory parole review coming up, and this time he didn't waive it. Extraordinary! I've been trying for five years to get him to at least go through the process, but he's always said there's no point because he'd have to admit his guilt. But now, not only has he asked for a meeting with the prison parole officer, he's developing a release plan."

Green swallowed his shock. "Has a hearing date been set?"

"Next week. I'm working with the IPO on the plan. It's not going to be an easy sell. James has a lot of ground to make up. As you know, he's been an argumentative sonofabitch all the time he's been inside, refused the treatment programs offered to help him come to terms with his offence, and also much of the rehab for his spinal injury at the treatment centre."

"Yes, it's hard to argue that he's developed much insight into his behaviour."

"No, but in the plus column, he's been no trouble on the inside. Except for the prison fight, of course, but that was ten years ago and he didn't start it — although he'd just lost his last appeal and I think he was itching for a fight. The guards should have seen that coming. He does his job in the library and even helps run the school literacy program. He stays away from drugs and badasses; he's co-operative with the routine. Personally, I'd say — and I *will* say in my report — he's at low risk to reoffend and a minimal risk to the community."

"The wheelchair would certainly cramp his style anyway."

Goodfellow chuckled. For a moment his voice was swallowed in the roar of a passing truck. "I'm pleased he's decided it's time to get out. I see this as a big step. He has always said he could never lie about his guilt, but I think, underneath it all, he was just afraid to get out. He had no hope of going back to the life he had before — no university or even private college would hire him, he'd never pass a crim records check anyway — and life for a poor, unemployed paraplegic can be really tough on the outside."

"None of that has changed," Green said.

"But you must have triggered some new idea," Goodfellow said. "You must have made him think there was something for him. And I've got him a place on the outside, a new halfway house in Belleville. It's fully accessible, he'll have his own room but share meals, and Belleville is big enough he has a hope of finding some sort of job. Because it's practically the only wheelchair-accessible house in all of Ontario, he could probably stay there for years if he wanted."

"Uh-huh." Green tried to reconcile this new vision of Rosten with the man who'd fought his conviction for twenty years. "All he has to do is say 'Yes, I understand and regret what I did.'"

"Yeah. I know. It's a big step."

Green could hear his own doubt echoed in the chaplain's voice. "Do you think he means it?"

As the silence dragged on, Green wondered whether the chaplain would reply at all or whether he was treading too far into confidential territory. Finally Goodfellow chose to be noncommittal.

"Honestly, I don't know. And I don't plan to ask."

"Did he mention the Carmichaels at all in his decision?"

"Not at all. It's never been about them, you know. He has nothing against them. He's often said he feels sorry for them and wishes they could get real answers."

"The mother will be notified," Green said, "and she's not in such a conciliatory mood. I suspect she'll prepare a victim's statement and attend the hearing."

"Oh, she's already been notified, although she hasn't sent in her reply yet. You boys would have been notified too."

"When were the notices sent out?"

"A couple of weeks ago? If your desk is anything like mine, it's probably buried in your inbox somewhere."

Goodfellow roared with laughter, but Green was too busy doing calculations to rise to the bait. The timing was perfect to explain Marilyn's tailspin. Just as she was struggling to adjust to a new life, news had arrived that the man who had killed her daughter and haunted her husband to his grave was applying for release. As she had always feared, Rosten would be free to get on with his life while her daughter was gone forever. Green knew without doubt that Marilyn would attend that review.

The mother tiger was back.

A small crowd had already gathered in the waiting room by the time Green arrived with barely two minutes to spare. He'd had to perform some fancy last-minute foot-work with Superintendent Neufeld, who didn't consider parole hearings part of an inspector's job descrip-tion, but he was damned if he was going to miss James Rosten's next move. All Green's private doubts, all the years of second-guessing the evidence, might be erased in a single afternoon.

Would Rosten admit his guilt? Express remorse? Apologize to the Carmichael family? Was he really a changed man with a fresh vision for his future, or was this just a ploy to advance his own interests?

It was a question of intense importance to Green, but, judging by the sparse crowd, to few others. After twenty years in prison, the man who had commanded media headlines for months barely merited a footnote. Green scanned the faces of the group, spotting Archie Goodfellow in huddled conversation with the parole officer beside him. Normally Archie filled any room he occupied, not just with his six-foot, three-hundred-pound frame but also with his booming baritone voice that could shake the rafters of the largest opera house. Yet today his voice was a mere whisper in the other man's ear.

Green was just debating whether to approach him when the door opened and James Rosten wheeled in. Green was immediately struck by his transformation. No longer did he look like a shrivelled old man. Muscles rippled down his arms as he propelled his chair across the room.

As he had been during his trial, this was a man gearing up for battle.

Rosten searched the room, nodding briefly to Archie and the parole officer before settling on Green. Something flickered in his eyes. Surprise? Alarm? Before Green could decipher the meaning, the interior door opened and the hearing officer ushered them inside.

It was an unadorned, institutional room with a table in the centre and a row of chairs along the back. Rosten, his parole officer, and a civilian sat at the table, observers and interested parties at the back. There was a shuffle of movement when Marilyn Carmichael entered through another door and took a seat in the farthest corner, her head bowed and her thin frame cradled as if to ward off blows. Unlike Rosten, she did not look geared up for battle, but Green observed with relief that although she was wearing her familiar navy suit, at least it was pressed.

Once everyone was settled, all eyes turned to the two Parole Board members on the other side of the table. The official reports on Rosten were in a file in front of them, documenting Rosten's insight into his crime, his conduct within the prison, his release plans and sources of support, the impact on the victim, and most important, his risk to the public.

From experience, Green knew how the game was played. Some reports would be favourable, others less so, especially given Rosten's long history of denial. But Green was only interested in what two people had to say — Marilyn and Rosten himself.

Once the introductions and procedural formalities were over, the lead board member, who had introduced himself as Pierre Anjou, invited the institutional parole officer to summarize the case. Green leaned forward curiously. From previous cases, he remembered Gilles Maisonneuve as an experienced PO with a reputation as a hard-ass. If he had bought Rosten's sudden conversion to remorse, perhaps the board would too.

After giving a brief sketch of Rosten's criminal history, which was essentially unblemished until his current offence, Maisonneuve sped through Rosten's twenty years of anger, protest, and endless legal wrangling before arriving at the past three months. Maisonneuve had personally worked on Rosten's release plan and administered a number of standard risk- and needs-assessment measures. In drawing the board's attention to the man's moderate scores, he explained they would have been even better had Rosten co-operated more fully in recommended treatments and not lost all ties to friends and family on the outside.

However, Maisonneuve was quick to add, despite his reluctance to assume responsibility, Rosten had never presented a discipline problem, had no history of substance abuse, and had co-operated fully with CSC rules and routines. He had used his advanced education and skill as a teacher to help in the prison school program by mentoring and tutoring students toward high-school diplomas and even advanced science credits. This was a skill he intended to carry into his community placement.

"But what about insight and remorse?" the lead board member said.

Maisonneuve paused and leaned across the table, conversational now. "As I mentioned and his records show, although Mr. Rosten has been a model inmate, exhibiting no violent or disruptive behaviour, some attitudinal problems have hindered his progress in the past. He has had difficulty accepting responsibility for his crime and coming to grips with its implications for himself, the victim's family, and the community at large. It has been a difficult admission for a man in his position, and one that until recently he has been reluctant to make. The professional opinion of CSC counsellors and psychologists is that the crime was so repulsive to him and so contrary to his values and self-image that he denied it happened. Perhaps he even blocked out all memory of it. We may never know. However, he has now come to accept that he committed this crime while under the stress of his new job at the university and the increased financial pressures of his family. His wife had recently given birth to twin girls and no one was getting much sleep."

Ridiculous, Green thought, just as Anjou echoed his thoughts. "Everyone has pressures, Mr. Maisonneuve. Some of us even have children."

"Agreed. It's not an excuse. But his circumstances are very different now. He has no family obligations, financial or otherwise — in fact there's been no contact with his family at all since his incarceration, and none is anticipated. He has no job pressures, other than the job he will be applying for if his parole is granted. He is no longer a young man, and his spinal cord injury has left him with considerably diminished sexual capacity. Certainly his capacity to physically assault and over-power a victim is greatly diminished, should he ever feel the urge."

"So what are your recommendations, Mr. Maison-neuve?"

"At this stage of his life, James Rosten wants to use his skills to help others with literacy and schooling. Based on extensive discussions with Mr. Teske here, who is the director of the prison school at Warkworth, with other CSC personnel, and with CSC psychologist Dr. Kim Lee, whose report is before you, I consider him a minimal risk to reoffend and I support the following plan:

"Number one. Release to serve the remainder of his sentence in Horizon House, a new, fully wheelchair-accessible, community-based residential facility in the City of Belleville. It has private rooms, communal meals, and 24/7 supervision. Belleville is nearly three hundred kilometres from Ottawa, where his offence took place.

"Number two. Employment as an online tutor and instructor with adult male clients in CSC programs, initially on a volunteer basis, but with the potential to expand to educational and employment centres if it works well and if funding can be secured. As a precursor to that, Mr. Rosten will be working hard to familiarize himself with digital and online technology, which was in its infancy when he was incarcerated.

"Number three. Financial support will be available through the Ontario Disability Support Program and private personal investments, and there is the potential to supplement that sum through his teaching."

During the PO's entire presentation, Rosten had barely moved a muscle. He seemed to be staring at his hands, which were clasped on the table before him. The board members asked a few questions but showed almost no interest in Rosten's belated change of heart, preferring to dissect the minutiae of his job plans and his potential to endanger the public.

Green's mind wandered. He was cast twenty years into the past, once again trying to understand how a promising young professor who had just completed his post-doc and landed a rare tenure-track position in the biology department of Carleton University, who had just bought a big new house in the upscale suburb of Whitehaven, and who had just become the proud father of twin baby girls — how a man on the brink of his dreams — could lure a young college student under the pretence of helping with her studies, drive her out into the country, strangle her, and bury her half-naked body in the woods.

Furthermore, he wondered, how could such a man could return home to hug his young daughters and show up for his class the next morning as calm and self-assured as ever?

No explanation had ever been put forward by the defence during the trial, because the possibility of guilt had never been entertained. So the police and the Crown had been left to wonder. All these years without a credible theory ... until now. Was the PO's theory of repression possible? Green wracked his memory for clues. Had there been any signs of stress in Rosten's life? Rosten's wife had stuck by him, loyally providing an alibi of sorts, until the exam comments were released. And until other students, mostly female, admitted receiving similar notes offering private help and described him as flirtatious and full of himself. Then a chill had descended over her demeanour, and, by the end of the trial, she had stopped visiting him in the detention centre. The very day of the guilty verdict, she had packed up the children, climbed into the family minivan, and headed home to her parents in Halifax.

Had she sensed an invisible darkness in him, even before all the evidence was out? Had it remained hidden even from himself, as the PO claimed, or was this latter-day insight just an elaborate sham to win his way out of prison? Green wished he could see Rosten's face and look him squarely in the eye as the story was told.

The prison school director, Theodore Teske, was speaking now about Rosten's patience and commitment to the inmates he'd helped in recent years. His involvement had begun slowly, even grudgingly, when he was spending much of his free time hiding out in the prison library, avoiding the threats from other inmates and poring over law books. Other inmates began to ask him questions and he helped them understand the material they were struggling to read. The librarian spoke to Teske and to the chaplain, who encouraged Rosten to form a tutorial group. Bit by bit, Rosten became engaged. His natural love of teaching took over, almost in spite of himself. He treated even the slowest inmate as a challenge.

Green listened first with disbelief but gradually with reluctant surprise. He had never seen any emotion from Rosten but resentment and contempt. If anything, Rosten had conveyed an arrogant belief that he did not belong in prison and had nothing in common with the losers who surrounded him.

How many sides were there to James Rosten, and would he ever reveal his true self? Green found his heart pounding as the school director wrapped up and the board members turned their sights on Rosten himself.

With the flair of a trial attorney, Pierre Anjou slapped his file shut and fixed Rosten with a disbelieving stare. Rosten stiffened, and Green saw Teske touch his arm. To caution him, or reassure him?

"Unlike most of the inmates in this prison, Mr. Rosten, at the time you committed your offence, you had been living a very successful life. You had advanced education and skill, a stable job, financial security, and a loving family. Yet despite all those advantages, you chose to murder a young woman. I've read the psychological reports and listened to Mr. Maisonneuve here describe the pressures of university teaching, the exhausting demands of twin babies, your repression of the memory of the crime, but I see little evidence in these reports of the steps you've taken to rectify that. No counselling, stress- or anger-management programs. No admission even of the need for them. Then, three months ago, with this review coming up, suddenly you change your tune. According to your file, you've spent years fighting your conviction and denying your guilt, and only three months facing the truth. That raises concerns for me. Raises doubts about your sincerity."

Rosten said nothing. Initially he had tried to meet Anjou's stare, but as the criticisms mounted, he bowed his head. *Wise,* Green thought. Staring down a member of the Parole Board of Canada would not advance his cause.

"Was all that denial of your guilt a lie?"

Collectively the crowd held its breath. In the silence Green leaned forward to catch every nuance. The moment had come.

Rosten cleared his throat. "I … I … It was too awful a crime for me to face or admit to. Not just for my sake, but for my family and my children. I have two daughters, and I couldn't bear the thought of them growing up with such shame in and revulsion of their father."

"So this repression idea is a fiction? You knew all along that you were guilty?"

"No. But a life sentence provides a long period for reflection, especially when you're in a wheelchair. Over the years, the reality sank in. I had so much invested in that denial, however, that I kept it up on the outside. I reasoned that as long as my children, my colleagues, and my old friends retained the slightest doubt in my guilt, there was hope for us."

"So what changed? What happened three months ago?"

Rosten raised his head, appearing more confident about this question. "I turned fifty. And I realized I was never going to get my life back. My daughters and my former friends were gone forever. One of the police officers who put me away helped me to see that. In fact, he's here in the room today. He pointed out that I still had years, potentially decades, to live. And I realized that, even in spite of myself, I had started to build a new life. Here and now. With the men I taught, the guys I made a difference to, guys who went on to earn a credit or diploma and who came back to thank me."

"Three months is a very short time to change old habits and make effective preparations. Do you think you're ready to be released?"

For an instant Rosten wavered. He glanced back at the observers and his eyes locked on Marilyn. A faint frown pinched his brow before he averted his gaze. "I do. I will have close supervision and support, and adequate financial means. I've been incarcerated a long time, but further incarceration will not make it any easier. I want to learn to use the Internet for teaching, to manage my chair in public, and face the outside world from this chair, with these scars and this baggage, while I still have good people to support me."

Anjou pursed his lips, looking unconvinced. At his side, the other board member, who until then had merely jotted notes, leaned forward. "You've given us a lot of reasons why you'd like to be released, Mr. Rosten. But why *should* you be released?"

A classic question and one Rosten had clearly been coached in. He leaned forward intently in his chair. "In prison, I saw the difference that basic literacy and a high school diploma can make to the futures of men who never had the chance earlier in their lives. If we teach them to read and write, maybe they won't end up back in here or on the streets. It's taken me a long time to stop feeling sorry for myself. My life is not over. There is still some good I can do, and I'd like that chance to make amends. I have walked both sides of the street and that gives me a unique qualification to lend a helping hand to others."

Damn it, Green thought as he sat back in frustration. Clever bastard. Nowhere in his carefully crafted appeal was there an actual, unequivocal admission of guilt. He had left that to his parole officer. Whether the board members noticed that subtlety, they did not dwell on the issue, choosing instead to ask about the logistics of Rosten's release plan and his ongoing medical needs.

Finally, Pierre Anjou thanked him and flipped back through the file. "As I said at the outset, the victim's family has declined to read their statement at this hearing, but requested that it be read out at the close of the hearing. Here then is the submission made by Mrs. Marilyn Carmichael, mother of Jacqueline Carmichael, the victim."

Anjou selected a single page from the pile and adjusted his glasses. For a long moment he peered over the rims at Marilyn, and then began to read. "When I gave a statement at James Rosten's sentencing, I tried to describe how Jacqueline's murder changed my family's lives. In many ways, ruined our lives. Twenty years later, nothing has changed. The murder took away the warm, vibrant young woman we all loved, made our world a brutal, terrifying place, and destroyed our trust in laws, justice, and basic human goodness. My husband went to his grave recently a broken man, and my remaining two children have left the country and become estranged from me in their effort to run away from the memories.

"I need to pick up the pieces and build a new life. Jackie was a loving, generous girl, and it is her spirit that I must keep alive. Not bitterness, pain, and emptiness. James Rosten has spent the prime years of his life behind bars and he has lost everything including his health in payment for this crime.

"I believe it is time for him too to make what he can of the life he has ahead, and so for my sake and his, I support his release on parole."

CHAPTER FIVE

"I think it's bullshit."

Hannah spoke with the cocky assurance that is the hallmark of the young. *Before all life's puzzles and contradictions have a chance to confound her*, Green thought wryly. He held his tongue, which prompted Hannah to roll her eyes.

"I mean, come on, Dad. Amnesia? How lame is that?"

"It happens," Sharon said. She was perched on the edge of her chair, her own dinner neglected while she attempted to wrestle a spoon away from Aviva. When the baby screeched, she abandoned the effort and picked up a second spoon. The floor around Aviva's high chair already looked like the morning after a street party, but the dog was happily stationed underneath doing cleanup duty.

It was Shabbat, but Sharon had abandoned much of the ritual of the Friday night dinner since the baby's arrival on the scene. They had retreated to the cramped but scrubbable kitchen and the silver candlesticks were relegated to the counter. Today, Green's father had declined to come, citing fatigue, but Green suspected — indeed, hoped — that Aviva's lungs were the main reason. Recently, however, his father's skin looked greyer than ever and his stoop more pronounced.

Amid the chaos, Green noticed his seven-year-old son casually slipping his Brussels sprouts under the table for the dog. A grin sneaked across the boy's face, whether at the dog's enthusiasm or his sister's profanity was unclear.

"In bad movies," Hannah countered. "But on a college campus? You should see what it's like, Dad. College profs hardly older than their students, strutting around campus like their dicks are a mile long —"

"Hannah!" Sharon snapped. Tony burst out laughing, and, to her credit, Hannah flushed.

"Sorry," she muttered before reaching under the table to tickle her brother. "But he should learn this stuff. He'll be after the girls himself soon enough and if you don't want him to be a jerk —"

"We have a little time yet before his education."

Hannah sighed. "All I'm saying is, these profs have it all offered to them on a silver platter. Hot young girls lining up to score with them to get the inside track, better marks, exam secrets, maybe just bragging rights. The whole place is floating in hormones."

"That doesn't make it acceptable," Green said. He could feel his lips tighten primly and he felt a hundred years old. It seemed a lifetime ago that he had been shamelessly prey to his hormones himself.

Predictably, Hannah took up the challenge. "Acceptable's got nothing to do with it. The temptation is there. Hard to resist. Some profs don't even try."

"That's why there are laws —"

"Exactly!" Hannah flailed her fork, sending a Brussels sprout flying. Modo snapped it from the air. They all laughed.

"Saved by the circus dog," Green said, rising to pick up plates. "Let's see what she thinks of dessert."

Hannah didn't move. "Why do you never take me seriously? Why is my opinion always a joke, just because you've got a hundred years as a cop? I know something about this!"

Green paused to study her. Spots of red stood out on her cheeks and her hazel eyes glittered as they met his. She was just finishing her first undergraduate year at Carleton University and had been frantically cramming for exams and completing papers. In recent weeks, she had rarely surfaced for dinner or conversation. He felt a twinge of worry that he had lost track of her. Perhaps this wasn't the usual contrary Hannah; perhaps something was truly troubling her.

He planted a quick kiss on her head. "Okay, let's you and me talk about it later while we do the dishes."

"I've got a paper to do. It's way overdue."

"Ten minutes? I could use your input."

It was half an hour before Sharon had shepherded the two younger children upstairs, leaving Hannah and Green to the peace of the kitchen. Now that silence had descended, Hannah was curiously tongue-tied.

Green busied himself at the dishwasher. "Everything okay, honey?"

"There's no prof hitting on me, if that's what you're thinking."

"Then...?"

"I just think it's way too convenient, this amnesia crap. The guy murders his student but he's such a hard-working, loving family man that he can't live with himself so he forgets the whole thing? For years? Even with all the evidence piling up in court to remind him? Then, twenty years later, when he's finally got parole coming up, he suddenly remembers? Boy, that's some trick!"

"I'm not saying I believe it."

"Good. 'Cause if you did, I'd say you needed a brain transplant."

"But the point is, the parole board seems to have swallowed it. At least some of the psychologists and counsellors."

"Then they're dumb. I'm doing a paper on criminals and amnesia. A lot of them make it up — it's the best defence, even when you've got blood all over you. 'I don't remember, it's all a blank.' How do you disprove that?"

He turned from the dishwasher to face her. Hannah was in her first year of a criminology degree, but in typical Hannah fashion, until now she had shared almost nothing with them. Now he realized she was wrestling with important issues of justice, evil, and the dark labyrinth of the human mind. Heady ideas for a twenty-year-old, especially after all she had been through in her young life.

She seemed to be asking him to help her rather than argue with her.

"That's the big question," he said gently. "I'm bushed. Let's make some tea and go sit in the living room."

She seemed embarrassed. Ready to flee again. He touched her arm as he moved past to fill the kettle. "I really could use your thoughts on this."

Rosten's psyche — the contradictions and incon-sistencies — had always confounded him. As a young detective, he had shrugged off his doubts. He was not a shrink, he'd told himself. It was not his job to analyze or to explain, merely to follow the trail of evidence.

Yet the psyche was at the core of it all.

Hannah said nothing as they prepared two cups of tea and headed into the living room. "I don't really know too much," she muttered, fussing with the cush-ions as she prepared to settle in. "It's just a first-year paper. Short."

"All the same, you've researched the theory of amne-sia. I know Rosten and the circumstances of the murder. Maybe we can tease it out."

She twirled her cup. "I know Rosten too. I used him as a case study."

His eyes widened, prompting her to scowl. "I'd have to be living under a rock in this house not to hear you and Sharon talking these past few months."

His jaw dropped in dismay, but she cut him off. "Calm down, I didn't report any of that stuff. I just read the court transcripts."

"Okay," he said carefully. "What's your take on him?"

She fidgeted. Blew on her tea. "I keep coming back to why he would have killed her in the first place? He could have slept with her; lots of profs sleep with their students without a bit of trouble."

"I always figured she was going to blow the whistle on him. Even back then, universities disapproved of faculty seducing students. He would have faced not only gossip and scandal but also disciplinary action. Possibly the denial of tenure when it came up. Not to mention repercussions with his wife. She might have left him and taken his children away. As indeed she did."

He could see Hannah weighing his words. Rejecting them. "But did you have any evidence that this girl, Jackie, was threatening to rat him out?"

"No. We never even had proof they were having a private relationship, other than the tutoring."

"So she didn't talk to girlfriends? Her mom? Even just hinting at it?"

He shook his head.

"See, that's the thing, that's not normal. Girls talk about stuff like that. Unless we're really ashamed or afraid, we'd be sounding out what we should do. She didn't even mention this to her sister? Weren't they almost the same age?"

Green rifled through long-forgotten memories. Julia and Jackie were four years apart but had never been close. Their temperaments were too different, and because Julia wasn't attending university, they had few experiences in common. But more than that, after the murder no one had wanted to push Julia to talk about her sister. At first she'd been convinced Jackie had run away to avoid dealing with her stepfather when he was drunk, and she'd been inconsolable when Jackie's body was found. She had blamed Lucas and become hysterical the moment anyone questioned her reasons.

"I don't think her sister had any idea that a relationship was going on," he said finally.

Hannah looked unconvinced. "That's a massive secret to keep from your friends and your sister. Maybe there was no relationship. Maybe Rosten hit on her that one time, she freaked out and threatened to tell, so he killed her."

That had always been Green's most likely scenario, but he was still dissatisfied with how the facts fit. "Murder is not as easy to pull off in real life as it appears in fiction," he began. "Even a desperate, spur-of-the-moment killing. It takes a lot of strength, nerve, and persistence to pin down and strangle a victim who's fighting for her life. She would have lashed out, scratched, or bruised him. Plus, most people would be agitated if they'd just killed someone, no matter how hard they tried to cover up. According to his wife, he hadn't a mark on him, except for a scratch on his forehead and some dirt on the knees of his jeans."

"Where did he get those?"

"He claims he went out to the cottage that day to close it up for the winter, and bumped his head crawling around underneath disconnecting the water. When we checked, it was in fact disconnected."

"Pretty feeble story," Hannah said. "And convenient too, picking that very same day to go out to his cottage."

"His wife corroborated his statement. She said he'd been looking for a spare afternoon to get out there before the pipes froze."

"She could have been lying."

He shook his head. "Maybe in her initial statement, but by the end she would have put the nails in his coffin herself if she could."

"So he's a killer who's so calm, cool, and collected that he can strangle a girl and act like he's been for a walk in the park."

"It happens," he replied, thinking of the killers he'd known. The predators and psychopaths for whom extinguishing a life that had become an impediment or a threat was akin to squishing a bug.

She was leaning forward intently. "But wouldn't *someone* know? His wife? Can you sleep beside someone every night and not sense something is wrong with them?"

"If you're really smart, good at acting, and good at compartmentalizing your life, maybe. And if your wife isn't looking too closely. She might have thought, *He's under pressure, he needs his own space, he needs to feel in control.* We don't usually think, *Gee, maybe my husband is a killer.* And the wife did say he was under stress. Everybody attributed it to the birth of the twins."

She shook her head, still skeptical. "But he'd show his true colours sometime. Surely! A guy doesn't just wake up at the age of thirty and become a psychopathic sex murderer!"

He grinned. "No, but if they're smart and careful, these guys can operate undetected for decades. And it escalates. He might have started off with just fantasies. Then stalking, then a few bouts of rough sex."

There had been a few hints of that. Rosten had married his lab assistant while he was doing a post-doctorate at Dalhousie University, suggesting that he was inclined toward relationships with those he could control. One former girlfriend had surfaced to report that he was an ambitious, unfeeling bastard who put women on a par with invertebrates in a Petri dish. A few coeds had testified to flirtatious remarks. But how many men would emerge with their reputations untarnished from their interactions with women over the years? *Certainly not me*, Green acknowledged ruefully.

"So maybe something pushed him over the edge?" Hannah said.

He reached over to tousle her soft curls, now red with turquoise tips that shimmered when she tossed her head. "You've learned a lot for this short paper of yours."

She jerked away. "Dad, I do know something about being pushed over the edge."

Shame stole over him. The previous summer she had barely escaped with her life from people pushed to the edge. "Of course you do." Despite his best efforts, he could hear the gravel in his voice.

"So could it have been the twins? His new responsibilities?"

"Certainly that factored into the various psychiatric theories. Who knows what it triggered deep in his psyche that drove him to a bigger, more dangerous thrill."

Hannah was silent, perhaps caught up in her own memories of danger and death. He sat quietly at her side, sipping his now lukewarm tea and letting her follow her thoughts. He heard Sharon's footsteps first in the kitchen and then in the hallway to the living room. Pausing there. Perhaps wondering whether she should interrupt this rare moment of father-daughter intimacy.

Hannah broke the silence finally. Her voice was hard. "So let's assume he's a cold-blooded psychopath pushed to a new thrill. Is it possible he'd block out the whole thing afterwards?"

Green shook his head slowly. This was the inherent contradiction he had struggled with. "If amnesia is intended to protect the person from a traumatic or intolerable memory, psychopaths don't need it. They don't feel guilt and fear like normal people."

Hannah snorted. "It's all circular, isn't it? Label him a psychopath for what he did, then explain what he did by calling him a psychopath. Doesn't help us *understand*, does it?"

"No. And I don't think we can really understand psychopaths. They are different from us, and no amount of trying to step into their shoes can help us understand. And God knows, I've tried."

"Amnesia can have different causes, though," Sharon said, stepping into the room with her own tea. "Sorry, I couldn't help overhearing."

He smiled up at her. "The munchkins asleep?"

"Tony's reading in bed."

Green glanced at his watch. Eight o'clock. It amazed him how quickly time flew by. The hours, the years … now he had a seven-year-old son who could read his own bedtime stories. How long before he was borrowing the car keys? Heading off into his own life?

Hannah was oblivious to the private detour of Green's thoughts. She swivelled around to look at Sharon. "Like what? I know about brain damage, tumours, concussions. But none of those happened to Rosten."

"No, but drugs and alcohol can also make you blank out. Give even a normal person enough of either, and their brain wouldn't register the memories."

Green weighed the idea carefully. He had met numerous men who had killed in a drunken rage, but all of them had been serious alcoholics with a long history of assaults. In all cases, they had left a trail of clues that even a rookie detective could follow. One had been found passed out in the adjacent bedroom with the kitchen knife still in his hand. Drunk or drug-addled killers didn't think clearly enough to cover their tracks as Rosten had.

"Was he drunk, Dad?"

He paused, trying to recall the investigation. In her initial statement, Rosten's wife had said that when he arrived home shortly after 9 p.m., she detected a faint smell of alcohol, but he was not staggering or slurring his speech. However, although she had been his strongest ally in the beginning, the defence had not called her as a witness. Green recalled the Crown crowing about her change of heart as the evidence mounted. By the time the defence began its rebuttal, she was no longer sure of his state of mind on the evening in question, nor indeed what time he had come home, because she had fallen asleep. Possibly he'd been as late as midnight. He had seemed tired, she said. Distracted and preoccupied.

His eyes had been red-rimmed and he had stammered slightly. He had brushed aside her concern by saying he'd dropped by the university after the cottage to pick up some lab reports.

No one had seen him there, however.

He could have been drunk, Green acknowledged. Drunk enough to lose his inhibitions, drunk enough to make unwise advances toward a pretty co-ed, maybe even drunk enough to get angry when she refused him. But drunk enough to black out the entire episode from his memory?

"I don't think so," he replied. "This killer was more careful and controlled than that."

Hannah swung on Sharon. "Is there a type of amnesia that could do that? Block out the entire thing but leave him in control? What about that multiple personality stuff? That's not just in the movies, is it?"

Sharon shook her head. "But it's extremely rare. The mind is capable of the most astonishing things. The more I see, the less I know for sure. Anything is possible, but usually this kind of dissociative amnesia — when the mind blocks out a traumatic memory — occurs in people with a history of chronic, severe abuse, so the forgetting becomes a mental escape hatch for them. It becomes their way of coping with the intolerable. Did James Rosten have a history of childhood trauma?"

Green dredged his memory again. In truth, unlike Green, the OPP and the Crown had not been interested in the man's psyche. They had constructed their case on circumstantial evidence: the cut on his head, the dirt on his knees and in the treads of the car tires, Jackie's hair in his car, the sighting of Rosten and Jackie together and later of his car near the scene, the exam note in Jackie's backpack, Rosten's flimsy alibi and his flirtatious behaviour with other students.

Now Green recalled that only one brother had come forward to offer character evidence for the defence. He had testified to Rosten's intelligence, drive, and rough, blue-collar roots. As the son of a Sudbury miner with no patience for book learning, he had delivered newspapers, mowed lawns, and shovelled laneways all through school to earn the money to continue his studies. He was the first in the family to go to university, the only one to earn a graduate degree.

The Crown had had only two questions for the man during their cross-examination. "Would you say that your brother's accomplishments and position were important to him?"

To which the unwitting man replied, "No question."

"Important enough to fight for?"

"He fought for them every day he lived in Sudbury."

The Crown had quietly taken her seat. Green recalled thinking that the brother had clearly not inherited the same brains.

The brother's testimony provided no hint of childhood abuse or trauma. On the contrary, he had described a capable and focused young man who'd carved his own path. But Green knew that beneath the veil of normalcy, a family could hide horrendous secrets. Children learned to keep them private from prying eyes and to act normal as if their life depended on it. Often it did. Perhaps James's father had expressed his contempt not just with belittling words but with his fists.

"Can a childhood of abuse be hidden behind a façade of competence?" he asked Sharon now.

"Absolutely. Sometimes even super competence. But dig deep enough, there are scars. Often anger issues. Lack of trust, trouble with intimacy."

"Pent-up rage?"

She studied him briefly, as if recognizing the implication. "That too. But amnesia suggests more than that. Usually people who dissociate are mentally fragile. They don't learn to handle stress, because they escape it. So they usually have pretty serious chronic psychiatric problems, like anxiety and depression. Every time there is a new stress, they are prone to crumble. Maybe even dissociate again."

If — *if* — this theory were true, Green thought, the stress of a new job and a new family could have been the trigger, and the killing of Jackie Carmichael the unconscious acting out of his buried childhood rage. Farfetched, barely credible, but, as Sharon said, the human mind was an astonishing thing.

And now this loose cannon was on the loose again. Without treatment and facing perhaps the worst stresses of his life.

CHAPTER SIX

Ignoring the laminated menu in front of him, Archie Goodfellow laced his fingers over his girth and smiled to catch the waitress's eye. She grabbed a pot of coffee before hustling over. "Meatloaf and mashed, hon?"

He chuckled. It was the Tuesday lunch special at the diner, and in all the years he'd been coming here, he'd never missed that special. "You got it, Nancy. With extra gravy on the mashed."

She laughed as she retrieved the menu. "No one joining you today?"

Archie did half his ministering over lunch at the diner, but today he pointed to his laptop. "Gotta catch up on my paperwork."

Once she'd left, he moved aside his motorcycle helmet, set his laptop on the table and booted it up. It was true that there were fifty-two unopened emails in his inbox but he scrolled past all of them. Paperwork, even the electronic kind, was not his strong suit, and most people knew him well enough to send three or four reminders if they actually wanted a reply.

This time, however, he focused on a single email

that had been sent to him only once. It was a forwarded message from Rosten's new parole officer, accompanied by one sentence of explanation. *Think you should handle this. She checks out.* The parole officer knew him well enough to keep all correspondence brief.

Archie had already skimmed through the message earlier that morning, enough to know that it could not be handled with a quick, off-the-cuff reply. This would require some planning, some weighing of alternatives, even some soul-searching.

> *Dear Mr. Vogel,*
>
> *My name is Paige Henriksson. I am writing to you in your capacity as James Rosten's parole officer. However if there is someone better suited to address my query, please forward this to them. I am James Rosten's daughter, although I haven't seen him or had any contact with him for nearly twenty years. I grew up in Halifax with my mother and my twin sister, Pamela, both of whom remain there. However, I recently married and moved back to the Ottawa area. We all received notices of my father's parole. Like my sister and mother, I have no interest in re-establishing contact with him but I do have questions about his medical history. Specifically,*

about any psychiatric evaluations and diagnoses that have been conducted on him. I understand that this information is confidential, but as his blood relative, it impacts my own medical history and that of my children. Are there reports I can read or, failing that, any mental health professionals who can answer my specific questions?

Thank you for your help,
Paige Henriksson

Archie considered the formal prose. It suggested an educated woman familiar with the language of bureaucracy, but, by his calculations, Paige Henriksson couldn't be more than twenty-three. The twins had been toddlers when Jackie Carmichael was murdered, barely four when he was sent to prison. Why was she asking about Rosten's mental health? Did she have problems of her own? Did her sister?

Archie hated email. Although it was efficient, it robbed communication of all spontaneity and emotional context. Paige's note was dispassionate, but beneath the carefully chosen prose lay a quagmire of pain, confusion, and fear. Beneath it all, she was a wounded young woman reaching out across the decades toward a father she barely knew.

Wherever possible, Archie preferred to meet people face to face, as much to respond to their yearning and fear as to their words. Words themselves were not his forte, but rather the emotions that lay at the heart of them, and that was what the PO was smart enough to understand.

Paige had not left an address, but there was a phone number at the bottom of her message. At least phone conversations were more personal than email. Pulling out his cellphone, he dialled the number.

It being the middle of the day, he expected it to go to voicemail and was just composing his message when the phone was snatched up on the fourth ring.

A young, breathy whisper. "Hello?"

"Paige Henriksson, please."

A pause. Wary. "Speaking."

He launched into his most professional tone. "This is Reverend Archibald Goodfellow. I'm the community chaplain at Horizon House in Belleville where your father —"

A sharp intake of breath, nothing more.

"His parole officer passed on your note. I hope I can help."

"I — I don't need a chaplain," she said, her voice gaining strength as she recovered her footing. "I just need access to some medical information. Psychiatric reports mainly."

"That information is confidential, as you noted. But with a signed release from your father —"

"Oh no! No, no. He mustn't …" She paused and he heard her draw breath again. "I don't want him to know."

"I understand," Archie said. "Maybe if we could meet in person?"

"That's not necessary. And in any case I can't get away to Belleville."

"But I'm going to Ottawa the day after tomorrow," Archie improvised. "I could meet wherever is convenient."

"No! I don't want … it's just … a couple of simple questions answered, that's all I need."

"What questions?"

"Is he a psychopath?"

Archie was startled. "That's not a simple question, Paige. It's not even an official psychiatric diagnosis."

"But it's a recognized disorder. That's what I need to know. Is he psychotic, or psychopathic, or a sexual predator?"

He could hear the fear in her voice as she breathed the words. "He doesn't know where you live, Paige."

"That's not the point."

"Then why do you want to know? What's wrong?"

There was a long pause, during which he half-expected her to hang up. When she spoke, her voice was low. "I have a son. He's two years old. I know these things are hereditary and I want to know if there are things I need to watch out for."

He barely noticed his meatloaf arrive. Nancy set it down in the small remaining space between his laptop and helmet, and gave him a wink before slipping wordlessly away. Archie's uncertainty vanished as the real issue emerged. Here was a young woman afraid for her child.

"Have you talked about it with your son's doctor?"

"No. He doesn't know. About my father, I mean. No one knows."

"Not even your husband?"

"Please! I just need to know...."

"That is a lot to handle on your own."

"I've handled it my whole life," she retorted. "I just need to talk to the professional who assessed my father, so I'll know what I'm dealing with."

"It's a very small risk, you know. Even with inheritable psychiatric disorders. He has your mother's genes and your husband's too."

"But there are warning signs, early on."

"Are you worried your son is showing them?"

"He *is* showing them! Tantrums, spiteful, lack of empathy."

He wanted to tell her the boy was only two, that all two-year-olds had tantrums and lacked empathy. That hers was a normal fear of a young mother dealing with her first child.

But most mothers did not have the blood of a murderer in their veins.

A child's wail could be heard in the background and she stifled a groan of dismay. Archie searched his conscience for a path through the minefield of legalities. He was not qualified to discuss medical diagnoses, and even if he were, the laws of confidentiality prohibited it. Yet here was a woman who had lived with this fear all her life and who deserved some genuine reassurance. The law be damned.

He took a deep breath. Shut his eyes the better to focus. "I can't give you any specific information about his health. I am not a doctor and I don't have his permission. I can tell you, though, that none of those words have ever been used in reference to him."

"None?"

"You heard right. Like anyone who's been in prison that long, he's a bit scared and overwhelmed right now, but —"

The child's wailing rose an octave. "You know him?"

"Yes, I've known him for years. And I think …" Archie surprised himself with the thought that came into his head. "Your son could do much worse than to inherit some of his genes."

Utter silence. In the background, the child screeched indignantly. Halfway through, the phone slammed down.

Archie sat at the table staring at his meatloaf unhappily. It had grown cold and the gravy was congealing in greasy pools. Despite the nagging unease about Paige, he forced himself to dig in. No point in good food going to waste. He was just polishing off a piece of strawberry pie and turning his thoughts back to Paige when his cellphone rang.

"I'm worried about James Rosten," Inspector Green said without preamble.

"Why?" The words were out of Archie's mouth before he could censor himself. As cops go, Green was a decent sort. His job was to protect the public and lock up the bad guys. It's true that Green had always shown an interest in Rosten and had even come to his parole hearing, although he hadn't said a word, but it was no secret that he and Rosten had waged a war of letters for almost twenty years. Archie doubted he was calling out of compassion.

"I'm concerned about his risk to reoffend. Or at least to do some harm."

"You were at the hearing. You heard the opinions of the professionals."

"Yes, and that's precisely what got me thinking. We're looking at two scenarios. Either he really blocked out all memory of the murder and in fact may have committed it in what my wife calls a dissociative state —"

"No one's suggested that."

"But that's the point. No one has figured this guy out, because he's never let anyone inside his head. The thing is, this kind of blocking is very rare and it's not just a one-off. It points to a very disturbed individual, the kind who might do it again if something sets him off."

Archie said nothing. He'd seen some terrifyingly disturbed inmates in his time, stark raving psychotic and out of control. Rosten had never acted remotely like that. He said as much to Green.

"Okay, but prison is a very predictable and regimented environment."

"That doesn't mean there aren't stresses," Archie said. "As a killer of an innocent young woman, Rosten met his share of scary guys. Don't forget what put him in the chair."

"But the signs may be subtle. He's not psychotic, but my wife is a psychiatric nurse, and here's what she wants to know. Did he ever seem zoned out? Not responding or not remembering something that happened? Did he have mood swings or personality changes, when he acted out of character or seemed not himself?"

"You mean like in the movies, where someone flips back and forth between different identities?"

"Probably not that extreme but along those lines. If he's been having little episodes where he blanks out or steps outside himself, he may act unusual or at least bewildered afterwards."

Archie thought back over the years he'd known Rosten. And most recently to the weeks in Horizon House. "Mike, I'm no shrink, but I have to say Rosten is the most consistent and predictable guy out there. Rational to a fault, maybe. He doesn't react to things, except to get out his books or his computer and figure out a response."

"Yeah, but what about after the prison assault? I seem to remember he had panic attacks, even suicidal thoughts."

"Put yourself in his shoes. Paralyzed and living in fear. Who wouldn't?"

"True." Green paused. Archie waited. "So forget what the shrinks and counsellors think. We've both seen our share of bad guys. We're seen them at closer quarters and for longer periods than most shrinks. There is another scenario."

Archie suspected he knew what was coming. "A con," he said.

"Not just any con. A master con. It's not easy to fool counsellors and psychologists and corrections officers and you, not to mention a tough old PO like Maisonneuve."

"I don't buy it, Mike. I've watched lots of inmates trying to adjust to the outside, and Rosten is just like most of them. He's scared, he's lonely, he's overwhelmed by even the little bit of freedom he has. I'd say some days, like many parolees, he wishes he was back inside. That's not the behaviour of a master manipulator."

There was silence on the phone, and Archie pictured Green trying to reconcile the conflicting faces of Rosten. Archie didn't try to think so hard. He took a man at face value and accepted that he had secrets and contradictions inside that he was never going to expose. But Green had always tried to climb inside the head of the criminals he pursued, the better to catch them. It was his strength as a detective, but at what cost?

"Okay, I hear you," Archie said. "You're worried Rosten is not what he seems and he may be up to something."

"Yes. I wonder about his sudden decision to seek parole. I wonder if he has an ulterior motive for wanting to be on the outside."

"He's under very tight supervision. I'll keep an extra eye on him, but right now he just seems like a lonely parolee trying to find his way forward in a strange city with no family that cares to connect. I'm trying to encourage socializing. He has no one except —"

Before he could change course, Green pounced. "Except what?"

"Except nothing." Archie heaved a sigh of resignation. "I got an email from his daughter. She's concerned about medical implications." He filled Green in his phone conversation with Paige. "But I have a suspicion there's more to her request. I won't tell James about it yet, because I don't want to stir up old feelings or get his hopes up. But I will follow up with the daughter. See if I can soften her up a bit, maybe build some bridges so he at least has that connection in his life."

"Jesus, Archie. Go easy on that. That was a very traumatized, betrayed wife and mother twenty years ago. God knows what kind of scars Rosten has left them with."

"You know me, Mike. If there's a bridge to be built, I'm going to get out the hammer and saw. In the end, that's the biggest healer there is. Next to ... you know."

The real estate office was a tall, old-fashioned house with white clapboard siding and a wide front porch. Red and yellow tulips were massed in beds below the porch and a shiny black pickup truck sat in the drive.

The sign on the screen door of Navan's only real estate agent said, PLEASE COME IN.

Sue Peters and Bob Gibbs did just that. In their nine-month quest for the perfect marital home, they had been through half a dozen real estate agents, ranging from eager twenty-somethings wearing power suits and stilettos to grizzled boomers on their second careers. Sue thought the new truck and the manicured garden sent the right message of prosperity and competence, so she was taken aback by the man who emerged from the back in response to the tinkling bell over the door.

He was well over six feet, with a country plaid shirt hung on his reedy frame and steel-toed boots on his size-thirteen feet. He had a sunken chest and a little potbelly that suggested a fondness for beer. Brushing crumbs from his belly, he blinked at them in surprise, as if they were the first customers to walk through the door in a week.

"Hi there!" he exclaimed, recovering enough to thrust out his hand. Sue winced at the grease and crumbs still clinging to it. The man's grip was bone-crushing.

"Paul Harris," he said, his name matching the sign outside. "Welcome to Navan. You two interested in a property around here?"

Sue glanced around the room. Photos and fly-ers of properties plastered the walls, and large binders cluttered the desk in the corner, nearly burying the computer. The photos depicted everything from water-front shacks to mansions. None of them, she noticed, had Paul Harris listed as agent.

"We're looking all over," she said cautiously. "We like the country feel of Navan."

"Well, you've come to the right place. I know every property listed within a 10k radius and quite a few that aren't listed. Yet." He flashed a grin, exposing a perfect white smile. *Dentures?* Sue wondered. She put Harris's age at around forty-five, which was rather young for dentures, but faint scars on his eye and lip suggested an old injury. Her opinion softened.

Belatedly, he gestured to two chairs in front of his desk and then folded himself in behind. "What kind of place do you folks have in mind?"

Sue glanced at Bob. He always let her do the

talking, which sometimes got tiresome, but she sensed Mr. Pickup-truck-and-steel-toed-boots might do better with a man. "You go ahead, honey," she said.

But right off the bat, Bob stuttered. "A — a place we can grow into. Quiet and out of the way. The house doesn't have to be big, as long as it has potential to add on. Most important is the land. Maybe five or ten acres? Wooded, natural. My wife wants to have horses."

Harris was already fiddling with his computer. "Will you be commuting? Where do you work?"

"Downtown Ottawa." Bob paused. "We're police officers."

Harris's eyes widened ever so slightly. Like all cops, Sue was used to that. People always did a quick inventory of their sins the minute they heard the word *police*. "So, not too far out into the country?"

"No. And with good access to the highway."

"It's a balancing act," Sue added. "We want the acreage and privacy, but we have to be able to get to town fast."

Harris typed and clicked through several links before swivelling the computer monitor toward them. "Here's a beauty that just came up. Two acres, new building. It's a divorce, so they're anxious to sell."

The price was outrageous. While Bob dithered, she told Harris so.

"No problem," he said, flashing those dentures again. "What range are you looking at?"

She gave him a figure. His smile evaporated and his brows drew together. "That does limit our choices."

"It doesn't have to be big and fancy. A little old house with some land attached would be perfect."

He led them through a few other properties, all of them atrocious. A shack that would be better off burned to the ground, and an old farmhouse stuck together with spit and cow dung as far as Sue could tell. Her hopes for country affordability began to fade.

"Isn't there some place that will at least stay standing while we fix it up?"

Harris pursed his lips in disappointment. "Maybe Limoges or Embrun? They're up and coming."

Sue gathered her purse and began to unfold her stiff body. "That's too far out. But thank you for your time, Mr. Harris."

Harris tugged his lip. Twiddled his pen. "Well … just between us, there might be something coming up. I can't promise anything, but I've been in to see it. The owner recently lost her husband …"

Sue plunked back into her chair. "The Carmichael place?"

Harris's eyebrows shot up. "Ah! You've seen the place?"

"Well, n — not inside," Bob hastened to add. "The owner wasn't interested."

More twiddling. "It's a beautiful little property. And the price … the price would be close to your ballpark."

"But it's not for sale," Sue said.

"Not yet. However …" He was tapping the pen now. "The owner's son was in here just yesterday asking what they could get for it. I told him there could be developer interest — which there could be, so you'd have to act fast if you're interested. The son seemed pretty pleased with the price and said he just needed time to work on his mother."

Sue remembered Marilyn Carmichael planted in the middle of her laneway with her arms crossed. Her son had his work cut out for him.

"We can't compete with developers, though," said Bob gloomily. "They've got deeper pockets and fancier lawyers than us."

Sue was already scribbling their cell numbers on her card. "Can you call us if it comes on the market? We might be interested."

The agent glanced at her card before slipping it into his breast pocket. He gave a knowing smile. "I'll let the son know."

Sue was at her desk catching up on routine reports when Paul Harris phoned the next day.

"We've hit a slight snag on the Carmichael property," the real estate agent said. "For now. The owner is still refusing to sell. I don't know why. The place is way too much for her, but the son says she's still clearing it out and refuses to let anyone in."

"So maybe in a few months ...?"

"Personally, I think if you're patient and you like the look of it, it will come up before the winter. She won't want to be there all alone once the snow hits. The laneway is a nightmare to plough and the power goes off every time there's a —" Harris broke off abruptly, as if recognizing the poor sales pitch he was giving. "Of course, most of the time it's fine. And the son's going to keep trying to make her see reason. He's pretty determined. Wants to get back to Paris, and, between you and me, he sounds like he really wants the money."

"But it's his mother's house, isn't it?"

"Oh yeah. But I guess she'll be giving some of the proceeds to her kids. That's what she always promised them, he says. I'll let you know the minute anything changes."

"Okay, but meanwhile we'll keep looking elsewhere." No point in appearing too eager. Harris started to rhyme off other properties, but she extricated herself and went to track down Bob.

She found him closeted with Inspector Green and Staff Sergeant Sullivan, but the door to Green's new office was half open so she poked her head in. They were poring over court testimony Bob had to give the next day. Bob was a competent detective, maybe even thorough to a fault, but defence lawyers terrified him. Tomorrow he was up against the lion of the defence bar and he needed all the coaching he could get to prepare for cross-examination. All three detectives stared up at her in disbelief.

"Sorry," she muttered when she realized her intrusion. "The real estate lawyer in Navan called. That house is still a no-go, for now."

"What house?" Green said sharply.

Sue glanced at Bob. Should they risk angering the inspector once again? "The Carmichael house. We didn't bother her," she rushed on hastily. "A real estate agent there told us her son is trying to persuade her to sell."

"Her son? Gordon?"

"I don't know the name. He lives in Paris."

"That's Gordon. I didn't know he was even in the country. But I can guess what his interest is."

"Money. But the agent does think he can persuade her."

Doubt and distaste flickered across the inspector's face. Sue hesitated before throwing caution to the winds. Nothing ventured, nothing gained had always been her motto. "Are you still in touch with Mrs. Carmichael, sir? Could you —"

"No, Detective, I won't. Marilyn Carmichael is a strong, sensible woman who will sell that house when and if she's ready, no matter what that son of hers wants. She's smart enough to see right through him."

The hospital call came at eight o'clock the next morning, just as Green was tightening the lid on his travel coffee mug in hopes of escaping the house. The kitchen clamoured with life. Modo was sprawled strategically across the centre of the kitchen floor, hoping for tidbits, and Aviva was pulling her ears. Over her squeals, Tony chattered about his upcoming summer soccer day camp. The microwave hummed and plates clattered.

Hannah, as usual, had yet to put in an appearance. Much to Green's consternation, she had taken a summer job waitressing at a Byward Market pub. After dusk, the heritage market area came alive with pub crawlers, street people, and prostitutes, along with the crooks who preyed on them all. In response to Green's fatherly fretting, she had cast him a dark, knowing look that he didn't dare question. A look that said she'd walked those streets herself and knew every trick.

Over the morning chaos, he didn't even hear the ring, but Sharon glanced at the phone and sobered instantly. "It's the Ottawa Hospital," she said as she picked up.

It could have been work-related — his or hers — but Green felt a jolt of fear. At last week's Shabbat dinner, his father had merely pushed his food around on his plate, even though Hannah had tempted him with Green's mother's legendary roast chicken. Afterwards he had asked to go home right away. Home was a small, lonely senior's apartment in Sandy Hill, mere blocks from the old tenement where he had raised his only son and nursed his wife through her long death.

In the years since her death, Sid Green had withered to a shell of himself, retreating inside his memories and his TV game shows, growing deafer and frailer. All his cronies were dead, and the vibrant, Yiddish neighbour-hood he'd once known was long gone. Even Nate's Deli, where Green had always taken him for cheese blintzes or smoked meat on rye, had been bulldozed to make way for a Shoppers Drug Mart.

Yet his battered body had refused to cede defeat, and he had insisted that as long as his brain and his two feet still worked, no one was going to park him in some soulless nursing home.

"One day we may have no choice," the ever-practical

Sharon had said after the dinner. "He will fall and break his hip or have a stroke."

Although Green knew she was right, it didn't bear thinking about. The idea of his father, who had survived the Nazi camps by sheer force of will, being leached away bit by bit by the cruel thief of age was unbearable. They had considered bringing him to live with them, but the five of them were already cheek by jowl in their old-fashioned house, with its one bathroom, narrow halls, and daunting stairs. Faced with the astronomical cost of the renovations, they had stalled.

All these thoughts rushed through his brain as Sharon handed him the phone. He steeled himself. A brisk, no-nonsense voice from Admissions verified his identity before he heard the words he'd been expecting for months.

"Your father has just been brought to hospital by ambulance. The medical team is working on him, but as his power of attorney for personal care, we need to discuss treatment options."

Two hours later, after filling in a mountain of forms and repeating his father's medical history to three different people, he was sitting in the ICU waiting room when an incredibly young woman in green scrubs approached. She looked grave.

"Your father has suffered an ischemic stroke and he's unconscious. We have administered a thrombolytic, tissue plasminogen activator, to dissolve the clot, but we won't know the extent of the damage until he regains consciousness and we perform some tests. He apparently collapsed some time during the night, but wasn't found until 7 a.m. this morning when his personal care worker arrived to help with his morning routine."

"So it could have been hours."

She met his eyes. Despite her youth, she didn't flinch. "Yes. The clot-dissolving medication is most effective during the first four to five hours, after which brain cell death begins to occur. We don't know in your father's case."

Green absorbed this. "Where was he? Did it happen in his sleep?" It was a faint comfort that his father might have slipped away painlessly.

She dashed it. "No. He was found in a chair in his living room. He probably didn't feel well, perhaps had some nausea, dizziness or headache, and got up to get something. Water or Tylenol."

"But he didn't call 911 himself?"

"He may not have realized how serious it was until it was too late and he lost consciousness."

"So in your opinion, how bad is it going to be?"

She shook her head. "Too early to tell. He is breathing on his own, but his vitals are unstable. We are giving him oxygen and aspirin and keeping him hydrated, but beyond that ... I see he has a DNR order and a living will."

Green nodded. "If there is no hope of meaningful recovery or decent quality of life. My father was very clear on that."

Again she shook her head. "The next forty-eight hours will tell. But if he has another stroke ..."

The doctor wasn't prepared to offer a prognosis, but Green didn't need her words to send his thoughts spinning. In one scenario, his father might recover enough to continue his slow decline. In another, he would never regain consciousness and would slip into death in a day or week. But as painful as either possibility was, the nightmare scenarios in between were worse. Paralysis. Loss of speech. A body robbed of volition, a mind of expression.

Feeling numb and disconnected, Green headed toward the nursing station. He knew he should have a hundred questions, but all he felt was a heavy weight of responsibility and loss. He had no siblings, no uncles or cousins, with whom to share that weight.

As he leaned over the bed and slipped his hand into his father's pale, unresponsive one, he found he couldn't speak. Couldn't think. Could only squeeze, and hope.

For what, he wasn't sure.

CHAPTER SEVEN

For once Archie Goodfellow was on time — early, in fact. The VIA train from Kingston didn't arrive until 3:22, but he wanted to snag a good handicapped parking spot at the side of the station with a clear view of the platform. He left the van with the air conditioning running to combat the sweltering afternoon heat. Late May could be unpredictable in Belleville, with rogue snowstorms one day and blazing heat another. Even with the air conditioning running full force, sweat trickled down his back and soaked his shirt.

As he waited, he fiddled with his cellphone, ostensibly responding to neglected voice-mail messages, but really keeping his anxiety at bay. He'd gone out on a limb to persuade James Rosten's parole officer to let him go unaccompanied to his medical appointment at the Kingston General. During the month since his release into the community, Rosten had barely been outside Horizon House. He had participated only reluctantly in a couple of the organized house excursions, during which he had barely spoken to the other residents, but in the main he had remained sequestered in his room with his books and his new laptop.

The house staff regarded him as a snob, but Archie had learned to see through that months ago. James was overwhelmed, and when he was overwhelmed he retreated behind his pedantic professorial façade. Archie suspected the world inside his head was much more manageable and comforting than the chaos outside.

Archie had been trying to encourage brief forays out into Belleville, which was a small city with modest commercial and retail strips within easy reach. However, James had been reluctant to go beyond the local library and the community medical clinic where his health needs were managed. Archie was more surprised than anyone when James asked his parole officer for permission to travel on his own by train to his specialist appointment in the larger city of Kingston. A forty-minute train ride.

James had argued that the trip was simple enough and that surely it was time for him to take full charge of his medical care. If this consultation went as hoped, he would be making frequent trips to Kingston in the months ahead for further rehab. During his years in prison, James had shown little interest in his rehabilitation, and Archie regarded this newfound determination to increase his independence as a positive sign. After planning and reviewing every step of the trip with him, Archie supported the request.

His small frisson of concern be damned.

A whistle blast jolted him from his ruminations. He looked up to see a pinpoint of light approaching along the track from the east. He switched off the engine and clambered down from the van, groaning as he stretched the kinks from his back. He limped across the walk behind the shiny new station to the platform just as the train clanged to a halt.

He knew James would be among the last to disembark, because he required the assistance of the station staff and a hydraulic lift. Nonetheless, he watched with increasing apprehension as the trickle of passengers made their way across the overhead walkway and out through the station. There was no station attendant waiting by the first-class car and no sign that preparations for a wheelchair exit were being made. Archie's small frisson of concern grew to full-fledged alarm. Where *was* he?

James's consultation with the spinal cord specialist had been at ten o'clock. A return trip ticket had been purchased on the one o'clock train back to Belleville. As agreed, Archie had waited at the station until that train pulled away from the station before returning to his office. He had not been worried. He and James had discussed the possibility that the appointment with the doctor might run late, that he might order additional test or consults, or simply that James might be in the mood for a taxi tour of Queen's University, where he had earned his undergraduate degree.

His unsupervised pass from Horizon House had accordingly been granted until four o'clock, so that he could catch the later train if need be. Now, however, that train had also come and gone. Archie stood staring at the empty platform in disbelief. James was now in clear violation of his unsupervised pass. The next train was not until 9:00 p.m., well past the time for any acceptable excuses such as delayed medical appointments.

James was supposed to phone Archie if he encountered any obstacles. He had not phoned. Archie's fingers hovered over his cellphone, as he considered checking with Horizon House in case James had somehow missed him at the station and made his own way back. Archie stalled. By all rights, the house would be obligated to report his breach of parole. Before Archie made his absence official, there were a few simple places to check.

His first phone call was to Dr. Ansari at Kingston General Hospital. After multiple frustrating attempts to break through the hospital's automated phone system, he was connected to the receptionist at the neurology clinic, who refused to divulge any information. Throwing all confidentiality to the winds, Archie explained James's violation of his day pass.

"I want to avoid getting the police involved," he said. "I don't need to know any medical information, just whether he showed up for his appointment and what time he left."

The woman muttered something indecipherable and put him on hold. After an interminable delay, she came back on the line. "He arrived at 9:50, saw the doctor at 10:40, and left at 11:30."

"Did he have any further appointments that morning? Can you tell me that at least?"

"One moment please." On hold again, another long delay. "No further appointments."

"Did he say where he was going?"

"He ..." She paused, probably weighing legalities again. "He didn't say anything."

"How did he seem?"

"Pardon?"

"His mood."

"Mood?" The woman sounded incredulous, as if this were a requirement well beyond her job qualifications. He heard a man's voice in the background followed by a muffled exchange before a clipped male voice with an English accent came on the line.

"This is Dr. Ansari. To whom am I speaking, please?"

Archie identified himself and explained his involvement and his predicament, with heavy emphasis on his concern for James's well-being. "This is Mr. Rosten's first excursion on his own and he's still easily overwhelmed. He had a lot invested in this consultation. What was his state of mind when he left? Angry? Depressed?"

There was a long pause. "I can tell you this. Mr. Rosten impressed me as an intelligent, knowledgeable man. He was not pleased with my conclusions, but I do not see him as at imminent risk for self-harm, if that is what you are asking."

"So you did not give him good news about further treatment?"

There was a sigh. "There are no new avenues of treatment."

"Did he argue?"

A faint chuckle. "You know him well."

"Did he mention anything that might give me a hint where he's gone?"

"Not to me. But you must understand, Reverend, that this type of bad news takes time to absorb. Often patients take a few hours to themselves and wander around the city, sit by the lake.... Sometimes time slips away."

"Do you know if he took a taxi from the hospital?"

"No, but there are only a couple of major companies." After Ansari supplied the names, Archie thanked him and signed off, feeling marginally reassured. Perhaps James had merely taken time to regroup. It was a glorious spring day. Lunch at an outdoor café or in a lakeside park might easily have stretched to three hours, causing him to miss even the later train.

Archie was even prepared to drive to Kingston to search for him, but before he did so, he phoned the taxi companies. This time he did not explain the violation of the day pass, but instead portrayed Rosten as a potential victim of foul play. This netted him the information he needed on the first call.

A middle-aged man in a wheelchair had been picked up outside the main entrance of Kingston General at 11:58 a.m. At the passenger's request, the taxi had driven him through the Queen's University campus and along the lakefront, stopping at Macdonald Park and at the Tim Hortons drive-thru beside the ferry dock. Forty-five minutes later, it had dropped him outside the Kingston train station off John Counter Boulevard.

Archie knew he was now out on a very fragile

limb. It was well past time to report Rosten as unlawfully at large. But once done, there would be no going back and no predicting what the parole office would do. Ken Vogel was a tough, by-the-book PO who did not cut his charges much slack for personal lapses or failures of character. Rosten could find himself back in Warkworth.

Archie, on the other hand, understood perhaps too well the struggles that ex-cons endured and their tenuous grip on success. He knew he was a soft touch. He knew he sometimes got played. But he refused to harden himself.

Fortunately, in his years as chaplain he'd built quite a network of friends, and he used it now as he went inside the Belleville train station. Bypassing the ticket booth, he approached the lone station attendant who was sneaking a cigarette around the back of the building. Freddie and he had volunteered at many a pie- and jam-judging contest over the years, and, like Archie's, his girth now told the tale.

They exchanged greetings and Archie asked after his wife and family. Freddie produced pictures of his new grandson and Archie detected a hint of sadness beneath his pride, for the grandson lived in Calgary. Twice yearly visits were all he could hope for.

Freddie had helped Rosten board the train that morning and Archie was able to jump in without much explanatory preamble. "You know that fellow in the wheelchair this morning? I am supposed to pick him up but he hasn't come back on the train from Kingston yet.

Can you check with the attendant in Kingston to see if anything went wrong at that end?"

Freddie pulled out his cellphone, flipped through his contacts, and placed the call. "This is a new guy," he said to Archie as he waited. "I let him know personally about your man's arrival and departure, so he should have been prepared. Plus it should all be on his computer manifest...."

He stopped as the phone was answered. Archie listened as he explained the problem. There was another break, during which he looked back at Archie. "He remembers your guy. Remembers him getting back on the train. He's just checking what time."

Back to the phone. "Okay. Okay ... about an hour ago, you think?"

He hung up and turned back to Archie to repeat that message. Archie frowned. "That would be the 3:22 that just went through. But my guy wasn't on it."

"Maybe he fell asleep and slept through the stop. I can call ahead to the crew on the train and they can check if you want." Freddie's eyes narrowed. "If you're really worried."

Archie nodded and stood by, gazing anxiously down the track at nothing in particular while he waited for Freddie to connect with the staff on the train, which was now hurtling toward Toronto. A big place if someone wanted to disappear.

After a brief conversation Freddie hung up. "No sign of your guy on the train. No sign of anyone in a wheelchair."

Archie felt a sick dread in the pit of his stomach. Something was terribly wrong. "Maybe they're mistaken about the time. About which train."

"I can phone Kingston again and get them to double-check."

"Please." Archie was already moving away, too anxious to do nothing. "I'll go back to the house. Maybe I missed him. Maybe he's already there."

The moment he walked through the doors of Horizon House, however, he knew Rosten wasn't there. The man on the front desk looked up sharply.

"Where's Rosten?"

"He appears to have missed his stop." Archie held up his hand. "Sometimes things don't move smoothly when you're in a wheelchair. I'm trying to track down —"

The man was already reaching for the phone. "We gotta report this."

"Give me half an hour." Bypassing the elevator, Archie was already halfway up the stairs. He didn't wait to see whether the young man had agreed or was already placing the call. Inside Rosten's room, Archie worked quickly. Rosten had brought only a small day bag with him that morning, presumably to contain his wallet and supplies for the day. The staff had seen no reason to search it, but now Archie moved efficiently around the room looking for telltale signs. Rosten's clothes, what few there were, were all folded in drawers or hanging in the closet as usual. His pyjamas were folded on top of his pillow, his shampoo, soap, electric razor, and skin lotions all in their place.

Two items were missing, however, and their absence quickened his pulse. Rosten's toothbrush and toothpaste.

At that moment of revelation, even as he was pawing frantically through drawers in search of them, his cellphone rang.

Freddie.

"Mystery solved," he said, but he didn't sound pleased. "Your boy didn't catch the train back to Belleville. He got on the 2:22 in the opposite direction. To Ottawa."

Green was already on the Queensway on his way home when his cellphone rang. He glanced at the call display, which read *A. Goodfellow*, and debated whether to answer. He was going to be home on time for the first time since his father fell ill, but even so, the schedule would be tight. It was Tony's night for Beavers and Green's night to do the car pool. He had cancelled at the last minute too many times to have any goodwill left with the other parents.

But Archie never phoned without good reason. Steering into the right lane for the next exit, Green punched the talk button.

Archie's voice was taut with panic. "He's gone."

Green nearly drove off the road. "What do you mean, gone?"

"He went on his own to a medical appointment in Kingston and on the way back he hopped a train to Ottawa."

"What the fuck!" Green wrestled his car down the exit ramp and pulled onto the shoulder, fumbling among the gas receipts and empty coffee cups for his Bluetooth. "Have you reported it?"

"Yes, and your guys have all the details. But I thought you should know. I don't know why he's gone there."

"What time was the train due in?"

"4:20."

Green glanced at his watch. 4:45. There was a very slim chance Rosten might not have left the station yet, if the train had one of its very frequent delays or Rosten had trouble disembarking or finding an accessible taxi.

"I'm on this. I'll get back to you." He whipped the car back onto the road. As he accelerated back toward the train station, he phoned the NCO for an update. Two units had been dispatched to the train station as soon as the alert came in, but they had missed him. Station staff remembered a man in a wheelchair leaving the station and getting into a taxi. No licence plate, no descriptions, but uniforms were canvassing the remaining cabbies in the line as well as any fellow passengers still in the station.

So far there were no answers.

Green scoured his brain for explanations. This made no sense! Rosten must know that he would be apprehended within hours, that one man in a wheelchair was no match for the police resources of a major city. What did he hope to accomplish? What — or who — was he looking for? Someone from his past? From his trial? From his family?

After twenty years, the list was very small. Green himself was the most obvious target, but surely it would be utter folly for Rosten to go after a high-profile police officer in person. There were the witnesses at his trial, most of whom were professionals from forensics or pathology, along with a few university students who had probably long since moved on.

There was Rosten's own family, but most were either in Sudbury, where he'd grown up, or in Halifax, where his wife had moved. Only one lived in Ottawa, the daughter whom he barely knew but who merited more attention.

But there was one person who positively screamed danger. "We need a unit out to Marilyn Carmichael's house in Navan. It's ..." He scrounged his memory for the address.

"Already on its way," the sergeant replied. "Luckily, the bastard can't do much sneaking around in that wheelchair." He paused. "You were the investigator on that case. What do you figure this is? Payback?"

Green felt a wave of relief. Sergeant Bowles came from a background in the Tactical Unit and quickly zeroed in on state-of-mind issues.

"I have no idea. But he's not a guy to let go once he gets something in his sights, and he remembers every damn word of his trial. We have to be prepared for revenge."

Green broke off as an awful thought occurred to him. Was this what Rosten had intended all along? Was this the real reason he had changed his story and sought his release from prison? Not for some belated desire to teach, but for revenge? Anger swept through him. Had they all been duped? Archie, the prison psychiatrists, the tough-minded PO, the director of the prison school?

"Get hold of his court file and check every witness whose testimony helped put him behind bars," he snapped. "We have to find out who's still in the city and get units over there. If he's going to strike, it will be fast. He knows he's only got hours before we catch him."

After signing off, he phoned Archie back. By this time, he was closing in on the train station.

Archie answered on the first ring, as if the phone had never left his hand. "Any news?" he said, quashing any hope Green had that Rosten had phoned in.

"Not yet. Archie, what the hell is he doing?"

"I don't know! I had no idea ... I told the cops, 'You think we'd have let him go on his own if we had any idea he was planning this?' He's been quiet as a mouse. Compliant, helpful ... *goddamn!*"

"Any unusual outings or visitors?"

"Visitors, yes. Two. One was his daughter, the one I told you about."

Green's hopes surged. "She actually came to visit?"

"Yes. I've been working on it and I finally persuaded her to meet with James and me. She only stayed fifteen minutes. I don't think they knew what to say to each other, but it was a start."

A huge start, Green thought. For Rosten, who had lived with nothing but the memory of a tiny toddler for all these years, this was a step beyond all he'd hoped for. Maybe that joy, that hope, had swept him away. Surely that was where he'd gone.

Archie was still talking about the meeting, but Green barrelled through. "What's her name and address?"

Once Archie supplied the address, Green rang off immediately to notify the NCO. He knew that within minutes a patrol car in the area would be on its way to the daughter's house. He was breathing more calmly as he swung into the long, curving entrance drive to the train station, now lined with impatient taxis. He pulled up beside a patrol car. The officer was inside on his radio, fiddling simultaneously with his in-car computer. Green tapped on the window and held up his ID.

"Any luck tracking down the cab that picked him up?" he asked the surprised officer who rolled down his window.

"Not yet, sir. The cabbies here didn't recognize him, said he wasn't one of the regulars. But we have calls in to all the taxi companies and they'll put the word out on their radios."

"Tell them to be careful about what they say over the air," Green said sharply. "This man should be considered dangerous."

The patrol officer nodded. "He didn't take an accessible van, just an ordinary sedan — the cabbie put the wheelchair in the trunk — so it's going to take more time. And some of these guys are only part-timers who borrow their uncle's taxi to make a bit of extra money. He might be off duty now and not listening to dispatch."

Green left the officer to his phone calls and headed into the train station to check with the man's partner. A few passengers in Rosten's first-class car had been intercepted and questioned, but no one noticed anything unusual or suspicious about him. The wheelchair had been immobilized for the trip, and one woman remarked he spent almost all his time looking out the window. Not gazing as if in a daydream, but staring as if he were drinking up every sight. Since there was little to see but barns, cows, and endless freshly ploughed fields, it seemed to her an odd scrutiny. His facial expression barely changed, she said, but she did detect a small smile as the first suburban houses of Barrhaven came into view.

The station attendant, having assisted him off the train and pushed him up the ramp, had left him at the exit gate, where Rosten thanked him and indicated he needed no further help. He was polite, the attendant said, not confused but nervous. He had a small bag on his lap, plus a book and a map.

"A map?" Green repeated. "Of the city?"

"Eastern Ontario," the attendant said. "I've got the same one myself. Very handy, shows all the little back-country roads in the whole region."

Backcountry roads — Rosten's specialty. In a flash, Green was back on the phone to Sergeant Bowles. "He's got a rural backcountry road map. Any word from the unit going to Marilyn Carmichael's house in Navan?"

"They're in place. No sign of him."

"Anything from the daughter's place yet?"

"No sign of him there either. Uniform spoke to the daughter. She's scared. Her husband wants her to take the baby and go to a friend's for the night."

"Might not be a bad idea." Green signed off, baffled and frustrated. Every line of inquiry led to a dead end. Had Rosten spotted the patrol cars and aborted whatever mission he'd been planning? If so, where had he gone? What were they all missing?

What the *hell* was Rosten up to?

The answer didn't come until the next morning. His phone rang before he'd even managed his first cup of coffee. Tony and Aviva were playing peekaboo in the kitchen and Green could barely hear the NCO over the shrieks of laughter.

"We finally tracked down the cabbie. He was at a night class at the university, slept over at his girlfriend's. He didn't pick up his message until now."

"And where did he take the bastard?"

"Some place way the hell out in the country."

"Navan?"

"No. West Carleton Township. The drive was almost an hour each way. Rosten paid him two hundred in cash, off the meter …"

Green's pulse leaped. He flew through his memories of twenty years ago. "West Carleton? Let me guess: 12 Timber Way in Vidon Acres near Morris Island."

"How the hell did you know?"

"That's his cottage. He's gone out to his cottage."

Where his nightmare began, Green thought.

CHAPTER EIGHT

Green raced west on the Queensway, at first ducking in and out of the rush-hour traffic that crawled toward the high-tech offices in Kanata. Once past it, he barrelled along the increasingly deserted highway through Ontario scrubland. Thanks to the "big is cheaper and more efficient" amalgamation craze of the 1990s, large swaths of Eastern Ontario bush and farmland were now subsumed within the boundaries of the City of Ottawa. When Jackie Carmichael's body was found, the remote bush by the Ottawa River had been outside the city limits, but it now fell under city jurisdiction, no longer policed by a small rural detachment of the Ontario Provincial Police, but by all the specialist firepower of a large urban police service.

That much was evident as Green reached the turnoff to the winding country road that led into the area. A cruiser was parked at the entrance, screening all vehicles entering or leaving. After being waved through, Green drove through the dense woods, noting a pair of startled deer watching from the verge. He slowed marginally. Soon the whole area would be awash in official vehicles and the deer would melt further into the forest.

The area formed a triangle at the junction of two rivers, the mighty Ottawa and the Mississippi, a much smaller tributary originating in the Lanark Highlands. The rocky point was lushly forested, but still showed scars from its distant logging and mining past. At one time, it had been crisscrossed with railway spurs, rough-cut logging roads, and bush camps, but nature had reclaimed most of the land, leaving clumps of cedar and mixed hardwoods to flourish in the rich, damp soil. As the logging receded, city dwellers had ventured west to tuck modest cottages into the rugged, undulating shore-line, while the outlying rocky islands and peninsulas were protected as a nature preserve.

It was one of the region's best-kept nature secrets. *However, no secret can remain hidden forever,* Green thought ruefully as he noted the large modern estates peeking through the trees and the developers' signs adver-tising lots for sale. As he neared the turnoff to Timber Way, he saw that many of the old cottages from his mem-ory had been replaced by modern homes, complete with paved drives and two-car garages. As he crested the hill and wove through the thick forest, he spotted the flash-ing red and blue lights of a cruiser blocking the lane to Rosten's little cottage. A uniformed officer was hunkered down behind the vehicle, probably awaiting instructions. He glanced back at Green drove up.

Green left his car on the road, well out of the way, and stood in the shelter of a tree, pulling his jacket tight against the damp chill of the morning. The blackflies descended in gleeful swarms. Waving them away, he scanned the cottage. Once an unadorned board-and-batten bungalow, it had been transformed to cottage chic. Where once the drive had been a dirt track, it was now finely crushed limestone, and the path to the front door was slate. The overgrown tangle of brush in front had been replaced by sculpted lilies and ferns. The wood siding had been stained deep mahogany and the trim painted green to match the new steel roof.

Someone was taking excellent care of this cottage. It looked deserted, however. No cars other than the police cruiser sat in the drive, and all the curtains were drawn. No sound could be heard except the intermittent crackling of a police radio.

He joined the officer and squatted behind his cruiser, trying to ignore the bugs. After identifying himself, he asked for a status report.

"We're securing the area, sir, and waiting for backup. My partner is circling to the back of the house. Our sergeant is on his way."

"Is the subject inside?"

"We're attempting to establish that, sir. We've seen no sign of movement and so far he hasn't responded to our calls."

Green nodded to the neighbouring house about a hundred feet away. Although it was barely visible through the trees, Green could make out another police officer talking to a woman. "Have the neighbours seen him?"

"Not this morning. They said there was some activity late yesterday afternoon, and they thought they heard a car later in the evening."

"Then perhaps he has driven away," Green said.

"The sergeant said to take no chances. We have him contained, so we can wait him out."

Green peered over the roof of the cruiser at the cottage again. It looked dark and still. How much danger could Rosten present, even if there was a gun at the cottage, which was unlikely? As he recalled, Rosten had disliked guns.

"What do we know about the cottage?" he asked. "Does he still own it?"

"According to land registry, yes, sir. But the neighbour says it's been rented out during the summer by a property management firm. No one's rented it yet this season, though."

That explained the cottage's facelift. All the time Rosten was in prison, he had been collecting a tidy rental income. Had the money gone to the wife and daughters, or had he socked it all away in a bank account he now had access to? *The bastard*, Green thought once again. *Has he played us all for fools?*

Anger made him step around the car and walk toward the house. From sheer force of training, his hand strayed to the handle of his Glock, but he doubted Rosten would shoot him. So far on this outing, the man was only guilty of breach of parole. Shooting a police officer would put him back behind bars forever. If he wasn't shot dead on the spot himself.

The uniformed constable watched in shocked silence as Green crunched up the gravel drive to the front door. Not a single shadow moved behind its glass. He pressed himself against the protection of the wall. "James! It's Inspector Green. We have to talk!"

No answer. He pressed his ear to the wall. No sound. Twisting the front door knob gingerly, he found it locked. He walked around the side of the house and peered through the window into a bedroom, which was neat and empty. The bunk beds were stripped. He called out again, to no avail.

Around the back of the house, a large patio door gave onto a new deck overlooking the river. Patio furniture had been stacked in the corner for the winter. The blackflies were ferocious, and he gritted his teeth as he mounted the deck stairs toward the door. Not a curtain twitched. By now, he was convinced Rosten had left. Whatever reason had drawn him to the house — nostalgia or a long-cherished memento — it no longer held him there. Green eased his hand from his gun.

He peered through the glass door. Under the canopy of trees, the cozy living room was dark, but he could make out a fieldstone fireplace and twin loveseats angled toward the lake. The fireplace too was new. Green remembered a smoky black woodstove that barely kept the place warm in the fall.

At first he could see no other details, but as his eyes adjusted to the darkness, he made out the shiny chrome of a wheelchair. The curve of the wheel, the footrests and the vague outline of a man's legs.

A chill shot through him. He grabbed his gun handle and ducked back against the wall, his heart hammering. He took a deep breath to regroup before peering through the glass again. The figure had not moved. Was the man lying in wait? In silent ambush? Had this been his plan all along? Lure Green out to exact his ultimate revenge?

Green unclipped his gun. Peeked in. The shadow did not move. He called out, banged on the door. Not even a reflexive flinch. Dread stole in past Green's fear. The patio door slid open soundlessly beneath his touch, and a rush of stale, pungent air flowed out. Gun drawn and eyes riveted to the wheelchair, he stepped inside.

He spoke softly. "James, it's over. Don't make it worse by …"

His voice faded as he crossed the room to the motionless man. James was upright in his chair, his head bent forward and his hands limp on the wheels.

Green pulled a pair of neoprene gloves from his pocket. Even before he touched Rosten's cold, rigid neck, he knew the man was dead.

"You couldn't find one lowly coroner out here, laddie?"

Green almost smiled in spite of himself. He had watched the forensic pathologist stride up the gravel lane toward the yellow cordon, swiping at blackflies and cursing in his colourful Scottish brogue. Dr. Alexander MacPhail was ageless, his face creviced by acne and booze, and his white hair flying from the elastic he used to capture it. Green could tell from the glint in the man's bloodshot eyes that he was enjoying the novelty of the call.

"What, and deprive you of this chance to sink your teeth into a real mystery? Dead man still sitting in his wheelchair, no sign of a struggle, no sign of anyone else on the premises."

"A dead man."

Green nodded, catching a whiff of stale booze as the doctor spoke.

"I haven't pronounced yet, laddie. You been earning a medical degree in your spare time?"

"No, but I've learned a bit hanging out with you. He's good and stiff, I'd say he's been dead since last night."

"So what's the mystery?" MacPhail asked, pulling on his white bunny suit. "People do die, lad, with surprising regularity."

Green said nothing. By now the scene was humming with activity. The uniformed team had strung yellow tape around the cottage grounds, and Ident had laid a trail of paper squares to mark the access route. Ducking under the tape, Green led MacPhail around the side of the cottage, careful to stay on the trail. MacPhail was gazing all around, taking in the dense tree canopy, the swarms of blackflies, and the chilly damp. All grist for a pathologist's mill.

Once on the back deck, Green gestured through the open patio door. "That's true," he replied belatedly. "But not all of them are paroled murderers on the run, three hundred kilometres from their halfway house. This is going to be a mess, Alex. We need to cross every *t* and dot every *i*."

MacPhail glanced up sharply. "Your case?"

"A lifetime ago."

With a grunt, MacPhail headed inside, ignoring the Ident team photographing the scene. He stopped to sniff the air, wiggled his bulbous nose, and nodded appreciatively. "Tandoori chicken, lamb korma, and expensive single malt. A man with good taste!" He paused to shake his head dolefully. "Pity." He leaned over to poke and prod Rosten's body, which was rigidly molded to the chair. Easing himself down on creaky knees, he shone his flashlight onto the face and hands.

"I do think you are right, lad. He is dead. Rigour is near its peak, so, given the ambient temperature of about ten degrees overnight, your ETD is probably also right. Yesterday evening. Not sure you need me any more, laddie."

"Can you determine cause of death?"

"Without examining him? Even for me, that would be a neat trick. He's very pale, your boy —"

"He's been in prison twenty years."

"Ah." MacPhail wielded his flashlight over the body and chair. "I don't see signs of cardiac arrest, asphyxia, or gastrointestinal upset. Your boy did not thrash about or struggle against death. He went gentle into that good night. Probably coma."

"Drug overdose?"

MacPhail straightened up, wincing as his back and knees unfolded. "Could be."

"Shit."

"But let's not be getting ahead of ourselves. For now, I will order the autopsy and rule the death suspicious, pending further investigation."

They were the words Green needed to keep the Ident and Major Crimes teams involved. It was not yet a criminal investigation, but it allowed him to gather crucial evidence that might be needed if it became one. Memories faded and physical evidence was often washed away in the critical few days it took to establish a cause of death.

The Ident team, headed by the consummate obsessive scientist Lyle Cunningham, had already ordered a search of the grounds for footprints and tire tracks. The half dozen or so official vehicles already on the premises had rendered that search nearly futile, but if there were the odd print unaccounted for, Cunningham would pounce on it. He had declared the cottage and grounds off-limits to everyone but MacPhail to avoid scene contamination, so any further evidence from inside the cottage would have to wait for his report. With one final look at the sad figure in the wheelchair, Green headed outside to touch base with Major Crimes.

His newest sergeant, Marie Claire Levesque, had caught the call at Major Crimes that morning and had arrived with her grande latte and her latest rookie from general assignment in tow. While she waited for Cunningham's preliminary report, she orchestrated a canvas of the neighbourhood. There wasn't much to canvas, she told Green. According to the first responders,

Timber Way consisted of ten homes strung out about two hundred feet apart along the twisting shoreline of the Mississippi River. Half the houses were empty, the other half inhabited year-round by commuters. Many of these had already left for work and their children had been picked up by the school bus.

Only the immediate next-door neighbours were still around by mid-morning, a retired couple with two dogs in a cozy little cottage surrounded by bird feeders. They had, as they told the first officers on the scene, not noticed anyone arrive, perhaps because they were out in their kayaks, but they had seen lights on in the cottage. At some point in the evening, they had heard a car and their dogs had barked. After that, because the lights were off in the cottage, they assumed the visitor had gone.

When MacPhail finally emerged around the side of the house, Levesque broke off her briefing to watch his approach. She tried to keep her face impassive, but a tiny pout pulled the corners of her mouth. *She still doesn't like my meddling*, Green thought with amusement. *She'd better get used to it on this case.*

"Dr. MacPhail? You called the big guns out today, Inspector?"

MacPhail executed a gallant bow, rendered comical by his bunny suit. His enthusiasm became palpable. Nothing to do with the mysterious death, Green knew, but with Levesque's willowy, long-limbed figure, perfect cheek bones, and pale blonde hair. Despite her severely tailored clothes and lack of makeup, many a competent male was rendered semi-incoherent at the sight of her.

"Victim is a middle-aged man, roughly 175 centimetres, sixty kilos, with significant atrophy of the lower limbs consistent with spinal cord paralysis, but well-developed musculature in the upper torso."

When he continued on to reiterate the routine details, Green found his attention wandering. He was startled when MacPhail raised his voice.

"Something you don't know, laddie. Sergeant Cunningham found empty bottles marked benzodiazepam and Scotch under the wheelchair. Aberlour ..." He closed his eyes as if to pay homage. "Expensive by anyone's standards, pure gold to a man who's been inside for twenty years. I will run tox screens, of course, but I had a quick whiff of our boy. The same heavenly smell."

"So he was mixing alcohol and diazepam."

"Could be. Did he have a prescription for diazepam?"

Green made a note to ask Archie but he doubted it.

"Diazepam is a tranquilizer normally used to treat anxiety and sometimes insomnia," MacPhail said. "Was your lad suffering from either?"

Green shook his head. He may have, but abstinence from drugs and alcohol was part of his release conditions. Diazepam made a nice high and was far too easy to abuse, or sell, to be prescribed in a custodial facility.

"Any sign of the drinking glass?" he asked.

"The place was very clean except for the bottles in the living room and the empty cartons of takeaway curry in the kitchen bin."

"What about the rest of the cottage?"

MacPhail shrugged. "Undisturbed. No linen on the bed or towels in the lavvy."

"It's not been rented yet this season," Levesque interjected. "Rentals and maintenance are handled by a property management firm based in Ottawa —"

"You'll need to interview them," Green said before he could stop himself. He was rewarded with another pout.

"I already have. They've been handling the cottage for twenty years; rentals are on a monthly or seasonal basis only."

"How are the accounts managed?"

"The firm works through the wife, but James Rosten set it up, and the money goes into a joint account at Scotiabank."

"Any recent activity on that account?"

Levesque made a show of consulting her watch. "It's only eleven o'clock, sir. We're working on the paperwork."

He grinned at her. MacPhail took that moment to interrupt. "I'll leave you two lovebirds to sort out the details while I get my own paperwork in order so my lads can remove the body to the morgue. Have you notified next of kin?"

Levesque nodded. "Wife's been called. Goes by her maiden name, Victoria MacLeod, now. She lives in Halifax and she doesn't want anything to do with the arrangements. She would have divorced him, she said, but for the financial entanglements. He refused to sell the cottage."

Out of spite or nostalgia, Green wondered. *Or as one last tie to the woman he still loved?*

"Rosten has a daughter here in Kanata," he said. "I suspect none of the family will be too happy to claim him, but you could start there."

Levesque's notebook was poised. "Name?"

Green supplied the name. "The community chaplain knows her. I'll see if he can smooth the way."

After the briefest hesitation, Levesque nodded. "Thank you, sir."

As she walked away, she flicked her blonde ponytail irritably. MacPhail chuckled. "Losing your touch, laddie?"

"She's a good cop but she doesn't like supervision."

"You mean meddling."

Green laughed. "Humour her, Alex. It's her case. But keep me in the loop. I have to liaise with Correctional Services."

MacPhail grimaced. "Better you than me. You'll be dropping by to observe the PM too?"

No response was necessary, for Green had never survived past the opening of the skull, but MacPhail was still laughing when he walked away. Green caught sight of the phalanx of media vans now lining the end of the driveway beyond the tape. It wouldn't be long before they had determined the owner of the property and began to link this new death with the old murder case. It was a media jackpot, and speculation on the dead man's identity would fill the airwaves and cyberspace. Twitter was a terrifying tool.

Rosten's daughter had to be informed immediately.

He phoned Archie Goodfellow's cellphone and was relieved when the big man answered right away. Archie too did not need to read this on his latest Twitter feed.

"Oh no, oh no, oh no," he said when Green broke the news. His normally jovial voice cracked. "How? Oh sweet Jesus, how?"

Green filled him in on Rosten's flight to the cottage and his apparent overdose. "It's looking like suicide, Archie."

Archie was silent but Green could hear him fighting for breath. "Does that seem possible, Archie?"

"No. No!"

"You yourself said he was lonely and feeling overwhelmed. You and I know it's a risk when guys get out after dreaming all these years about being free, only to discover they have nothing."

Archie took a deep breath. "You're right. But I didn't see any signs. How could I have missed the signs? I wouldn't have let him go on his own if ..." He broke off. Green could hear him muttering.

"Archie, what?"

"No, it still makes no sense."

"What?"

"He didn't get the news he was hoping for from the Kingston specialist. He'd been reading on the Internet about new neural stimulation research, and he'd been hoping he might regain some limited use of his legs with this new therapy. Enough to get around his room, in and out of cars. The doctor said no."

"So instead, he hops a train to Ottawa, goes back to a place he loved, and kills himself."

"No! Damn it! I would have seen something."

"Not if he didn't want you to. Tell me, was he on diazepam?"

"Are you kidding? In a house full of cons?"

"Could he have got hold of some there? Any dealers, any connections?"

"In my world, Mike? There's always someone who knows someone. But James had no history of drug use, never shown any interest either."

"What about alcohol?"

"No. James didn't like anything that messed with his brain. He'd lecture all the guys about it too. Point out how many brain cells were being killed with every drink, how many of the guys owed their troubles to one drink too many." Archie paused. "He'd never think to drown his sorrows in a bottle of pills or booze. If he was going to kill himself, he'd do it in one grand sweep. Roll his wheelchair off the dock."

When Green pondered the idea, he conceded Archie's point. James Rosten would go down fighting, his death as much an act of defiance as of despair. Peacefully consuming an entire bottle of pills and Scotch while looking out over the bay suggested resignation. Not a mood Green would ever associate with him.

Yet Rosten was a biologist. He would know exactly what effect would be achieved by combining diazepam with alcohol. He would also likely know how much of each would be lethal and how long it would take.

"Speculation for now, Archie. Let's wait for the autopsy before you beat yourself up over this. I need the phone number for the daughter."

"Paige? Hang on." His asthmatic breathing whistled in the silence as he searched. After reading out the number, he sucked in his breath. "That's another thing! He was just beginning to reconnect with her. Remember I told you she came for a visit a couple of weeks ago. It …" He faltered. "It didn't go great; they were both too nervous, so it was awkward. But sweet Jesus, after twenty years of hoping, it was a start!"

Green cut through the sentiment. "What did they talk about?"

"Not much. Small talk, mostly about the work he was planning to do. His medical condition. He asked about her family but she clammed up at that. I told him it was going to take time and he didn't seem discouraged."

"Did they talk about future visits?"

"Nope. But I think there would have been more. You could see them both kind of feeling ahead in the dark." Archie caught his breath. "But he did mention the cottage. Asked if she or her sister ever went there. She asked what cottage, and so he told her about how they used to play on the sand beach he made. She had no memory of it, of course."

"Did he seem sad about that?"

"Yeah, but … Mike, I wouldn't read anything into that. They both seemed a little sad, like it was a part of their lives lost in time. I still think … It wasn't a comfortable reunion, but I think afterwards James had hope. And so did his daughter."

* * *

Green had to use the GPS on his cellphone to navigate the labyrinth of crescents in the new subdivision of Stittsville where Paige Henriksson lived. When Green was growing up in inner-city Lowertown, as far removed from suburbia as it was possible to be, Stittsville had been its own little village, with a main street, a whistle-stop train station, and a handful of local shops. When the city first began to stretch its tentacles toward the old village, developers championed it as "just beyond the fringe."

It was now well within the fold. Acres of pasture and corn fields had been sacrificed to tract housing that looked indistinguishable from any other suburb on the continent. Like its neighbours, Paige Henriksson's house boasted two storeys of bland beige brick, a double garage, and a scattering of marigolds, petunias, and spindly new shrubs under the bay window.

Green recognized the flowers only because he had bought the same ones at the local supermarket garden centre two weeks earlier. He figured he'd done well to choose colours that matched, but Sharon apparently wanted flowers that weren't on half the lawns in the neighbourhood. The lowly flats were still sitting on the back deck waiting to be planted in hidden corners of the yard. Now, with his father's health crisis, that likelihood had faded along with the blooms.

With an active toddler, Paige probably had no more time or inclination than he did to worry about the finer niceties of landscaping. He climbed out of the car, dreading the task ahead but curious to see what kind of woman James Rosten had produced.

He had paid scant attention to the twin girls when they were little, except a cursory question to their mother concerning their adjustment and mental health. He had known almost nothing about children in those days, but Rosten's wife rightly guessed that he was looking for signs of physical or sexual abuse, and she froze him out. Her interaction with him was limited to terse monosyllables, and even when she picked up and fled at the end of the trial, she never betrayed a word of concern about the mental health of her own girls.

He hesitated on the doorstep. Although he was now facing a stranger, he felt he knew the deepest, most formative secret of the young woman's life. It gave him an odd feeling of kinship. When she opened the door, he found himself staring into the watchful grey eyes of a younger, softer Rosten. The rich brown hair was the same, as was the long slim neck and the proud tilt of the head.

She looked trim and fit, but was dressed for comfort rather than style in a grimy T-shirt and old jeans. A pink, well-fed toddler was propped on her hip, clutching a piece of cheese. Unlike the mother, the boy was grinning ear to ear.

"Mrs. Paige Henriksson?" To forestall her incipient protest, Green produced his ID and introduced himself.

"Inspector Green," she repeated. "Michael Green. Aren't you the one who …?"

He nodded. "May I come in?"

"What's this about?"

He inclined his head politely. "Perhaps we can talk inside."

She didn't move. "I don't plan to see him again, if that's why you're here. If it's against the rules or something."

"No. I have news."

Belatedly, she seemed to hear the gravity of his tone. She clutched her child closer, opened her mouth to ask what news, and then turned instead to go back inside. He followed her into the brightly painted but minimally furnished interior. A chemical smell of new house still clung to the air.

The living room looked as if a hurricane had blown through. Paige looked flustered as she tossed toys aside to clear a space for Green on the sofa. "I'm sorry. I —"

He held up his hand. "I have three children. Believe me, I understand."

She sank onto the sofa opposite, still hanging on to her son, who had begun to wriggle. She fixed her eyes on Green, no longer wary but frankly fearful. "What news?"

"Bad news, I'm afraid. Your father is dead."

She didn't react. She continued to gaze at him as if the words had no meaning.

"He appears to have died last night up at his cottage near Morris Island."

Now she blinked. "The cottage? I knew he'd escaped. But dead?"

"He took a taxi out there yesterday. I thought he might have contacted you."

"No." The toddler squirmed and pushed her away. Numbly she opened her arms and released him. She took a deep breath. "My God," she murmured. "What happened?"

"We don't know yet. There will be an autopsy, probably in a couple of days."

"Was he sick? I mean, I hardly knew him, but he didn't say anything about that. He looked fine." She shook her head, grappling. "Was it an accident? Did he roll off …? I've never been to the cottage, I don't know if it has a deck or stairs …"

"No, nothing like that. He was inside."

She was watching him intently, as if trying to see through his evasions. Her son had clambered onto a lamb toy on wheels and was beginning to scoot around the living room, crashing into furniture with delight. Paige didn't seem to notice, so focused was she on absorbing the news. Slowly her eyes widened.

"Was he murdered?"

"There's no sign of that either. But we'll know more once the autopsy is complete."

"He was just lying there?"

"Well, sitting in his wheelchair, actually. As if he was looking out at the view."

She pressed her hand to her mouth to hide its trembling. "He talked about that cottage. He wanted to see it again."

"Did he mention plans to come up here, maybe show it to you?"

"We didn't get that personal. It's odd, you know, meeting a stranger who you know is your father but who's also a monster, and you've grown up all these years with this huge shameful secret hanging over you like a shroud. Most of the time, he was nothing to me. I didn't think about it. I didn't remember him at all and my mother didn't talk about him. No one in my mother's family did."

She paused, as if trying in vain to stem the memories. "No, that's not quite true. When we were little, the official story was that he was dead. That worked until I got to school and somebody spilled the beans. Our mother pulled us out of that school and put us in another, but the damage was done. I couldn't pretend he was dead, because he wasn't. I couldn't even have a make-believe father like some of my friends with single moms, because I had a murderer instead. For a while I pretended he was dead, but that only takes you so far when you're ten."

Green tried to look understanding. He'd handled dozens of struggling survivors over the years and watched families come to grips with a murderer in their midst. It never got any easier for him. But unlike many survivors, who grew up in what amounted to a family war zone, Paige was an innocent, protected by a mother who had known how to escape.

"How did he seem when you met him?" he asked, to steer her away from her memories.

For the first time she noticed her son, who was racing down the hall and smashing into the end wall with shrieks of glee. She seemed to hesitate before choosing to ignore the destruction.

"The thing that struck me the most was how ordinary he was. Not at all the monster I'd imagined. In that wheelchair, with his grey hair and sad, tired eyes, it was hard to picture him killing anyone. I know that's the trouble. Killers and monsters do seem like ordinary people.

"He drank his coffee black and worried about whether my coffee was hot enough. He seemed ready to take the staff to task on my behalf." She smiled faintly. "The coffee was awful, and when I told him it was fine, he smiled. It was such an ordinary smile. Reminded me of my sister, Pam. He said, 'No, it's appalling, but it's nice of you not to say so.'

"I guess I was surprised by how well-spoken he was. I was expecting some semi-literate thug because that's how we think of murderers, and I forgot he was a professor with a Ph.D. from Princeton. Not that that makes him any less a murderer, of course, but his intelligence didn't seem manipulative." She flushed and bit her lip. "I don't have any experience with murderers, but he … Well, he just wasn't at all what I expected."

"How did you leave things with him?"

She rose abruptly to intercept her son just as he was heading for the wall at full speed again. The wall already had several dents and, as Green glanced around, he saw other signs of toddler destruction. Gouges on the legs of the dining room table, scratches on the white baseboard, and broken stalks on the houseplant in the corner.

Paige snatched him off the moving toy with a sharp reprimand, which evoked a screech of rage. The boy thrashed and kicked in her arms but she pinned him tightly to her chest. Averting her head to evade his fists, she met Green's eyes. He thought there were tears in hers.

"I just left. Said I had to think about things and consider the effect on my son. And on my husband."

"And how did your father take that?"

As she struggled to soothe her child, she looked very young. Barely older than Hannah, and much too young to be handling such a fiercely wilful son. Yet she held on. "He was very quiet. He said he was happy to meet me. That's all." She eyed him keenly. "These questions ... are you suggesting he may have killed himself?"

"I don't know, Paige. I honestly don't know. He had a lot to contend with, a lot of adjustments to make after twenty years of lost life."

"That's what my husband said. That I shouldn't get too close. Too involved. Give us all space. He ... he did phone, once, and left a message. I didn't return it." Her voice dropped to a whisper. "I'd hate to think ..."

As soon as he was back in his car, Green phoned Archie Goodfellow again. The chaplain sounded harassed and worried, a shadow of his usual jocular self.

"Boy, have I dropped myself in the middle of it this time, Mike! Corrections is all over me. First for letting him go to Kingston by himself in the first place, although technically his PO authorized it, but more importantly for not reporting him absent when he didn't show up on his train."

"Bureaucratic ass-covering, Archie. It's moot. He was already on the train to Ottawa."

"I know, but if I'd reported it, they'd have caught up with him before he got off the train in Ottawa, and got him back into custody safe and sound."

Green gazed out the window in search of a reassuring answer. The truth was there wasn't one. Archie had screwed up, and it would likely cost him. Not the least with his own conscience.

The venetian blind in Paige's living room twitched. She was watching him, probably wondering what he was putting in his report and what judgment he was passing on her actions. Not so harsh as her own judgment, he suspected.

"Archie, I've been to see the daughter," he said. "She says he tried to contact her once more after their visit. Did you know about that?"

Archie paused. "Nothing came of it. She never returned the call."

"But it may have influenced his state of mind."

"I know what you're thinking, but he wasn't discouraged. She hadn't cut him off. You know James, Mike. This is a guy who doesn't give up, who hangs on to the tiniest thread of hope. All those years in prison, that's what got him through. He's not going to give up now, not with his daughter and grandson almost within reach. Not to mention ..."

"Not to mention what?"

Silence stretched across time. An old grey SUV revved around the corner and shot up the street. It braked beside Green and the man at the wheel stared at him for a moment before pulling into Paige's drive.

"Well, I'm in enough trouble," Archie said finally. "I don't know if it means anything, but you better know. James had another visitor."

"Who?" As Green watched, the man got out of the SUV and glared at him before heading in the front door.

So she called her husband, he thought. *I guess that's natural enough.*

"He wasn't supposed to have any contact with her," Archie was saying, "but she's the one who came to me. I set the meeting up off the grounds in a public place — Tim Hortons. I didn't stay, because she didn't want me to, but I kept watch through the window from the parking lot. He was really surprised by the visit. More puzzled than suspicious, I'd say. Excited even, like maybe she had something significant to say."

"Archie. Who?"

"The last person either of us would expect. Marilyn Carmichael."

Green was flabbergasted. "What did she want?"

"James never told me. Never said a word about the meeting except that she had a lot of courage. She didn't stay long, but when he came back outside, he was different. Visibly shaken."

"Ashamed? Guilty?"

"No. I can't put my finger on it. More like his world was suddenly upside down."

CHAPTER NINE

G reen was already halfway across the city on his way to Navan before he remembered Marie Claire Levesque. She had not been pleased that he'd barged into her case to take over notification of next of kin, but since her only other option was to send her rookie sidekick along with a local uniform, she had capitulated with as much grace as she could muster.

She would not be so forgiving of his taking over a key witness. Nor would he have been, in her shoes. Which he had been once — a new detective filled with righteous conviction, out to make his mark. Ignoring the reprimands of both the OPP and his own sergeant in his determination to follow his gut.

His rationale now, which he formulated as he rang her cellphone, was that, first of all, this was not yet an active murder inquiry and, second, Marilyn Carmichael was likely to be far more forthcoming with him than with a stranger.

Not to mention he knew exactly what questions to ask.

When Levesque answered with her trademark bilingual "*Oui, âllo*, Sergeant Levesque," Green filled her in first on his interview with Rosten's daughter. She listened without comment until he mentioned Rosten's later call to her.

"And this was what date?"

"Two days ago. He left a message which she didn't return."

"A disappointment for him, for sure," she said. "And he told her how much he loved the cottage?"

"Yes. She doesn't even remember it."

"Another disappointment." He could almost see her ticking off the suicide checklist. "We will need a formal statement from her and instructions on the release of the body."

"Those sound like tasks for your new detective," Green said. As casually as he could, he tossed out the next line. "Any new developments in the investigation at your end?"

"Small details. Ident has lifted usable prints from both the Scotch bottle and the pill bottle. Rosten's prints are on file, of course, so it will be an easy match once Cunningham gets back to the station. They did a search of the house, but there were no signs that any of the other rooms were disturbed. Rosten's bag was on one of the beds and it contained nothing unusual." She rhymed off toiletries, a sweater, and a paperback thriller.

"No pyjamas?"

"No. We have found two neighbours further up the road who saw the taxi drive in and out again. About dinnertime, one said. The other thought it was later. They heard and saw no activity at the cottage, because it is too hidden by trees."

"What about the taxi driver? Has he been interviewed?"

"He is in class. We have arranged to meet him in an hour."

"Don't forget to ask him —"

"I know what to ask him. Sir. Rosten's mood and demeanour, did they make any stops, how did he obtain the takeout curry, the Scotch, and the drugs?" She let the silence hang a moment. "Did I pass, boss?"

Green laughed. "Perfect score, Sergeant. I am on my way out to Navan to break the news to Marilyn Carmichael. That's his victim's mother. Apparently she visited him a week ago —"

"She *what*?"

He had hoped to slip this tidbit in quietly, but Levesque was too quick. He sketched in the few details he had on Marilyn's meeting with Rosten.

"And the priest permitted this?" Still incredulous.

"Chaplain. Yes. He felt there might be some healing in it for both of them. He is very big on the healing power of bridges."

"*Tabernac,*" she muttered. "How far is Navan from Morris Island?"

"They are at opposite ends of the city. At least ninety kilometres apart."

"*Sacre bleu*, an hour."

He could almost hear her calculating pros and cons, so he gave her a gentle nudge. "You've got the taxi driver to interview, Marie Claire. I'm already halfway there. And Marilyn Carmichael knows me. This is going to be difficult news for her. I will fill you in on any relevant information."

She signed off with a brusque thank you that made Green smile. Levesque had been on the Major Crimes Squad for over a year and a half now, and she was proving herself a competent detective, albeit precise and procedure-bound. Green was still hoping trust and humour would follow with time, although he suspected he'd be the last to know.

Marilyn Carmichael's laneway was empty when Green pulled in, and her aging green CR-V was nowhere to be seen. Green cursed. He stood in the lane, studying the little house, which looked transformed from the dreary winter months. The front door and shutters had been painted a cheerful green and the window boxes were bursting with flowers. Marigolds and petunias, he observed with a wry smile. The grass was lush, the perennial gardens massed with colour, and the lilac bushes were in full flower. Their fragrance wafted on the country breeze.

He felt a wave of relief. The proud, industrious Marilyn appeared to be back with a vengeance. Perhaps the era of gin was over. He was just bending over to examine a clump of unfamiliar, bright-pink flowers when, to his surprise, the front door opened.

"Inspector! What are you doing here?"

He looked up to see Marilyn standing in the open doorway, pale, tired, and even thinner than ever. He appraised her as he approached, but her eyes were clear and her clothing neat.

"Marilyn, the garden looks beautiful."

"This is its best time of year," she replied. Rather than inviting him in, she stepped out onto the porch.

"I didn't think you were here," he said. "Your car is gone."

She waved her hand dismissively. "Gordon has it. Gone to town for some more paint."

"Gordon's still here? That must be nice for you." Green kept his voice neutral. "Is it him who's been doing the work?"

"The heavy work, yes."

"Is he staying much longer?"

Her lips pursed. "He's not sure of his plans. Paris is ... not what it used to be, he says. Are you just in the neighbourhood, or is there a reason for your visit?"

"There's a reason. Can we go inside?"

Alarm flared in her eyes and she tightened her arms across her chest. "Inside is a bit of a tip, I'm afraid. What's this about?"

"James Rosten."

"Of course. Has he turned up?"

"Yes." He gestured past her toward the door. "Please?"

She searched his face before turning reluctantly to lead the way inside. The interior was in stark contrast to the outside. Dark and dingy, it was still piled high with boxes and garbage bags of clutter. Dishes, beer bottles, and discarded clothes littered the living room. She rushed ahead and busied herself collecting the bottles.

"Kids. They never do grow up, do they? I'm relieved he's turned up. I won't be visiting him again, if that's what you've come about. I wanted to see ... how he was. It felt like something I had to do — to face him square on."

He chose a corner of the sofa, moving a buttery leather jacket aside to make room. "Why?"

"Why?" She turned to head into the kitchen, calling over her shoulder. "I wanted to see what kind of man he'd become. During the trial, I never really saw *him*, only this monster who had killed Jackie. But now he's a middle-aged man, isn't he? No longer the handsome charmer, just an invalid in a wheelchair. I didn't stay long. Tea, Inspector?"

He rose to help her in the kitchen. "Is that why you supported his parole?"

A cup slipped and nearly fell from her grasp. He rescued it and set it down. "I need to move on," she said. "That means letting go. Seeing Rosten for the broken man he is, telling him it was time for him too to move on."

"How did he react to your visit?"

She said nothing while she poured milk into her cup and placed a sliver of lemon beside his. "He thanked me for supporting his parole. He said he was managing and asked me how I was. How the children were."

"What did you say?"

She turned to him then, her back against the counter and her brow knit in alarm. "What's this about? What's happened?"

"Marilyn, James Rosten is dead. He died last night."

She pressed her hand to her mouth. Stared at him, blinking as if in disbelief. "How?"

"We don't know. He was at his cottage on the river."

She absorbed this in silence, no doubt battling a barrage of memories about that infamous place. Green knew she had driven out to the woods after Jackie's body was found and had sat on the damp, leafy ground, sifting the loam through her fingers as if seeking the closeness of her daughter's last moments.

Now she was visualizing another death. Fear, anguish, and ultimately horror flitted across her face. Eventually she pulled herself together with an effort and shook her head. "He didn't seem ill. Was it an accident?"

"We're still investigating. So far there's no evidence of that."

"Then he ..." Her eyes widened. "Oh my lamb, did he kill himself?"

"Did he seem depressed to you?"

"Oh! No. It's just he seemed healthy enough, so ..."

"All I can tell you, Marilyn, is that until the post-mortem, we don't know. We have to keep all possibilities open."

"How did he get there? What was he doing there?"

"He took a taxi. We don't know what he was doing there."

"So he didn't go with someone? Or meet someone there?"

Green hid his surprise. "What makes you think that? Who would he meet?"

"I — I don't know. I just thought ... maybe his daughter?"

"Did he mention that possibility to you when you saw him?"

"No. Well —" The water began bubbling vigorously and she turned her back on him to attend to the tea. "He didn't mention the cottage, but he said he'd met his daughter."

"How was his mood?"

She arranged the tea on a tray but when she tried to pick it up, her hands trembled too badly. He rescued it from her. To his surprise, there were tears in her eyes.

"He *did* kill himself, didn't he? That's what you're saying. Alone, back at the scene of it all, unable to face his life ahead."

"Marilyn, we won't know —"

"I know, I know. Until the autopsy. But surely there are some signs! A gunshot to the head, an empty bottle of pills? A needle by his arm? How?"

"There were some pills, but ..." He stopped himself.

"Then that's it." She headed down the hall toward the living room, her hand on the wall as if to steady herself. "You asked about his mood? He was sad. He didn't say so, but I think he was sad that life had passed him by, that his family and friends had moved on and he had to start from scratch." She sank heavily into a chair. "Poor man."

She made no effort to pour the tea, but merely sat in her chair with her hands clutched in her lap as if she were fighting back a wave of horror. The depth of her emotion puzzled Green.

"An unusual sentiment, coming from you," he remarked.

"Well, I'd only just seen him. Just spoken to him. It gives me the chills."

A car sounded in the drive, and before he could inquire further, the front door flew open. Gordon's thin, high voice filled the house.

"She wasn't on the flight! Sent me a fucking text when I'm nearly at the airport to say —" He stopped abruptly in the archway to the living room. A scowl crossed his face. "So that's a fucking unmarked cop car outside."

Green rose to offer his hand. Gordon had put on some weight, perhaps now that he was back under his mother's wing, and he had abandoned all pretence of the Bohemian *artiste*. He was dressed in flip-flops, torn jeans and an ancient stained T-shirt from the rock band AC/DC. The album title *Back in Black* seemed to match his mood, and three days' worth of patchy stubble did not improve the look.

He gave Green's hand an incredulous stare before addressing his mother. "What does he want?"

Marilyn responded in a rush. "James Rosten is dead. He committed suicide last night at his cottage."

Gordon froze, fighting shock and disbelief before rearranging his face in his customary indifference. "Good riddance, I say."

"Gordon!"

"No, Mum. Eye for an eye, tooth for a tooth. Now I'm going to get myself something a bit stronger and colder than that tea, if you don't mind."

He headed to the kitchen, where Green heard the fridge open.

Marilyn followed, her voice carrying down the hall. "What about Julia? She missed her flight, you say?"

BARBARA FRADKIN

"No, she switched it and flew to Syracuse instead — said it was cheaper — and then rented a fucking car."

Marilyn murmured a response Green couldn't hear.

"Said she wanted to visit an old friend on the way and anyway we'd need more than one car while we're all here. I told her don't expect me to pay half."

"So when is she coming?"

Green heard the sound of a beer top being popped and clattering onto the floor. "You know Julia. Only ever does what's good for Julia. She'll be along in her own sweet time, depending on whether this old friend is a guy or not." Cupboard doors creaked and plates thudded on the counter. "I'm going out back."

Marilyn gave a barely audible whisper.

Gordon raised his voice further in answer. "He's your friend, not mine. Don't expect me to talk to him."

The back screen door screeched and Marilyn returned to the living room, her face pink and her eyes evasive.

"So you have both your children visiting," Green said. "That's unusual."

"I don't know why you say that. I am their mother."

"I didn't mean they shouldn't. But both at the same time?"

"Nothing unusual in that either," she said, reaching for her tea. "It's my sixty-fifth birthday next week, and I'm going to have a celebration. I decided it was high time."

"Happy birthday," he said with a smile. "Lucas would want that."

She sucked in her breath. Put her teacup down with a clatter. "Yes. Yes, he would."

On Monday, after ten days in hospital, Sid Green was finally moved from the Neurology ICU to a regular room on the neurology ward. Nursing and rehab staff buzzed in and out throughout the morning but Sid spent most of the time in bed staring at the ceiling. In the four days since Rosten's death, the team social worker had been trying to set up an appointment with Green but he'd been dodging her calls. He told himself he had no time to spare at the moment, but he knew better. They wanted to ship his father to a nursing home.

Green had always hated hospitals. Even the smell of them filled him with dread. It had been a quarter century since he had sat at his mother's bedside, listening to the monitors beep and watching the life slowly ebb from her shrunken frame. She had not gone gently. If the Holocaust had given her unimaginable scars, it had also given her rage. She had not survived Hitler's death plan just to be robbed by an enemy smaller than the head of a pin.

In the end, all her rage had been no match for the cancer, but the battle left Green with scars of his own. Now he had to fight memories as he tiptoed into his father's room for a quick visit during his lunch hour. His nostrils closed against the smell of flowers, stale food, disinfectant, and urine. By the bed Sid's lunch tray sat untouched, twin globs of congealing mush. Monitors beeped a steady, peaceful rhythm, and Sid Green's breathing was quiet. He lay propped among pillows, slack-jawed and dozing, but at the whisper of Green's shoes, he opened his eyes.

They focused slowly on his son and only then did his jaw work in his struggle to form words.

"Hi, Dad." Green leaned over to kiss his father's papery cheek. "You're looking good today."

Sid waved his functional left hand in irritated dismissal. The right hand was still a claw curved against his chest.

"Was the doctor in this morning?"

Sid nodded. Green watched him gather his words but he didn't intervene. All the therapists said his recovery depended on his will to try. He finally produced two mangled words. "What use?"

"Give yourself time, Dad. Your brain has a lot of healing to do." He gestured to the wheelchair by the bed. "Did they give you a ride today?"

Slowly Sid wagged his head back and forth.

"Do you want a spin? I can take you down to the sunroom." Anything to escape this stifling room and give purpose to the visit. "I'll ask the nurses to help you up."

Sid sank into his pillows with a sigh. Green, however, took that as agreement and went to find some staff. His father was little more than a hundred pounds and Green was learning to transfer him, but it still took two people to accomplish it safely. Sid was more than a dead weight; his damaged body was stiff and resistant, so that all of them, Sid included, were sweaty and panting by the time Sid was strapped in.

His father's face twisted and there were tears in his eyes. Sharon had warned Green that weeping was common among stroke patients, since their emotional control was weakened not only by their sense of loss but also by their damaged brain.

Nonetheless, Green felt a stab of pain. His father had already coped with so much over his life that this seemed an unfair blow. "I know it's frustrating, Dad. Tomorrow I'll take you outside. Spring's here."

Sid hit the armrest of his wheelchair. "No," he said, shaking his head and sending spittle flying. "Not in this."

"It's not forever, Dad."

Green had no idea whether it was forever. The doctors were pessimistic that he would ever use a walker again, given his advanced age and frailty, but at this moment, hope was all his father had.

"Hate this, hate this." Sid continued to flail at the wheelchair until Green reached out to stop his hand. He folded it gently around the armrest.

"Hang on tight, we're going for a ride!"

He wheeled his father slowly around the ward, dodging gurneys, supply carts, and patients wrestling their walkers down the hall. The smell of hospital disinfectant and bland food soured every breath, but Green soldiered on, gaily commenting on the staff and other patients Sid had met before.

Sid greeted everyone with the same uninterested stare. Even the sight of the noon sunshine outside did not rouse a smile. Once he was back in his bed, with his blanket tucked up to his chin, he finally looked up at Green. He said nothing, but the wordless plea in his eyes was eloquent enough. *Fix this*, he seemed to say. *Fix it, or end it.*

Instead, Green cheerfully announced he'd be back tomorrow with Hannah. He was hoping for a flicker of joy, for Hannah was his father's favourite. When Sid merely frowned, Green fled the room. He stopped in the parking lot to recover his equilibrium, and with a heavy heart he finally returned the social worker's call. It's preliminary, she said, but we need to talk about placement options.

Placement options, he thought grimly. As if his father were a carcass in need of storage. Sharon had raised the same issue on the weekend, gently but firmly, and they had even driven out to look at a couple of homes. As he listened to the social worker describing the cheerful gardens and caring staff, all he could see were wheelchairs with their desiccated charges lined up along the wall. Bodies dying, eyes already dead.

He was still subdued when he arrived back at the station. Waiting to greet him was Marie Claire Levesque. She followed him to his office with her notebook in hand and studied him so warily that he wondered if his despair was written on his face.

He forced his face into neutral. "What is it, Marie Claire?"

"Sir, the preliminary post-mortem results are available on James Rosten. Staff Sergeant Sullivan asked me to inform you."

Green was surprised, for James Rosten had died only four days earlier and his was not a high priority case. MacPhail must have been bored enough to work on the weekend. Green invited her inside and gestured to the chair opposite his desk. On the surface, his office appeared more orderly now, but files and manuals had been shoved into the bookcase willy-nilly.

As she settled in and crossed her legs, Levesque's gaze roamed over the titles. "You have some interesting old documents, sir."

He grinned. "If you mean my shelves need clearing out, you're right."

"You've been in Major Crimes a long time."

His grin faded and he felt a quiver of paranoia. Was this Levesque's attempt at rapprochement or was there a sinister innuendo in her words? A suggestion that perhaps it was too long ...

"It's the best place to be," he replied before steering her away. "What did MacPhail find?"

She pursed her lips and opened her notebook. "James Rosten was a fifty-year-old white male in —"

"Just the good stuff, Marie Claire."

Straightening her back, she began to recite. "Rosten was a healthy man. Heart, lungs, liver, bones, GI, everything was normal. Better than normal for a man of his age, because he consumed no drugs or alcohol most of his adult life. He died where he was found, sitting in his chair. There were no marks on the body, no bruises or lacerations that suggest a struggle, and no changes in lividity that suggest he was displaced after death. However, there was sufficient alcohol and diazepam in his system to kill a horse, mostly in his blood and tissues, some still in his stomach — along with a partially digested mix of Indian curry. Dr. MacPhail estimates he died about an hour after he ate."

"Suggesting the meal was eaten at the same time or slightly earlier than the alcohol."

Levesque nodded. "A killer chaser, sir. It appears the pills were swallowed with straight Scotch."

Green pictured Rosten, alone in his beloved cottage, sitting in the living room and gazing out at the spectacular view. Trapped by his past, trapped by his future. Green already knew from the scenario what MacPhail's conclusion would be, but he had to ask.

"Death by suicide," Levesque replied, sounding disappointed the case was over when she'd barely started. "There was too much alcohol and drugs in his system to be accidental. He had one intention, and one intention only."

Green nodded. "Did Ident find anything?"

"No. The prints on the bottles were Rosten's, and there was no sign of disturbance or struggle."

Green's shroud of gloom grew heavier. Life had to be pretty bleak and painful for a man to choose death as a solution. When had Rosten made the decision? When his daughter had avoided his latest call? When Marilyn had visited to remind him of his horrific deed? When the doctor at Kingston General had dashed his hopes of greater recovery? When he'd found life on the outside even lonelier and more purposeless than life inside?

But Green had a nagging fear that it was none of those reasons. He feared Rosten had known all along, from the moment he applied for parole and pretended to make plans for the future, that he was going to kill himself. All he needed was the freedom and opportunity to arrange the deed.

In which case, Green and Archie had played right into his hands.

There would be official repercussions, given that Rosten had died under the Correctional Service of Canada's watch, but unless the family or the media raised a fuss, Rosten's sad story would soon be buried under paperwork.

"Has the family been informed?"

Levesque nodded. "The coroner's office notified them the body is ready for release. The wife doesn't want it. Doesn't want anything to do with the funeral either. The other sister" — Levesque consulted her notes — "Pamela, also doesn't want it. Paige Henriksson is going to take the body, but even she doesn't seem too happy about it." Levesque flushed. "I imagine she wouldn't be, would she? Her father just killed himself and that's bad enough. But she hardly knew him and now there is all this media attention on herself, her kid, and her husband."

Not what the worried, overwhelmed mother living in the fishbowl of suburbia would wish for, certainly. "Let's try to keep this low key, Sergeant. Let the coroner's office handle the media; they might bury the story on the back pages."

Levesque frowned. Green suspected she at least wanted her moment in the limelight to demonstrate how efficiently her team had co-operated with the coroner and wrapped up the case. But she snapped her book shut and rose with a curt nod before gliding out of his office. Leaving a faint scent of spice in her wake. Indefinable, rather like Levesque herself.

Shaking his head sharply, Green picked up the phone. Archie needed to be told so that he could brace himself for the fallout. To his surprise, Archie wasn't worried about his own hide at all.

"That's nonsense!" he exclaimed. "Suicide? I don't buy it. Mike, I've searched his room, my records, and my soul, but I can't make that fit. There are no hints of suicidal ideation in his room or on his laptop. He left all his belongings arranged as if he were planning to return in a day or two. His computer search history is all about science and modern Internet skills, and his Documents file is full of lecture notes and lesson plans for the courses he was hoping to teach. Plus, he's been reading up on literacy challenges and employment qualifications at the library. This was a guy who was looking ahead."

"Something must have happened to tip the balance."

"Like what? His visit from his daughter? Unless she said something absolutely crushing, I don't think so. He had zero expectations about his chances with his family when he got out, so any contact — any chance — was better than he'd ever hoped."

"Then maybe Marilyn Carmichael's visit brought out all the guilt he'd been avoiding."

Archie was silent a moment as if replaying the visit. "He's not a guy to open up easily. We talked a bit about his feelings in the past few weeks since he's been out, but mainly about him missing the activities and people on the inside, and how surprised he was by that. But he never talked about feeling guilty about his crime. When he was going to meet Mrs. Carmichael, he kept wondering why she wanted to see him, even why she supported his parole. He was nervous she was up to something. But afterwards ... no, he didn't act guilty. He acted upset, agitated, like he was seeing something for the very first time. I suppose, once that sank in, maybe guilt would follow, but I never sensed that. And I've got pretty good radar. Even the morning I drove him to the train station for his medical appointment, he was energized. Determined."

"But then he got one more blow."

"Yeah, but you know this guy. He's not going to take the first *no* for an answer."

Green had no argument for that. "But, the fact is, after that appointment he climbed on a train, drove to the place of his happiest memories, and drank himself into oblivion."

Archie muttered a soft, sad prayer. "I know. And I let it happen. I was blind."

"You don't know that. It might have been a moment of impulse."

"Oh no! Whatever his intention was when he got there, he planned that trip days ahead. He persuaded his PO to let him travel alone and he packed his bag with just enough overnight supplies that staff wouldn't get suspicious."

A curious thought popped into Green's head. "When did he ask if he could make that trip by himself? Before or after Marilyn Carmichael's visit?"

"Gee, I ..." Archie muttered and wheezed. "After. That's when he got really excited about the doctor's visit too. You think that might be important?"

"I don't know," Green said. "It does make me really curious about what Marilyn said to him, though. If somehow it tipped him over the edge." He thought of Marilyn's reaction to the news of Rosten's death. He'd expected mixed emotions, including relief, but not horror. As if she knew more about his death than she let on.

Archie broke through his puzzled thoughts. "Another person who's going to feel really bad is Paige. She was on the fence about seeing him again. I'd like to speak to her personally, but there's no way I can get away from here right now. Things are a mess."

He didn't elaborate but Green could guess. Archie had to tread a fine line with the rigid, almost paramilitary bureaucracy of Corrections. This time his rule-bending had cost a man his life. Green squinted at his calendar on his desk. Superintendent Neufeld had called a meeting of her minions for 3:30. That would give him at most an hour before his meeting with the hospital social worker.

"Are you asking me to go see her?" he said.

"If you could, yeah," Archie replied. "Tell her ... tell her none of us saw this coming. And if it's any comfort to her, I still can't believe it."

Neufeld's meeting dragged on for two hours. The woman was obsessive, combing through every comma in her mandate, including some Green had never known existed.

CID had been under temporary management for over a year, so some of her housekeeping was justified, but Green chafed as the discussions of minutiae droned on. In the end, he was forced to cancel his meeting with the social worker and it was well past seven o'clock by the time he drew up to the curb outside Paige Henriksson's house. In the life of a family with young children, it was crazy hour. Cranky, tired children, baths, pyjamas, bedtime stories, and then the fight to get them to sleep. He sat in his car debating the wisdom of speaking to her now. But his own family, and his own tired wife, awaited him too.

Even from halfway up the walkway, he could hear the screaming which he recognized all too well. Toddler meltdown. Aviva hadn't reached that stage yet, but by the age of two, Tony had developed a pair of lungs any tenor would die for. Green hesitated yet again before steeling himself to press the bell.

More bellows from inside, this time from the adults disputing who would answer "the fucking door." In their place, he doubted he would even bother. Most evening callers were peddling some dubious charity or even more dubious religion.

The door jerked open, and he found himself staring up at a very tall young man with flaming red hair and cheeks to match. He glowered down at Green. "Yeah?"

Green introduced himself. "I realize this is a bad time, Mr. Henriksson, but —"

"We don't want the body," he snapped. "It will cost us ten grand to bury him. Let the government pay for it; you're the ones who screwed up in the first place!"

"Tom? Who's that?"

"Some cop!" Tom shouted back before skewering Green with another glare. He had a tangle of red eyebrows that almost eclipsed his blue eyes. "We don't owe that man a damn thing! He ruined Paige's childhood and he deserved everything he got. I'm glad he finally saw it that way."

Paige appeared in the doorway, trying to peer around her husband's broad shoulders. She was pale, and deep charcoal circles under her eyes gave her a haunted look. Green wondered if she'd slept at all since her father's death.

Tom swung on her. "Where's the baby?"

"Upstairs in his crib." Screaming reverberated through the halls. "That's what the doctor said to do."

"Yeah. And when he wrecks that crib too? The doc going to pay for that?"

"Tom, let me handle this. You go check on Oliver."

The beleaguered husband hesitated, his gaze flitting from Green to his wife before he shoved the door open and stalked away. Paige stood on the threshold. Despite herself, tears gathered in her eyes and she dashed them away as if ashamed.

"He's only trying to protect me. He knows the scars my father left on me — on both of us — growing up, and he's read the newspaper reports of Jackie's murder. Even in death, he says, my father is screwing us."

"Can you spare a moment to talk about it?"

She glanced back over her shoulder. The screaming had abated but her husband was hovering at the top of the stairs, bouncing the toddler on his shoulders. Green realized they had little chance for a meaningful discussion with Tom poised to swoop down.

"How about some fresh air? It's a beautiful evening for a walk."

Gratefully she nodded and stepped onto the porch, drawing her sweater around her, more for protection than for warmth, he suspected. The sun was just sinking below the rooftops and the sky was bathed in amber streaks of light. The suburban lawns were rich green and a soft breeze brought the fragrance of spring flowers and freshly cut grass. Neighbours were out in their gardens with trowels and bags of compost.

They strolled a moment in silence before he spoke. "Can your mother and sister contribute to the burial costs even though they won't come?"

"My mother and sister want my father to rot in hell."

"It's not that easy, is it?"

She tugged at her sweater. Buried her chin in its collar. "It would be easier if I hadn't met him, if I hadn't seen him as an ordinary, middle-aged man in a wheelchair — my son's grandfather — instead of a sex-fiend monster. If I didn't see my grey eyes, my hair, even my long neck. My mother never mentioned that Pam and I look like him. She always said, 'Oh, you're throwbacks to my grandmother.'"

"Do you know the official cause of death?"

She caught her breath. "The coroner told me it was definitely suicide." She faltered. Paused to wave at a neighbour, feigning cheerfulness. "That doesn't make it any easier. Tom says it's just one more way he's sticking it to us. A coward's way out, leaving us with nothing but guilt."

"Tom didn't meet him. What do you think?"

"I think my father was the one feeling the guilt and wanting to make amends. That's what I don't understand. I got the impression he wanted a relationship, but only if I wanted it too. He was determined not to push me. But he was … like a kid … barely holding his excitement back. And I was scared. Who wouldn't be? I had Tom's objections to contend with. But I hadn't closed the door. That's what I don't get."

"But you didn't return his call afterwards."

She stopped short. Eyes searching, jaw open. "I needed time! It didn't mean …" She shook her head back and forth. "That doesn't explain it. Killing himself now doesn't make any sense! That chaplain, did he see this coming? Does *he* say my father was depressed because of me?"

"No. Quite the contrary."

"Maybe the coroner was wrong. Maybe it was an accident. Anyone can mix booze and pills in a careless way."

That doesn't seem likely, Green wanted to say, but he kept his opinion to himself. If Paige needed this sliver of possibility to lessen the guilt of her father's death, the small deception was worth the price. He wanted that sliver of possibility too, for Rosten's suicide made accomplices of them all. Not just Corrections staff, parole officers, Horizon House staff, and Archie, but Green himself. None of them had seen the risk.

Yet he knew, all wishing to the contrary, that Rosten's overdose had been no accident. MacPhail had said the man had washed the pills down with straight Scotch in a quantity and time span that could only be deliberate.

"Suicidal people don't always let on what they're up to," Sharon said later that evening, once he finally arrived home to overcooked, twice-heated chicken. Aviva was already asleep and Tony was playing video games in his room. "They can hide it really well, especially the serious ones who want to make sure they succeed. And once they've made that decision, sometimes their mood even improves. They feel relieved and liberated, and people mistake that for getting better."

He pushed aside his half-eaten food and reached for his wine. "So all the lesson plans — that was a burst of energy?"

"Or part of the deception. Rosten obviously planned this whole scenario carefully, from the cottage locale to the delicious meal to the fine Scotch. A perfect, painless exit. He spent days laying the ground work, setting up the deception of the chaplain, and figuring out where to buy diazepam." Sharon's chocolate-brown eyes glowed with warmth. "Don't feel bad that none of you saw this coming, honey. You weren't supposed to."

Green nodded, but without conviction. From his years of training and experience, he knew all the hallmarks of suicidal intent. If they had been there, he should have seen them. "But don't seriously suicidal people take action to tidy up their lives? They leave notes of explanation, they write wills or give away valued possessions. Rosten did none of that."

"What personal possessions did he have to give away, or to will to anyone? He'd been twenty years on the inside."

"A note then. Some kind of final commentary. Rosten loved the last word."

"Who was he going to write the note to? He had no family who cared to get one."

"His daughter! She deserved an explanation."

"Come on, you said he was an intelligent man. What explanation could he give that would make her feel better?"

"Anything! Like this isn't your fault. Some reassurance and encouragement, after all he'd put her through."

"He probably thought he had nothing worthy to say, that a quiet exit from her life would be best for her."

"But —"

"I'm not saying it's true, Mike. It's how depressives think."

He sat back, frustrated. "The chaplain, then. Archie deserved a note. Rosten must have known he'd get the blame."

She was silent a moment as she sipped her tea. "Yes," she admitted finally. "But it doesn't mean he'd care."

"And what about me! My God, Sharon, this is a guy who's been sending me letters for the last twenty years. How would he even be able to resist? His last hurrah!"

She twirled her glass. In the silence, faint bursts of

tinny music echoed from Tony's room, but otherwise the evening peace was bliss. "Maybe ... maybe he did write a note, and no one's found it yet."

CHAPTER TEN

At eight o'clock the next morning, Green strode through the station and into the Ident labs at the back. He found Cunningham squinting at fingerprints on his computer. The forensics officer had eagle eyes that once could have spotted a stray hair from across the room, but years of staring at minutiae, not to mention encroaching middle age, had begun to take their toll. He was now fiddling with a brand new pair of rimless reading glasses.

"Did you guys search every inch of the cottage and grounds at Rosten's place?"

Cunningham looked up, surprise turning to affront as he peered over his glasses. *What a stupid question*, his expression seemed to say. When have you ever known me to skimp on a scene? He confined himself to asking why.

"For a note."

"A note. Imagine me not thinking of that."

Green smiled in spite of himself. "Sorry, Lyle. I'm just dotting *i*'s."

"The dozens I leave undotted, you mean."

"Just one. No one is perfect all the time."

"Is that right?" Lyle responded. He returned to his computer. "It's all in my report, including the absence of a note."

Green resisted the urge to return the salvo. The truth was, Cunningham's reports were so tedious and excruciatingly detailed that they put even the keenest detectives to sleep. Instead, he made his exit and headed up to his office, where the usual piles of emails and memos greeted him and the message light blinked on his phone. Ignoring all this, he put in a call to Archie Goodfellow.

"Have you cleared out Rosten's room yet?"

The chaplain sounded not exactly cheerful, but back in control. "Yes, we just got the go-ahead on that yesterday when the coroner's verdict came in. We're going through it now. Not much to clean up."

"Any sign of a will, disposition of property, suicide note?"

"I've been looking for that. Or at least for some clue what he was thinking. But there's nothing."

"What about on his computer?"

"Like I said, nothing but lesson plans and research."

"What kind of research?"

"High school curriculum. Biology labs. Stuff you'd expect."

"Nothing on overdosing? Drug effects?"

"No. Well … there was one weird thing. He visited some websites like the *DSM-5* — that's the diagnostic manual for psychiatrists — and the American Psychological Association. Looking at criminality, sexual deviance, violence, nature vs. nurture."

Trying to reassure his daughter, Green suspected. Had she told him she was worried about her son? Or had he himself harboured his own fears about the twisted genes he'd passed on?

"Most of it was science curriculum, though," Archie was saying. Voices interrupted him in the background. "Hold on."

A muffled conversation ensued, during which Green began to paw through the piles of paper in his inbox. Reports, memos, yesterday's mail buried under new reports from today.

Archie's voice returned. He sounded excited. "There is one thing. One of the day staff just told me. Rosten wrote a letter. We don't know who it was to, but Rosten asked for permission to go down the street to mail it. About a week ago. Maybe to his daughter?"

Green's hand froze. Hovered over a plain white business envelope with familiar writing.

Inspector Michael Green
Ottawa Police Services
474 Elgin St.
Ottawa
K2P 2J6

He's added my professional rank this time, Green noted with bemusement. Not so dismissive anymore. "No, it was to me," he said as calmly as he could before signing off.

His impulse was to rip open the letter on the spot,

but fortunately his police training kicked in first. He rummaged for a pair of neoprene gloves in his drawer and snapped them on before picking up the letter. It felt like the last one he'd received. Thin, perhaps no more than one sheet. Apart from the full address and title, the writing was the same. Slashing, stabbing, precise.

He slid the letter into a manila envelope and rushed downstairs to Cunningham's lab. No doubt dozens of postal and police employees had left their fingerprints but he needed to be sure James Rosten had as well. He wasn't sure why. The death investigation was closed, the pieces all in place. Perhaps it was just part of his lingering dissatisfaction with the picture they made.

Luckily Cunningham was even more of a by-the-book investigator than he was, and required no half-baked explanation to photograph and fingerprint the letter.

"Come back in an hour. I'll have it all done."

Green fidgeted. "Can't you slit it open and have a look first?"

Cunningham gave him a look. He peered at the paper with his illuminating magnifier and shook his head. "The less disturbance the better. I'll probably have to fume it. You want it done, or you want it accurate?"

Suppressing his impatience, Green headed upstairs to wait for the call. While he waited, he forced his attention to his inbox. True to his word, Cunningham called in less than an hour. For the dry, obsessive technician, he sounded excited.

"You're going to want to see this."

Green took the stairs two at a time, bursting through the lab doors in less than fifteen seconds. The choking stench of glue still hung in the air.

"The prints aren't his?" he demanded.

Cunningham held out a single piece of paper, safely encased in a plastic evidence bag. "Not the prints. This."

Green snatched the paper. Like the others, it was a short note, without salutation or closing. Only a date and five short lines.

> *I've been blind. I've spent twenty years pursuing the wrong villain. Lucas didn't kill Jackie, but I have a horrible suspicion who did. I just have a couple of tests to run and I will prove it to you!*

Green reread the letter several times in disbelief. His head began to spin. "What the fuck is this?"

Cunningham shrugged. "Not a suicide note, that's for sure."

"Did you copy it?"

"Didn't think of that." Cunningham gestured to a pile of copies on his desk. "Help yourself."

Green handed back the original note and snatched three copies from the desk. "Keep this with the rest of the stuff from the scene until we get to the bottom of this."

He was out the door before Cunningham could muster a sarcastic retort. Upstairs, Green spotted Brian Sullivan bent over Levesque's computer, conferring with her. Green jerked his head toward the office, and without a questioning word, Sullivan followed him inside. Silently Green handed him the note, which Sullivan studied without reaction.

"What do you think it means?" Sullivan asked finally, looking up.

"It means a week ago, suicide was the furthest thing from his mind."

Sullivan inclined his head in doubtful agreement. "A lot could change in a week. Don't forget his medical appointment."

"But this is the old Rosten, still on the warpath. That whole repentance thing was a sham so he could get out on parole."

"Could be."

"Could be?" Green was incredulous. "What do *you* think it means?"

Sullivan pursed his lips. "I don't like his final statement. *I will prove it to you!* This is personal, Mike."

"Of course it's personal. It's always been personal for us!" Green corrected himself. "For him."

"Maybe this is his final payback. His best payback yet."

Green took the note to study it again, trying to imagine James Rosten — relentless, never-say-die combatant — crafting these words. Gauging not their truth, which may have been irrelevant, but their impact on Green. Despite himself, the note quivered in his hand.

"You think he wrote this whole letter just to mess with me? To leave me in permanent doubt about Jackie's murder and about the circumstances of his own death?"

Sullivan steepled his fingers and nodded softly. "Is that possible?"

Green stared at the ceiling. Searched his whole understanding of Rosten. Not just as the tenacious, obsessive professor on trial, but also as the humbled, lonely man trying to start over.

"Fuck," he whispered. "I don't know."

"Because if it's not possible, then you realize what this note tells us?"

Green nodded. A slow horror spread through him. It had lingered at the edges of his consciousness since he'd first read the note, but he'd been loath to acknowledge it. "It wasn't suicide or accident after all."

For the rest of the day, Green drove all vestiges of emotion from his thoughts as he summoned the investigating team to his office, quietly, one by one. Only Sullivan remained throughout, his chair tipped back against the wall in the corner as he lent an objective ear. Levesque was the first person Green called. She arrived clutching all her notes and planted herself just inside the door. Green held out the note.

"This came to me from James Rosten this morning. Postmarked in Belleville a week ago."

"Bravo for Canada Post," she said drily as she took the note. Her disdain vanished the moment she read the words. Crossing the room, she dropped into a chair and her mouth fell open.

Green held up his hand. "I don't want to speculate

on what it means. There are numerous possibilities. What I need from you is the answer to one question. Is there anything we missed?" He chose the word *we* deliberately. No point in backing her up against a wall. "A small detail from the crime scene — an observation by a neighbour, a random comment to the taxi driver — that suggests that someone else might have been involved? That it might not have been suicide, but murder?"

Levesque swallowed. The investigation had been closed, the crime scene released. Green prayed that like Cunningham, she had dotted every *i*. "It wasn't a full-scale murder investigation, sir. It was a death investigation, and once the coroner ruled —"

"But you did interview neighbours. You did search the grounds."

"Yes, sir." Levesque bowed her head and fingered her papers. She seemed to be thinking rather than evading. No pout, no denial or affront, Green noted with relief. Just an immediate grasp of the implications. He let the silence grow. Finally she flipped open her notebook and began to scan.

"There is one thing, sir," she said finally. "A small discrepancy, but since this was the country and the neighbours couldn't actually see anything through the woods, it was easy to explain it."

"What?"

"The time of his arrival, sir. Detective Okeke interviewed the taxi driver, who stated he delivered Rosten to the cottage at about 6:30. He says he helped him up the drive and wheeled him inside —"

"How did Rosten get in?"

"Apparently the driver was vague. Couldn't remember exactly. Thought Rosten had a key."

Green calculated the timeline from the train station. "The train got in at 4:20. That's more than two hours, a long time, even for a trip all the way out there."

"Well, there was the stop for takeout, probably for the Scotch as well."

"Probably? Did they stop for Scotch or not?"

"The taxi driver wasn't sure."

"Nonsense." He knew an evasion when he heard it. It was more likely the cab driver had stopped not only for Scotch but for drugs as well. But Levesque's rookie detective had missed it. "Did you draw up a detailed timeline?"

Levesque merely looked at him, the answer in her silence. He had to fight to keep his voice even. "I want every second of his time accounted for from the time he got off the train until his body was found. Was that two-hour delay the discrepancy you mentioned?"

Levesque roused herself. "No sir. The neighbour's dogs barked at about 8:30, and the neighbour thought she heard a car arrive at that time. However, she couldn't actually see which house it went to —"

"How did she pinpoint the time so exactly?"

"She was a bit curious. Typical country busybody, I think. She said the cottage is normally unoccupied at this time of year because of the blackflies, and she looked at the clock because she thought they were arriving pretty late. It was becoming dark."

"Headlights?"

"I ... don't know."

"Go back and ask her," Green said. "Did she hear the car drive away?"

Levesque pressed her lips together in dismay. "Her dog barked again much later, and she thought she heard a car. She was already in bed and she thought whoever was there must have left. Later, when the body was discovered, she —" Levesque stumbled. She wasn't reading from her notes now and Green suspected she hadn't even written it down. "She said the car must have been visiting another house."

"Did you turn up any trace of another vehicle? Tire tracks? Footprints?"

"No sir. But Ident processed the scene."

Green bit back a reprimand and let her go with orders to re-interview the taxi driver herself, as well as all the neighbours. Then he called up Cunningham, who arrived within moments with a flash drive in hand. If he sensed the tension in the room, he gave no sign.

"I wondered when you'd get around to taking a second look, so I've been reviewing all our findings." Cunningham fished his glasses from his pocket and propped them on his nose. "We can start with the scene photos."

The three men clustered around as Green pulled the photos up on his computer. They watched in silence as the video panned the living room, first in long shots and then close-ups. Cunningham's dispassionate voice could be heard providing commentary. It was a remarkably benign scene, far removed from the chaotic, blood-spattered scenes they usually encountered.

Cunningham flipped through less important photos of empty rooms and ended with the close-ups of the Indian takeout containers in the garbage bin under the sink. Apart from this, and the restaurant receipt, which Cunningham had also bagged, the bin was empty. The receipt confirmed that the food had been picked up at 5:16 p.m. and paid for with cash.

A single dirty plate and fork lay in the sink.

Green wrestled with an increasing sense of incongruence. "Anything strike you as unusual about this scene, Lyle?"

"Unusual?" Cunningham pulled off his glasses. "I give you the facts and leave the speculation to you guys."

"But there are not a lot of facts to process."

"True. The guy had only been there a few hours. Hadn't even unpacked."

"Did you see any evidence that it had been cleaned up?"

"It was clean, that's all I can say."

"Recently swept? Counters sponged down?

Cunningham hesitated. "Yes."

"And didn't that strike you as odd?"

"Maybe he was cleaning it up after the winter. Mouse droppings, spider webs — all kinds of creatures move in over the winter."

"When he was planning to kill himself within hours?"

Cunningham clamped his mouth shut as if realizing too late that he had been drawn into speculation.

Green turned to Sullivan. "Levesque needs to find out whether the property management team employs cleaners and when the place was last cleaned."

Sullivan nodded. "She's on top of that. Her sidekick checked, as I recall. The company had renters lined up for the month of June, so they had a team in there opening up the place two weeks ago."

"Two weeks. How much dust can accumulate in two weeks?"

Cunningham shrugged, unwilling to commit. "Depends how airtight the place is. I'd say that old place is full of chinks."

"Enough that there should have been a fine layer of dust — and this time of year, tree pollen — on the floor. Was there?"

The Ident officer's eyes flickered. Settling his glasses back on his nose, he scrolled back through the photos, enlarging, comparing. Slowly he grew red. "In the bedrooms. Not in the kitchen or living room."

Green sat back. "*Goddamn it!*"

"Maybe he swept it up."

"From a wheelchair? A lot of work for his last hours on earth." Green tapped the last photo on the screen. "This looks staged. Look at the position of the wheelchair, facing out over the view. It just screams, 'poor guy's last wish.' Look at the empty bottles on the floor beside the chair. No glass, implying the guy chugged pure whisky straight from the bottle. The empty pill bottle is under the chair, like it was carelessly dropped. Nothing else in the room. Nothing else in the whole place. Clean as a goddamn whistle."

He gritted his teeth, trying to keep his rising outrage at bay. "I suppose now that the scene's been released, every Tom, Dick, and Harry, including the cleaners, has trekked through the house?"

"Well … MacPhail ruled it a suicide."

"Yes, and he's next on my list. Meanwhile, get back out there and see what you can salvage. Prints in unusual places, footprints in the dirt, and go over every inch of the man's wheelchair."

Cunningham unplugged his flash drive and headed for the door. His face was unreadable but deep red mottled his neck.

"He's going to blame himself," Sullivan said quietly once the door had closed.

"We all should," Green retorted, snatching up his phone to call MacPhail's private line and putting the call on speaker phone. The pathologist answered after five rings, his brogue unnaturally thick. Green glanced at his watch, which read just after one o'clock. Too early for MacPhail to be impaired, unless he had graduated to liquid lunches.

"You caught me just getting back, laddie," he said. "Another meeting with James Rosten's daughter. I think she's going to take the body."

Green felt a rush of relief that the body was still in the morgue. "Alex, new evidence has come up. Is there any chance — any marks on the body — to suggest he was forced to take the Scotch?"

"Scotch like that, no one in his right mind would refuse." MacPhail laughed.

Green waited.

"You're saying I missed something?"

"No. Just trying to see if there's another explanation."

"Because I didn't, lad." The brogue grew rougher. Raspier. "I've been doing these PMs since before you put on your first uniform."

"But we all —"

"No defensive wounds, no scratches, no bruising — in the mouth, on the throat, anywhere! — nothing under the fingernails but Tandoori sauce. I don't read minds, laddie, but I'd say he drank that Scotch willingly."

"Under threat, perhaps?"

MacPhail snorted. "I don't read tea leaves either! Why would I even think that? The man was a killer and a cripple, his life in ruins. Why would I go off into the wild blue?"

Green clenched his jaw to hang onto his civility long enough to thank him and get off the phone. He looked at Sullivan grimly.

"He's piss drunk," Sullivan said.

Green nodded. "He's been on the edge for years, but he used to accomplish more dead drunk than the rest of us could sober. This is the first time I think it's impaired his workday. Fuck, Brian, what if he missed something? What if we all missed something?"

"This isn't anybody's fault."

Green shook his head slowly. "It's nobody's fault and it's all our faults. We let who this man is colour our commitment. He was a killer, supposedly remorseful now, and having trouble adjusting. And because of that, we didn't see the other possibility. That there is another killer on the loose."

It was a tense, whirlwind afternoon. First he called the entire team together in an incident room. Photocopies of the note, the death scene, the immaculate cottage, and the discarded bottles were already pinned to the wall, along with the beginnings of a timeline and a list of actions to be pursued.

"We need to treat this as a murder investigation," he said. "Re-interview every witness, re-examine every fingerprint, re-analyze the residue in the Scotch and pill bottles, review every inch of the pathologist's report. If Rosten didn't take the diazepam willingly, look for evidence it was forced or injected."

He saved the bulk of the investigation for Marie Claire Levesque. She had managed to confirm both neighbours' statements, but was still waiting for the taxi driver.

"I want to observe that interview," he said. "We need to find out how Rosten bought the curry and the Scotch and whether any other stops were made along the way. We need to comb through Rosten's computer, check his search history, and talk to the other Horizon House residents. We need to re-interview all the taxi drivers who drove him in Kingston and Ottawa that day. Find out every word he said to them. Did he mention any places or people, did he ask them any questions? Did he make or receive any phone calls, or make any stops to use a pay phone?

"We need to track down all the first-class customers who saw or spoke to him on the train, and ask them the same questions. I want a complete record of what this guy said and did during the last week of his life."

Levesque had begun the briefing diligently jotting down every lead Green suggested, but by halfway through she was staring at him in open disbelief, and by the end she tossed her notebook on the table.

Green held his temper. "We need a thorough investigation, Sergeant. I will get you all the help you need — Gibbs and Peters for a start and some uniforms for the Prelims. Belleville Police can handle things at their end."

Throughout the briefing, Sullivan sat with his chair tipped against the wall and his arms crossed, listening. He interrupted only occasionally to offer suggestions. Midway through, Superintendent Neufeld opened the incident room door and peered in. As usual, not a silver hair was out of place and her dark, tailored suit was impeccable. Her eyebrows shot up in astonishment but she uttered only three words.

"When you're done, Inspector."

At the end of the meeting, Sullivan remained behind while the team filed out. "A lot of manpower," he said quietly. "Neufeld is not going to be pleased."

"*I'm* fucking not pleased. They screwed it up. So we're going to do this right this time, Brian. Before memories fade and all the physical evidence is washed away. Neufeld can't object to that. If there is something there — if Rosten *was* murdered — by God, Brian, there will be hell to pay!"

Sullivan shut the door. "It's not your fault, Mike."

Green frowned at him, not needing to ask what he meant. But Sullivan told him anyway. "You didn't send an innocent man to jail."

Many thoughts were on the tip of Green's tongue. An angry dismissal, a protest of innocence, a sputtered denial. But he quelled them all as he sank into his chair.

"I was the original investigating officer. I helped to determine what leads were pursued and what evidence was found. What suspects were identified."

"Junior investigator, Mike."

Green grunted in dismissal. "The OPP were obsessed with their random sex killer theory, and tracking down every sex offender on the continent. Remember, this was just after Jerry Paulson led all the police forces in southern Ontario on a merry chase. The media were terrified it was a copycat, and the senior brass wanted to get someone behind bars as soon as possible. DNA had taken nearly two years to nail Paulson and his wife, giving them time to kill three more young women. I'd put Rosten in the frame during the MisPers investigation when I learned she was last seen walking with him to his car. I had all the pieces of the case." He raised his hand to tick off the points on his fingers. "The exam paper with Rosten's note with the date of her disappearance jotted beside it; confirmation he'd tutored her at least once; student statements about Rosten's ego and his flirtatious behaviour. Plus, a cottage neighbour remembered seeing Rosten's car, and his wife confirmed he'd gone to the cottage that day.

"At first the OPP laughed in my face. Rosten was a successful, professional family man. No one would believe he might also be a killer, until I reminded them about the handsome, charming couple from small-town Ontario who turned out to be serial killers."

"Paulson and Miranda Jean."

Green nodded grimly. "Then forensics matched the dirt in Rosten's jeans and tire treads to the scene. They found a strand of her hair in his car. Suddenly the case blew wide open. The OPP ran with it and nailed down all details. But it was my case, Brian. I connected the dots."

"You were twenty-seven years old."

"Which is no excuse. I thought I knew everything back then. I thought I could see through anyone!"

Sullivan studied him thoughtfully. "Fair enough. You were young and cocky. But you didn't send an innocent man to prison. The Crown attorney prosecuted the case. He —"

"She. Beth Jensen. Now Justice Jensen."

Sullivan whistled softly. "Okay, so Justice Jensen of the Jugular got the conviction. She could turn even a mediocre case into a winner. And then there was the judge who charged the jury and the jury who convicted him. There are a lot of cogs in our wheels of justice, Mike. Including Rosten's defence lawyer."

"The first lawyer was a moron. Some boyhood friend of Rosten's who didn't know a thing about criminal law. Rosten fired him halfway through the trial. But the jury would have convicted anyone we told them to. Everyone was still freaked out about that Martins creep who got off on a technicality. Not to mention Miranda Jean pleading battered-wife syndrome after she helped her husband rape and kill those girls."

Green stared into space, remembering back to that horrific time. The lies, the depravity of the pair, the destruction of public trust. "*I* was freaked out. No one, no matter how normal and upstanding they seemed, was above suspicion. Without me, without my relentless digging up of dirt on James Rosten, he'd be an important professor by now, enjoying a fruitful career and his daughters and grandson."

"Fine. Beat up on yourself." Sullivan rose. "We don't even know that Rosten was murdered, let alone why. It's a big stretch to say he's innocent. He might have been killed as payback. But we'll be turning over every rock between here and Belleville, and on the off chance there is justice to be done for James Rosten, we'll do it!"

After scheduling a progress meeting for the next morning, Green reluctantly turned to the task he could avoid no longer. Superintendent Neufeld. It was nearly six o'clock but he knew she'd be waiting in her office. He found her sitting in a club chair, with her stocking feet propped on the coffee table and a cup of cold coffee at her elbow. Her own copies of the case reports were strewn on the coffee table in front of her, plastered with Post-it Notes.

She made no effort to take her feet off the table, merely waved him to the chair opposite with a weary flick of her hand. The moment he began his explanation, she let him have it. She was appalled that he was second-guessing the coroner's verdict and exposing the police service to public outrage, not to mention lawsuits, by casting doubt on an old case.

"All the facts we need are right here in MacPhail's report," she said, tapping the top report for emphasis.

"No one is questioning any of this but you, Inspector. Why poke a stick into the hornet's nest that can only end up causing harm?"

He resisted the urge to lecture her about moral obligation and the pursuit of higher justice. Neufeld's job was to guard the departmental purse strings and the police force's ass. Few people, certainly not the force's brass, would see the vindication of Rosten's name as being worth the cost. Nonetheless, he showed her Rosten's last letter and sketched the gaps in the investigation he was attempting to fill in, leaving the moral issue unvoiced but implicit.

She listened without a flicker of reaction, and at the end she picked up another file. "You've been in charge of Major Cases a long time, haven't you."

Alarm bells rang. Was that a shot in the dark, or had Marie Claire Levesque put a bug in her ear? He didn't reply as he waited for the other shoe to drop.

She thumbed lazily through the other file, which he realized must be his own. "Six years," she said.

Deliberately he unclenched his jaw and forced himself to be calm. "It takes time to acquire the expertise that's essential to the position," he said.

"But it appears you haven't done much else. Perhaps it's time for a change. There may be an opening in Support Services."

He nearly choked. He wanted to shout his objections but instead he dredged his very depths for words that were both persuasive and deferential. "Things are at an extremely sensitive and complicated juncture right now, ma'am. The credibility and professionalism of the Ottawa Police Service will be under scrutiny. I assure you the investigation will be conducted discreetly, but we have to investigate. We have to see things through to the end. Transparency and accountability are key concepts in today's policing." *As our police chief reiterates at every opportunity*, he wanted to add, but he hoped she was smart enough to add them herself.

To her credit, she did, but her expression hardened. "Agreed. For now. But if this blows up in our faces, Mike, you will wear it. You. Is that clear?"

CHAPTER ELEVEN

That threat loomed huge in the middle of the night as Green lay in bed staring at the ceiling. In the stillness, Sharon's breathing rose and fell softly, and leaves rustled against the windowpane. This wasn't just about searching for justice or righting a possible wrong, it wasn't just about his own personal guilt and redemption. It was about his career. With two children under the age of ten and a daughter just entering university, he was staring into an abyss.

Through the darkness, the small alarm clock on his night table glowed 3:42. The last time he'd looked, it had read 3:34. Before that, 3:16. The night inched forward, black and bottomless. Into that dark void, thoughts rushed in, crowding out sleep and replaying his fears in endless, haunting loops.

He had barely moved in over an hour as he tried to will himself to sleep, but still his heart raced as if to outrun an invisible foe.

What if James Rosten had been murdered? That possibility was bad enough — the possibility that he had finally gained his freedom only to be targeted by a killer.

There were several people who could have wanted him dead, people who didn't think his punishment severe enough for his crime or who feared he might kill again. But as unpalatable as that revenge motive was, Green understood it. Accepted it with the kind of sad resignation that cops have to master if they are to survive the sheer unfairness of people's lives.

But what kept him awake was the other possibility — that Rosten had been killed not to balance the scales of justice but to silence him. To stop him from checking into Jackie Carmichael's death and digging up information someone was desperate to hide. Which could only mean one thing; James Rosten was not the original killer.

And Green had railroaded the wrong man.

His whole career had been launched by this case. After the embarrassment of botched investigations and failed prosecutions, the senior brass had seized the opportunity to praise him to the skies. Only a junior detective, the police chief had crowed, but a man clearly skilled beyond his years. Green had found himself fast-tracked into Major Crimes and he had never looked back. Until now.

He'd been so damn sure of Rosten's guilt. Had he been so blinded by his own importance, and by the chance to break this case when the OPP were trying to sweep him aside, that he had failed to see the truth staring him in the face?

Had his whole career been based on a lie?

He tried in vain to wrestle back his panic. Rosten's death could still be a simple suicide by a man who had finally hit a wall. The favourite food and drink, the beloved cottage locale, the lack of supplies for a prolonged stay — indeed, he had not even brought coffee or cereal for breakfast — all these pointed to a final, deliberate choice. So far, besides the possible evening visitor, the overly clean and freshly swept cottage, even MacPhail's sloppy work on the autopsy, there was precious little hard evidence to contradict the verdict of suicide.

Just a letter from the dead man and a deep, yawning feeling of dread.

With that dread, at four in the morning, came anger. Irrational, blood-pounding fury. At himself for being so goddamn proud and cocky that he'd put winning ahead of truth. At the OPP, who had frozen him out of the final stages of the investigation. They had not let him follow up on the few loose threads that had niggled at him; Rosten's claim that he'd spotted a car like Lucas's on the road near Morris Island; the missing belt used to strangle Jackie, which had not been found in a search of Rosten's house and which his wife said he'd never owned; even Julia's initial theory that Jackie had run away to escape her stepfather.

Perhaps if he'd been allowed to continue the investigation himself, he might have found more flaws in the case. And now, once again, he had to rely on the skill and wisdom of others. On Levesque, whose sloppy timeline had obscured crucial gaps, and on Cunningham and MacPhail, who had let preconceptions blur their acumen. They had made the mistakes, but as Neufeld said, if the case blew up in their faces, the blame would land squarely on him. That's what they paid him for.

He'd made enemies during his twenty-year rise through the ranks. He'd stepped on toes. He'd trumpeted justice and refused to compromise for expediency. He'd been intolerant of mediocrity and indifferent to authority. Every defence lawyer who'd ever lined up against him would be filing appeals. The jackals would be out in force, waiting to feast on the tatters of his reputation.

At 4 a.m., he felt like a trapped dog. Finally he flung off the duvet, slipped out of bed, and tiptoed down the dark staircase. After putting the kettle on for tea, he found a fresh pad of yellow foolscap. *You can't follow every lead in this investigation yourself, but you can damn well see where they're going.*

With shaking hand, he began to put his thoughts to paper. He started off by casting the net as wide as he could. No matter how remote the chance or how obscure the motive, there was no fucking way anyone would escape his scrutiny this time. Rosten had spent the last twenty years trying to exonerate himself, and his last letter suggested he was gathering evidence on a new suspect. If he hadn't gone to the cottage to kill himself — which Green strongly doubted — why had he gone? Why pick the cottage?

To use it as a secret base of operations while he pursued his investigation into the person he suspected of killing Jackie? As a base of operations, it was hardly secret. Surely he realized that once the police tracked him to Ottawa, they'd soon check out all his known hangouts, including the cottage. If he were hiding out to give himself time to investigate, a no-name budget hotel would be smarter.

Had he gone to the cottage because he wanted to check out some evidence at the scene of the crime? This seemed a more likely rationale, although his wheelchair seriously limited his mobility to navigate the rough logging terrain where Jackie was killed.

Or had he planned to use the cottage as a rendez-vous place? Not just any place but one with powerful emotional impact. Had he wanted to shake up a witness or confront a suspected killer on the very site of his original crime? That would be so like James Rosten. The man was so intense and focused that he would have met the challenge head-on without thinking of the danger. Or maybe he didn't give a damn.

Green's pen hovered over the page. *Keep your options open*, he reminded himself. As tempting as it was to assume Rosten had identified Jackie's killer and had been killed to silence him, that wasn't the only possibility. Even if Rosten was innocent, he might have been killed by someone who believed he was guilty. In either case, however, it had to be someone who knew he'd be at the cottage. Who might he have told? The suspected killer? A witness? Or perhaps he had invited one person but someone else had overheard or been told of the intended meeting.

The most obvious person for him to invite was his daughter Paige. He'd contacted her before and had even left an unanswered message. Perhaps he hoped to show her the cottage she'd enjoyed as a baby. But would she have killed him? Her father's crime had devastated her childhood and made her fear for her son's normalcy, but she had seemed more bewildered than horrified by her own visit with him and she had been buying herself time to decide how much she would let him back into her life.

A far more likely suspect was her husband, Tom, who clearly wanted no part of his father-in-law's life. If Rosten had told Paige he was going to the cottage, Tom could easily have found out. He had a temper and a fierce protectiveness toward his wife and child. Green wasn't sure he himself would feel any different in his shoes.

Green put Tom Henriksson at the top of the suspects list.

Next on the list were Rosten's wife, Victoria, and second daughter, Pam, neither of whom wanted him back in their lives. They'd refused all involvement, even after his death. Rosten may have been anxious to build bridges, but would he have risked rejection by contacting them? If so, which one?

Once again Green tried to put himself in Rosten's shoes, and his answer to the first question was a definite *yes*. Rosten never backed away from conflict, and he was well beyond being hurt. When the news of his wife's desertion reached him at the end of the trial, he'd reacted with rage rather than despair. Not at her but at Green. Green was to blame; his incompetence and his personal need to win the case against all the contrary evidence had led to the prosecution and verdict.

If Rosten wanted to reconnect with his wife or child, even if for no other reason than to discuss the future of the cottage, he would have plunged right in.

Of the two, Green favoured the wife. Rosten had had an intimate, seven-year relationship with her, and he'd had twenty years inside a cell to wonder what had become of her. Had she found a new man? Re-established her career? Before the birth of the twins, she had worked as an emergency room nurse in a hospital in New Jersey. While he was at Princeton, apart from his stipends and research grants, her income had been their main means of support.

A familiar story, Green had thought at the time of the trial. The wife supports her husband through his schooling and once he's reached the gates of success, he tosses her aside her for a nubile co-ed ten years her junior. In this case, Victoria had experienced more than simple betrayal; she had also had to face the soul-destroying self-doubt of having shared her life with a killer. During the trial, the media and the gossip circles had been ruthless. She must have neglected him or turned a blind eye, they said, or, worse, she must have been utterly emotionally divorced from him in order to miss the clues to his true nature.

In the end, shattered and full of shame, she had fled back to her parents.

It was clear that she had neither forgiven nor forgotten in the past twenty years. A nurse would have easy access to diazepam and know all about its lethal effects. Moreover, she was perhaps the only person who could have made Rosten distraught enough to chug the whole bottle of Scotch.

Green put her name below Tom's. She was a strong suspect, possibly the strongest, but much depended on how fiercely she had clung to her outrage and how willing she was to re-open the wounds by visiting him. Having put fifteen hundred kilometres and twenty years between them, perhaps she'd prefer to leave it that way.

The most straightforward way to verify that was to check her phone records. Rosten had no phone of his own but had used both the Horizon House phone and nearby pay phones to make the few calls he had. If he had contacted her, the trail should be easy to trace. However, Green would need a warrant for that — and on the basis of MacPhail's suicide verdict and his team's sloppy investigation, no judge would ever grant one. Green would have to find another way to check her whereabouts. Neighbours and work colleagues could be discreetly interviewed, but in the end, someone would have to confront her directly.

The second daughter, Pam, was a long shot. What kind of person had she become and how likely was it that she would still harbour a bitterness intense enough to fuel murder? Her father had never been in her life, and unlike Paige, she clearly wanted it that way. Did she have the same soft, anxious core as her identical twin, or was she tougher? Could Rosten have said something to make her travel fifteen hundred kilometres to kill him rather than simply hanging up on him? But Green didn't know the woman. He didn't know how damaged and irrational she was, and he didn't intend to dismiss her without a routine check.

Conduct background inquiries via Halifax Police, he wrote next to both Victoria's and Pam's names.

He rested his head in his hands and took a deep breath. The clock now read 4:56 — still more than an hour before his alarm was set to ring, if Aviva didn't wake him and Sharon first. Sharon was still on maternity leave. She would nap in the afternoon while Aviva did, whereas he faced another whirlwind day as the investigation swung into action. He had ordered a blitz; now he had to deal with the consequences.

His black mood had lifted slightly, but his head ached, his eyes felt like sandpaper, and sleep still seemed as elusive as it had at 3 a.m. He abandoned all hope of it and rose to make a pot of coffee while letting his thoughts range over other possible suspects. Among them, the Carmichaels.

No one ever recovered from the murder of a loved one, be it sister or child. Life was forever on another plane, the ache as bottomless after twenty years as on the first day, the rage and despair as corrosive as ever. A survivor became used to living with the pain, so that eventually it did not consume their days. But the least reminder could reopen the floodgates, as Green knew from his own parents, who would retreat into days of impenetrable silence.

Rosten's mere release could have triggered such floodgates. Or perhaps it was something even more potent, such as a phone call from him or a visit to the place where Jackie had died.

Returning to his seat with a freshly brewed cup of coffee, Green applied his thoughts to the first, and most palatable, Carmichael suspect. Gordon. He had never liked the man. Twenty-two years old at the time of his sister's death, he had preferred to hang out with his buddies, playing music and smoking dope, rather than providing support to his mother and stepfather. Lucas had retreated into a stunned alcoholic stupor and Marilyn had gone on the warpath, so neither had been easy to comfort. Perhaps it was expecting too much of the young man to see through their behaviour to their need. Nurturance was not a strong point for most twenty-something males.

Certainly it hadn't been for Green himself. He hadn't known how to comfort the family, and had responded to Marilyn's rage by redoubling his efforts to bring Rosten to justice. In the dead of night two decades later, he saw just how poorly he had handled his own emotions as well. Beneath the cockiness, the bravado, and the cop attitude, he'd been scared. It had been his first case, and as it wore on, the expectations of the police, the media, and, most of all, the family had left him terrified. Marilyn would tolerate no less than the case solved and the killer brought to justice. Preferably over hot coals.

He realized now that he'd lost his objectivity. Three years earlier, he had watched helplessly as his own mother fought a war against a killer. Like his mother, Marilyn was Old World and honed by hardship, and he'd felt the echo of his mother's pain and the same impotence to make the world right for her. But unlike

Gordon, he had tried. No matter how overwhelmed he'd felt, he had tried to give Marilyn what she demanded. Not in handholding, but in action. Gordon had not. He had escaped into the false balm of bars and drugs, dropped out of college to take a job as a bartender, and as soon as he had saved enough for a plane ticket, he had headed to Paris. Never to return.

Until now.

Green's brief glimpses of the man two decades later had not improved his opinion of him. Gordon had not grown up during his sojourn in Europe, and now he was back home, drawn not by filial affection but by the whiff of inheritance money, hovering like a crow around carrion, hoping for easy pickings. He had done some work to fix up the house, but more likely with an eye to increasing its sales value rather than to help out his mother.

Those very same qualities of laziness and detachment, however, made Gordon a poor candidate for vengeance. Rosten's killer had passion, intensity, and a memory as tenacious as an elephant. Reluctantly, Green conceded that Gordon probably didn't care enough — about his sister's death or Rosten's undeserved freedom — to right the scales of justice himself.

The stairs creaked and Green looked up just as Sharon appeared in the doorway to the kitchen, rumpled with sleep.

"I thought I smelled coffee."

"Oh, honey, I'm sorry. I didn't mean to wake you."

She came into the room to peer at his scribblings. "What's going on?"

"I couldn't sleep. The case was going around and around in my head, so I thought …"

She went to the coffee maker and poured the dregs into a cup. "You thought, *Why fight it?*"

He shrugged, unwilling to reveal the depths of his struggle. "But don't you get up. Go back to sleep. I'll get Aviva if she wakes."

She sank into the chair opposite him and cradled her cup sleepily. "It's kind of nice at this hour. Peaceful. I can actually finish a thought." She waved a languid hand toward his notes. "You still worrying about the suicide verdict?"

He hesitated. He'd always wanted barriers. Between the turmoil of his job and the peace of his home, between the 4 a.m. blackness and the bright warmth of family. But who understood people, or listened better, than Sharon? "I got a letter in the mail from Rosten today."

She set her coffee down so quickly it sloshed over the cup.

"Sent just before his death," he hastened to add, smiling in spite of himself as he rose to mop up the mess. "It suggests he may have been murdered. Do you really want to hear all this?"

"Now I do," she replied.

"Then I'll make you some new coffee." As he set about brewing a fresh pot, he filled her in on the events of the day and on his attempts to narrow down motives and suspects. He kept his voice dispassionate and his private fears to himself.

"Much as I dislike Gordon," he concluded, "I don't see him getting all worked up about Rosten at this point. And …" He tapped the next name on his list. "The same applies to the other daughter, Julia. I felt sorry for those kids back then, having their lives blown apart like that just as they were starting to make their own way. Gordon was at Algonquin College, studying something to do with sound technology, and he never made it through. They lost almost two years of their lives between the investigation and the trial — years when they should have been dating and exploring and generally goofing around — and they never got those years back.

"Julia hadn't really found her feet in the first place. She had trouble sticking with things, and at twenty-four she was still bouncing around, waitressing a bit, working odd jobs like house sitter and dog walker while she picked up random university credits all over the map. She seemed to always quit or get fired. She might have straightened out in time if her sister hadn't been murdered …"

He stopped to pour Sharon coffee, buying himself time to organize his thoughts. She was drooped over the table with her eyes at half-mast and her chin propped in her hands.

"Marilyn always said the kids had a rough start in life. Their father had been abusive — old story, the kids witnessed it, hid under the table, she stayed with him because she was broke and new to the country and figured she'd lose her kids and be sent back to England if she left him. Eventually, the husband got fed up living in a cramped bungalow with three screaming children and he disappeared. Took the truck and left her with a mountain of debts and not a penny in the bank. The woman moved heaven and earth to raise those kids and give them a good home. But I guess those early years left their scars."

"And maybe …" Sharon roused herself and sipped her coffee gratefully. "To make up for it, she tried too hard, made excuses for their laziness, and didn't expect enough of them, so they ended up with no appreciation of hard work."

He shot her a smile. "You planning to be a slave driver?"

"Absolutely. I see how easy it is for parents to over-protect and rescue their kids. I do it all the time; it's a mother's natural instinct. But it does the kids no favours for learning how to manage the real world. And in the end, they don't respect you for it."

"That's it exactly! It's what I've always felt about Julia and Gordon. It's all about me, me, me. They never saw their mother — or even more so, their stepfather — as anything more than the cook, cleaner, and money-bags. And neither of them, deep down, really mourned Jackie's death."

"You don't know that."

He doodled beside Julia's name, trying to articulate his instincts. His head was swimming, and instead of clearing his thoughts, the coffee had only filled him with buzz. "No, I don't," he admitted finally. "But I got the impression they mourned the loss of their nice peaceful life and their mother's attention more than they did their sister. Jackie was the youngest. She'd been spared most of the fallout from their father's abuse. She was better adjusted and didn't get into nearly the fights they did with their parents. I think both the older kids resented the fact she had an easier ride."

"So neither of them would be hell-bent to avenge her death."

"Well, Julia has the passion, and she can definitely hold a grudge. There were certainly times she got really mad at me."

"Why?" Sharon asked in surprise.

He tried to think through the sludge. "Partly because she felt rejected. She was clingy and needed a lot of support, which her family wasn't giving her, so she called me often at first. I was a young man, and the red flags were going up."

She chuckled sleepily. "Since when did you pay attention to red flags back then?"

"When my sergeant warned me. Julia was vulnerable, he said, and so was I, because Ashley and I were really rocky. I think Julia was also hurt when I got closer to her mother instead. There were odd tensions in the family even before Jackie's death. Lucas and Marilyn were close, and so was Jackie, whereas Gordon and especially Julia were on the outs. But Julia was much more unpredictable and needy than Gordon, who seemed to drift along. Life was a big 'whatever' to him."

Sharon craned her neck to read Green's list. "It seems to me the mother has by far the strongest motive of them all."

"For vengeance, yes. But if Rosten was killed to stop him from unmasking Jackie's killer, Julia and Gordon become much more credible suspects."

"But that implies one of them killed Jackie?"

He nodded.

She looked askance. "Why?"

"They were immature, self-centred, and jealous of her."

"Welcome to Sibling Relations 101," Sharon said drily. "Usually a motive for tattling and petty payback, not murder."

He smiled. As an only child, he'd yearned for a brother to play with and to share the burden of his parents, even to play petty pranks on. But as Brian Sullivan, one of eight in an Irish Ottawa Valley farm family, often said, "You're not missing much."

But he'd promised himself not to overlook any suspect, however obscure. "Sometimes in a moment of anger or miscalculation, petty payback can turn deadly. And as I said, there were a lot of tensions in the family. Jackie was clearly the favoured child."

"She was the baby of the family. Older siblings always grumble they're the favourite," she countered. "But this was not a murder of impulse or accident. You've said so yourself many times. This killer was devious and methodical, and planned out every detail."

She had a point. Julia and Gordon had been considered at the time of the original investigation, and their movements and alibis verified, but neither had been taken seriously as suspects for the very reasons Sharon gave. Nonetheless, he wrote a note to double-check their alibis in the morning. Sipping his coffee, he tried to remember the original serious suspects in the case. Other than the OPP's random sex killer, only two stood out: Erik Lazlo, Jackie's boyfriend at the time, and Lucas Carmichael.

Lucas had been an early contender when Jackie first disappeared. Adult male family members, particularly stepfathers, come under automatic scrutiny. Originally Julia thought Jackie had run away to escape Lucas. She'd never actually seen anything sexual between them but Jackie had always been his little pet. The hugs had been too long and too frequent, the offers to be her chauffeur too eager. Rosten himself claimed to have seen a car resembling Lucas's in the Morris Island vicinity on the fateful day. But other than Julia's suspicions, there were no signs of sexual abuse, and Marilyn had provided Lucas with an alibi for the entire day. He had been at home with her, she insisted, preparing the gardens and firewood for the winter. The car had been in the shop.

All these suspicions and alibis were moot, however, because Lucas had been dead almost five months when Rosten was killed.

Which left Erik Lazlo, a callow youth whom Green and the OPP had dismissed as a serious contender because he had an alibi — he had been working with two other students on a project most of the evening. Had they all underestimated him? Lazlo had been bewildered by Jackie's disappearance and had mouthed all the right platitudes about their flawless relationship and deep respect for each other. He'd been momentarily affronted when Green questioned his sincerity, but after a brief flare of temper, he had tripped over himself trying to co-operate.

He'd been the first to point the finger toward Rosten. The professor had been giving Jackie private tutoring in the evenings, Lazlo said. Also, Rosten had told Jackie, whose class was studying algae growth in different water conditions, that the Morris Island area near his cottage provided interesting contrasts. On the day of her disappearance, Jackie had planned to hike in there to collect water samples. Maybe Rosten knew she'd gone, Lazlo had said. Maybe he knew she'd be alone.

This, coupled with the confirmation of his alibi by his fellow students, had been enough to point suspicion away from him and squarely at Rosten. A clever sleight of hand? It had been difficult to pinpoint Jackie's time of death precisely, given the week's delay in finding her body and the highly variable ambient temperature in the woods in late October. A forensic entomologist had been consulted, and maggot reproduction had estimated her death within a twelve-hour window shortly after she went on her fateful hike, but that time frame was still tentative.

There was still plenty of time for Lazlo to slip through the cracks of his alibi. Green put a bold asterisk beside Erik Lazlo's name on the suspects' list, with a note to review every scrap of his evidence and to ask Gibbs, the Internet wizard, to track him down.

Significantly, Erik Lazlo was the only suspect who qualified for both motives.

CHAPTER TWELVE

The boxes of microfilm and court transcripts were sitting in the incident room when Green arrived at 7a.m. He was buzzing with caffeine, but the arrival of daylight had brought a little equanimity as well. He eyed the boxes warily. The Carmichael murder case had generated hundreds of reports and witness statements, most of them irrelevant to the case at hand. A rookie would have to do the initial search.

Instead, he busied himself putting his lines of inquiry up onto the whiteboard while waiting for the briefing to start. Levesque arrived shortly afterwards and he barely had time to fill her in before the rest of the team arrived. Levesque led them quickly through the updates and new assignments. Peters was to re-interview all the witnesses from the trains and the hospital by phone, while Gibbs had been tasked with tracking down Erik Lazlo and getting Rosten's phone and bank records. He had already secured the warrants for the latter.

"We're still waiting for the Horizon House phone records because of the other users involved, but the pay phones at the Kingston and Ottawa train stations should be in soon. And the bank records on that joint cottage account are already in." Gibbs looked excited as he flourished a faxed page. "There's a hefty balance of $76,901 in that account. The wife never seems to touch it. Almost all the activity is with the property management firm. Large deposits, presumably rental cheques, go in and small ones go out, including a withdrawal of five hundred dollars earlier this month —"

"Probably for the spring cleanup," Leveque said. "But verify it."

Gibbs nodded. "Yes, ma'am. But there is one really interesting withdrawal made from the bank's Belleville branch four days before Rosten's death, for fifteen hundred dollars."

Green had been listening quietly from the back of the room, letting Levesque run her case, but now he sat bolt upright. Only a few twoonies and loonies had been found at the cottage. "Fifteen hundred dollars! For curry, Scotch, and a couple of taxi rides?"

Everyone absorbed this startling twist. "Perhaps he bought something to give to his daughter," Levesque offered.

"She never mentioned it, and if he bought something, where is it? Did either the Kingston or Ottawa taxi driver mention any other stops that day? Like the post office? Detective Okeke?"

Levesque glanced at her new detective, who met her unspoken query with a bewildered frown. Green suspected he hadn't thought to ask. More sloppy detective work.

"The Ottawa taxi driver was pretty vague, sir, and I ... I didn't ask."

Before Green could open his mouth, Levesque headed him off. "Then let's get him back in. ASAP!"

Okeke slunk out of the room, leaving an electrified excitement in the room. Everyone sensed a potential major breakthrough in the case. An extra thousand dollars in missing cash was a huge mystery. By comparison, the rest of the briefing was mundane. A luckless rookie from General Assignment was given the dull but crucial task of combing through the original Jackie Carmichael case records. As everyone was filing out, Green overheard Peters grumbling to Gibbs about being stuck at her desk on the phone, re-interviewing witnesses. Green smiled in secret sympathy. Peters was a bulldozer and he did not envy her mild-mannered husband the task of keeping her frustrations in check.

"Tracing Rosten's last day and all his conversations is important, Sue," he said. "What if he made some innocent remark or let something slip that could save us days of legwork?"

"But it's old ground —"

"It's fresh eyes, and you don't have to look at it all. The General Assignment detective will look through it for anything suspicious, any loose ends or questionable alibis. Just keep an eye on him. I'm especially interested in Jackie's boyfriend."

"Boyfriend?"

"Erik Lazlo. He may be more devious than we

thought. But look for any disputes or jealousy, anyone who might have motive to kill her —"

"Like the wife, sir?"

Green was startled. "What wife?"

"Rosten's wife. If he was trying to get it on with Jackie … Mrs. Rosten was stuck at home with two babies, probably feeling ugly and fat and old, while hubby is chasing twenty-year-olds. A woman scorned and all that."

Green cursed his own 4 a.m. stupidity. He had considered her during the initial investigation years ago, for exactly the reasons Peters gave, especially given the proximity of Jackie's body to her cottage. But he had quickly dismissed the idea. Victoria Rosten had been home without a vehicle or babysitter, and he recalled a friend had dropped in for a drink at some point in the evening of Jackie's disappearance. But the actual time of Jackie's death was approximate and parents had been known to let their children sleep in the car when they went out.

Victoria Rosten had been neither ugly nor fat, and at twenty-nine hardly old, but he knew from Sharon and Ashley's experience as young mothers that reality had little to do with it.

"Good catch, Sue," he said. "Wife, too."

Down the hall, the elevator door opened and Detective Okeke emerged with a very nervous young man in tow. The taxi driver, Green surmised, impressed by the fast detective work. As soon as he could, he headed to the video control room. Levesque and her sidekick were already crowded inside, conferring with Bob Gibbs, who was fiddling with the video equipment. On the monitor was the image of the interview room where the witness sat alone, rigidly still with his hands in his lap.

"Who's doing the interview?" Green asked as he squeezed inside.

She looked at him, unreadable. "I am. Okeke will observe." She brushed past him out the door with Okeke on her heels. Gibbs stole an uneasy glance at Green, obviously not wanting to be caught in the middle. Green smiled his most disarming smile.

"Good work on Rosten's warrants, Bob."

Gibbs flushed crimson. "Thank you, sir."

He was saved from further conversation by Levesque opening the interview room door. She stepped into the frame carrying a file and her notebook. Gibbs and Green watched in silence as she ran through the formalities. The taxi driver flashed his gaze toward the camera, swallowed, and blinked several times. Green leaned in, puzzled. What did the cabbie have to fear? His papers were all in order. He had immigrated from Pakistan six years earlier, and his landed immigrant status and taxi licence were both valid. Incredibly, he had not so much as a parking ticket on his record. Was this just an immigrant's natural fear of the police? Had he helped Rosten buy the diazepam? Or had he told someone else that Rosten was at the cottage?

"Mr. Akhtar," Levesque was saying, her voice like silk. "Can you please take me through your entire trip with Mr. Rosten, starting from the moment you first saw him?"

Akhtar nodded. Swallowed. "I pick up so many fares, I don't remember all."

"But this man was in a wheelchair."

"Yes, yes. Uh … he came out of the doors, I helped him into the cab, he told me where to go —"

"How did he act?"

"Act, Miss?"

"Sergeant. Was he nervous? Excited, upset?"

"I — I didn't notice. I was driving. The traffic was heavy. It was rush hour."

Levesque leaned in uncomfortably close, forcing him back against the wall. He lowered his gaze, whether to avoid her blunt, blue-eyed stare or to look at her breasts, Green wasn't sure. Obviously irritated, she led him through the rest of his remarkably vague testimony. There seemed to be many details Mr. Akhtar had either not noticed or remembered. Levesque pressed him on every one, to no avail, until she finally caught him in a lie.

"Who picked up the takeout curry, sir?"

"I don't remember."

"How is that possible? You would have had to get the wheelchair out of the trunk —"

"Oh yes, yes. I remember doing that."

Levesque frowned, as did Green. The restaurant owner had already confirmed that the taxi driver picked up the food and paid for it with two twenty-dollar bills. Why was the driver lying? What was he hiding? When the answer dawned on Green, he knocked on the interview door and strode it.

"Mr. Akhtar, I'm Inspector Green," he said, pointedly ignoring Levesque for maximum shock value. Luckily she caught on and swallowed her annoyance. "You did not drive your cab that afternoon, did you?"

Akhtar snapped his jaw shut and gaped, like a trapped animal.

"Who did you lend your cab to? A friend? A relation?"

"No one," Akhtar replied with careful dignity. "I drive hundreds of fares. I don't remember them."

"This is a murder investigation, sir. False statements not only make it difficult for us to find the killer, but they are also illegal. Much more trouble than letting someone use your cab without a licence. We can investigate all the drivers in your company if you prefer."

"I don't have to talk to you. I want a lawyer."

Green stood over Akhtar, his arms crossed. "At a thousand dollars a visit, that's your right. But you're not under arrest here, and your friend will not be either if he co-operates, even if he's here without papers. We're not immigration; we need answers about his passenger, that's all. Then he walks out that door."

Akhtar was silent a moment. "I will call him," he said finally. "He will decide."

Green shook his head. There was too much risk the man would run if he were tipped off. But from Akhtar's reluctance, he guessed the mystery driver was a close family member. Perhaps even the man's own brother.

Green softened his stance. "He is not in trouble, Mr. Akhtar. Just let us talk to him."

Akhtar scowled. He huffed and squirmed before sitting back in his chair and gazing up at the ceiling in surrender. "Kamran Akhtar."

* * *

Barely half an hour later, Levesque was escorting Kamran Akhtar into the same interview room. A glimpse of him confirmed Green's suspicions, for the family resemblance was unmistakeable. Although this young man was clean-shaven and barely twenty, he had the same slender body and frightened eyes as his older brother. However, he lacked the bravado.

Green took up his position in the video control room while Levesque began her routine. The young man's fear gave way to relief almost immediately. He spoke softly, his English fluent and almost unaccented.

"I told my brother I wanted to speak to the police. The doctor is wrong about the suicide."

Levesque smiled encouragement. She sat back as if for a chat, while Detective Okeke tried to blend into the corner. "I appreciate you coming in, Kamran. Your information is important in helping us figure out what happened to him."

"He was a nice man, Mr. Rosten, and not depressed. He looked very happy to be at his little house."

As with his older brother, Levesque invited him to start at the beginning and take her through the trip, step by step. "Tell us everything he said and did, no matter how unimportant it seems."

Dutifully, Kamran began his recitation in flustered, disorganized detail, beginning with his having to ask repeatedly where the destination was, because the cab's

GPS was broken. Rosten eventually suggested he turn off the meter and offered him a two hundred–dollar flat fee for the trip.

"Once we were driving, he said he hadn't visited Ottawa in twenty years and asked if the best Indian restaurant in town was still the Light of India in the Glebe. He borrowed my cellphone to make an order — a feast, he told me — and then we went to pick it up. I mean, he gave me the money and I picked it up. It was forty dollars with the tip —"

"Was it a meal for one or two people?"

"I don't know. Possibly two. I gave him some suggestions for dishes. He asked me where I was from and I said Pakistan, and he talked about the troubles there and asked if I was doing okay in Canada. I am studying computer engineering. I told him life was paradise here." He paused, his limpid eyes growing solemn. "Mostly."

"And did you make any other stops? At the liquor store, for example?"

"No, but he ordered two bottles of Kingfisher from the restaurant. That's what I recommended."

"He didn't buy a bottle of Scotch?"

Kamran looked affronted. "Oh, no. Scotch wouldn't go at all."

Green could see Levesque frowning as she jotted some notes. No beer bottles, either empty or full, had been found at the cottage. Just as Green was willing her to ask about diazepam, she looked up sternly. "Did you make any other stops? I remind you this man has died. Did he ask you to buy anything illegal?"

"Illegal?" Kamran's eyes widened and he whipped his head back and forth. "We — we did stop once more, but I don't know what he bought. He told me he was interested in security systems. First he asked me about my cab and did I know where he could buy a good home alarm system here in Ottawa. I think he wanted a small shop where they wouldn't ask a lot of questions, so I took him to a shop on Gladstone Avenue in Little Italy."

Levesque leaned forward. Green could hear the controlled excitement in her voice. "And what did he buy?"

"I don't know. I don't know anything about it! This time he asked me to set up his wheelchair and he went in by himself. He was there a long time. I was worrying about my two hundred dollars, and my class that night. He came out with only a very small bag."

"Did he say what it was or why he bought it?"

"He just said you can't be too careful in the country these days. And we drove to his cottage."

"What's the name and address of this store?"

Levesque was already rising as she jotted down the address. "This is very helpful, Kamran. Detective Okeke here will finish up and ask you to write a formal statement. If you remember any more details, let him know."

Then she was out the door. It took all Green's restraint not to follow her. At times like this, he hated his job. Hated the oversight, the administrative minutiae, and the so-called big-picture planning that comprised a day in the life of middle management, while his subordinates did the only job he truly loved. Seizing a case in his teeth and following every tantalizing tidbit to the triumphant end.

Instead, he watched her dash for the stairwell with a glint in her eye that he recognized all too well. She met his gaze as she passed and gave him a faint nod. *Of triumph or of understanding?* he wondered.

He suppressed a very unprofessional quiver of arousal and confined himself to a single request. "Keep me posted."

She didn't answer and he was grateful he had his own inquiries to make.

He returned to his office to study his list of suspects. Several lines of inquiry were still calling out for answers. The boyfriend, Erik Lazlo, still had to be located and brought in for questioning, Rosten's wife needed to be interviewed and her whereabouts at the time of his death verified, and Paige's husband needed an alibi. On the evening when Rosten went missing, Tom had sent Paige to stay with a friend, ostensibly because he feared for her safety. But it had left him free and clear the whole night. As a major person of interest, his actions that night had to be investigated immediately.

The hunt for Erik Lazlo had already been assigned to Gibbs, the wizard of the Internet, but so far without success. The team was already spread thin following up the multiple lines of investigation, leaving few experienced officers to carry out the rest of the delicate face-to-face interviews.

What a pity, Green thought with a secret smile as he reached for the phone.

Ten minutes later he was sitting with Brian Sullivan over coffee in the Tim Hortons down the street from the mother ship. Sullivan looked equally excited by the prospect of climbing back into the trenches.

"Do you have this guy's work address? No point in tipping off the wife."

Green nodded. Paige was high-strung, but she was also fiercely protective of her family. Green suspected she would cook up an alibi for her husband without a moment's hesitation.

"He works for Scotiabank in Stittsville, junior loans manager, but I think 'junior' is code for poorly paid. Their single vehicle has seen better days, their big, fancy house is mostly empty, and he was upset by the idea of the ten thousand–dollar funeral."

"Can't say I blame him. Happy to shake his tree." Sullivan tossed back his black decaf coffee with a grimace of distaste. Health had its price, and gone were the days of double-cream coffee with a chocolate-dipped doughnut. He gave Green a sly smile. "What are you going to be doing?"

How well he knows me, Green thought. "Phoning Rosten's wife in Halifax. I'll get the local police to do background inquiries, but I don't want them doing the interview. I know what questions to ask and I want to hear her reactions."

Sullivan chuckled. "I'm betting you're not on her list of favourite people."

Green thought back to his meetings with Victoria Rosten two decades earlier. Her initial hostility had been palpable, but as the trial wore on, she retreated into silence. Although she resolutely refused to share her doubts with him, he had sensed she knew something more about her husband's guilt.

"But it will be interesting to get her take on who might have wanted her husband dead." He paused. Fiddled with his paper cup. "I also have to interview Marilyn Carmichael."

Sullivan's eyes narrowed. "Is that wise? You've had a pretty close relationship with her."

"I know, but …" He shrugged as if to say, *Who else?* "I can do it."

"You could. And this may be a mistake —"

"It is. You're already compromised in this investigation. And we don't want some defence lawyer accusing you of bias or lack of objectivity. Worse, conflict of interest."

"If it gets sticky, Brian, I'll call you. But I'm fed up with others getting it wrong, and for now, my relationship with Marilyn is going to be useful." He paused, wondering whether it was wise to open up the topic he'd kept at bay all morning. In the end, it was Sullivan who broached it. He eyed Green keenly.

"How is Neufeld taking all this?"

Green ducked his gaze. He twirled his cup. "She thinks it might be time I had a change."

Sullivan's jaw gaped. "Goddamn. *Goddamn*! I was afraid of that."

"Support Services, Brian. Fucking Siberia."

"Oh, there's a perfect use of your skills. Courtroom security and prisoner transport."

"Don't forget all the liaison and inter-jurisdictional negotiations." Green threw his hands up. "You know how much I love that stuff."

"What are you going to do?"

Green began to tear his coffee cup into little pieces. He shrugged. "Nothing. Not now. You know she can do whatever she damn well pleases. But if she sticks me there, who knows? I may decide it's time for an even bigger change."

Before Sullivan could protest, Green's cellphone rang, startling them both. *Levesque.* Grateful for the distraction, Green picked up. Before he could even say hello, Levesque burst in, fairly singing with excitement. "He bought two miniature hidden cameras, sir! The latest high-tech, battery-operated types, with built-in SD cards."

Green was momentarily speechless as he raced over possibilities. Security cameras? Had Rosten feared someone would come after him? Had he in fact been hiding out at the cottage?

"Did he tell the clerk what he wanted them for?"

"Yes, sir. He wanted them to be invisible, wireless, and capable of recording in weak light. Sound and motion activated."

"Did he buy any other security equipment like trip alarms or motion sensors?" Beside him, Sullivan had snapped to attention.

"No, sir. The store owner remembers him very clearly, because he tried to persuade him to invest in a proper alarm system with their company. The disabled are sitting ducks, he told him. But Rosten wasn't interested. 'Doesn't matter,' he said. 'I just want security cameras, audio as well as video.' The best resolution he could afford in a miniature device. Spy stuff."

Spy stuff indeed, Green thought with a rush of excitement. All his doubts and worries vanished in the thrill of the moment. Rosten had wanted his visitor on tape. Yet Cunningham had found no cameras in his search of the cottage grounds. Had he gone over every inch, or had he screwed up again?

"Great work, Marie Claire," he told her. "Get a team back out to the cottage and go over it with a fine-tooth comb for those cameras. They may be hidden in plain sight in a smoke detector or clock radio. Even a garden rock."

"We're already on our way, sir. I'll call you the instant we have anything."

Sullivan was watching him, eager for an update. But Green couldn't resist a smile as her words sank in. They were both so enthralled with the hunt that she'd forgotten to be offended.

CHAPTER THIRTEEN

On his walk back to the station, Green glanced up at the third floor and debated paying a visit to Superintendent Neufeld. In light of this latest revelation about the cameras, perhaps she would ease up. In the end, he opted to wait until he'd phoned Victoria Rosten in order to avoid any censure or interference on that front.

He was doubtful Victoria Rosten would be home in the middle of a workday and even more doubtful that she would answer when she saw the call display. Hence, he was surprised to be wrong on both counts. He identified himself.

"Goodness," she said, her voice more honeyed and resonant than he remembered. "*Inspector* Michael Green."

"It's been a long time, Victoria," he said. "I hope you are well."

"I am, although fifteen hundred kilometres helps. I assume this is about James? You won't change my mind about his funeral."

"I'm not even going to try."

There was a pause. "Then what can I do for you?"

"We're still pursuing some lines of inquiry in his death."

"Lines of inquiry? Why?"

"Have you had any contact with him recently? Phone call? Letter?"

"No. I don't think he'd dare. It's bad enough he phoned Paige."

"So he didn't phone you at all, not even in the past week or so?"

"No." Her voice took on a slight edge. "I'm sure he realized I wouldn't have answered."

"I'm sorry, Victoria. I just need to be thorough. Did you know where he was living?"

"I did know that. The authorities keep me informed. But I don't understand what difference it makes. He committed suicide."

Realizing he was getting nowhere with the "official inquiries" approach, he changed tactics. "Some information has come to light that calls into question the coroner's original verdict of suicide." He let the implications sink in, but she said nothing. The woman had clearly learned to play her cards very close to her chest. He gave another nudge. "We need to clarify what happened to him."

"You're saying someone killed him? I can't say I'm shocked. Surely there's a lineup for that."

"Not a very long lineup, given the circumstances."

She seemed to process that. "Ah. And I'm on the list."

"To eliminate, yes."

"And my daughters?"

"Can you tell me where you were the evening of Thursday, May 22nd?"

She chuckled. It was a throaty laugh that radiated confidence. He tried to reconcile it with the panicked, angry young woman of twenty years ago, but could not. "Not at that cottage, I assure you," she said. "I couldn't stand the place. Bugs, mice, outhouse, boiled water, ugh! That was James's thing, not mine. So, Thursday May 22nd I was right here with my friend — my new partner. We had plank salmon on the barbecue with a delightful New Zealand Sauvignon Blanc, and then we watched TV."

"Can anyone else confirm that?"

"Our neighbours. We had some wine with them on the patio before dinner. Unless I am capable of teleporting, that should put me in the clear, I hope."

He hesitated, trying to pinpoint the hint of secrecy he'd sensed from her in the past. She mistook his silence for disapproval.

"I'm sorry if I sound flippant, but the truth is James nearly ruined my life and more importantly my daughters'. I'm afraid I can't muster much sorrow at his passing."

"You know he never gave up claiming his innocence."

"You know James. He always had trouble admitting he was wrong."

"In this case, there's a chance he was right."

He let the words float into the silence, wishing he could see her face. He heard a faint intake of breath. Then, "What are you talking about?"

"New evidence has come to light."

"What new evidence?"

I'm not at liberty ... was on the tip of his tongue, but he checked himself. "I can't say just yet."

More silence. She swore softly. "That's impossible."

"Believe me, I'm just as shocked as you."

"*You*? You got it wrong?" Her voice rose. "He was innocent and you got it wrong?"

"I don't know."

A wail sliced through the line, quickly cut off. "But he could still be guilty."

"Yes. But in light of this, can you think back? Did James ever say anything about who he thought might have killed her?"

"You ... you drop this on me and you expect me to think back?" Another stifled wail.

"Yes. This is important."

A muffled curse. He could almost see her mentally thrashing about. "Her stepfather. Always the stepfather. No, briefly it was the boyfriend."

"No one else? No one he mentioned in passing, like a colleague or another student?"

She took a deep, steadying breath. "He was suspicious of everyone. Lucas Carmichael because James had seen his car, the boyfriend because he was the first to finger him. James kept saying someone very clever had set him up."

"Ms. MacLeod, this is an intrusive question but I hope you'll answer it. You started off believing in your husband's innocence —"

"What woman wants to think she's been sharing her life with a killer?"

"But by the end of the trial you had changed your mind. Why?"

"Because …" she sputtered. He could hear her struggling to control her voice. "Because of all the evidence, those other girls saying he'd met with them. Do you think it was easy turning my back on him?"

"No. That's why I think there was something else."

He expected more protest but instead there was silence. Then some muttering. "I found a note," she said finally, her voice barely audible, more like the panicked woman he remembered. He could almost picture her, bowing her head and drawing in on herself. "Later, at the cottage among some of his papers. I was getting the place ready to rent. He had obviously forgotten it there."

Green gripped the phone. "What did the note say?"

"It was from the girl. Jackie Carmichael. It was short, just said she'd be collecting water samples on Morris Island for her lab and maybe she could meet him. The date, the time — it was the same as the day she disappeared."

It was Green's turn to be struck dumb. He took several seconds to collect himself. "Did you ask him about it?"

"No. I never spoke to him again. I just …" she faltered. "I just ran."

"What did you do with the note?"

"I threw it away. I knew right away it would be the final nail in his coffin. I didn't know what else to do. My children, my girls … I couldn't be that final nail."

* * *

What the *hell*, Green thought after he'd rung off. Why had the OPP search team never found this note? Why had Rosten never mentioned it? If he were innocent and being set up as he claimed, surely the note could have been crucial evidence!

And most importantly, had Rosten met with Jackie as arranged? Had he murdered her after all?

He paced his office, running through alternate explanations. The search team had been incompetent. Rosten had feared the note was too incriminating. Or perhaps there had been no note at all; perhaps Victoria had made it up. He had only her word for it. Why would she lie? What purpose did the lie serve for her?

It served to make Rosten look guilty again, just when Green was beginning to look for other suspects.

Including her. Had she thrown in this red herring in a desperate bid to deflect suspicion from herself? Or had she simply lied about when and where she'd found it? If she'd found it before Jackie disappeared, then it gave Victoria herself a good motive to murder her. And, last week, to murder Rosten too. What had Rosten said in his final letter to Green? *I have a horrible suspicion who it is.* Horrible. Implying the suspicion was abhorrent to him.

Green phoned the Halifax Regional Police to ask them to confirm her alibi with her neighbours and partner. Before his suspicions ran completely wild, that was a small, rational step he could take.

* * *

Half an hour later, he sat in his staff car outside the little bungalow, collecting his thoughts. Noon sunshine beat down. There were two vehicles in the lane in front of him: Marilyn's rusting CR-V, which had once been dark green but was now a mottled black, and a late-model, white Accent, parked at a crazy angle, half-crushing a peony plant at the edge of the bed. With that exception, the yard was clean and neat, all the shrubs trimmed and the flowerbeds mulched.

Just as Green was approaching the front door, it flew open, framing Julia against the dark hall. Amusement glinted in her eyes.

"Mum will be happy to see her favourite cop. She told me Rosten killed himself."

"How's your mother doing?"

She shrugged as if to dismiss his concern. "She's had so many deaths. Everything upsets her, but her party ought to cheer her up." She hadn't moved. To get inside, he would have had to brush past her. From deep inside, he heard the murmur of voices.

"Are you and Gordon staying for long?"

"As soon as the party's over this weekend, I have to leave. But Gordon will stay on. He's got no place to go since his French lover kicked him out."

Green did a quick double take. Lover? Such an ambiguous word. Male or female? Had there been any hints in his youth as to which way Gordon leaned? Green recalled he seemed to have lots of friends who flirted and groped each other indiscriminately in the haze of music and drugs. Had there been any special women? Special men?

He became aware that Julia was watching him, a smile hovering on her lips as if she were enjoying his confusion. But she chose not to elucidate.

"I hope you'll come to the party. It will mean so much to Mum."

"I'm not sure that's wise."

"Does it violate some cop code of conduct or something? I wouldn't tell, you know."

He ducked the question. She was like the Julia of old, flirtatious and clearly enjoying keeping him off balance. "May I come in? I need to —"

"Julia, what are you doing?" Marilyn said as she appeared behind Julia. If possible, she was even thinner than before. She was wearing old shorts and a T-shirt, and her arms and legs protruded like knobby sticks. "Why don't you invite the inspector in?"

Julia brushed past him out the door, her keys jangling. "Sorry, Mum. We were talking. I have to go out."

"Can you pick up some bleach? I used it all."

"More bleach?"

"The basement is full of mould."

Julia stopped midway across the peony bed. "Mum! I told you, don't touch the basement. I'll get to it."

"Yes, but when," Marilyn muttered at her daughter's retreating back. Without waiting for an answer, she turned to lead the way inside. As usual, the house was stuffy and, on this sunny June day, stiflingly hot. But the clutter of bags and boxes was gone, and any whiff of gin was overpowered by the acrid stench of bleach.

"So much mould," Marilyn said as she gestured him to a seat. He noticed she made no offer of tea. "I'm cleaning places I haven't touched in years."

"Basement mould is nothing to trifle with," he said. "I hope you'll take Julia up on her offer."

She laughed, without humour. "Right. And I'll just build a pen for the flying pigs while I'm at it. Julia and Gordon are doing their part, planning the party and sprucing up the yard. We're praying for fine weather so we can hold it outdoors. The irises and peonies are in bloom. You will come, won't you? It's this Saturday."

He hesitated, searching for a way to decline. Now that it was a murder investigation, the boundaries of their relationship had changed.

She misinterpreted his silence. "If Julia put you off, forget what she said. I want you there."

"This is not a social call, Marilyn. We're still tying up loose ends in Rosten's death."

She froze. "Why?"

He didn't answer. "When I told you about his suicide last week, you seemed very upset. Why?"

"Why? *Why?*" An angry flush rose to her cheeks. "Why wouldn't I be, for pity's sake? That man had tied my life up in knots for years."

"You said when you went to visit him, he asked about your children. What specifically?"

She struggled to drag her feelings under control, starting to speak several times before settling on a response. "He — he asked how they were coping. How we were all coping."

"Did you get the impression …" He took his time, trying to temper the edge of his questions. "That he had any ulterior interest in them? Any desire to contact them too?"

"Nay! I … I mean no. He asked how they were handling Lucas's death, whether their own father was still in their lives. He seemed interested in what kind of man he was. I thought he was fishing for suspects again. Looking for someone else to blame."

Green masked his excitement at this unexpected twist. Rosten hadn't mentioned the children's father in years. "What did you tell him?"

"That I had no idea where their father was, we hadn't had a word from him in thirty-three years, let alone a support payment, and for all I knew, he was dead or in jail. He was a selfish, violent man, and I am very grateful he left us alone. He did enough damage to the children while he was around."

The angry spots of colour had returned to her cheeks. Green trod very carefully into the next question. "Did he ever behave …? Marilyn, I'm very sorry I have to bring this up, but did he ever abuse the children either physically or sexually?"

She stared at him, eyes sparking. "I know everyone wonders about Julia, but I took beatings to spare her that. If he'd ever laid a hand on any of them, I'd have killed him myself!"

"But you couldn't be there all the time."

"Aye, I was. I had three little ones — Jackie only a baby — and I never left him alone with them. I knew he had other women; he'd disappear for days and come home stinking of sex and booze and pot, but I never let him bring any of that stuff home."

Green doubted the diminutive young mother could have done much to stop him, and he wondered, not for the first time, whether Julia's problems stemmed from his abuse. The oldest often gets the brunt of an abusive parent.

Rosten's sudden interest in the man was curious. At the time of Jackie's disappearance, the investigators had tried to trace the father, but his last known address had been in Labrador several years earlier. He could be anywhere, or as Marilyn said, he could be dead.

Marilyn broke into his thoughts. "Why?" she demanded. "What's going on?"

He chose his words with care. "Rosten had a visitor at the cottage before he died."

Her eyes widened. "And you think Percy —?"

"We have to eliminate all possibilities, including him." Green tried to sound casual. "When Rosten met with you, did he mention he'd be at his cottage that night?"

A floorboard creaked in the back of the house. Marilyn sucked in her breath. Gave her head a brusque shake.

"Maybe later, in a phone call?"

"He never called. I told you that."

"Just for the record, can you tell me where you were last Thursday evening?"

She blinked, as if trying to refocus. "I was here."

"Anyone see you or talk to you?"

"Well, no. I was in the basement cleaning. Good heavens, why would I …?"

"What about your children?"

"What about them?"

"Maybe they can confirm that?"

"Oh." In the silence, he could hear distant rustling. Her hands tightened in her lap. "Julia hadn't arrived yet and Gordon was out with friends. Drinks and a movie, I think."

"Is he here?"

"No. I mean, he is, but he's asleep."

Green suspected the furtive noises he'd heard in the back hall were from Gordon. "What time will he be awake? I'll send a cruiser out to pick him up and bring him to the station."

On cue, a door banged in the back of the house and Gordon appeared down the hall, looking groggy and bewildered. The stink of stale booze and cigarettes wafted around him.

Marilyn jumped up to intercept him. "Inspector Green has some questions for you about the night you went to the movies with Phil."

Gordon feigned confusion, a performance Green doubted would earn him an Academy Award. "Why?"

"We're tracing Rosten's movements on the evening he died," Green said. "Who he might have met with, what transpired during the meeting. So if you can give me Phil's contact info and tell me what movie you saw — a receipt would be very helpful —" Green flipped open his notebook.

"We didn't go to a movie. We got there too late, so we just went to a club."

"What club?"

Gordon flopped into one of the aging armchairs, put his bare feet on the table, and pulled out a half-empty pack of Gauloises. Marilyn pursed her lips. In small defiance, he tucked one into the corner of his mouth, unlit. "I don't remember. Several, I think."

In the silence, Green's cellphone buzzed. Levesque. With an effort, he ignored it. Waited, pen poised.

"Maverick's. Zaphod's."

"Phil's name and number?"

Gordon scowled. "I don't want my friends hassled by the cops. Check the clubs, they'll remember me."

"His name is Phil Rudinsky and he lives in Orleans," Marilyn said.

Green was just about to record that when Gordon heaved a sigh. "I wasn't with Phil. I ditched him at Maverick's and went off with some other guys."

"Names?"

"Like I said, I don't want them hassled."

I bet you don't, thought Green. "What about Erik Lazlo? Do you ever see him anymore?"

A brief flicker of alarm crossed his face. "Erik? Fuck, no. Haven't seen him in years."

Why the alarm, Green wondered? "Do you know where we can reach him?"

Gordon blinked several times, as if weighing his answer. "Not a clue. I heard he was married and living in Hungary." He straightened as his wits took hold. "What the hell is this, anyway? Why are you dragging up Erik and all this old shit? You think …?" His eyes narrowed. "You think someone killed the guy?"

Green closed his notebook and stood up. "We're pursuing several lines of inquiry. Routine. If you remember the names of anyone you saw on Thursday night, or the whereabouts of Erik Lazlo, ask them to contact me." On his belt, his cellphone buzzed again. Levesque again. Two calls in less than three minutes. He excused himself and stepped into the hall to check.

Levesque's voice vibrated with excitement. "Sir, I'm out at the cottage. We've found the camera, and I think you should see this."

CHAPTER FOURTEEN

Even in the fast lane of the Queensway, the drive across town to Morris Island took almost an hour. Too restless and keyed up to simply stare at the highway, he phoned Gibbs for an update.

"Any progress on locating Erik Lazlo, Bob?"

"Not yet, sir. We know he graduated from Algonquin in 1996, but he has almost no Internet presence. No traceable social media accounts. Nothing. Weird for an IT guy. He worked for Nortel in Ottawa until it went under, then he moved overseas to some start-up in Eastern Europe. He comes back and forth but we don't know where he is right now."

"Family?"

"His parents retired back to Hungary."

"Business contacts here?"

"That's who I'm waiting on now, sir."

"Sounds good. If you've got some spare time, see what you can track down on Marilyn Carmichael's first husband. Apparently Rosten was showing an interest in him."

"What's his name, sir?"

Green rolled his eyes at his own stupidity. Years behind a desk had dulled his investigative instincts. He rang off to dial Marilyn's number. As luck would have it, she was out and Gordon answered.

"What's our father got to do with anything? He's been gone for years."

"Not even birthday cards? Christmas?"

"Not a peep. We're nothing to him. Mum was nothing to him either."

"I'd still like his name."

Heavy breathing. "You *do* think he was murdered, don't you."

"We're pursuing several —"

Gordon interrupted him with a bark of laughter overlaid with contempt. "You're wasting an awful lot of effort for the slimeball who murdered my sister."

Green was forced to dodge around an SUV that lumbered onto the highway with a massive boat in tow, oblivious to the traffic. During that moment's silence, he heard Gordon's muttered oath. "Are you telling me … *now* … that he didn't?"

Green wrestled with the steering wheel. "I'm telling you no such thing, Gordon. I'm filling in blanks in our investigation."

Another soft curse. A deep breath rattled through Gordon's smoke-wracked lungs. "Percy Mullenthorpe. Can you imagine?"

Green wondered how he could have forgotten. It was a comically elegant name for a thug of a man, but at least it should be easy to trace. Thanking Gordon, he hung up before the man could make any more lucky guesses. Gordon was not as dim-witted as he pretended.

Green had just passed the name on to Bob Gibbs when the turnoff to Morris Island loomed ahead. Several uniformed officers were conducting a methodical grid search of the property around the cottage but Green found Levesque inside. All the windows had been thrown open, but even so, the lingering stench of booze, curry, and death pinched his nose. Levesque and Cunningham were bent over a laptop, peering at an image they had enlarged on the screen. To Green, it looked like abstract art. Nothing but fuzzy streaks and spots.

"Impossible to make out on this machine," Cunningham was saying. "But maybe with digital enhancement —"

They both looked up as Green entered the room. Levesque's cheeks were flushed with excitement and even Cunningham looked alive. "This is the closest we've got to a licence plate, sir," Levesque said. "Looks like an Ontario plate, but it's muddy and the light is too poor in the trees."

"The old story," Cunningham added. "Camera's okay as security cameras go, but no match for this kind of challenge."

"Rewind," Green said. "What are we looking at?"

"The SD card from this little camera, sir." She held out a small black rectangle, barely larger than a key fob. "This was positioned in the eaves just above the porch light. It's sound- and motion-activated." Levesque pressed rewind, and Green watched the jumbled images race backwards through time. Once it stopped, she pressed *Play.* The time display in the corner registered 22/05/14 19:05.

In the video, shafts of sunlight played off the slate in front of the house and lit the overarching boughs of pine and maple that bordered the path. Simultaneously, Rosten's disembodied voice broke the silence. "This ought to do it," he was saying, and a moment later, the back of his head came into the frame, followed by the rest of his chair as he wheeled himself out onto the porch. With deft flicks of his wrists, he turned his chair around and tilted his face up to look at the camera.

"I have put the game in motion. I have put out the invitation, using phone and Facebook. Whoever drives up that lane behind me, whoever parks and walks up this path, I will capture them. One way or another. Even if they search the place and find the camera inside, they won't know about this one. My backup. My fail-safe. So that no matter what happens to me, this camera will be my witness. And my proof, Inspector Green."

Green was jolted. Rosten stared hard into the camera, as if directly into Green's eyes, for a full five seconds before wheeling himself slowly inside. After a brief delay, the picture flicked off and when the next scene appeared, the shadows were deeper and the sunlight more golden. The time display read 20:31 on the same evening. Almost dusk. The scene was motionless save the soft rustling of leaves, but the rumble of a car engine and the crunch of tires on gravel must have triggered the recording.

In the distance, the dark silhouette of a vehicle approached through the trees. Green leaned close, holding his breath as the vehicle drew closer. A minivan or an SUV, judging from the shape. Black, navy, charcoal? The deceptive gold of sunset played off the paint, obscuring its colour. The vehicle came to a cautious halt some distance from the cottage and the driver switched off the engine. Sat a moment in the car. Assessing threats? Plotting strategy?

Finally the door opened and the driver stepped out, dark and shapeless against the forest at dusk. *Too far away*, thought Green with frustration. He and the others were mesmerized as the person began up the walkway, his head bowed to concentrate on his footing in the deepening gloom. He carried what looked like a paper bag in one hand. Halfway up the path, he froze and turned slowly in place, scanning the woods. Searching for what? Green had heard nothing, seen nothing.

Could it have been the neighbour's dogs barking? he wondered. *Too far away to be captured by the recorder? Or the kayakers returning to their dock next door? Or perhaps the stillness of the cottage itself, betraying the trap that lay in wait.*

The figure stepped sideways out of the frame into the woods, leaving nothing but the empty path and the dark hulk of the vehicle in the drive. Green was about to speak when Levesque signalled. "There's more, sir."

At that moment, the recording picked up muffled footsteps and the swish of a sliding door, followed by Rosten's startled voice. "Ah! An unorthodox approach, as always."

The door slid shut, cutting off further sound, and five seconds later the picture clicked off. When it resumed at 21:47, the camera could distinguish nothing but flitting shadows in the dark, the rasp of heavy breathing, crunching gravel, and a distant engine starting. No headlights, no revving, just a quiet, furtive drift back down the lane before the camera clicked off.

"Careful bugger," Cunningham said. "He didn't even turn the headlights on."

"Is there more?"

Cunningham shook his head. "Battery ran out. But this model lasts four hours, so nothing else happened within our time of death parameters."

Green was still staring at the laptop, trying to recapture the images in his mind. "Looked like a woman," he said.

Levesque frowned. "Why? You can't even make out their clothes."

"The walk. It was delicate."

"But they were picking their way across the stones in poor light. It wasn't a natural gait."

Green had to acknowledge that. "It also looked like long, dark hair."

"But it could have been a hood, sir. Or even a collar turned up against the chill."

"What about the other camera? He bought two, and he mentioned another inside."

Levesque shook her head. "No sign of that one. We've looked all over."

Which means the visitor found it, Green thought.

Which means he knew Rosten was trying to set him up and foiled him yet again. Green swore silently. They were so close! He tried to match the image of the darkened figure against his list of suspects. Marilyn's hair was white and Julia's was short and blonde, but both Paige and Gordon had longish dark hair. Tom was red-haired and balding, but stooped over with his collar turned up, even he was a possible match. Green had no idea of the hairstyles of Erik Lazlo and Percy Mullenthorpe.

"So this is all we got," he said. "Facebook! Marie Claire, how did we not know Rosten was on Facebook?"

"Belleville police handled that end of things, sir. But there was no account under his name, for sure."

"Get Bob Gibbs on it. He's a wizard. If Rosten was hiding a Facebook account, he'll find it." Green tapped the murky image on the screen. "Lyle, see what you can tease out of these images with your software downtown. The vehicle and the suspect. Let's see if we can narrow things down."

"The bag in his hand is an LCBO bag," Cunningham said. "The sunlight hit it just right for a moment."

The Scotch. So this visitor had come prepared, not to celebrate but to kill.

"And the vehicle looks like a Honda or Hyundai. They have similar hood logos."

"Minivan or SUV?"

Cunningham shook his head, as usual reluctant to commit himself further, but Levesque had no such qualms. "I believe SUV, sir. It sits higher than a minivan."

Green felt a strange mixture of thrill and dread; Marilyn owned a dark-green Honda SUV, which both she and Gordon drove. Rosten had set the trap, and like it or not, the noose was tightening.

Levesque put his thoughts into words. "One thing's for sure, sir. You were right. Rosten *was* murdered, but it looks like he set it up himself."

Bob Gibbs studied his page of jotted notes, trying to figure out his next line of inquiry. Phone calls and Web searches had filled in a lot of the blanks in Percy Mullenthorpe's last thirty-five years, revealing an erratic work history of temporary, unskilled jobs. His most lucrative job, as a long-haul trucker, had ended when his licence was suspended just after Jackie's death for driving while impaired. Gibbs wondered whether there was a connection. Mullenthorpe had not contacted the family or come to the funeral, but Jackie's murder and the subsequent trial had been in the news for over a year. He'd been a drinker for years according to his ex-wife, but perhaps this had pushed him further down the slope.

After that, there had been work in the Maritimes as a general handyman and roofer before he had followed the economic boom out to Alberta. He'd worked in the oil sands, with brief jail stints for assault and causing a disturbance, before being laid off and moving to Calgary. On his latest arrest two years ago, the Calgary police listed him as of no fixed address.

The man had hit bottom.

But he did not appear to be dead. Homeless people moved from city to city and province to province in search of greater warmth, better social services, easier drugs, and less harassment. With his temper, he could easily have worn out his welcome in Alberta and come back east. The police in Toronto, Montreal, and Ottawa had no record of him, but he could have blended into the obscurity of a smaller town.

The more Gibbs learned about the man, however, the less likely he looked as a candidate for Rosten's killer. Mullenthorpe was impulsive, disorganized, and probably brain-damaged from years of alcohol. Drunks were driven not by carefully planned revenge but by the when, where, and how of their next drink.

Nonetheless, because the inspector had assigned the task, he put out a routine inquiry. Then he glanced at his watch, shut down his computer, and rose to go. A handful of detectives were still bent over their computers, writing up their day, but Sue was waiting for him. They had a lead on a modest family farm near Navan that claimed to have a horse barn and paddock. They were going to grab an early dinner at the Elgin Street Diner up the street before heading out to Navan, hoping to avoid the worst of the rush hour.

Luck was not on their side in that regard, however, and they found themselves sitting on the eastbound Queensway, baking in Sue's little Echo, whose air conditioning had long ago conceded defeat to the Ottawa summer. Sue had all the windows open, welcoming in the gas fumes and the rumble of idling engines. Sweat glued her hair to her forehead in a cloud of red frizz. Her head bobbed to the catchy rhythm of Belle Starr, her latest Celtic folk craze.

"I hope we get rain," she shouted, peering out at the restless sky, which roiled with pink, white, and charcoal clouds. "It would get rid of this heat."

"Don't wish too hard 'til we get back home," he said.

"Bring it on! Nothing is more beautiful than a summer storm in the country. The smell of damp earth, the warm drops on my face …"

A fork of lightning sliced the clouds ahead and he winced. Warm rain was one thing but thunderstorms quite another.

"I have high hopes for this place," she said, undaunted. "The pictures look beautiful."

"Except for that 'Awaits your personal touch.' Code for 'Needs a lot of fixing up.'"

She laughed. "We can do that. Any place we can afford will need fixing up. But it will be a fun project for us while we …" She trailed off. Gibbs stole a glance at her and saw the flush on her freckled face. He knew she was afraid of childbirth. Afraid that her broken body and old scars would make it painful or even impossible. The doctors were encouraging but they had not lived through the pain she had.

He twined his fingers through hers. "Anything with you will be fun."

They bantered languidly about dream kitchens and man caves as the steamy traffic lurched toward Orleans. By the time they approached the real estate office in

Navan, the sky had darkened to billowing charcoal and lightning tongues lashed the fields.

"We're early," she said. "Let's drive around to see if there are any private sales."

She made a pretence of turning down a few back roads and looping south below the village before approaching the one back road he knew she'd had in mind all along. Sue had never forgotten the little Carmichael bungalow. Over the weeks, they had watched it transform slowly from neglected, overgrown shack to a fairytale cottage of perennial gardens, overflowing window boxes, and bright green gingerbread trim.

Sue stopped the car at the bottom of the lane, leaned out the window, and drank up the sight in the moody twilight. Marilyn Carmichael's Honda sat in the drive but the bungalow was quiet and dark. She heaved a wistful sigh. "So cute."

He rubbed her neck. "We'll find something."

She took another breath. Deeper. Frowned. "Smoke? Who would light a fire in this heat?"

He thrust his head out the window. She was right; the acrid whiff of smoke was unavoidable. She climbed out of the car and turned in all directions, searching. The thick brush along the roadside obscured most of the view, but Gibbs knew there were barns and hay fields nearby.

"In the country people are always burning something," she said. "Dead leaves and brush in the fall, old crops in the spring."

"That could be it."

"But in this heat, a grass fire could easily get away from you. Or maybe lightning struck a hay barn." She climbed back in the car. "We should check the main highway."

Gibbs was just about to join her when a plume of black smoke boiled up behind the bungalow.

"It's right behind the house!" He slammed his door shut and pulled out his cellphone, already on the run down the lane as he dialled 911. He could hear Sue behind him, grunting as she forced her body to move. As they drew nearer, the smoke grew thicker, swirling around the roof and roaring up through the treetops. Orange flickered in the basement window.

"It's *in* the house!" Gibbs ran to the back door. He could scarcely hear the dispatcher through the growing roar that filled his ears. He laid his hand on the door, which was warm but not burning. He reached for the knob. Locked. He shook the door, kicked, fought to get in.

"Bob!" Sue's voice, screaming. "Don't! The fire is all over!"

"But someone might be in there!" Still on the line to the dispatcher, he shouted breathlessly about the vehicle in the driveway. The dispatcher was talking, snatches of her voice audible over the din. Any shouts for help? Pounding on the walls? Moving shadows inside? He circled the house, peering through windows but could see nothing through the dense smoke.

By now, the basement was engulfed. One tongue of flame leaped at the back door near the basement stairs and blew out the window before shooting up to the eaves. He stumbled back, stung by flying glass. Pulled his shirt up over his face before forcing himself back to the door. Saw nothing inside but a wall of flame.

Sue grabbed his shirt from behind. "It's growing too fast! The trees overhead, the forest behind — it could all go in an instant!"

She tugged him coughing and stumbling back down the lane toward the safety of her car. Halfway down the lane, she turned back to look at the bungalow. Tears from smoke and sorrow poured down her cheeks.

"Goodbye, little house," she whispered.

Through the thunder of the flames came the distant wail of sirens. "Let's just hope … let's hope there's no one in there," he managed before falling to his knees.

Green got the call just as he was paying an outrageous ransom to get his car out of the hospital parking lot. Aviva was in the back seat, screaming at the restraints of her car seat, and nearby a landscaper was running a very loud lawnmower. Green was surprised to see Gibbs's private cell number on his call display. The young detective was off duty and by now should have been out in Navan on yet another quest for his dream home.

Dusk had fallen and Green was anxious to get the baby home to bed before a full-fledged temper tantrum developed. He was in a grim mood. His father's physiotherapist had cornered him to say that his father lacked the will to recover, and without that he would not progress.

"He doesn't fight," she'd said in her lilting French accent. "A long-term care facility would be best. I will ask his social worker to arrange this with you."

Green had hoped the sight of his newest grand-daughter would lift his father's spirits, but Sid barely raised his head when he brought the baby into the room. He lay like a shrivelled husk among the over-sized pillows, grey-faced and slack-jawed. His pale eyes tracked Green across the room and his brows quivered in a frown,

"Not sight for baby," he said.

"She wants to see her *Zaydie*," Green replied, swooping Aviva in the air until she giggled with infectious glee.

"What? These bones?"

"Her family, her history."

Amid the translucent blue flesh of his wasted body, Sid eyed him wearily. With Aviva tugging at his ear, Green could barely concentrate, but he wondered whether he'd been wrong to bring the baby. Aviva brought joy, life, and the promise of the future, but his father wouldn't live to see her grow up, he wouldn't share in the anticipation or celebration of *simchas*.

But then Sid surprised him again. "My stories not for her. Don't tell, *Mishka*. Look ahead, not back. You too, *Mishkeleh*."

"I know, Dad. But Hannah loves you, Tony loves you. I want Aviva to know you too."

Sid wagged his head back and forth. "Enough. Tired." His eyes filmed with tears. "My Hannah waits. My children, my brother."

Green sank into the chair by the bed. There was a simple truth in his father's words. The time for pleading and pep talks was passed. "I know, Dad. But tomorrow let me bring *my* Hannah and my Tony." He gripped his father's hand, as fragile as a bird's wing. "For us, not for you."

Sid's pale eyes searched his solemnly. He gave a tiny nod. "Yes. Bring."

The certainty and finality of his tone sent a quiver of alarm through Green. He leaned over to kiss his father's bristly cheek and left the room, dodging the social worker as he fled.

Sensing his distress, Aviva cried lustily as he fumbled with her car seat and muttered reassurances he barely heard. His father was slipping away. Green had been expecting this for years, but he'd hoped the passage would be gentler. A simple heart attack and loss of consciousness, without being forced to stare down the end of his life. But for his father, as in the Holocaust, death had never let him off easily.

Hence Green was swearing quietly and emphatically when the phone call came. He was in no mood to talk to Gibbs. No mood to play boss or mentor when floundering in the role of son. He considered letting it go through to voice mail, at least until he was back home, with Aviva in bed and a hefty glass of red wine at his elbow, but Bob Gibbs would not have phoned him on his private cellphone unless he really needed him.

So after four rings, duty won out.

* * *

Green smelled the fire long before he turned onto the country road and spotted the cluster of emergency vehicles up ahead. Red and blue lights strobed the darkness and played off the billows of smoke and steam that spiralled into the night sky. He pulled in behind a police cruiser blocking half the road. The officer was trying to keep the small crowd of neighbours, thrill-seekers, and local media at bay.

Green showed his badge and began walking up the road, taking in the scene. Four fire trucks, the district chief's vehicle, two ambulances, and three police cruisers lined the road and laneway leading up to the hissing ruin of Marilyn Carmichael's house. The brick walls, although still standing, were blackened, the windows were shattered, and the roof was a charred, gaping hole. The stench was choking.

Firefighters were picking their way around the soggy perimeter, looking for hotspots, while two men conferred at the edge of the lane. Green recognized one as a duty sergeant in East Division. The other, dressed in a firefighter's uniform, was a brick of a man with a barrel chest, florid face, and handlebar moustache, whose ramrod stance bore the unmistakeable air of authority. *No doubt the district chief*, Green thought. He was on his way to join them when he spotted paramedics tending to fire victims at the edge of the scene and recognized Peters's strident voice. Her face was red and smudged with soot, but she was swatting away a paramedic intent on bandaging her hand.

"I'm fine, for God's sake! This little burn is nothing,

trust me. Look after my husband. He inhaled a whole houseful of smoke trying to check inside."

Drawing closer, Green saw Gibbs lying on a stretcher in the back of the ambulance. A sheet covered most of his body but his hair and eyebrows were singed and his face bright red from the fire. He was wracked by coughing as paramedics tried to keep an oxygen mask in place.

Alarm raced through Green. No wonder Gibbs had been unable to give him any details over the phone. He hurried over and Peters leaped up, knocking her stool over. "Sir! We're all right. Bob tried to be a hero and got too close to the fire — jumping catfish, those flames are hot! Never realized how hot it gets or how fast it can spread. One minute we're trying to see in a window and the next minute — whoosh, flames are flying out at us. We didn't know if — there was a car in the drive and we were afraid ..." She ran out of air and took a deep, gasping breath that ended in a cough.

"Take it easy, Sue. There's no rush." Green laid a careful hand on her scorched sleeve. He had seen the aging Honda in the drive. "Was there anyone inside?"

"We don't know. They don't know." More coughing silenced her. The paramedic tending to Gibbs frowned at her. "Rest that throat. Whoever you are, sir, can you ask your questions of someone else?"

From his stretcher, Gibbs struggled to croak an answer. Green stopped him with a word of thanks and headed over to introduce himself to the men in charge.

"Harry Flannigan," the district chief said, wrapping Green's hand in a fierce, calloused vice. "What's CID's involvement? You guys know these folks?"

Green nodded. "From an old case."

"Criminals? Grow-op?"

"Victim's family."

"How many people reside on the premises, Mike?"

"Three. A woman in her mid-sixties. Widow."

"Mobile?"

Green nodded. "That's her vehicle in the drive. And her two adult children are there visiting."

"Well, so far there's no sign of them on the premises. We can't be sure until the scene cools and we can get in there, but usually victims are found near the exits trying to escape, unless they're incapacitated. Your two officers who called in the fire heard no fire alarm, so CO poisoning or smoke inhalation is a possibility. Or drugs or alcohol. Any of the residents likely to do that?"

All of them, Green thought with dismay. But before he could reply, a scream split the air and he turned to see a distant figure pushing past the police barricade down the road. White hair glinted red and blue in the emergency roof lights, and Green felt a rush of relief.

"That's the owner," he said. "Marilyn Carmichael. Looks as if she just arrived." Leaving the other two, he hurried down the lane to head her off. When he took her arm, she was rigid with panic. Beneath the pungent stench of smoke and burned plastics, a whiff of alcohol assailed his nose.

"Mike, what happened? What happened to my house?"

He guided her toward the supervisors. "There was a fire, Marilyn. My officers spotted it. Was anyone home? Julia? Gordon?"

"Julia? Gordon?" She repeated the names as if they had no meaning. Her eyes bulged in panic and her hand clutched his arm. "I don't know. Oh dear God!"

"Where are they this evening?"

"They took the cars. Julia was out." Her grip eased as her memory came back. "Yes, Julia went out earlier to meet a friend. And Gordon was going to meet someone downtown later, so he wanted my car." She frowned as if trying to keep track of the evening. "I needed to buy something in the village so I phoned my friend Laura to pick me up. I stopped over for dinner. It was a hot night and I wanted to clear my head, so I told her I'd walk home." She craned her neck to get a glimpse of her house and her chin trembled. "It's all gone. Everything's gone."

"But you are safe," he said, trying to block her view of the Honda. "That's what matters." He signalled the fire chief aside and reported what Marilyn had said. "There may be one person inside. He was there when she left but was supposed to take the car into town."

"I need to confirm that, Mike." Tight-lipped, Flannigan shouldered past him and headed over to introduce himself to Marilyn. "There was one individual in the house when you left, ma'am?"

"Yes, but he was going out. He took my car." She forced her way around Green's shielding body and stared at her car in the drive. "He must have got a ride."

"If he was in the house, where —"

"No. He got a ride. If he was here, he would have put the fire out."

"Were there working smoke detectors in the house, ma'am?"

"Oh yes, two."

"Was there a fire extinguisher?"

"On the wall in the kitchen."

"Is it possible an appliance was left on? Stove, microwave, barbecue?"

She was shaking her head. "I was going to do some baking. I had the ingredients out on the counter but I hadn't turned the oven on. I needed vanilla. Only pure vanilla works well, so —"

"You're sure the oven was off?"

She shot him the scowl Green knew very well. "I would never go out with the oven on."

"Any electrical problems? Sometimes these old places have old wiring."

"My husband replaced all the old knob-and-tube. Put in proper ground wires. It was a sturdy little house; it should have lasted a hundred years."

"When things cool down tomorrow, the fire investigator will get inside to look for cause and point of origin."

She blinked. "Why?"

"Always important, ma'am. Every fire teaches us something. Where and how it started. Your insurance company will need that information too."

She wrapped her arms around herself as if she were cold, even though the steamy heat from the fire was suffocating. Flannigan's face remained impassive. *He's seen*

too many fires and too many victims, to be easily moved,
Green thought as he slipped his jacket around her and
guided her toward a cruiser.

"Marilyn, let's get you some place to sit down. And
give me Gordon's cellphone number. I'll try to reach him."

"He — he doesn't have one. He's been overseas. Well,
you know that. Julia has one."

"Okay, give me her number."

Marilyn huddled in the back of the cruiser, shaking
her head. "It's in my book. Inside." Tears filled her eyes.
"With everything else."

"We'll find her. Don't worry."

He left her cradling herself while he went in search
of the duty sergeant. Police and emergency Red Cross
support had to be mobilized. Besides tracking down
Julia and Gordon, they had to ensure Marilyn had
a place to stay and someone to stay with her. Beyond
that, Green wanted to be informed the moment the fire
investigators found anything. A point of origin, a cause,
any evidence of a crime.

"There may be a connection to an active case," was
all he said.

CHAPTER FIFTEEN

The next morning dawned benign and beautiful. Azure skies, puffs of cloud, and a sultry breeze that rippled the soft, new grass of the suburban lawns. Brian Sullivan propped his Tim Hortons travel mug on the dash and stretched out his long legs in a vain effort to ease the cramping. He'd been sitting in his car down the street from the Henriksson house since 7:00 a.m., waiting for Tom to emerge for work. He wanted the element of surprise. He didn't want to tip off Paige, and he especially didn't want to give the two of them a chance to coordinate their stories.

The fire at the Carmichael house had made the news that morning, but so far no names had been mentioned and no connection had been drawn to the Rosten case or the man's recent death. If some inquisitive reporter, or worse the Twittersphere, started to speculate, however, they might converge on the Henriksson's street looking for a reaction. A juicy quote. An unguarded emotion. Sullivan knew he had to get to them before fear and paranoia shut them down.

All up and down the street front doors were slamming, cars were revving, and school kids were spilling into the sunshine, backpacks on their backs and out-sized sneakers on their feet. He smiled. It had been a long time since his own three had greeted the day like young colts released into the paddock, ginger cowlicks bobbing and freckled faces shining. Unlike Green, he and Mary had started young, and so now, instead of coping with car pools and terrible twos, they were juggling car keys and college tuition. Sometimes Sullivan longed for the simplicity and daily wonder of small children.

Half an hour with Green usually cured him.

Movement in the rearview mirror caught his eye and he watched as Tom came out of the house, swinging his briefcase and shrugging on his suit jacket. He barely looked around as he climbed into his vehicle and revved it down the drive. Sullivan stepped out and flagged him down just as he was gathering steam. The man's mouth opened in an astonished *oh* as he brought his bulky Hyundai to a shuddering stop.

His protest halted in midsentence when Sullivan held up his shield. Tom was a tall man but no match for Sullivan either physically or psychologically. His belligerence died to a sputter and he glanced back toward the house before following Sullivan meekly into the police car.

"Some questions about your father-in-law, Mr. Henriksson," Sullivan began.

"More? Why?"

"Routine follow-up, sir."

Tom gazed through the front window, masking any reaction. "I never met the man. I don't know what I can tell you."

"Did you ever speak to him on the phone?"

Tom hesitated, his nostrils flaring. "No."

"How many times did he phone?"

Again he hesitated. He seemed to be trying to guess what Sullivan knew. "I'm not sure. Two or three times? I saw the number on our call history."

"How many times did he leave a message?"

"Just once."

"When?"

The nostrils flared again, like an animal assessing a threat. "The day ... the day before his death."

"Did he contact the house on the day he died?"

Tom blinked. Sullivan could see him once again weighing the safest response. Finally he gave a terse nod.

"What time?"

"In the morning. Maybe 11:30? We didn't answer."

Sullivan made a show of checking his watch. It was barely eight o'clock. "Were you home?"

Again a pause. A faint head shake.

"Then your wife might have answered."

"She said she didn't."

Sullivan nodded. So far he hadn't taken a single note but now he jotted down a few words. *Paige may have spoken to Rosten at 11:30.* Tom, craning his neck, grew pink beneath his freckles.

"When and how did you learn that your father-in-law had come to Ottawa?"

"When I got home from work that day. Paige told me the police had shown up looking for him."

"And what was your response?"

"What's this all about, Officer? I don't get the point of your questions."

"Some information has come to light, Mr. Henriksson."

"What information?"

"I understand your wife was afraid to be at home that evening."

"No, she wasn't afraid. I was concerned."

"Where did she go?"

"To her friend Melissa's house."

Sullivan poised his pen again. "Full name?"

Tom flushed. "I don't get this. She had nothing to do with his suicide. She didn't even know where he *was* and she would never have taken our son there anyway."

"You can't be sure she didn't speak to him that morning, or later in the day."

"She wouldn't lie to me."

"Full name, please."

Tom grumbled in futile protest before providing Melissa's name and contact information. "But Paige didn't *do* anything. She wouldn't."

"Were you home alone that evening?"

"Yes."

"The whole evening?"

Tom caught himself in mid nod. His eyes widened. "You're looking for alibis, aren't you!"

"Accounting for everyone's whereabouts, yes."

"But why?"

Sullivan pretended to flip back through his notes. "Can you account for your whereabouts that night, Tom? Thursday, May 22nd, from 6 p.m. to midnight?"

"I was in there!" Tom pointed his finger in the direction of his house. "Guarding my house in case he showed up."

"Anyone with you? Anyone verify that?"

"You think one of us had something to do with his suicide?" Tom stiffened. "Wait a minute. You think we … we killed him?"

Again Sullivan didn't reply. "Can anyone verify you were home?"

"Is that the new information? That he was *murdered?*"

"That he had a visitor."

Tom's jaw snapped shut. Alarm flared in his eyes as he processed the implications. "Whatever you think, it wasn't one of us. I didn't like the guy, but he was Paige's father. Like I said, I didn't leave the house, because if the guy showed up I was going to tell him flat out he wasn't welcome in our home. And Paige would never drive out into the country by herself, especially at night. Anyway, she didn't have the car." Braver now that he had settled on his story, he put his hand on the door handle. "Now are we done? Because I gotta get to work and I'm already late."

"We're done, Tom. Thanks." Sullivan smiled as he closed his notebook. He watched Tom rush back to his SUV and peel away from the curb in a screech of rubber. Once he was out of sight, Sullivan started his own car and drove slowly away as if he hadn't a care. Out of sight, he circled a few blocks; five minutes later he cruised past the Henriksson house again.

He noted with satisfaction that Tom Henriksson's grey Tuscon was parked in the drive.

* * *

Archie Goodfellow expected to be on the phone all morning, trying to negotiate a graveside memorial service involving two feuding families, and he knew he would need all his strength and patience. He pulled into the diner for his usual breakfast special and Nancy cleared his favourite table by the window. As she poured him a large coffee, he placed his laptop and cellphone on the other side of the table. He was in no mood to deal with administrative trivia. Once the caffeine began to course through his blood, however, he revived enough to pick up his phone to make his first call, this one to a nephew who might be able to talk some sense into the dead ex-con's brothers.

As he thumbed through his recent calls for the nephew's number, he was startled to see that T Henriksson had called while he was driving to the restaurant. Now that Rosten was dead, Archie had not expected to hear from either Paige or her husband again, and he wondered whether they wanted his help with Rosten's funeral.

Curious, he checked his voicemail, flipping through the automated links until an anxious voice broke through the line.

> Reverend Goodfellow, it's Paige Henriksson. I'm sorry to bother you, I don't know if you can help or if you even

know … Well, anyway, I'm wondering if you know what's going on. The police are still asking questions about the suicide. One was outside our house this morning, grilling Tom on his whereabouts. And mine. The night my father died, I mean. The cop said my father had a visitor, and Tom got the impression they're suspicious about his death. The detective talked about new information. What information? What have they learned? This all seems very unfair, to be treated like common criminals when we didn't ask to have him back in our lives. Oh, I don't mean that, since he's dead now. But we'd like to know where we stand.

You and me both, Archie thought, gazing at the phone in surprise as the various message options played out. He saved it. His first instinct was to phone Mike Green for an explanation, but after a moment's reflection and a few more swigs of coffee, he opted for a more oblique approach. Constable Pitt of the Belleville police had shared many a strawberry social and charity auction with Archie and they were both on the board of a local youth literacy initiative. The two men frequently worked together to find creative solutions to keep minor juvenile violations off the official books. Bad knees and an excess of pounds kept Pitt on the front desk most of the time, where he learned every-thing worth knowing.

After the customary exchange of news and jokes, Archie broached the subject of Rosten's investigation.

"Yeah," Pitt said. "They did ask us to re-interview a couple of people and double-check phone records. We just got the ones from your Horizon House, so we sent those on to Ottawa directly. Needle in a haystack if you ask me. They're welcome to it."

"Any idea why? I'd like to help if I can."

"They're still looking for people Rosten was in con-tact with. Can't see what you can do."

"Anyone interesting on that phone list from Horizon House?"

"No one suspicious. We all had a look, mostly to check for known local drug dealers, because Ottawa was inter-ested in that too."

Archie frowned. Could that have been the new information Paige referred to? The mystery visitor? Were they trying to trace the diazepam and link the source to his death? Was it a bad batch, perhaps? "Were there any local drug dealers on the list?"

Pitt laughed. "Well, we're talking about a commu-nity custodial facility here, Archie. Lots of those guys and their pals are known to us. But between you and me, I think that's a blind alley."

Archie didn't argue. He had spoken to all the other residents in the house, and none of them had seen or heard Rosten show any interest in drugs. But a dim memory stirred from the day he had searched and packed up Rosten's personal effects from his room. A pharmacy receipt for toothpaste and body lotion, crumpled in the pocket of his windbreaker. He had thought it of no consequence and had shoved it back in the pocket before packing the jacket into the box. Now he remembered there had been a name scribbled on the back of the receipt.

And a phone number.

Last he'd seen, the box had been sitting in the staff office at Horizon House, waiting for pickup by Corrections.

Collecting his cellphone, laptop, and motorcycle helmet, Archie rose from the table and almost collided with Nancy, who was delivering his platter of fried eggs, sausage, and hash browns. With a quick apology and a twenty-dollar bill slapped down on the table, he barrelled toward the door.

Slaloming in and out of the Belleville traffic with an expert eye, he made good time and arrived at Horizon House to find the staff office open and Rosten's modest box of personal effects still sealed in the corner. The worker at the desk looked startled when he grabbed some scissors and sliced open the packing tape. He suddenly felt foolish. This could be a fool's errand, yielding nothing but a slip of paper with a doctor's name and number written on the back. Discarded once the appointment had come and gone.

With an effort he forced himself to slow down so that he could unpack with minimal mess. He found the windbreaker at the bottom of the box. Bunched up in the third pocket was the pharmacy receipt. He unfolded it to reveal the name and number written in Rosten's trademark jagged hand.

Erik Lazlo 613-555-6853

Did that mean anything? he wondered as he reached for the phone.

CHAPTER SIXTEEN

The smell of smoke and damp ash was still suffocating, but by the time Green returned to the site in the morning, the fire investigation crew was tromping through the ruins, ferreting out any lingering hotspots and looking for the point of origin.

Marilyn too had arrived, and was hovering at the end of her laneway. Despite the warm sun, she hugged a baggy sweater around her and cradled a hot cup of tea. Green left his vehicle on the road and walked over.

She managed a wan smile. "It never was much of a house."

"Any word from Julia and Gordon?"

She nodded. "Julia showed up at Laura's in the middle of the night. The crew here had told her where I was. Gordon has no phone but Julia thinks he's with a friend."

"That's a relief."

She nodded ruefully. "No casualties. Just my little house." She tugged her sweater tighter. "We can't all stay at Laura's indefinitely, however."

Green knew that a place to stay, at least temporarily, was the least of Marilyn's worries. The Red Cross would help with crisis support, but it was the aftermath — the insurance wrangling, the replacement of priceless mementos, the restocking of possessions and clothes, the sheer paperwork — that would wear her down. But for now, everyone had to focus on the immediate.

"Where were they last night?" he asked.

"Oh, I don't ask. I've learned not to ask. I left Julia asleep at Laura's, and Gordon — Gordon is heaven-knows-where. Some mystery friend. He always had mystery friends."

They both looked up as the fire chief strode down the lane with a grim expression. "Inspector, a word."

Marilyn tensed. "What is it?"

"Just part of the investigation, ma'am." With a tilt of his head, he drew Green out of earshot.

"You found something?"

Flannigan nodded. "Multiple points of origin in the basement, and evidence of an accelerant. We've taken air samples for analysis, but I'll bet my paycheque it's gasoline. This fire was deliberately set."

Green frowned. "Is there a pattern of arson in the area?"

"Not around here, and starting in the basement like that is unusual. The insurance company will be really interested. The basement was crammed with old paint cans, turpentine, and other flammable liquids. Pile a few rags nearby and it would have been easy to get a good blaze."

Green pondered the implications. The arsonist would have had to have access to the house and perhaps knowledge of the flammable potential in the basement. Flannigan was right. This was not a random act of destruction, but a deliberate targeting.

He glanced back at Marilyn, standing watchful guard by the road. Did she know who did it? One of her mercenary children, grown restless with waiting for their share of the profits and deciding to speed up the process by which developers would take over the land? It happened all the time, netting the homeowner a tidy insurance payout as well as the profits from the sale of the land. Julia and Gordon had no attachment to the house and very few possessions to lose inside it.

Green felt a twinge of anger at the thought. According to Marilyn, Gordon had been the last to leave the house the evening before, but Julia had a car and could easily have come back. But how could she have known her mother would be out? And could she or Gordon have had all the equipment ready in reserve to seize the moment when Marilyn left the house?

"It was a bit of overkill," Flannigan was saying. "Either this is an amateur or he really wanted to make sure to get the job done fast. If your officers hadn't spotted it when they did, there'd be nothing left but a pile of bricks."

Green contemplated the blackened shell. From Gibbs's description, the whole house had been engulfed in moments, with no smoke alarm going off. Perhaps whoever did this hadn't cared whether Marilyn was inside. Or worse, perhaps they had intended her to be there.

He shook off the thought. Surely that was too callous even for Marilyn's children. A moment later, Marilyn herself marched up to join them.

"What are you two up to? What's going on?"

Flannigan pulled no punches. "I'll be turning this investigation over to the Arson squad as a suspicious fire, Mrs. Carmichael."

Her face was a mask. She tightened her jaw as if to prevent a word from escaping.

"Do you have any idea who might have wanted to burn it down?"

"Must have been kids out for a lark."

"Was there a working smoke detector in the house?"

"Yes. As I said, two."

"Then they were disabled, ma'am."

She absorbed this, blinking rapidly. "Maybe I forgot to change the battery."

"Do you have insurance on the structure and the contents?"

"There is nothing worth insuring inside, but yes, I have some. Can I get inside to look for some things in the ashes?"

"It's not safe, ma'am. But we will be going through the whole place carefully ourselves."

"Why?"

"Arson is a serious offence. Can you make a list of valuables we should be searching for?"

"There is nothing worth searching for." She turned away, her jaw quivering. "I don't want anything from there. Just … just bulldoze the whole thing!"

"Even so," said Flannigan impassively, "I'd like you to sit with one of my men and draw up a list. Items may come to you."

Reluctantly she turned to follow the man across the clearing to his truck. Green pondered her reaction as he watched her progress. Did she suspect that one of her children might have burned it down? And that they might have intended her to be in it? He needed to interview both children as soon as possible, before their mother could warn them. Before they had a chance to cook up a story.

Quickly he set off down the lane. He'd probably be waking Julia up, but it would be worth it to catch her off guard.

He found Laura Quinn's house on Trim Road on the edge of Navan. The Victorian clapboard, two-storey building was located next to a cemetery and defiantly painted pink with purple trim. It was engulfed by flower gardens, and hand-painted leprechauns, bunnies, and butterflies peeked out between the flowers everywhere. A pink, heart-shaped WELCOME sign hung on the door and a large brass bell said, PLEASE RING. No one answered when he did, but the door was unlocked. Inside, he was greeted by more animals — painted, stitched, and carved. Floral air freshener filled the air.

Once his senses had recovered, he heard the sounds of a shower. Bedding and clothes were piled in a jumble on the couch and a cellphone lay on the coffee table. While he waited for Julia to emerge, he picked it up to peek at recent activities, but a password blocked his access.

Her open purse spilled receipts, candy wrappers, broken pens, and makeup onto the sofa. From the jumble, he picked up a battered old address book held together with an elastic band and flipped through it, trying to locate a phone number for Gordon. There were several numbers under his name, all scratched out, but Green also noted in passing a number for Erik Lazlo. It might be old, but just in case, he jotted it down.

Just then, Julia entered the room, swathed in fluffy towels that slipped off her shoulder. Her face glowed pink, and a flirtatious smile was playing across her lips. It vanished at the sight of her address book in his hand. "What the *fuck* do you think you're doing?"

He set the book down calmly. "I need to talk to you, Julia. Do you want me to make us coffee while you get dressed?"

"You don't have permission to go through my bag!"

"If you prefer to be interviewed without coffee, that's fine with me." He gestured toward the couch.

Stuffing everything back into her purse, she grabbed it and her phone before retreating to the bedroom. Inside the kitchen, as he hunted through meticulously labelled cupboards in search of coffee, he kept his ear tuned to hear whether she would use the phone. He was absent-mindedly rooting through tins of specialty teas in the pantry when he came upon an antique-looking metal box. He popped open the latch.

A snub-nosed Smith and Wesson .38 was nestled inside.

The gun was in perfect condition, oiled and shiny, its grip worn smooth by countless hands. The box wasn't locked, not remotely secure, but Laura Quinn lived alone and probably thought nothing of it. He was not a fan of handguns — in his hands nor in the hands of civilians — but this was the country, where help was sometimes far away. How much havoc could a little old lady who painted leprechauns actually wreak? Besides, it looked as if it had been in the cupboard since before the modern era.

When the dust settled, he would advise her to lock it up, but meanwhile he shoved the box back and moved on to the next cupboard. He finally located the coffee canister sitting in plain view on the counter and had just finished brewing the coffee when Julia re-emerged. She was dressed in a silky blue top that plunged deep into her cleavage, her damp hair fell in artful curls and her lips glistened red. He poured coffee into two mugs shaped like bunnies and held one out to her. She took it without a word of thanks and leaned against the counter, stretching her long, tanned legs before her.

He waited, sizing up the best plan of attack. She grew impatient. "I don't know anything about the fire, if that's what you want to ask about."

"What time did you leave your mother's house yesterday?"

"Why?"

"I'm trying to establish the chain of events."

"Chain? What chain?"

He said nothing. She took a sip and made a face. "I don't even know when the house burned down, but it

was so full of junk, I'm not surprised. Luke saved everything. Every can of paint, every broken stick of furniture.
I'm just grateful Mum wasn't there."

"What time did you leave?"

She pushed herself away from the counter, strolled
across to the sofa, and sank into it with a dramatic sigh.
"I left at six o'clock. Took my car and went into town to
meet a friend." She smiled. "And no, Mike, I did not
burn the house down. The first I heard of it was 4 a.m.,
when I got back and found it … barbecued. A cute firefighter told me where to find Mum."

"Who was still in the house when you left?"

"What did you make this coffee with?"

He grinned. "Coffee, I hope. Who was in the house?"

Another dramatic sigh. "Gordon and Mum. Gordon
was waiting for his ride and Mum was … Mum was
passed out on the couch."

"Passed out as in …?"

"Drunk. Hammered. It's not just bad girls like me
that go over the top, Mike. Nice, proper British mums
do too."

"Gordon wasn't taking the car?"

Julia sipped her coffee and ran her tongue over her
red lips. "Gordon wanted to party. And he doesn't think
tooling around in a battered old Honda has enough cool
factor anyway."

"So he left the car for your mother."

"Oh, he took the keys. In case. We do that sometimes
when she's having an especially bad day."

"When you phoned him this morning, where was he?"

"He doesn't like to be disturbed when he's having a fling. He's probably in bed somewhere."

"Can you give me a name and address?"

"If I knew that, I would call him myself. He doesn't confide in me. He has a new lover — man this time, I think. Always his first choice. But it's all very hush–hush. Some married businessman from out of town." She was watching him coyly, no doubt hoping for a reaction, but he gave her none.

"He still needs to be notified. Where is he?"

Irritation flitted across her face. She set her mug down with a thud, sloshing coffee onto the table. "Is this part of the chain or are you just being nosy? There is nothing more I can tell you. I left at six o'clock and I got back at 4 a.m. The house was already totalled. I wasn't there, Gordon wasn't there, and luckily Mum wasn't passed out on the couch anymore. It was an accident. Period."

He didn't reply. Her eyes narrowed. "What — you're implying it wasn't?"

He shrugged. "A convenient accident for those of you who wanted to sell."

She uncurled herself and stood up. "What the hell do you mean by that? Mum set the fire. She was drunk, she turned on the stove, the microwave, the barbecue — whatever — and forgot about it. You know how many kettles she's burned dry making her damn tea? Stupid, but not 'convenient,' as you put it."

"You may be right," he said blandly. "I'm sure it will all come out in the investigation. It's amazing what they can tell from the ashes these days."

* * *

On that note, Green left the house and pulled his vehicle around the corner, curious to see what Julia might do now that he'd stirred things up. His phone vibrated on his belt and a quick glance revealed it was Archie Goodfellow. Surprised, he picked up.

Archie's operatic voice blasted through the little phone. "Paige Henriksson called me. She said you guys have new information? Rosten had a visitor that night and you guys suspect her and her husband?"

Green hesitated. Sullivan was far too experienced an interviewer to give information away by accident. He had planted this tidbit for a reason. Green ducked the question. "Archie, we've uncovered a lot of things. We believe he contacted someone in the days before his death, and we're trying to determine who."

"Well, you certainly freaked her out."

"It's complicated. Did Rosten have a Facebook account?"

"Are you kidding? We monitor stuff like that."

"So you found no trace — on his computer or in his emails?"

"Not unless he used the library computer and a fake account. The guys do that, but Rosten's never been that devious."

"Archie, Rosten did a whole lot of things we knew nothing about."

Archie fell quiet. "Okay. Does the name Erik Lazlo mean anything to you?"

Green nearly dropped the phone. "Where did you get that name?"

"On a scrap of paper in Rosten's jacket, along with a phone number. The man isn't anyone Rosten has been dealing with since his release, to my knowledge."

"Did he mention the name to you at all, ever?"

"Nope."

Green asked for the phone number and, as Archie read it out, he compared it to the one in Julia's address book. They didn't match. He was so excited he barely paused to thank Archie before dialling the station. He was surprised to find Gibbs at his desk despite orders from the paramedics to take the day off. The young detective's voice was hoarse and he struggled to suppress a cough.

"Bob, you should be at home."

"I'm taking it easy, sir. J — just desk work, tracing Lazlo and Mullenthorpe."

"Don't overdo it. I want you home by noon. Any luck locating Lazlo?"

"No, sir." Gibbs coughed. "But his business colleagues are upset. He missed an important meeting with their Eastern European partners a couple of days ago. When he shows up, he's going to be fired. They gave me a cellphone number, but it seems to be turned off."

Movement outside Laura's house caught Green's eye and he glanced up just in time to see Julia sweeping down the front walk and knocking over a china bunny before climbing into her rental car. Two seconds later, the white Accent shot down the road. He debated following her but his tailing techniques, such as they were, were woefully out of practice. Furthermore, this new lead on Erik Lazlo was more important.

"Is Lazlo's cell number either of these?" Green read off the two numbers from Archie and Julia. "They're both local."

"No, sir. But I'll get right on these."

"Keep me posted." Green paused, reluctant to push him further. "If you get a chance, dig around to see if Rosten had a Facebook account under a fake name."

"That's pretty hard, sir, without ..." He was stopped by a fit of coughing.

"Don't try to talk, Bob. I'm on my way in to the station now to talk to the Arson squad."

"Arson, sir?" Bob sputtered.

"Looks like the Carmichael fire was deliberately set. You and Sue hadn't a hope of stopping it, Bob. You could have been seriously hurt."

"Who? Who would do such a thing?"

"Did you and Sue see anyone around the scene? Perhaps running away? Or a vehicle driving away?"

"We weren't looking for that, sir. We came up the road the back way and when we saw the fire, all we thought about was getting people out. But I'll ask Sue."

With a word of thanks and an admonition to be gone by noon, Green signed off and started his car. Just as he was pulling away from the curb, an aging pickup rattled into the drive of Laura's house and a plump, middle-aged woman with orange hair clambered out. She struggled up the walk as if she had bad knees, pausing to pinch a dead iris from the border and to pick up the china bunny that had toppled over into the flowerbed.

She swung around with wide eyes as Green pulled into the lane behind her. She pressed her hand to her heart until his hasty introduction brought an instant gasp of relief.

"You're Laura Quinn, Marilyn's friend?"

"Yes, and you must be the inspector she talks about all the time. Come in, come in. Poor Marilyn, what a shock. After all she's been through and not even back on her feet yet. Your heart just breaks for her, doesn't it? I've left her going over household contents with the fireman. Poor lamb looks done in."

Laura had a faint Irish lilt that had been worn down by years in Canada. Despite the outlandish orange hair, she looked older than Marilyn, and had probably immigrated in the post-war boom of the 1950s. From cozy Irish village to cozy Ontario one.

Laura led him back inside, where she stood surveying the clutter left by Julia. Wet towels bunched on the sofa, mug leaving a wet stain on the coffee table, tote bag on the floor, overflowing with discarded clothes. Laura tightened her lips but refrained from criticism as she silently mopped up the coffee.

"Difficult for them all, of course, although I haven't seen Gordon or Julia since ... well, not since poor Jackie, God rest her soul. I've been hoping their arrival would be a comfort to Marilyn, but ..." Her voice trailed off. After straightening some crystal lambs on the coffee table, she turned to the kitchen.

"Yes, I know she's been having trouble coping," he replied, hoping to encourage her. She shot him an uncertain glance. He ventured further. "This fire is a terrible blow. I'm trying to figure out what happened. She phoned you to pick her up yesterday evening, is that right? What time was that?"

"Just gone six."

"Did the house look okay then?"

She nodded, placing the two bunny mugs to the sink. "It looked lovely. All dolled up for the party. The children have been helpful that way, I suppose."

"Did she lock the house when she left?"

"Oh, I didn't actually go up to the house. When I got there, Marilyn met me at the end of the lane."

"How did she seem?"

Laura paused. Cast him an oblique look. "Seem?"

"Was she angry? Sad?"

"Ummm, perhaps upset. Out of breath. A little … unkempt, as if she'd been in a rush."

"Had she been drinking?"

Laura drew a deep breath. Tightened her lips and gave a small nod. "She's been through so much that I'm not going to fault her. But she was very unsteady. She wanted to go shopping and do some baking for the party, but I persuaded her to come here for some coffee and dinner, get herself cleaned up —"

"Cleaned up?"

"Well, she reeked."

"Of what?"

"To be honest, alcohol. And I think she'd been sick as well. Anyway, she needed a good scrub."

"Any other smells?"

She frowned. "Like what?"

"Smoke?"

"I didn't notice that. But I didn't try very hard, if you know what I mean."

"Gasoline?"

Her eyes widened. "Gasoline! What would she be doing with that?"

"It might have been the reason the fire started," he replied vaguely. "Lying around or whatever. If she'd spilled it ..."

"There were a lot of smells here in the house. I had to use half a bottle of air freshener this morning. But I couldn't tell you what they were. Now that I think about it, gasoline? It's possible."

Green was on the Queensway on his way back to the station from Navan when his cellphone rang again.

"Your father has stopped eating," the nurse said. Over the phone, her tone sounded accusatory, as if it were somehow Green's fault.

He pictured his father — pale skin draped over brittle bone, muscle and fat long since melted away. Barely a hundred pounds even before the stroke. He couldn't afford to refuse a single calorie needed to keep the fading embers of his life alive.

"What does he say?" he asked.

"Nothing. That's the point. He's doing nothing. Won't touch his food, won't open his mouth when we offer it. We may need a feeding tube."

Green glanced at his watch. He was hoping to talk to Sullivan and the others about their progress in the case before reporting the latest developments to Superintendent Neufeld. But it was just after noon and the hospital meals would have made their rounds.

"Don't," he said. "Is his tray still in his room?"

"Yes."

"Leave it there. I'm coming."

He hesitated at the Metcalfe exit ramp, from which he could see the police station with the website emblazoned across its brutal concrete facade; however, instead of exiting, he reluctantly continued west. En route he phoned Hannah's cell.

"Why don't you ever text, Dad? It's cheaper."

He tried to laugh. "You know me and thumbs. Can you get away? I'd like to visit *Zaydie*."

"Great minds. I'm just getting off the bus outside."

"You're an angel! I'm on my way. See if you can persuade him to eat."

"That slop? I have a cheese bagel from Vince's in my bag."

His laugh was genuine this time. Cheese bagels had been the food of choice on their weekly father-son outings, in the old days when Nate's Deli on Rideau Street offered the full range of artery-clogging Jewish delights — smoked meat on rye, chopped liver, knishes, and *varenikes*. Vince's Ottawa bagel shop was not in the old Lowertown neighbourhood, but it did its best.

"I love you," he said, signing off before she could summon a wisecrack response. Hannah would perk his father up. If there was anything Sid loved more than cheese bagels, it was his older granddaughter — the namesake and living replica of the woman he'd loved for over forty years.

When he walked into his father's room, however, Sid's lips were resolutely shut and the cheese bagel lay untouched on his bed table. Hannah, never the pillar of patience, was sitting with her arms crossed, scowling at him.

"*Zaydie*, that cost me four bucks!"

"Then you eat it."

"I don't even like cheese bagels. They're like lead, thudding down to the very bottom of your stomach." She leaned toward him. "They take three days to digest. Still …" She picked up a spoonful of anaemic yellow pudding from his tray. "You want this *drek* instead?"

Sid spotted Green coming across the room. "*Mishka*, you tell her."

"Tell her what?" Green leaned over to kiss his pallid cheek.

"This. All this." Sid waved a frail hand to encompass his food, his IVs, and the monitors beeping discreetly in the corner. He yanked at his IV. "I don't want."

"*Zaydie!*" Hannah looked stricken and Green regretted having dragged her into it. A twenty-year-old who had been to the brink of death and back herself did not deserve this burden.

"Dad." Green stopped his hand. "Hannah is just trying to help."

"Jesus, Dad!" Hannah said, snatching the bagel away. "Let me have my own thoughts. *Zaydie*, I get that you're tired. It's hard to keep going and it's not much fun. I get that you fought off death many times already, and this time you're not sure why you should."

Sid turned his head to her. His soft, rheumy brown eyes reflected sadness and joy together. He reached his claw-like hand over hers. "Tell him. Tell your father."

Green found he couldn't speak. He rose and walked out into the hall, leaving his wild, rebellious, angry but infinitely wiser daughter to handle the goodbyes. She came out a moment later, tears brimming now that she was away from him.

"We don't get a say, do we, Dad."

"No, we don't." He folded her to him and held her tightly.

"No one's going to put a feeding tube in him, are they?"

He shook his head, his face still buried in her turquoise-tipped hair.

"Good. I left the cheese bagel there. Just in case."

CHAPTER SEVENTEEN

Back at the station Superintendent Neufeld ambushed him just as he reached his office. She strode in, shut the door, and leaned against it with her arms crossed as if barring anyone else entry.

"Status report on Rosten, Inspector."

"I was just about to call you." With an effort, he put the hospital behind him and focused on the investigation. He filled her in on the discovery of the hidden camera and the secretive late-evening visitor to Rosten's cottage. "It seems clear he set a trap but it backfired on him."

She looked grim. "But there's no proof this visitor killed him. The PM still points to suicide."

"The visitor went to extraordinary lengths to avoid detection, and obviously removed the other camera located inside."

"Still —"

"There's more. The Carmichael house burned to the ground last night. Suspected arson."

From her expression, he could tell she already knew. *Does this woman keep tabs on everything?* he wondered. "That was my next question," she said. "How does that connect?"

Green shrugged. "Perhaps only peripherally. The children want the mother to sell, but she's resisting."

"Then it's Arson's case."

"Yes, and they'll handle it. But as long as there's a killer out there and the fire involves persons of interest, I'm going to keep a hand in. Besides, I know this family's history. Arson will need my input."

She tightened her arms and pursed her lips as she weighed her response. Finally she nodded. "Fair enough. Media Relations is going to need some copy. The press may make the connection to Rosten's death, and we need to control the rumours."

The latest news update on the fire had identified the Carmichael house but so far had focused on a possible lightning strike. But it only took one enterprising reporter.

"I'll get Staff Sergeant Sullivan on it," he said. Sullivan was a pro at press interviews. Imposing, impenetrable, and unflappable, he could stonewall with the best.

Behind his closed office door, Green could hear noises in the hallway. A woman's voice raised in agitation, murmurs of reassurance, his name requested. Neufeld raised her eyebrows and turned to leave. A faint smile seemed to flicker at the corners of her mouth.

"The hounds are at your gate," she said, and she was gone.

Leaving him in disbelief. Had that really been a smile? Was there hope?

Searching for the source of the commotion, he found Marilyn Carmichael standing by the elevator, arguing with a very red-faced Gibbs.

Gibbs turned fuchsia at the sight of him. "Sorry, sir. I — I was going to —" he began but Marilyn dived in.

"What's going on, Mike? What are you keeping from me? Why were you questioning Laura and Julia? We've barely had a moment to recover from the fire."

"Evidence is destroyed very quickly, Marilyn. We need to know what to look for."

"What evidence?"

"Accelerants, for one."

"You mean gasoline? That's what you were asking Laura about, isn't it? Do you think I burned down my house?"

"I don't think anything at this point. The Arson Unit has to look at all possibilities."

"But you ... you ..." She quivered and struggled to breathe. Around them, activity had ceased as all eyes focused on them.

"Marilyn," he said, taking her elbow. "Let's talk in my office." He waited until he had closed the door behind him before he spoke again. "I know this is difficult. We have to investigate all possibilities."

"And you think it's possible the fire was deliberate?"

"The fire investigator smelled gasoline."

Her eyes searched his. Her lips still trembled but her eyes were clear and sharp. No smell of gin floated around her. Fear and uncertainty warred across her face, as if she were looking for an answer inside her own thoughts.

"Do you know something?" he asked gently.

"I did it."

Her voice was so soft he wasn't sure he'd even heard. "What?"

"I burned it down."

"How?"

"Gasoline, just as you said."

He longed to push for details, but resisted the urge. This was Arson's case, not his. "There are procedures to follow. Before you make any statement, you should speak to a lawyer."

"No lawyers, no procedures. Just you."

"Marilyn, please."

Her head jerked up. "Mike! I don't care what happens. I don't want all the past dug up again, the media following us around, Julia and Gordon harassed. I burned my house down. I hated it, hated the memories, the pain, the horror of it. I just wanted it gone!" Her voice grew shrill and fresh colour stung her cheeks.

"You've lived there twenty years since Jackie died. You were fixing it all up for your party. This doesn't make any sense."

"Nothing makes any sense anymore! I'd been fighting it and fighting it, but I couldn't do it anymore."

"Were you …?"

"Drunk? Yes. But that wasn't the reason. It was just the courage."

"How did you do it?"

"Luke had jerry cans of gasoline in the shed for the lawnmower and the generator. He often started fires in our pit that way. I started it in the basement because I know fire rises."

"Where in the basement?"

"I don't remember, Mike. It's all a blur."

"How did you ignite it?"

She frowned as if he were exceptionally dim. "With a match."

He knew that contrary to television wisdom, lighting a match in a room doused with gasoline would produce an instant conflagration as the fumes ignited. Many an inexperienced arsonist was burned to a crisp making that mistake.

"From where?"

"From the top of the stairs. I threw the match down and … up it all went."

He eyed her thoughtfully. He knew he should have stopped her confession and brought in the Arson team. At the very least, he should have insisted on cautioning her and recording the interview. But something did not feel right.

"I'm not sure I believe you, Marilyn."

She was gripping her hands in her lap as if to keep herself still. Now she stiffened. "I'm sorry, but it's the truth."

"The whole truth?"

Her gaze wavered. She looked down at her hands and twisted her fingers. It was then he noticed her wedding ring was missing, leaving a pale indent on her fourth finger. He softened his voice. "What's going on?"

Her lips trembled. A large tear spilled over and dripped off the end of her nose. She did nothing to wipe it away. She drew a deep, halting breath. Another. Looked around the room as if searching for escape.

"Marilyn?"

"I found something," she whispered.

"What?"

"When I was cleaning. Hidden in the basement among Luke's old magazines. I found …" She shook her head as if to banish the memory. "I found photographs."

Green's blood chilled. "Of what?"

"Of Jackie."

"Sexual photographs?"

"Some. Jackie with no clothes. With her boyfriend um … on the bed. In her room. Close-ups. Disgusting."

The question had to be asked. He searched for gentle words. "Were there any photos of Luke with her?"

She whipped her head back and forth.

"Then, as awful as that was, maybe he was just spying —"

"And of the body. Of Jackie in the woods."

All his years spent knee-deep in depravity counted for nothing. He was frozen. "Alive?" He managed.

A single sob shuddered through her. "Dead. Strangled. A belt — Luke's belt — around her neck."

Green forced himself to focus despite his dawning horror. The ligature used to kill Jackie had never been found, although the buckle had left a distinctive square imprint and forensic analysis had revealed traces of leather fibre in her bruised flesh. "Did you find the belt?"

Another sob, dry and wrenching. "I did look. Other things were hidden in other places. Jackie's clothes and hair ribbons, her childhood teddy bear. I had given it to her for Christmas, and we thought it was lost. Jackie was so upset. He saved all these things. Trophies — isn't that what they're called?" She took a deep breath as if to cleanse herself, and straightened her shoulders. Her voice was flat now, the emotion spent, the worst expunged.

"I've lived a lie all these years, believing it was Rosten, believing Luke was as much a victim as myself. Believing I needed to protect him and hold him together because he was not as strong as me. I defended him against all the gossip and against all my own little doubts. Even Julia's hints. That's what I hate him for the most, for allowing me to protect and love him when all that time he'd killed my baby girl. He sat through the trial and watched that poor man go to jail for life. Some days I am so filled with hate that I go down into the basement and scream."

He cut into her tirade. "Where are these photos now?"

"I burned everything I could find. Not in the fire but earlier, in the fire pit. Along with all his old clothes."

"When exactly did you find these photos?"

"When I was cleaning out his things from the basement."

He thought back to that abrupt change in her mood, when she had ordered Bob and Sue off her land. To the scream he had heard inside the house. Stubbed her toe, she'd said. Deep in his gut, anger stirred. "Back in March?"

She nodded.

"And that's why you supported Rosten's parole?"

Again she nodded.

"Why didn't you tell me?"

She bowed her head at the veiled rebuke. "A lot of reasons. To protect Julia and Gordon, to put it all behind me. No, that's not true. I just couldn't face it. I'd lied to give him an alibi. He wasn't home all evening because I'd sent him out shopping. I couldn't face the media and all the village gossip. All the shame. It was too late to do anything. Luke was dead, and all the dreadful backlash would land on me. Rosten was going to be released anyway. So I kept quiet."

"Did you tell Rosten when you met him? Is that *why* you met him?"

"No. I only wanted to see how he was doing, and to tell him I wished him well. I'd watched him at his trial and I knew he'd never let this go. But … I did end up telling him I wasn't sure he was guilty."

"How did he take that?"

"He wanted to know why, but I didn't tell him. Just that I'd found some things."

But that hint would have been enough to launch the tenacious professor on his new mission to track down the real killer. A mission that had cost him his life, all because this woman had chosen to keep her appalling discovery a secret. Green had to fight hard to remain calm.

"You realize you can't keep it quiet any longer. I will ask one of my officers to take a formal statement from you and it will become part of the investigation into both the fire and Rosten's death. You withheld — no, destroyed — crucial evidence that could have resulted in a very different outcome for him."

She raised her head to face him. She looked exhausted, but calmer for relinquishing the burden. "We were all duped by Luke, you know. He made us all party to his atrocity, accessories after the fact to all the tragedies that poor man suffered. I burned down my house not to destroy any other evidence he might have hidden, but to destroy the memory of him. To destroy the place where I'd shared my life with him."

Green managed to maintain his dispassion long enough to hand her over to Levesque for her statement, but afterwards he slammed his door and paced his office for a good five minutes. His guts were roiling with fury. Marilyn deserved all the censure he had given her for her part in Rosten's death, but he knew his rage came from a deeper place than that. Damn it, he had been wrong. So wrong! All those years that Rosten had railed at him about Lucas's guilt and he'd been too pig-headed to reconsider. To double-check Lucas's alibi. Lucas's vehicle had been a loose end. The shop mechanic had been unable to swear it was in the lot all day, which meant that Lucas could have picked it up, driven Jackie to Morris Island, and had it back on the lot without the mechanic even noticing. How could he have missed the signs, when all the hallmarks were there? Almost all children are abused and killed by a family member. And all too often, spouses lie to protect them.

In the end, it didn't matter how and why he'd screwed up. It only mattered that because of his mistake, an innocent man had been robbed of his freedom, his health, and ultimately his life. But this was no time for personal reproach or analysis; there was a murder to investigate, evidence to collect, and investigators who needed to know the facts. Once his head was clear enough to report them without anger, he reached for the phone.

The fire investigation team was still out at the fire site, slowly sifting through the ashes and tagging and bagging possible evidence as they went along. Listening to Green's update, Harry Flannigan grunted.

"She's lucky she didn't incinerate herself by throwing matches down the basement stairs like that."

"When do you think your report will be finished?"

"We should be finished our on-site examination tomorrow. The analyses won't be in but I can probably get something preliminary to you by the end of today."

"That long?"

"That's fast! It's hot as a bitch out here today, which is slowing us down. What's your hurry?"

"I'd like the Arson Unit to have it on hand when they question Mrs. Carmichael."

"Has she been charged?"

"Not yet. I want the Arson Unit to handle that aspect. There are a lot of elements to this case."

"Fair enough, but she's already admitted she set the fire."

Green thought about the hidden evidence and Marilyn's reluctance to let anyone into the house over the last few months. "I'm just not sure she's telling us the whole story. Do me a favour? If you find anything else in your search — anything odd or suspicious — give me a call."

Green had just hung up the phone when there was a soft knock at his office door. *Fuck*, he thought, *not more*! Before he could find a civil response, the door opened and Sullivan entered, carrying a brown paper bag.

"I hear you've had a wild day," he said. "When did you last eat?"

Green sagged back in his chair with relief. "I don't know. Breakfast?"

"Breakfast was eight hours ago." Sullivan opened the bag on his desk and took out two smoked meat sandwiches on rye. "From Bobby's Table. Not quite Nate's, but …"

Green smiled. "Yeah, but they're trying. Thanks." He reached for the thick, meaty sandwich, his mouth already watering. Bobby's Table had been opened by the staff of the iconic Nate's Deli after it closed. "Did you hear —"

Sullivan held up his hand. "Not now. Eat first. You have a lot on your plate, Mike. You have to take time for yourself, or before you know it, you've burned out your body. Believe me."

Sullivan propped his big feet on Green's desk and tucked into his own sandwich. It reminded Green of the old days, except that now Sullivan was fifty pounds slimmer and the sandwich was roast turkey with lettuce on multi-grain.

"How's your dad?" Sullivan asked as he sipped his water.

Green reached back through the mists of the day to recall the disastrous noontime visit. God, how could he have forgotten so quickly? "Bad," he said with a grimace. "Worse than bad."

As he sketched the worst of the story, an idea that had been hovering half-formed in his thoughts began to take shape. Sullivan listened without interruption, but when Green was done, it was he who put the idea into words.

"You know what you're saying, Mike. You have to bring him home."

Green nodded. "But we have no room, and our life is so busy. Three kids —"

"You have the sun porch."

"It's a mess. And it's freezing in winter."

"This is summer. And there's nothing a bit of carpentry and a lick of paint won't fix."

Green laughed. Sullivan had finished his water and was looking yearningly at Green's Coke. "Me? Carpentry?"

"I'll bring over my tools Saturday. We'll have the place set up in no time. Get a hospital bed, a portable toilet —"

"There's Sharon too. She'll be left with all the work. No matter how much I promise to help, I'm not there."

"Mike …" Sullivan paused. "Realistically, how long are we talking? A couple of months?"

"If that." He couldn't voice the sense of loss that hovered beyond his words. Unless his father found a new reason to go on, he likely wouldn't live out the month. That cinched it. There was no way his father was going to die alone in some dismal hospital bed. "Let me talk to the family about it tonight."

"Good. My truck will be waiting." Sullivan bunched the paper bag into a ball and lobbed it over Green's desk, hitting the basket dead on, just like the old days too. He grinned. "Now that you're fed and you have a plan for your dad, we can talk about Marilyn Carmichael's bombshell."

Green filled him in on Marilyn's confession and her horrific discovery in the basement of her home. As he talked, his anger toward her faded. She was right; they had all been blind. Only Rosten, who had known his own innocence, had seen the truth.

Sullivan was frowning. "But what about the letter Rosten sent you? He changed his mind at the end and decided the killer was someone else."

"He had a new theory, yes." Green broke off, his head spinning. This didn't make *sense*. "I haven't had a chance to fill you in on the camera. He had a visitor the night he died, and caught some of the details on camera. Not enough to identify his killer …"

Sullivan looked astonished. "But that creates another problem! Because even if Lucas killed Jackie, he couldn't have killed Rosten."

"I know. It means we have two killers."

Sullivan picked up his water bottle and twirled it absently. "Maybe," he said finally. "If we believe Marilyn."

"*If*? It was a hell of a difficult admission for her to make!"

Sullivan held up his hand as if to plead for patience. "But she destroyed the evidence, so we have no independent corroboration. But assuming she's correct,

Lucas killed Jackie and someone else killed Rosten. That's a stretch."

"Not necessarily. Payback for killing Jackie was always one of the possible motives."

"Okay." Sullivan still looked dubious. "Who do we have in the frame?"

Green sketched his thoughts on the short list of potential suspects. "I've got Halifax tracking down alibis for Rosten's ex-wife and daughter, and Gibbs trying to find Lazlo. We do know that the suspect likely drives a dark-coloured Honda or Hyundai SUV and may have long dark hair. The Carmichaels' vehicle is a forest-green CR-V, and Gordon has long hair and no reliable alibi."

As Sullivan listened, his eyes narrowed and the skepticism in them faded. At the end he leaned forward thoughtfully. "Tom Henriksson drives a charcoal-grey Hyundai Tuscon, and he's got no alibi for the time frame either. This is a very protective guy."

Green felt that familiar surge of triumph when a new lead appeared, but before he could track the implications, his phone rang.

"Sir?" It was Sue Peters's voice, breathless with excitement. "Sorry to interrupt, but ..."

Sullivan frowned and reached to open the door, revealing Peters on her phone just outside. To her credit, she turned pink with embarrassment. "Is this a bad time, sir?"

In spite of himself, Green laughed. He saw the muscles twitch at the corner of Sullivan's lips as well. "What is it, Sue?"

Peters waved her notebook. "You know those phone numbers you gave Bob this morning?"

"What did you find?"

"One of them has belonged to someone else for ten years, but the other one went to voice mail." Peters rushed on, as if afraid she'd be cut off at any second. "It was a woman. She didn't give her name but Bob did a reverse phone look-up and it's registered to a Donna Zionti. Turns out she's Erik Lazlo's wife, which is why we never found a home number for him. Bob left a message saying if this was Erik Lazlo's number, could he please contact police. The woman just called!"

"Which number was it?"

She held out her notebook and Green recognized the number Archie Goodfellow had found. "What did she say?"

"Well, that's the thing! She said she hasn't seen or heard from him in almost a week. She wants to report him missing!"

"Ask her to come in."

"Already done. She's on her way."

"He's gonna kill me," Donna Zionti said once Green and Peters had her settled in a comfortable interview room. She overflowed the easy chair, a lumpy sausage of a woman with jet-black hair that frizzed in the heat. She was perspiring freely, whether from the heat, anxiety, or the exertion of her travels, Green wasn't sure, and she mopped her face and her ample pink cleavage with a big, red polka–dot scarf. As soon as the words were out, she laughed. "I mean, he's probably off with his latest girlfriend and when he finds out I called the cops …"

Green let Sue Peters handle the interview so he could observe quietly from the sidelines. His involvement was unorthodox, to say the least, but all the other experienced investigators on the case were occupied elsewhere. He had sent Sullivan off to deal with Media Relations, Levesque was taking Marilyn's statement, and Gibbs was back in the station, readying the paperwork for search warrants. Yet this case had so many tentacles that a tight rein and a thorough knowledge of it were essential.

"Better to be safe than sorry," Peters told Donna. "When did you last hear from him?"

"Last Friday morning sometime." She paused and scrunched up her face. "Maybe noon. I'd slept in. He came into the bedroom to say goodbye, said he was heading overseas to Budapest to meet with some investors. I can never keep up with his business and frankly I don't care. Money doesn't interest me," her eyes twinkled, "unless I'm spending it. But he was supposed to be back in time for a big meeting here a couple of days ago and he never showed up. Never called or emailed. I've tried his cell, our kids have tried, his business partner has tried. No answer. It falls on deaf ears."

"What makes you think something is wrong?"

"Well, if it were just me, I'd say yeah, okay, we don't have the greatest marriage right now and he's always liked the ladies. I know for a fact when he travels he's got his regulars on his route." She shrugged and fanned herself with a pudgy hand that sported rings on every finger.

"I knew that going in, years ago. He just wanted a wife to give him kids, hot meals, and a nice house. I was handy. I'm no prize ..." She shot Green an oblique smile. "Unless you want a lot to grab on to. I was getting past my best-before date. Hell, I never had a best-before date. I think he knew I wouldn't ask too many questions."

Beneath her dimpled grin, her expression grew sad and she stared at her hands. At her wedding band, which was plain and modest compared to the flashy rocks on her other fingers.

"What seems different this time?" Peters asked, in a surprisingly subtle tone for her.

"Because even if he didn't phone me, he'd never ignore the kids. He's crazy about them. A boy and a girl, twelve and ten. Impressionable ages, you know? And he wouldn't screw up a business deal. He likes money way too much to turn his back on a chance."

"So there's been no communication with him since he left six days ago? No phone calls, no email, no texts? Nothing on social media?"

She was shaking her head. "Nothing. And he refuses to go on Facebook."

Green leaned forward, curious. Fortunately Peters herself caught the lead. "Any reason?"

"Invasion of privacy, he says. He doesn't want the kids on it either."

"I notice the phone is in your name. Does he have his own line?"

"He has a BlackBerry he uses for business. But he wanted to keep our personal phone at home separate."

Peters asked for the cellphone number and jotted it down. "That's the number his partner gave us. Once we get a warrant, the records will tell us about any recent activity, any calls made or received, and from where. What about other devices? Tablets, computers?"

"He does everything on his laptop, but he took that with him."

"What's his email address?"

Donna supplied that, but balked at the password, claiming he'd always kept it secret from her.

"We can get it," Peters said. She seemed to sense Donna's discomfort, because she switched gears. "The evening before he left, where was he? Did he go out?"

She hesitated. Twisted her rings again. "I was out. Bingo." A shy smile sneaked across her face. "My guilty pleasure, once a month with my girlfriends. He was supposed to be home with the kids."

"Was he?"

She shrugged. "I don't know. He doesn't like it when I get nosy. Suspicious."

Peters jotted a few notes. Privately, Green doubted whether twelve-year-olds would even notice if their father went out. "Tell me about the day he left," she said finally. "Was it a planned trip?"

"No. Actually it was a lie. There was no trip and his company didn't know anything about a trip. He just packed a bag, took his passport like he was going, climbed in his car and took off."

"He took his car? Does he usually take it when he goes overseas?"

She shrugged. "That was the first fishy thing. Usually he'd take a taxi to the airport. Cheaper, unless it's just an overnighter."

Peters made another note. "What was the second fishy thing?"

"You mean besides him not calling the kids? He'd been acting weird lately. Jumpy. He doesn't confide in me — you probably got that clue if you're any kind of detective — but he told me not to answer the phone unless I knew who it was. Said it was money troubles."

"When did this start?"

"About three or four days before he left?"

"Is there any unusual activity in your bank account? Any big debts or big withdrawals recently?"

"Big debts, always. But Erik handles all that. I don't pay much attention. My credit card still works, if that means anything."

"Can you access your accounts online?"

Donna held up her jewelled hands in surrender. "Oh no. Never want to touch that stuff. I'd spend it all!"

"We'd like to look at his bank records too," Peters said. "That will tell us if he's made any transactions recently and from where."

"Oh right, like *CSI*. Boy, all this stuff, it's like nobody has any secrets anymore, do they." A small frown of uneasiness puckered her brow. "He's really going to kill me. He's such a privacy nut."

"All this is routine in Missing Persons cases, Ms.

Zionti. Everyone leaves electronic footprints nowadays, and they'll help us find him and make sure he's okay."

She still looked uneasy. "And if he doesn't want to be found?"

"We find him, we verify he's safe, and we respect his privacy."

Her lower lip wobbled slightly and she looked away. "To be honest, now that I've talked about it, it seems silly. I guess I've been kind of worrying because of all this stuff in the news. About that Rosten guy, and the Carmichael house burning down. He's never really gotten over that experience, you know? Not that he talks about it, but it's like he's always looking over his shoulder." She bent down to gather her things. "But it's more likely some pissed-off husband is coming after him with a shotgun. Either that, or this time he actually found true love. Maybe both. Maybe that's why he's laying low."

"Do you have any idea who the woman might be?"

"No clue. Like I said, we were never much for talking. I suppose in his own way he figured he was sparing me. But ..." She looked up, hesitating. "That's another thing. He did get a call. I think it might be someone from the past. I overheard him saying something about it being a long time. Then he shut his office door on me."

A random, far-fetched thought occurred to Green out of the percolating recesses of the case. He leaned toward the woman, trying to be casual. "Ms. Zionti, has the thought ever crossed your mind — even for a moment, from something he said or did — that maybe his lovers were men?"

Donna Zionti didn't recoil in indignation as he'd expected. Her eyes narrowed, and she was just opening her mouth to protest when a sharp knock sounded on the interview room door. Sullivan stuck his head in. His ruddy face shone with excitement.

"You're going to want to hear this."

It was all the disruption Donna needed. She collected her purse and stood up to leave. Green stopped her with a quick hand. "Your information could be very important, Ms. Zionti, and we appreciate your co-operation. Detective Peters here will just take a few more minutes with you to complete the Missing Persons paperwork."

He left her blinking in dismay as he slipped out the door. Sullivan stood in the corridor.

"The fire investigator just called from the site. They found bones in the rubble. MacPhail's on his way out to the site right this moment."

Green sucked in his breath. "What kind of bones?"

Sullivan shook his head. "They don't know. A couple of long, thin bones that could be human femurs."

"Or deer bones. Or coyote. It *is* the country."

"Right. And the fire boys can't tell how long they've been there either. As soon as the investigators found them, they stopped everything and called the cops. The first responders were on the ball."

"So it's been secured as a potential crime scene?"

"Yup. Until MacPhail tells us they're human or not."

Green glanced at his watch. By now the time was creeping toward five o'clock. Time for him to be home discussing his father's house plans with Sharon while she still had some energy.

Unfortunately, it was also time for MacPhail to be well into his fourth or fifth whisky of the day. Not a reassuring thought.

CHAPTER EIGHTEEN

Green arrived to find Dr. Alexander MacPhail already on scene, knee deep in soggy ash. His rubber coverall and cap were askew but he was shouting orders in a firm, clear voice. Four Scotches or not, the adrenaline brought on by the unusual remains had whipped him to sobriety.

The charred remnants of the walls, roof, and floor beams had been removed, leaving the foundation hole a jumble of debris. MacPhail and a fire investigator were poking carefully through the rubble in the corner, lifting burnt planks and bricks one at a time to look underneath. Half a dozen police and fire crew were standing around in excited vigil.

The stink of wet ash was still strong but the blue sky and late afternoon sun lent a benign air to the clearing. Beyond the ring of scorched trees, a gentle breeze tickled the leafy canopy, and the yellow police tape fluttered.

As Green approached, MacPhail brandished two black objects, one the size of a stubby pencil. "I believe this is a finger," he announced triumphantly. "And this is a femur."

Green felt a heavy weight descend on him. This case grew more complicated at every turn, the noose around the Carmichaels tighter. "Human then."

"Unless cows and moose have fingers. Or is it meese?"

Not as sober as I thought. Green sighed.

MacPhail, still sputtering at his own joke, attempted to rein himself in. "Unless you're wanting to challenge my professional opinion on this too, Inspector."

Green ducked the salvo. "So it's a major crime scene?"

"Possibly. Or possibly the poor bugger was just in the wrong place at the wrong time."

Green pondered his next move. MacPhail had his huge Wellington boots planted firmly in the middle of the evidence but tact was required to extricate him. "Can you determine anything else about the remains? Length of time they've been there?"

"I imagine they've been here at least since the fire, lad."

"Age and gender?"

"I can't possibly know that until I dig them up and get them on the table."

Green abandoned tact. "I'd like to get Dr. Jeffry Synes's assistance with the excavation. He's a physical anthropologist at the Museum of History —"

"I know who he is, Inspector. He's a little man who displays an inordinate amount of glee at the discovery of every minuscule piece of bone. It will take him days and an army of graduate students to dig all the bits out of this black muck."

"All the same, we need to know the age of the bones, the position of the deceased when they died, gender and size …" Seeing MacPhail about to dismiss Synes's exacting work as voodoo science, he pressed forward. "For eventual court, you know. The more by-the-book we are, the more airtight the case."

MacPhail rolled his eyes. "Inspector Green by the book? There's a new one. You do realize this is probably the bugger who set the fire in the first place, trapped by his own stupidity, and it will never get to court. But suit yourself, lad," he muttered as he tossed the burnt finger down and began to trudge out of the muck. "Get your expert down here and I will go back to the fine Merlot and barbecued steak that are waiting for me. Synes can work all night for all I care; this lot isn't going anywhere. And once you're good and ready, bring the box of nice, clean bones to the morgue and I'll have a proper look."

Green offered thanks, allowing MacPhail to save face as he headed back to his car, where fortunately his assistant-cum-driver was waiting. MacPhail was right about one thing. Jeffry Synes was an expert in bones, and he brought the same level of boyish enthusiasm to fossils that were several thousand years old as he did to the occasional human skeleton he was called to analyze.

These bones were unlikely to be thousands of years old, having been found in the basement of a house built in the 1940s, but Lucas and Marilyn had lived in that house for thirty-five years, during which time the basement had been Lucas's private man cave. Had there been other victims that Lucas had buried in the cellar? Was that what Marilyn had found? Was that what she'd been so desperate to hide?

It was going to be a long night.

Anxious to avoid a media frenzy, Green tried to keep the news of the remains as quiet as possible, telling only the Arson Unit, Sullivan, Neufeld, and Jeffry Synes. In the era of Twitter and cellphone videos, however, he knew he couldn't keep the social media groundswell at bay for long. So, before heading gratefully for home, he called for a team case conference first thing in the morning.

By the time he arrived at 8 a.m., most of the team were already gathered in the incident room. At the front, Levesque was scribbling on the Smart Board, filling in more points on the timeline of events surrounding Rosten's death.

Green studied the dates. Laid out chronologically, the story of Rosten's last days came alive. It had all begun with the letter from his daughter Paige six weeks ago, followed by their meeting two weeks later. Only fifteen minutes long and by Archie's account filled with awkward silences, but life-changing enough to give Rosten a spark of hope. Enough for him to make an appointment with Dr. Ansari in Kingston for a clearer view of his prognosis.

Two weeks after the meeting with Paige was the meeting with Marilyn Carmichael — a meeting held at her request — which appeared to set him on his fateful track. He persuaded Archie to let him travel alone to his appointment in Kingston, he withdrew fifteen hundred dollars from his bank account, and he set off on his final day. On that day, there had been a phone call to his daughter, which went unanswered, a letter mailed to Green promising proof of the real villain's identity, a trip to Ottawa, purchase of food and security cameras, but not Scotch, and a taxi ride out to his cottage at 6:30 p.m.

At 8:31 p.m. an unknown visitor arrived, driving a dark-coloured SUV and carrying what appeared to be a liquor-store bag. The visitor ducked the camera system but seemed to be recognized and expected by Rosten. Why expected? Had Rosten called them or had they communicated through Facebook?

At 9:47 p.m., the visitor left, again hiding from the camera.

At 8:15 the next morning, Rosten's body was found, and death was estimated at between 6 p.m. and midnight. No other arrivals and departures were noted on camera during this timeframe.

On a separate screen, Levesque had written a list of persons of interest — Rosten's ex-wife Victoria and twin daughters, Paige and Pamela; Tom Henriksson; Erik Lazlo; Percy Mullenthorpe; and Julia, Gordon, and Marilyn Carmichael. She had filled in known alibis for the time frame of Rosten's death. Pamela and Victoria were both confirmed to have been in Halifax, and Paige was at her friend's house knocking back wine. Mullenthorpe had left a trail of petty convictions across the country before ending up a semi-vegetable in a hospital in Red Deer, Alberta. Life on the edge had apparently caught up with him.

Gordon's presence at nightclubs was partially con-firmed by the bartender but his time estimates were vague. Julia's alibi was also partially confirmed. According to Hill Island border control, she had crossed the St. Lawrence River the morning of Rosten's disappearance, and, by a stroke of luck, Peters had uncovered a parking ticket issued to her rental vehicle in nearby Brockville the evening of his death.

"A parking ticket. I thought that only happens in the movies!" Peters exclaimed as the whole room laughed. Only Levesque did not smile.

"Any confirmation on where she was staying?"

Peters's face fell. "Local uniforms are working on it. But Brockville is an hour and a half drive —"

The incident room door flew open and Gibbs rushed in, clutching a sheaf of papers. Levesque's eyes lit up.

"Lazlo's phone and bank records?"

He nodded as he brought them to the front. "I had a quick look. His credit card has been active since the day he disappeared, but not often and not for big pur-chases." Gibbs looked less fried today but his voice still sounded like chains dragged over gravel. "Food and gas mostly. I checked the pending charges with VISA and the card was last used yesterday at the Ultramar gas sta-tion in Pembroke."

What the hell was Lazlo doing in Pembroke? Green wondered. The small town was about a hundred and fifty kilometres northwest of Ottawa along the Ottawa River, essentially en route to the hinterland of northern Ontario. As an escape route, it was an unwise choice. If

Lazlo was hoping to disappear by fading into the crowd or catching a quick flight out of the country, he was going in the wrong direction.

"Find out from the wife whether he has any history or contacts there," Levesque said, making a note on the board. "Friends, family, former residence. What's in his phone records?"

"That's going to take some time," Gibbs said. "There are dozens of calls and texts in the last month, the last one yesterday. I checked that one. It's to a motel in Pembroke."

"Phone them," Levesque said. "Find out if he's there."

Gibbs took out his phone to make the call. Tuning half an ear, Green wandered up to peruse the phone records he'd left on the table. He tracked his finger down the list of calls Lazlo had received in the two weeks between Marilyn's meeting with Rosten and the man's death. If Rosten had phoned Lazlo to set up a meeting at the cottage, the call would have been made during that timeframe.

Belleville and Kingston had the same 613 area code as Ottawa, but a call from either place would be logged as long distance. Sure enough, there was one long-distance call from a 613 number, made to Lazlo four days after Rosten's meeting with Marilyn and ten days before his death. Time enough for Rosten to track down Lazlo's number and set the trap. A quick computer check revealed the call was from a Belleville payphone not far from Horizon House.

Levesque added that call to Rosten's timeline just as Gibbs finished his call to the motel. He shrugged. "The motel says they had one late-night check-in last night, but wrong name and description."

"Could be a disguise or a diversion," Green said. "To throw us off the track. Let's check it out and get an alert out on this guy ASAP as a suspect in Rosten's death."

A buzz arose in the room as Levesque began firing off assignments. Green picked up the phone list and continued to scan the numbers. Most were meaningless and would take long, painstaking hours to eliminate, but one had a familiar ring. He wracked his memory before pulling out his own phone to search through his contacts. And sure enough …

His chest tightened. Erik Lazlo had made two calls to Marilyn Carmichael's house — the first a few days before Rosten's death, and then again on the morning after.

As Green left the incident room, he considered which of the many tentacles of this case he had to pick up next. Neufeld was pushing for a high-level meeting with all the players implicated in Rosten's wrongful conviction case. Although it was not technically a wrongful conviction yet, since the man had not been definitively cleared by new evidence such as DNA, Neufeld rightly wanted to warn the Crown Attorney's office, the Justice Department, and the legal departments of the various police services involved that there was trouble brewing so they wouldn't be blindsided by a media leak.

Green knew she also wanted to protect the Ottawa Police Service's flank and ensure the blame was spread around should accusations and lawsuits begin to fly. Neufeld was new to the force and this would be the first major test of her mettle.

Green, however, had no wish to be the straw man set up by the brass to absorb the blame. It was bad enough that the threat of Support Services hung over his head.

He fell in step beside Brian Sullivan. "I'm heading out to the fire site to see if the bone doctor has any information for me yet."

Sullivan cast him a doubtful look. "Didn't Neufeld want —"

"I'll have a whole lot more answers for her if Jeff Synes can tell me about the remains — age, sex, time in the ground, manner of death, and such. And we have to set up a separate major case investigation."

"Isn't that premature?"

"Regardless of who the body is and when they died, it's a suspicious death. Warrants a major case file."

"Maybe some poor guy just got caught in the fire."

"Uh-huh. And I've got a swamp to sell you."

Sullivan chuckled. "Okay. We're running out of personnel. I've got two detectives on holiday. How about Gibbs?"

"Gibbs is a witness. He called in the fire."

"Right." Sullivan paused outside Green's office, mentally reviewing the officers in the unit.

"How about you?" Green countered. "At least until we know for sure whether it's a homicide."

Sullivan folded his arms and looked down at Green, his blue eyes twinkling as if twenty years had been taken from his life. As if the two of them were back in the trenches together, caught up in the thrill of a case. "I'm fine with it if you are, Inspector."

"Good. Done. And right now, I'm going out to Navan to see what Synes has uncovered. Love to watch those guys work. And while I'm there, I might just check out a few leads in the Lazlo MisPers." He grinned at Sullivan's raised eyebrows. "That's the great thing about being the inspector. As the boss, I get to do whatever the hell I want."

When Green arrived at the Carmichael fire site, he found Jeff Synes conducting a mini-archaeological dig. The diminutive scientist had gridded off the entire foundation, and two impossibly young-looking students, properly suited up and under the supervision of the arson investigator, were doing a methodical search while Synes concentrated on the remains themselves. Even from the edges of the cordon, Green saw that he had already excavated much of the body, and he wondered whether the man had begun at the first blush of dawn.

The skeleton lay wedged in the corner, curled by the fire into the classic pugilist pose. Synes was brushing off the skull with short, soft strokes, as if it were a piece of priceless, thousand-year-old pottery. He looked up with a jaunty wave.

"Almost perfectly intact," he said. "No animal activity, no shifting with frost. The fire didn't burn hot enough to destroy the bone. House fires typically don't.

My students are learning a tremendous amount from Sergeant Keller here."

The arson investigator glanced over with a grin. "And I from them." The rest of the basement was dotted with little yellow evidence markers, and a large plastic bin sat on top of the foundation wall. It already contained several tagged containers.

Green pulled on some rubber boots and ventured closer. "Find anything interesting?"

"Shards of glass, exploded cans, charred lids, piles of tools. The whole kitchen is down here too, the stove and fridge nearly intact. It's all interesting to me as a record of their daily life, which was messy. Someone sure was a pack rat. But who knows what's relevant?"

"Welcome to the world of crime scene investigation," said Green with a laugh. "What about the remains, Jeff? Can you tell me anything yet?"

Synes began to dance excitedly about his skeleton, gesturing. "From the narrow pelvic bone and his height, I'd say definitely adult male. He's medium height, femur length suggests five ten to six feet, but I can be more exact later. Your pathologist will have a fine set of teeth, although not pearly white, to make an ID. Judging from the wear on the teeth, as well as traces of osteoarthritis in the joints, I'd say middle-aged, but again, once we get him out of here, cleaned up, and into the lab, we can tell more."

"How long has he been there?"

"Oh, not long. There is still soft tissue especially on the underside. This was a body, not a skeleton, when the fire occurred."

"Can you tell how he died? Heat, CO_2 poisoning, smoke inhalation?"

"That's beyond my realm of expertise, but Keller here says most fire victims die trying to get to an exit. On the stairs or on the way to a door, not curled up in a corner —" He pointed to part of a charred staircase on the far wall, "at the opposite end from the means of escape. Besides ..." he paused and squatted on his haunches beside the skull, "this guy's got a great big crack on the back of his skull."

Green peered closer. Even from the edge of the basement wall he could see the jagged bone. "Skulls often explode during a fire from the heat of the brain inside," he said.

"Ah yes, but this ..." Synes traced the lines of the fracture. "This was not caused by a force pushing outward. See these edges? The skull was splintered inward."

"Could some bricks or a beam have fallen on him?"

"Nothing heavy enough in the vicinity. Except this." Synes pivoted to point to a large, blackened rectangular block.

"What's that?"

"A lid from a toilet tank. But there's no toilet anywhere near here. The bathroom appears to have been upstairs."

Green swore softly. "So someone hit him with it."

"Well, lots of heavy things fell through into the basement. It's possible the toilet did."

"I know this house. The bathroom is not in this corner of the house. This didn't land here by itself. This was deliberate."

Synes grinned. "You want to step on Alexander MacPhail's toes, be my guest. I'm not going there."

Green left him and the other investigators to their work and walked to the edge of the crime scene, where he peeled off the heavy boots with relief. Even without the fire, the rising heat of the June morning was sweltering. Once he could breathe freely, he phoned MacPhail to update him and obtain direction.

He was on the phone thirty minutes, first with MacPhail, then with Neufeld and the Ident Unit. He was just discussing plans with the East Division duty inspector to deploy a mobile command truck when he spotted a black pickup truck driving up the road toward the site. As it drew closer, he recognized Marilyn at the wheel. She veered onto the verge at the end of the lane and climbed out, gaping with surprise at the sight of all the extra officials swarming over her land. He hurried down the lane to steer her away but she struggled to peer over his shoulder.

"What's going on?"

"It's still an ongoing investigation, Marilyn. The premises are still off-limits."

"I know. I just came to see whether I could pick up my car. I mean, if it isn't damaged by the fire." She eyed the SUV that still sat in the middle of the lane, streaked with ash and water stains. "It looks okay."

He studied her closely. Her face was ghostly white and she vibrated with restless anxiety but her eyes and speech were clear. There was no hint of alcohol on her breath. Did she know that a body had just been discovered in her basement? Had she come to see for herself whether the police had found it, or had she really just come to get her car? If so, where was the additional driver?

"Marilyn, I know the waiting is difficult but let's leave the experts to get on with their work. Is there someplace we can go to grab a coffee in the meantime? Maybe at your friend's place? I have a few more questions."

"I told you everything yesterday."

"Something new has come up."

Her gaze shifted from his impassive face to the activity behind him. Her breath quickened. "I hate to keep imposing on Laura. She's been very helpful, but now that Julia is there too, it's really a lot to ask."

"Fair enough, but —"

"And I do need to get her truck back to her. Can't the questions wait?"

He was still angry at her and at her constant obfuscation. With a firm hand, he gripped her elbow to steer her aside, but she pulled free. In exasperation he abandoned subtlety.

"Why didn't you bring Laura or Julia back with you if you were coming to pick up your car?"

"Why?" She looked puzzled, then gave a little laugh. "I'm sorry. I — I guess I'm rattled."

"Why?"

"Why? I told you why. I told you what I did. What more do you want?"

"Have you or Julia heard from Gordon?"

"No, but that's not unusual. Gordon has always … disappeared for days, even before Jackie's death. He's like his father that way. Drugs, alcohol, tomcatting, most likely. Until he's had his fill."

"Do you remember his friend Erik Lazlo?"

She looked genuinely surprised. For a few seconds she gazed vacantly at him. "Erik? Of course I remember Erik. Jackie's boyfriend. The kids were all friends together growing up, and Gordon and he were in a band."

"Do you know if he and Gordon stayed in touch?"

She looked genuinely baffled. If she was the one Lazlo had spoken to, she was hiding it well. "Oh, I don't think so. I think there was a rift. Over Jackie, or Julia ... Most of Gordon's friendships fell apart during the trial. He wanted to put all those days behind him. I think we all did."

"Did Gordon mention that he'd heard from Erik recently?"

Marilyn frowned as she searched his face for clues. "I don't see what Erik's got to do with any of this — Rosten's suicide or this fire or Gordon."

"Because he phoned your house twice. Once before Rosten's death, and again the morning after. That call lasted seventeen minutes, so someone talked to him. Was it you?"

She swayed and thrust out her hand to steady herself. She shook her head as if trying to make sense of the news.

"Julia?"

"Julia wasn't here. Besides, she wouldn't have given him the time of day."

"Why?"

"She thought he was shallow and manipulative. She'd gone out with him a short while herself, and she told Jackie she was wasting her time. I guess — I guess it must have been Gordon he spoke to." Her brows knitted in worry.

"It's essential that we locate Gordon, Marilyn. Where might he have gone?"

She stared at him and frank fear gradually widened her eyes. "You think something's happened to him, don't you? That's why —" Her gaze swept behind him to the buzz of activity at the fire site. Before he could stop her, she had covered half the distance to the police cordon. Close enough that she could glimpse the search in the basement below.

He dived for her arm and spun her around. She struggled and thrashed, shrieking. "What is that? What have you found?"

Resolutely silent, he wrestled her back toward her pickup. "Marilyn! Go back to Laura's and wait. I'll be there as soon as I can. But we need to find Gordon, so if you think of anything, please call my cellphone."

She was still ashen and she stumbled a little as she climbed into the truck. To his dismay, he saw a pair of media vans speeding up the road and he swore loudly at the power and speed of modern communications. He was running out of time to keep this latest death quiet. Marilyn herself might find out by turning on the latest afternoon talk show.

He watched her with concern as she tried three times to manoeuvre the truck in a circle back the way she had come, stomping on the brakes and gas alternately so that it bucked like a wild horse. Belatedly, he wondered whether he should have had someone drive her home and stay with her in case the news hit the airwaves, but he reassured himself that the distance was short and Laura was waiting for her.

In any case, he had a far greater worry on his mind. He had to get an alert out on Gordon Carmichael as quickly as he could.

CHAPTER NINETEEN

Brian Sullivan was on his hands and knees on the floor, grunting as he tried to wedge his six-foot-two footballer's frame under the computer table in the corner. Cables and cords snaked around him in a bewildering array and the computer tech was trying to direct him on which plug to plug into which jack. Sullivan felt his temper fraying. *Budget cuts*, he grumbled to himself. *Can't even set up a decent incident room in this decade without doing half the work myself.*

There was a sharp knock at the door, and Sullivan scrambled to extricate himself, bumping his head on the table in the process. Mike Green was standing in the doorway, taking in the scene without even a flicker of a smile. *Must be serious.*

"I've just upgraded the arson to a major criminal investigation," Green said. "Synes confirmed it's a probable homicide."

Sullivan listened to the details as Green summarized his discussion with the anthropologist. "The body's on its way to MacPhail for the official word as we speak, but Jeff is pretty sure."

"Middle-aged male," Sullivan said. "Got a theory?"

Green ran a weary hand through his fine hair. "There may be some players we don't know about, but I'm betting on Erik Lazlo or Gordon Carmichael. Both are AWOL."

Sullivan sighed." I thought this was my case."

"That's why I'm telling you. We need to get dental records on both those men without sending the relatives into a panic, so be as vague as possible."

"Gee, I would never have thought of that."

To his credit, Green managed a laugh. "Marilyn Carmichael is compiling a list of Gordon's friends and hangouts." Sullivan detected a furrow of worry in Green's brow as he mentioned her name. This is personal, he realized, and Green was going to be a loose cannon.

"What else are you planning to do?" he asked. "Just so I know."

"I'm going to talk to Dispatch about intensifying the search for Lazlo and Gordon. We need all eyes on this one. And then —" Green scowled with distaste. "The media have caught wind of the body. We need to have a credible response to contain the rumours." His cellphone rang and Green glanced at the call display. "Neufeld," he muttered, heading for the door. "The circus has begun."

Catching Green's urgency, Sullivan hurried to set up the equipment and assemble a team. Of sorts. The unit was stretched thin, with two detectives on leave, some assigned to tracking down Lazlo, and most of the others busy on the Rosten case. There better not be any more murders in this town for at least a month, he thought, or we'll be borrowing from the janitorial pool.

Within an hour, he'd left the incident room in Sue Peter's eager hands and headed out to Navan. As he drove, he formulated a plan. He'd never been to the village but suspected it was no different than all the other old farming villages scattered through the Ottawa Valley. Years ago, it would have been a bustling hub for the surrounding farms, founded by hard-working, God-fearing settlers fleeing the American Revolution and the potato famines of Ireland. It would have been bursting with mills, foundries, cheese factories, and shops. Now, it would be fading, with the old mills and factories boarded up or taken over by kitschy boutiques and art studios.

Big box stores and community health clinics in the nearby suburbs would have replaced the country doc and the old general store-cum-post office. But Sullivan had Googled dentists and discovered that there was still an office right in the core of Old Navan. It was there he was heading. His memory of his own Ottawa Valley hometown of Eganville was not a warm one, but that had more to do with his hard-drinking father and their hard-scrabble farm than with village life itself. He forced himself to approach Navan with a less jaundiced eye.

Eganville had had a dentist who yanked teeth and filled cavities in his office on the main floor of his own house, and although he had young associates who came and went, he had stayed on to practise his own ancient art well into his eighties, bartering a chicken or a fresh bass with those who couldn't afford to pay. All eight of the Sullivan children had trooped through his office at one time or another.

Sullivan hoped Navan had a similar dentist who had tended the teeth of the Carmichael children. Thirty years ago, neighbouring Orleans would have been mostly cow pastures, and Navan would have been its own community.

He was encouraged by the sign posted on the front of a century-old house on Trim Road near the central crossroads. It was brightly painted in red and white and listed two dentists of the same last name, Dhaliwal. Old generation and new, with forty years of combined practice under their belt, he hoped.

There was a CLOSED sign in the front window, but the interior was wide open behind the screen door, which he pushed open with a screech of hinges. Immediately, a young woman popped her head out of a back room. Her black hair was pulled back into a ponytail and her rich black eyes were partially obscured by stylish, thick-framed glasses.

"I'm sorry," she said in a lilting Indian accent. "We're closed until 2 p.m."

Sullivan produced his badge, introduced himself, and asked to speak to Dr. Dhaliwal.

"I'm Dr. Dhaliwal. Do you wish me or my husband?"

Not forty years of practice after all, he thought. "It doesn't matter. I'm looking for dental X-rays that are probably twenty years old. For —"

"Ah, for forensic identification?" she asked, emerging from the other room. She was wearing a white lab coat but a chubby toddler was propped on her hip. "Oh dear. In connection with the fire?"

He should not have been surprised. No Internet was as efficient as the small town gossip chain. Reluctant to fuel it further, he didn't reply. "Has this dental practice been in operation that long?"

"Not by us. We have only been here three years, but we bought it from a dentist who was retiring after many years. We still have many of his old records stored in the back. We have been gradually moving them to proper storage off-site, but we have been very slow about it." She chuckled and planted a kiss on her baby's cheek. "It may take a while to locate the file, but if you give me the name, I will call you when I find it."

"Thank you. The name is Gordon Carmichael. If you find anything, I will get the necessary paperwork."

Her eyes widened. "Oh, no! Not Mrs. Carmichael's son!"

He nodded. "You know him?"

"Not him, really, but her. Such a lovely woman and so many tragedies. She welcomed us to the neighbourhood the day we arrived. Showed up with a big basket of strawberries and a bouquet of flowers from her garden." She looked sad at the memory. "She said it would be wonderful to have a dentist here who didn't spend half his days off fishing or tending his bees."

Sullivan felt the pull of other demands. "We don't know if it's Gordon, but we need the X-rays for elimination purposes."

"Of course, of course. And I can get those immediately because Gordon came in for a consult only last month. His teeth were very neglected. Poor diet, no regular dental care, those dreadful French cigarettes. He wanted everything fixed. It was going to be expensive but he said that would be no problem. My husband took X-rays at that appointment and I can get hold of them right away."

"Thank you. I'll get the official paperwork organized, and the pathologist's office will be in touch about delivery shortly. Call me if there is a problem."

They exchanged cards. "I will make sure these are sent before the day is out," she said, hugging her child close as she bowed her head. "Poor woman."

Green was in Neufeld's office sitting around her conference table with her, the duty inspector, and the deputy chief. Neufeld's office was practical and unadorned, and if she had any personal art, professional citations, or family photos to hang, she had not yet done so. The bookcase held neat rows of books arranged by subject and a single African violet sat on the table. It looked bedraggled. A small flaw in her orderly regimen, Green wondered, or had it just travelled across the country?

The group was reviewing the whole picture as well as results of the search for Lazlo and Gordon Carmichael, which were dismal. The alerts had gone nationwide: border crossings, airports, and train stations had been put on notice, but without any hints to narrow down the search, it was a daunting task.

A local OPP officer had been dispatched to the Pembroke motel with a photo of Erik Lazlo, but the night clerk roused from a deep sleep had been unable to confirm or deny the resemblance. The late-night customer had apparently worn dark glasses and a hoodie despite the hot night.

Numerous leads had tracked Gordon to assorted friends' houses, but each had yielded nothing. The friend he was to meet the evening of the fire said he never turned up. Never called either, but that was Gordon. Likely a better offer came along.

"Staff Sergeant Sullivan has arranged for Gordon's dental records to be delivered to the morgue, and I assume Dr. MacPhail has already lined up the forensic odontologist."

Green paused, choosing his words cautiously. Alexander MacPhail had a distinguished reputation, particularly in the courts and among the senior police ranks, and Green had no wish to cast it into doubt. "I expect we will have an ID on the burn victim by tomorrow afternoon. After which, we should be searching for one man, not two."

"For my money, I say we concentrate on this Lazlo guy," the duty inspector said. "He's gone to ground. He disabled his cellphone GPS and checked into a remote hotel in the middle of nowhere, wearing dark glasses at midnight for f— Pete's sake. Actions of a guilty guy to me."

Neufeld pursed her lips and gave Green a questioning look. *Rebuttal?* she seemed to say. She was the one who would have to justify the resources, both human and financial, that were being thrown at this search.

But Green was not going to jump to conclusions, no matter how obvious they appeared. He'd made that mistake once before. "Or a frightened one."

The inspector snorted. "Frightened of what?"

"Any number of things. Us, for instance. He's been a suspect before and he doesn't want to repeat that experience. According to his wife, he's paranoid about privacy, which probably stems from that. Maybe he knew we'd find out Rosten was in touch with him, maybe he has no alibi for the time of Rosten's murder. I know this guy. He's not a hero. He's not going to stand up and fight; he's going to run."

"Even the biggest cowards will fight when their backs are to the wall," the inspector said. "Bashing someone's head in with a toilet seat — that's not planned. That's grabbing the opportunity that presents itself and acting before you can think."

Green had already reviewed that scenario in his head and considered a similar conclusion. It did seem like an impulse killing. If indeed the victim was Gordon Carmichael, then the killer must have decided on the spur of the moment that he had to die, perhaps because of something incriminating he'd discovered in that basement.

It made a good theory, except there was no toilet in the basement; therefore, unless the killer dragged the body downstairs afterwards to increase the chance of it burning, he must have brought the murder weapon downstairs with him. At this point, however, speculation was not the top priority for them. Locating the man was.

"I'm not discounting Lazlo," Green said. "I just think it's unwise to discount Gordon Carmichael either. Lazlo doesn't have a pattern of impulsive behaviour, at least none that has brought him into conflict with the law. He's got a few traffic violations on his sheet — seatbelts and cellphone use — and he was a victim in an assault case involving an angry husband, but other than those incidents, he's never broken the law."

"Maybe he's just smart."

Green inclined his head. "Could be. But I'm not taking any chances. We're going to take a bath on the Rosten case as it is. The Ottawa police, the Attorney General, and the OPP are going to be on the hook for serious compensation to his family once the dust settles, and rightly so. We screwed up."

The deputy chief frowned and the duty inspector opened his mouth to protest. Neither of them had been on the force during the original Jackie Carmichael case.

"I screwed up," Green amended.

Support came from an unlikely source — Neufeld herself. "That was before we amalgamated the police services and before we had the major case management system to coordinate cases across jurisdictions. But you're right, Mike. This is a mess. Both searches continue. It would be nice to know where to look, however."

Green felt a rush of relief. He'd felt himself beginning to swing from a very thin limb. "We'll question both sets of friends again. I have an officer combing through cellphone calls. Sooner or later something will break."

He held on to that hope as the meeting wrapped up and he headed back toward his office. Descending the stairs, he almost ran headlong into Sue Peters on her way up to get him. Peters could be impetuous, but even she knew better than to interrupt the senior brass unless all hell had broken loose.

Perhaps the answer to his prayers. She clutched his arm, her voice an octave higher than normal. No apology, no preamble.

"Sir! You're never going to guess who just walked in!"

Sullivan felt the sweat trickling down his spine as he walked up the lane to watch the Ident team sift through the basement debris. The human remains had been removed to the morgue and the Arson team had finished their examination of the site, but senior Ident officer Lou Paquette and his rookie partner had just begun, taking over the grid analysis that Synes's students had set up.

Sullivan wanted to be thorough. If there were other clues left behind among the rubble and detritus of the family's home, he intended to find it. Paquette was down on his hands and knees near the site of the body, grumbling loudly as he pawed through mush. Paquette was a battered, grey-haired veteran with thirty years on the force, now counting down the months to his retirement dream of fishing at the cottage. Unlike his colleague, Cunningham, Paquette relied on his intuition from thirty years and had no fondness for the dirty minutiae of crime scene analysis. Fortunately, his intuition was worth a lot.

For Sullivan, it was a process about as exciting as watching paint dry, and he was beginning to think he could make better use of his time when Paquette straightened up, slowly as if his back were killing him, and shouted out to him.

"This looks interesting!"

Sullivan approached to peer down into the hole. Paquette gestured to a portion of the basement wall crudely finished with plywood panelling that was now peeling away in jagged, charred chunks. Near the base, Paquette had pried loose a square of panelling that the fire had barely touched.

"Looks like this piece was cut out of the wall some time ago." He poked at the debris inside the cavity. "And there's something inside this hole. Get the camera, will you, Shooter?"

After his partner had taken numerous photos and samples of the material in the hole, Paquette reached inside and as carefully as if he were handling an explosive device, he extracted a small metal toolbox. It looked antique and untouched by the fire, but all distinguishing markings had been obliterated by rust and water stains.

Shooter took more photos. After failing to loosen the rusty latch, Paquette shoved a screwdriver under the lid and pried it open. When Sullivan jumped down into the basement, he didn't say a word of protest. A dozen firefighters and graduate anthropology students had already messed up the scene beyond hope.

Up close, a dank smell arose from the box, but the interior was surprisingly dry. They all peered inside. At first the contents were unrecognizable — clumps of stained material, shredded and partially decomposed.

"Clothing of some kind?" Sullivan asked.

Paquette nodded and moved it gingerly with the tip of his stylus. "The lab might be able to do something. There's a zipper here, and what looks like a button. And this looks like a belt buckle." He slipped his stylus through it and held it up to be photographed. It was thick and square. Sullivan sucked in his breath. He'd seen that shape before, in a close-up photo of Jackie Carmichael's neck.

So the mystery ligature had been secreted away in the basement of her home all these years. A mere three feet from where the latest victim had been found. Sullivan felt a heady rush of triumph as he reached for his phone to call Green. At that moment, there was a shout from up above and the log-in constable guarding the crime scene peered down.

"Sir, dispatch just reported a 911 call from 3629 Trim Road, right here in Navan. We're closest, so should I respond?"

Sullivan's mind raced. The address rang a bell; he'd seen it just that morning in a report.

"What's the nature of the call?" he asked.

"Unclear, sir, They were cut off, but the woman demanded police and ambulance. Sounded serious."

Belatedly the memory clicked into focus. That was Laura Quinn's address, where Marilyn Carmichael was staying.

"Go!" He swung on Paquette. "Can you and Shooter hold the fort here till backup arrives?"

Without waiting for an answer, he was out of the basement and on the run to his own vehicle, yanking off his protective clothing as he ran. Up ahead, the young uniformed constable was already peeling down the road, roof lights flashing.

Laura Quinn's house was on a quiet block of old houses with huge lots. Thick flowering lilacs and tall spruce screened both the house and laneway from the houses on either side. The young constable was stationed behind his cruiser reporting on his radio by the time Sullivan slewed into the lane behind him.

Sullivan took in the surroundings at a glance. The old-fashioned two-storey house looked well maintained by someone with a craftsy bent and a very green thumb. The laneway was empty and the house looked quiet, but the front door gaped open. At his feet, however, were three very large dollops of blood. Further up, another. His eyes traced the trail of spatter up toward the porch. Crouching over and careful to sidestep the blood, he hurried up to join the constable, who looked tense but focused.

"Dispatch is getting no answer at the number, sir," he whispered. "Phone's off the hook."

"Have you tried calling into the house?"

"Yes, sir. No response. No sign of movement through the windows either."

Through the main floor window, Sullivan could see the type of lacy white curtains well loved by farm families throughout the valley. They dressed up a modest house but let the light in. These ones were embroidered with birds.

"Backup on the way?" he asked.

"Yes, sir. Five minutes out."

"That's time to bleed to death," Sullivan replied. "We're going in."

As he walked up the lawn to the front porch, he rested his hand on his Glock. More blood and a bloody handprint on the open door. There was still no movement or sound from inside. Signalling to the constable to follow suit, he drew his Glock and shielded himself behind the wall. "Police!" he shouted through the open door. "We're coming in!"

No answer. Not even a whisper. Even the birds in the trees seemed still. The hair rose on the back of his neck. A bloody domestic scene was one of the most dangerous situations an officer could face. If there was an assailant inside, he was waiting in silent ambush. But if someone was injured, they needed help immediately.

Using hand signals, Sullivan led the rush through the front door and pressed himself into the corner of the hall. Intent but quivering, the constable took the other corner. In rapid, soundless tandem, they made their way forward, keeping a wall at their back and checking each room as they moved down the hall. The living room was empty, but a lamp lay shattered and bloodstains marred the creamy carpet. Sullivan followed the blood down the hall, crunching on a broken plate and rounding the corner to the kitchen, where a phone receiver had left a streak of blood across the linoleum before coming to rest under the country pine–table.

From the corner of the kitchen, Sullivan sized up the situation. The room was empty, the back door closed. Broken figurines littered the tiles, and behind the counter, collapsed in a smear of blood down the wall, lay the body of a woman. Ducking low, Sullivan rushed over to check on her, leaving the constable to check the back door and to radio dispatch. In the distance came the wail of sirens.

Sullivan knelt at her side. A brutal wound gaped at her throat. She was deathly pale, and her orange hair ran dark red with blood, but as he groped through the blood for a pulse, he mentally ran through photos on the incident room wall. Not Marilyn Carmichael or her daughter Julia. Possibly the poor friend who had taken them both into her home.

Beneath his fingers, finally, he felt a faint flutter of life.

CHAPTER TWENTY

By the time Green made it down the stairs, even two at a time, the new arrival was in the interview room. Sue Peters was down the hall in the control room, helping to verify the recording equipment, but she abandoned the task to follow him into the interview room. The man stopped pacing and swung around in alarm. He looked as if he had endured a month of nightmares that had carved deep circles under his eyes and robbed him of ten pounds. Despite the passage of twenty years, Green would have recognized him anywhere.

"Erik Lazlo," he said. He held out his hand, which Lazlo stared at in disbelief.

"It's you!" he exclaimed.

"Yes, it's me. Have a seat, Erik."

"You're in charge of this case? Holy fuck!" Lazlo fell into the chair. Green positioned his own chair directly opposite, blocking Lazlo's exit and pinning him against the wall. At this distance, he could smell the stench of the man's stale cigarettes and unwashed clothes.

"Yes, I'm in charge. We have a nationwide alert on you, Erik. You've been hiding."

"It's all over the news," Lazlo said. "About the fire, I mean. Is it true they found a body?"

Green said nothing but his expression must have given him away. "Holy fuck!" Lazlo said again.

"Where have you been? Your wife hasn't heard from you in a week."

Green sensed Sue Peters eyeing him curiously, probably wondering why he was taking such a confrontational approach. His mantra had always been, when a witness comes in to tell their story, let them tell it. But he knew Lazlo and he wanted to make sure the man felt vulnerable.

"I travel a lot for my work."

"No bullshit, Erik. You disabled your GPS, you didn't call your kids, you holed up in a motel in Pembroke. You've been hiding. From us?"

"From you? No, no."

"Rosten is dead. What a coincidence you went missing the morning after he died."

"I heard that on the news too."

"He called you ten days before he died. A few days later, you called the Carmichael house. Now it's burned to the ground, someone — probably Gordon — is dead, and you've been on the lam."

Lazlo stared at him in shock, his moist lips slack and his once-handsome dimpled chin quivering. "You're twisting this all around! You've decided I'm guilty, just like you did Rosten all those years ago, and you're not listening to a fucking word I'm saying!"

Green allowed a faint smile as he sat back in his chair, giving Lazlo a little more room to breathe. "Then tell me."

"I know!" Lazlo shut his eyes and took a deep breath. His jowls trembled. "I think I know who burned down the house, and why. And who killed Rosten too."

Voices could be heard whispering outside the interview door. Green leaned in, trying not to lose the moment. "Who?"

"Julia."

"Julia." Green held his gaze, masking his own astonishment as he processed the idea. Seductive, needy, changeable Julia? "You think Julia killed her own brother. And burned her house down. And killed Rosten."

"And she killed Jackie too!"

"Why would she do that?"

"Because she's a psycho! Rosten thought so too; that's what he called me about. He knew I'd gone out with her eons ago, and I was pretty tight with the family. He wanted to know what she was like and why I broke up with her."

Green felt a chill sweep over him. "And what did you tell him?"

"That she was way too possessive. She's all sweet on the outside but don't cross her. She used to go ballistic if I even looked at another girl. Sometimes she'd wait a whole month but she'd find a way to get even. Little things, so no one else would know it was her, but I knew."

"What kind of things?"

"Once a girl in our class got some pretty earrings from her parents for her sweet sixteen. All I did was tell her they looked nice, and suddenly they disappeared from her locker. A few days later a photo of them smashed into pieces turned up in her backpack."

"Sounds like twisted teenage stuff."

Lazlo raised his haunted eyes. "It was her biggest thrill. Next to — she liked her sex rough. Rough for the guy, that is, not for her." He broke off, shifting in his seat. "I was young and inexperienced. I didn't realize how twisted it was."

More whispering. New voices, among them Levesque. Green swore silently as he tried to keep focused. "Why didn't you tell police about any of this at the time?"

"Because she was never really violent, you know? Calculating, cruel even, but I never thought — I mean, it was her own sister! Besides, I thought she'd gotten over our breakup. She seemed cool with me and Jackie starting to date. At least ..." He grew quiet. Stared at his shaking hands. "She said she was cool with it."

"What was Rosten's reaction when you told him all this?"

"He was pretty quiet. He said it was very interesting and he was going to be at his cottage for a few days to sort all this out."

"Did he say he was going to contact Julia?"

"No. But when I heard he was dead, I freaked out. I phoned Gordon to ask if Julia had talked to Rosten. He didn't think so because Julia wasn't in town yet. But I was afraid somehow she'd gotten to Rosten anyway. I was scared I'd be next."

Green was already on his feet. Julia needed to be stopped. If Lazlo was telling the truth, she was teetering on the brink of total destruction. Nothing and no one in her path was safe. After a quick word to Peters, he headed out of the interview room.

He found the squad room swirling with excitement and Levesque on the phone. Her eyes lit at the sight of him.

"Sir, Staff Sergeant Sullivan is on the line and he says it's urgent. There's been another development."

"I've got the NCO out here with me, organizing a search and a street canvas," Sullivan said, once he'd filled Green in on the attack. "What can you tell us about this situation?"

Green was already signalling to Levesque to boot up a large-screen computer in the squad room. "No one else in the house?"

"No, but it's like a war zone here. Looks like someone else may be hurt. They got in a car."

Green's heart sank. "She's taken her mother. They were both staying there."

"Who?"

"Julia."

"What's she likely to do to her?"

"Kill her," Green said without hesitation.

"Jesus." Sullivan paused. "I've got you on speaker here, Mike. What are we dealing with? An EDP? Is the public at risk?"

"Absolutely. This is an extremely dangerous woman."

"Can you give us descriptions? And make of vehicle?"

Green had been watching Levesque click through links on the computer. "Pull up Navan on the sat map!" he told her before turning his attention back to Sullivan. "Julia Carmichael is a white female, about forty-five, short blonde hair …" He paused to picture her. "About 125 pounds, athletic build. Driving a white, late-model Hyundai Accent. You can get the plate from Enterprise Rent-A-Car. Wait a minute, are there any vehicles in the laneway?"

"Negative."

Green took rapid stock of the possibilities. Three small details stood out. First, given the chance, Julia would have killed her mother on the spot. Secondly, there was the trail of blood from the crime scene to the driveway. Thirdly, both vehicles — Julia's and Laura's — were gone from the drive. Green clung to the faint hope that Marilyn was still alive.

"I think Julia's chasing her, Brian."

"What's the other vehicle?"

"An old black Chevy pickup."

"Got it." After some mumbling in the background, Sullivan came back on the line. "The sergeant is passing that info on to the Comm Centre. We're looking at the sat view here, Mike."

"Me too." Green bent over to squint at the computer screen, tracing the network of roads emanating from the scene of the crime. Cars could be seen beetling back and forth along them, turning this way and that like an army of ants on the move. "There are several country roads, most paved but some not. Traffic will be light on them, unless she's travelling north toward Orleans or south toward the expressway to Montreal. Sergeant, can you station units at both access points?"

A woman's voice echoed over the speakerphone, crisp and focused. "Already in process. Any idea where she's likely to go?"

"My guess is Orleans," Green replied. "Easier to lose a pursuer in the maze of suburban streets than on the wide-open highway to Montreal. And there's a greater chance of encountering help. But that assumes she's thinking rationally. She's just seen her daughter slit her friend's throat." He broke off as a memory struck him. "Oh fuck! Brian, there's a handgun in the residence."

"*What*? What kind?"

"A .38 snubbie. It was in a metal box in ..." Green tried to concentrate through his rattled nerves. Jesus, why hadn't he insisted Laura secure it when he saw it? "Middle shelf of the kitchen pantry."

He heard clattering through cupboards, Sullivan's voice low and tense over the phone. "Box is open and empty. Was the gun loaded?"

"We have to assume it is," Green replied. "Sergeant, update the Comm Centre that the pursuing suspect should be considered armed and dangerous. And get a zone alert out to the OPP in case she heads for the city limits."

More banging and talking in the background. The clipped tone of orders. Trying to screen it out, Green stared at the map with its dozens of rush-hour cars buzzing along the roads around Navan. All driving too fast, all seemingly in pursuit.

Sullivan came back on the line. "We're just had a report from a neighbour about a black pickup driving like a bat out of hell out of town."

"No white car in pursuit?"

"Nope. But we've got uniforms out canvassing."

"What direction was it driving?"

"East along Colonial."

Green located the road, which headed east out of town but not toward either Orleans or the Montreal highway. Instead, it went further into the country, where there was nothing but back roads, farms, and bush. After thanking Sullivan, he hung up and continued to stare at the map. She had a small head start, but that old Chevy pickup would be no match for a nimble sub-compact, especially on the open road, even if Marilyn had the nerves of steel to push it to its limits.

Where are you, Marilyn? What's going through your mind? Are you panicked, horrified, or outraged?

She might be injured as well, he realized, and running out of time. In which case, what would she do? Try to get help? Or try to find someplace safe to hide and treat her wounds?

On impulse, he headed back to the interview room where he had left Lazlo. The man jumped to his feet, eyes wide as Green snapped his fingers at him. "Julia's on the run in Navan, Erik. Where might she or her mother go?"

Lazlo stared at him blankly.

"Think, Erik! You know the area. Somewhere private and off the beaten track." He pressed the point. "Are there any places close to Navan but isolated? A favourite place of the family, maybe?"

Lazlo whipped his head back and forth. "I don't know! It's years since I've been out there! It's all ploughed under by developers. I mean, we used to have our favourite places as kids. An old watering hole in the creek, a hilltop with a fire pit. But —"

Green hustled him down the hall into the squad room. "Show us!"

By this time, a small ring of detectives had congregated around the computer, watching the drama on the screen. Lazlo stood in silence a moment in front of the satellite map, trying to get his bearings. Green pointed out the Carmichael bungalow and Colonial Road, and circled the area to the east. Much of it was checkered with farm fields, interspersed with dark clumps of forest. Slowly Lazlo began to trace his finger along the roads, as if feeling his way back in time.

He tracked a creek, his finger hovering over a bend near a narrow track. "Here. We used to fish here. Swim. Make out."

"Did you go there with Julia?"

"Yes. And Jackie."

Green called Sullivan back. "Anything from the field?"

"Negative. So far no sightings on either of the expressways. But Dispatch just had a call about a couple of vehicles driving much too fast on County Road 8. The sergeant is sending a unit out there."

Green found County Road 8 on satellite. It ran east-west, not far from Lazlo's swimming hole. "Okay," he said to Sullivan. "I may have a lead. Try this location."

As he read out the coordinates over the phone, he watched Lazlo run his finger down another road. A dead end leading nowhere but scrub. Lazlo tapped the screen. "And this too! This is the hill with the old fire pit and fort."

Green squinted. He could just make out a clearing in thick trees. "Zoom in," he told Levesque. As the scene enlarged, he could distinguish an odd-looking smudge of grey and black that sat in the middle of the clearing. It was partially obscured by leaf cover, but the shape stirred a faint memory. He pointed with his finger. "What's this?"

"That's the stone foundation from an old homestead on the hill. We used to imagine it was a fort to defend against the Iroquois."

A fort, Green thought. *Like a last stand against impossible odds.* "Do you think Julia's mother knew about it?"

"Oh yeah, she did a painting of it once."

The memory fell into place. Marilyn Carmichael's vibrant painting depicting an old stone chimney against a sunny backdrop of daisies and clover. Once proudly displayed over the mantle, but later relegated to a dark hall corner of the bungalow.

Sullivan's voice crackled through the phone line again. "Mike? The sergeant just got a call from her inspector. He's lining up a helicopter and the Tac team."

Green fed him the new coordinates. "Tell him this location is a priority! If Marilyn's wounded and losing strength, she may be trying to hole up." *Or else she's making one last stand*, he thought. "Don't forget there's a gun!"

"That's why the Tac team. Things are really heating up here, Mike, so I'm going to sign off. If you come up with anything else —"

After Green hung up, excited conversations broke out in the squad room as the detectives continued to gather. Filtering out the noise, and his own fears, Green stared at the map. After all Marilyn had endured, to die this way, alone and cornered by her own daughter, was beyond thinking about. The countryside was so huge and the tree cover so dense that, even with half a dozen cruisers crisscrossing the roads and helicopters overhead, two lone women might be impossible to find.

He sent Lazlo home. He paced. Cursed his inaction on the gun. What if Julia had seen him handling it?

Goddamn!

Time crept forward. He checked with Dispatch. Checked his phone. Called the hospital for updates. Laura Quinn was still in surgery, still critical. MacPhail was still working on the human remains. Finally, his phone rang. Julia's white Hyundai had been located parked off the road near the base of the hill where the old homestead was located.

"We're on our way there now," Sullivan said.

"Any sign of Laura Quinn's truck? Or …?"

"Nothing. No sign or sound of human activity. We're waiting for the Tac team's go-ahead and then the guys will move in."

Green bit back his impatience. A proper tactical operation took planning. "Any sign of injury, blood, or other tire tracks?"

"There are a lot of tire tracks. No damage to the vehicle, but there are what appears to be blood smears on the steering wheel and upholstery."

"Okay, secure it and I'll get Ident —"

"Already done, Mike. Things are moving really fast here, better get some extra Ident and maybe Major Crimes personnel lined up on standby, for whatever we find at the top of that hill."

Sullivan's last words rang ominous in his ears. *Don't even think about it*, he told himself as he hung up. Finally there was something he could do besides stand around and pace. He bounded down the stairs toward the main floor and was just passing through the lobby toward the Ident lab when a commotion at the front doors caused him to turn.

Marilyn Carmichael was limping across the checkered floor, her head rigidly high and her arms cradling her side. Blood covered her clothes and seeped onto the tiles. Ignoring the officers who rushed to intercept her, she fixed her sights on Green. Her eyes were huge. Haunted. Black with grief.

"It's done," was all she said.

CHAPTER TWENTY-ONE

They found Julia's body on the hilltop, slumped at the base of the stone fireplace. The saplings and wildflowers within the foundation walls were trampled and bloodied, as if a hurricane of rage had ripped through, but Julia had died from a neat bullet between the eyes. Marilyn had left the pistol on the top of the fieldstone wall by Julia's head and had walked away without concern for the trail of evidence she left behind.

Sullivan assigned Gibbs to manage the investigation into Julia's death, and within hours the scientists were all hard at work at the scene. Ident teams were busy retrieving fingerprints from the pistol and blood samples from the site of the old homestead as well as Julia's car. MacPhail, complaining that Green's body count was now so high he wouldn't get to Julia until next week, delegated her autopsy to a junior associate.

No one was disputing how Julia died, nor at whose hand. Green and Sullivan took a peek at Ident's photos of the gunshot wound and privately concurred from the stippling pattern that she'd likely been shot from less than three feet away, with the muzzle close but not directly against the skin.

Self-defence, or execution?

Marilyn herself had been whisked from the police station to the hospital to undergo surgery for a stab wound to the abdomen that had missed her liver by millimetres. Since her initial statement in the middle of the police station lobby, she had barely spoken a word, and when Gibbs was finally granted permission by her doctors for a preliminary interview, he found her uninterested and unco-operative, answering only in shrugs and monosyllables.

"Have you any children?" she finally asked him. When he avoided the questions, she looked at him squarely and said, "Then you don't understand. None of this matters."

Gibbs returned to the station frustrated and cowed. "I'll try again, sir," he said gamely. "Give her some time to recover."

Green suspected time would change nothing. Marilyn had retreated to that dark, desolate place within herself where all ties that bound her to the outside world were gone.

And who could blame her?

It was nearly eight o'clock in the evening before Green and Sullivan had the tangled threads of the investigations sufficiently under control to leave the station. Just before Green shut down his computer, a memo from Superintendent Neufeld popped up in his email.

My office, 8 a.m. Monday morning.

He logged off before he could shoot back a reply he'd regret. His career was already in free fall. Neufeld had been conspicuously absent through most of the afternoon drama, closeted with senior brass on high-level planning. She was going to let him swing, and as if he didn't have enough on his plate, she'd given him the whole weekend to stew about it.

When he stumbled home to a late dinner, he was finally able to broach the subject of his father. To his immense gratitude, Sharon didn't hesitate. Of course he comes home, she said, and let's not leave him another day!

Green slept badly that night and was on his third cup of coffee the next morning, trying to summon the energy for the day, when his front doorbell rang. It was Saturday and he faced a long list of chores in preparation for his father's move. A rare interlude of peace and quiet had descended on the house. Hannah was still asleep and Sharon was in the backyard with the two little ones, ostensibly planting petunias. With great reluctance Green dragged himself to the door.

Cunningham stood on the doorstep, holding his laptop and two transparent evidence bags, through which Green could see a wad of twenty-dollar bills and a tiny security camera like the one found in Rosten's cottage. Cunningham's expression was deadpan, but something close to a smile twitched on his lips.

"We found these stashed in the back of the glove compartment of Julia Carmichael's rental car," he said. "The video's pretty damn interesting. Do you want to see it?"

In truth, Green wasn't sure he could stand watching how Rosten died. The thought of Julia savouring her victory turned his stomach. But this new human side of Cunningham, and his unexpected abandonment of protocol, deserved recognition. Green stepped back to invite him in.

"I'm guessing it shows how she tricked him into drinking the Scotch," Green said as he led the way through the kitchen to his sun-porch office, now in complete disarray.

"Not tricked," Cunningham replied, shoving aside boxes to set up his laptop. "Just made him an offer he couldn't refuse. She was happy to confess to the murder. Proud of it, in fact. Proud of outsmarting all the police and even her family."

He clicked through links until the familiar scene of Rosten's cottage living room filled the screen. Julia was entering through the patio door with the bottle of Scotch in her gloved hand. She was wearing dark pants and a hooded rain jacket, chosen, Green realized, not only to conceal but also to leave no fibres.

They bantered about welcome-home gifts, about the power of Facebook to reconnect old friends, about his accommodations courtesy of Her Majesty's government.

"Better you than me," she said with a smile. She fetched him a glass of water from the kitchen, offered it as a chaser to the single malt, and then lounged on the sofa as if settling in for a long chat.

"You'll get yours," Rosten's voice replied. The camera didn't pick him up, but occasionally the Scotch bottle filled the frame as he lifted it.

"You think so? No one has any idea. That dumb cop wouldn't know the truth if it whacked him on the head. No one did. Not my precious mother or her idiot husband, who thought Jackie was just this perfect little princess. Not that cheating dick Erik. I fooled them all."

"All except me," he said.

She leaned toward him. "But it took you a while. You thought it was Luke."

"Because that's what you wanted me to think. That's why you used his car and his belt."

"Red herring. A classic magician's sleight of hand."

The bottle raised. A sip. "Why me?"

"Actually, I would have liked to use Erik, but I thought it might splash back on me. He … knows things." She yawned. Stretched as if she were bored. "So when Jackie started blabbing on about you and your cottage, I thought, well, that works even better. Nobody would connect you to me. A couple of damning notes, the exam paper planted in her backpack. It was easy."

"So I was just … handy."

"And you liked her." Julia's lip curled in distaste.

"I barely *knew* her! There were three hundred kids in that class."

"But she was your teacher's pet. You thought you were such hot shit." She wagged her finger at him slyly. "And now you think you've outsmarted me. You think I don't know about that camera peeking out of your pocket?

"The camera isn't the thing," Rosten said. "Your being here is the thing. It's all the proof I need. And if you kill me, Inspector Green will —"

She rolled her eyes in scorn. "I'm not going to kill you. You're going to kill yourself. No camera, no incriminating marks on you, no troublesome murder clues for that dumb cop to pick up on. And me? I'm in Brockville. If I'm lucky, my car will even have a parking ticket. Easy enough to borrow another from the used car–lot guy who was too busy staring at my chest to ask questions. A nice SUV like Mum's, just to throw the cops off if they have doubts about your suicide."

When he didn't answer, a small frown creased her brow. "Drink up your Scotch."

"I like to savour it," he said. He was sounding a little slurred now, and Green wondered if she'd already slipped him the diazepam in the glass of water she'd brought.

"Does your daughter like Scotch?" she asked.

Silence. She waited. Growing impatient. "Because if you don't want it all, maybe I'll bring the rest to her. Paige, right? She looks like she could use the lift. That baby has her quite stressed out."

The Scotch bottle quivered in his upraised hand. "And if I drink it all?" he asked.

"Now you're getting the message," she said. "Smart man. You've lost."

"Have I?" The bottle lifted again, and she watched in silence as he drank. Gulping now, no longer savouring. After a few moments, the bottle clattered onto the floor. She rose and came forward, looming in the camera frame like a monster. She picked up the water glass and pulled the camera from his shirt. After slipping the glass into her pocket, she paused and in final triumph she panned the camera over him, slumped in his wheelchair, looking up at her through hooded eyes. His expression was unreadable. Fear, perhaps. Awe. But just before his eyes drifted shut, he smiled. A tiny, secret smile that Green suspected Julia did not even see.

After Cunningham left, Green sat in the kitchen a long time, unable to shake the memory of that smile. The one small moment of victory for the man whose entire life had been destroyed by the woman before him.

The melancholy still hung thick around him as he walked down the hospital corridor later that afternoon on his way to his father's room. He'd not planned to visit Marilyn, knowing he should let Gibbs have another try, but some indefinable bond drew him to her. Her privacy curtain was closed, and when he pulled it back, he found her sitting on the edge of her bed in her hospital-issue gown, her head bowed and her bare feet dangling. Every part of her seemed to droop. A thin IV tube snaked across the sheet to the stand by her bed.

She raised her head to look up at him. Eyes hollow. Bleached of life. "What do I say? Where do I begin?"

He paused. He wanted to tell her he wasn't here to talk but merely to offer support. But the words came as if of their own volition. "Wherever you want."

"I'm sorry hardly seems like enough for all the destruction I brought down upon the world."

"Not you. Julia."

She eyed him. "You're a father. You know what I mean."

"I know we bring them into the world and we try to give them a good start, but who they are and what they become ..." He shook his head. "We have surprisingly little say."

"But I conceived her, nourished her in my womb, nursed her at my breast, and she grew up to murder three people, including her own brother and sister."

"You couldn't have known that."

"Couldn't I? My mum warned me that Percy Mullenthorpe was no good, that he was cruel and vindictive, and that the beatings would only get worse. 'The Mullenthorpes are all a bad lot,' she said. 'Crooks and thugs.' If I had aborted Julia as my mum wanted, instead of stubbornly running off to Canada with him, none of those people would have died."

"Those same genes produced Jackie as well as Julia, Marilyn. We can't control what happens."

"I should have seen it."

Wincing at the effort, she began to ease herself back onto the bed. As she sank back amid the pillows, he tugged awkwardly at the sheet to cover her pallid thighs. She breathed in shallow bursts, holding her abdomen as she gathered the strength to continue.

"I knew Julia was different. Not happy or loving like Jackie. From the time she was a baby, she wouldn't let me hold her or comfort her. She lashed out if she was frustrated. If she didn't get what she wanted, she threw temper tantrums so ferocious she'd break things. She had her dad's cruel streak. She'd hit Gordon or steal his toys, just to make him cry, and then she'd laugh. I thought she was just jealous. I thought she was reacting to her father's violence. I even thought … perhaps … perhaps he did molest her after all and it made her twisted and manipulative just so she could survive. I read that's what happens with abused children. When her dad went on one of his rampages, she used to watch him. I thought it was fear in her eyes, but it wasn't. It was fascination. All those years, all the mean and thoughtless things she did, I kept telling myself she was unhappy."

"We don't know why she did all that, Marilyn. Your motherly instinct was probably correct. She was unhappy, jealous, and frightened."

She whipped her head back and forth against the pillow. Colour blotched her cheeks and sparks flashed in her eyes. "No. I was deluding myself. Trying to ascribe a normal child's feelings to explain her. No mother wants to think she's spawned a monster." She paused, weakened by her outburst, as if the word itself had sucked the strength from her. "That's what she was, Inspector. A monster. And I … I refused to see it."

He was silent a moment, letting her catch her breath while he turned her observation over in his mind. The truth was no one had seen it. Green had met plenty of cruel and vindictive people in his life, many sporting the meaningless diagnosis of anti-social personality disorder. The idea that Julia — scarcely more than a girl, troubled and victimized herself — was capable of the premeditated murder of her sister while at the same time setting up an innocent young professor had never crossed his mind.

"None of us saw it, Marilyn."

She eyed him grimly. "No. And now all my children are dead, my house is burnt to the ground, an innocent man has been murdered, and his family deprived of the future they should have had together." She hung her head, her voice a whisper. "That poor man. How do we even begin to make amends?"

He'd been asking himself the same question. Beyond the vindication of his name, beyond the inevitable financial compensation to his family, how could anything make up for the tragedy of Rosten's life?

Marilyn broke into his gloom. "I've been thinking. My land is worth a few hundred thousand. Now that Gordon and Julia are gone, what would I do with it? It's not much, I know. It doesn't make up for a father taken from them, but I was thinking I'd give it to his girls. Maybe they'll throw it in my face, but I hope they'll understand. I was a mother, I loved too much, and I'm sorry."

He thought of Paige, bewildered, overwhelmed, and fearing she too had spawned a monster. "It's an excellent idea, Marilyn, and I don't think Paige will throw it in your face. She's a mother too."

A ghost of a smile flitted across her face. "Good. That's settled." She sat reflecting a moment and slowly her face crumpled. "But there's so much more. Laura, my poor, dear friend…"

"She's going to be all right."

"All right?" A bitter laugh died in her throat. "She will live that awful moment for the rest of her life. I brought that monster into her home, and she, like all of us, didn't see its true shape. She made the mistake of remarking on the gasoline smell in her clothes and asking if she wanted her to drop them in the wash."

Marilyn pressed her eyes shut. "Julia thought I was out. She used the butcher knife, and if I hadn't walked in ..."

"You saved Laura's life, at great risk to your own."

She shrugged off the comment. "I had to. I had smelled the gasoline on her clothes the day before too. When the fire chief told me it was arson, I realized Julia had set the fire. She knows no limits when she wants something, but I thought she just wanted the money." She broke off, trembling and overcome.

Outside in the hall, soft-shoed staff bustled to and fro amid the chatter of the hospital PA system, but inside the room a hush descended. Green waited her out. He reached over to squeeze her hand but she jerked it away.

"I knew she'd burned my house down, and still I made excuses for her."

"You took the blame for her."

She nodded. "I'd already lost one daughter. So I protected the only one I had left — my damaged, frightened, hurting child. Until the body was discovered. I knew right away it was Gordon, because he was still in the house when I left to meet Laura. But I thought, maybe Julia didn't know he was there. Maybe it was an accident.

Still making excuses! But when I rushed back to Laura's house, I found Laura with her throat slit …"

She rocked herself, cradling her bandaged side as if to keep the pain contained. Gradually her breathing slowed and her eyes grew bleak. "I suppose you need to know what happened."

"Not me. In due course Detective Gibbs will take your statement, when you're stronger and have a chance to consult a lawyer."

"None of that matters. There is nothing left for me but to tell the story, for all those victims who no longer have a voice. For Lucas, whom I doubted when I shouldn't have." Her voice thickened. "Julia took those photos, not Luke. She'd been taking nude photos of Gordon and Jackie for years, a sick little hobby she kept secret from us all. She told me all about it when she found me up at the old stone ruins. She said she had lots of hiding places in the basement and she burned the house down when Gordon found some of the evidence and she had to kill him. I … I think Gordon knew something. Or suspected. I heard him asking her where she was staying the night Rosten died. But even he could hardly believe … until it was too late."

Earlier, MacPhail had confirmed what Marilyn already knew — that it was Gordon whose body was in the basement, dead before the fire even started. Green's thoughts raced ahead, past her endless loop of self-recrimination, past Gordon's death. Dreading the answer, he asked the question nonetheless. "Did Julia have the gun, Marilyn?"

At first, it was as if she hadn't heard him. "She had to brag, Julia always had to brag, even when it got her into trouble. She didn't know I'd taken the gun before I ran from the house. She had the butcher knife and I was bleeding and older and smaller. I told her Gordon had died in the fire and asked her if she knew he was there. I was still hoping it was an accident — I guess it was my last little bit of blindness. She said, 'Oh damn, didn't he burn to a crisp?' That's when the last bit of veil fell away. Her tone, her contempt — it was like the monster had finally dropped her act. I realized —"

Her voice broke. She gasped for air. "I realized, oh dear God, it was Julia all along! I asked how could she let that poor professor take the blame? And she turned all soft. 'It all just got away from me, Mummy. You know me and my temper. Jackie and I were out at Morris Island, working on her project, and she started talking about how this professor had offered to tutor her and how his cottage was right near here. I don't know what happened, I just saw red. Everyone always loves Jackie. Erik, this professor, Luke, you. I just flipped out, and next thing I knew, Jackie was dead. I got scared and I tried to cover it up, but I just got myself in deeper and deeper.'"

Green listened without interruption, but he was checking off the inconsistencies in Julia's account. The note Rosten's wife had found, purportedly from Jackie, arranging to meet him at the cottage, which ensured he would be near the scene. The exam paper with its damning invitation, which had been found in her backpack. Lucas's belt. And most of all, Julia's triumphant admission to Rosten, which clearly showed how she planned it all.

"Did you believe her?"

"Not a word. Julia lies as easily and convincingly as she breathes. I do believe she was jealous of Jackie, especially over Erik, but even over Luke and me. Everyone did love Jackie. She was lovable. Julia was not. It made me feel so guilty. What mother doesn't love her own child? But as for the rest of her tale — the blackout, being scared, the plea for my understanding — that's all self-serving fabrication."

Green nodded. Waited.

Marilyn sucked in more air. "I'm sure she thought her act would work as it always had, but I'd reached the end. I had created a monster, and it had cost me everything I love in this world. My children, my husband, my house. My whole reason for being! I got to my feet and I started walking toward her. '"Who are you?' I asked. 'What do you mean?' she said. I pointed the gun at her and said, 'We're going to the police.' She laughed, 'You won't pull the trigger. I'm your daughter.' 'You killed my daughter,' I said, 'and my son.' 'What are you going to do,' she asked, 'take me to your pet inspector?' '"No,' I said.

"And I pulled the trigger."

The sentence hung in the silence, deafening. With it hung two unspoken questions. *Did she come at you? Did you fear for your life?* This time he did not dare ask either.

* * *

Green returned home from the hospital to find Sullivan waiting, full of purpose and armed with a wheelchair, grab bars, and commode from the Canada Care Medical supply store, as well as a gallon of bright yellow paint. By dinnertime, the little add-on sunroom had been transformed from home-office-cum-junk-room into a cheery bedroom, just in time for his father's arrival.

He knew he was running out of time, because his father was still refusing to eat, but he was hoping the noisy affection of his family and the cheerful view of the garden would give him renewed hope. Unlike Marilyn, a reason to go on.

The struggle to get his father into the house and settled into bed took every spark of Green's depleted energy. Sid had turned down dinner, but Sharon tried to assuage Green's fears with murmured reassurance about the disruption to his routine and his need for time to adjust.

What routine? Green wanted to shout. The routine where he's on his way to dying? But he nodded emptily and clung to the one bright moment of the evening. Sid, after snapping at everyone who came near enough, smiled when the dog came into the room and stole a piece of cheese off his plate. Like many Holocaust survivors, his father was afraid of dogs, but here, in his son's house, surrounded by the love of family, would it be Modo who lured him back from the brink?

Throughout the evening, Hannah was uncharacteristically subdued. She had phoned in sick to work, ostensibly to help settle her grandfather into the house, but afterwards, she had retreated to her room and the cocoon of her music. At midnight, long after the rest of the household had gone to bed and Green was sitting alone in the living room nursing a Scotch and trying to unwind, she appeared in the doorway.

She hovered there, as if uncertain whether she wanted to commit.

He forced a smile. "Going to bed, honey?"

"I don't understand how she could do it."

Green shut his eyes. He was exhausted, in no mood to discuss the psychology of evil. "We're not meant to understand, honey."

"How do you do it, Dad? How do you deal with these awful, twisted people and investigate all the terrible things they do to each other, and keep your sanity? How do you not slit your own throat?"

He opened his eyes again, recognizing the doubt and fear in her question. Hannah was studying criminology with the hopes of becoming a police officer herself, but she was now questioning the emotional cost.

"Come here," he said, patting the sofa beside him. She entered the room but perched on the armchair nearest the door. "You build walls," he said. "Between your job and your home. Between your eight-hour shift and the rest of your life. You surround yourself with things that make you healthy and happy. A family, good friends, a proper home you can feel good in, and a hobby that frees your mind and lets you blow off steam."

"You don't have a hobby."

He gave her a wan smile. "I don't always follow my own advice. But watching Tony play soccer, taking Aviva down a slide, sharing music with you ..."

She shot him a glance. "Even Avenged Sevenfold?"

A lump formed in his throat. He paused, unsure how much sentiment they could both handle. "Even Avenged Sevenfold."

She fell silent but he could see her thinking. Wrestling with something more.

"Most people, even the ones we deal with, have heart," he said. "They're just desperate or angry or foolish. Hurt, lonely, bitter, screwed over by life ... you can usually see a reason. That's another way I cope. Never lose sight of their humanity."

"But how could she kill her own sister? Her own brother? I get the jealousy and the temper; I know what that's like. But I was looking at Aviva and Tony tonight and no matter how mad I might get ... how does she just snuff them out? Deliberately?"

"Because she's not like us, honey. She doesn't feel. She doesn't love."

"My head gets that. But my heart ... how could she feel nothing? Even a dog gets upset when someone is in pain."

"Most of us, even dogs, are hard-wired to mirror feelings. We laugh when others do; we feel fear and sadness when we see it in others. Psychopaths seem to be missing that hard-wiring. They only learn to play-act."

"You think she was a psychopath?"

It was the question he'd been pondering all evening. "I knew she was manipulative and often deceitful. I knew she played people to get what she wanted. But I looked into her eyes a hundred times during the past twenty years and never saw the fundamental sham. The fake neediness that wormed through my defences, the play-acting at grief and sympathy. I never saw the emptiness. It's scary to think there is nothing inside there that we can touch or understand. No common human bond. Nothing that stops them from using us. Some people call that evil, but pure psychopathy is actually a tragedy."

"Yeah. For everyone else!"

He nodded. "That too. But the flaw is probably mostly in their genes, a missing humanity if you like, that keeps them from feeling and linking with others. Reminding myself of that, even when I feel like ripping their head off, helps me to cope as well."

She scowled. "But we still have to hold them accountable. We can't use this so-called missing humanity to excuse them."

"That's the difference between law and psychology. Between my job and Sharon's. We don't need to take sides. Both are important, both play their part in making society fair." He rose to pull her to her feet and hugged her close. "If it's what you decide, you'll make a great cop. But you've got years to think about it."

He watched her climb the stairs to bed, her steps lighter now, and then he went to pour himself a rare second Scotch. The truth was, the walls were often breached, and he'd never known a cop who didn't struggle now and then with the depravity they encountered. Many people, even the ostensibly law-abiding, had a touch of the psychopath in them. They conned and swindled and lied for their own gain. They shrugged off the suffering of others, even beat their loved ones without a qualm.

But pure psychopathy was a rare and elusive beast: master of deception and illusion, terrifying in its absence of soul.

It was those shape-shifters living among us as innocent school children, sons and daughters, who are the hardest to recognize. The hardest to trap. Marilyn Carmichael and James Rosten had both paid a terrible price in their attempt to take on the monster. For Marilyn, it meant facing her own guilt and cutting out the poison that was part of her. Rosten had paid with his very life, but that choice had been a deliberate one. He had known he might not survive, but he had already lost his dreams, his health, and his freedom to her. His life was all he had left to barter.

Green sipped his Scotch and thought about his meeting with Neufeld on Monday. Wondered what price he would pay, beyond sleepless nights and haunting self-doubts, for his own part in the destruction the monster had wrought.

ACKNOWLEDGEMENTS

There are many stages in the journey of a book from ethereal concept to final product. Along the way, authors are indebted to many who voluntarily contribute expertise, creative input, or critiquing to make it better. At the earliest stage of my research into *None So Blind*, Dan Haley, Executive Director of the Peterborough Community Chaplaincy, shared his invaluable insight, compassion, and experience with prisoners and parolees, and later Don Wadel, Executive Director of the John Howard Society of Ottawa, provided information about procedures in half-way houses. Thank you as well to Ursula Lebana of Spy Tech in Toronto for her expertise in security cameras.

The police have always willingly shared their expertise. I'd like to thank Constable Eric Booth of the Ontario Provincial Police for his knowledge of historical policing, Inspector Don Sweet of the Ottawa Police Service for his expertise in forensics and police pursuits, and especially, as always, my friend Mark Cartwright of the Ottawa Police Service for his ongoing advice, feedback, and support. And thanks to Sheila Minogue-Carver and the Navan Streetwalkers for giving me the perfect location. Any factual inaccuracies in the representation of official procedure or geography, whether accidental or intentional for dramatic purposes, are mine alone.

I am privileged to have a wonderful critiquing group, The Ladies Killing Circle — five talented writers and lifelong friends who provide not just insightful feedback but also wine, hugs, and laughter as needed. Huge thanks to Joan Boswell, Vicki Cameron, Mary Jane Maffini, Sue Pike, and Linda Wiken.

I am indebted to my publisher, Dundurn Press, for its staunch commitment to Canadian writers and stories and for its continued belief in my work. I'd like to thank Kirk Howard, Beth Bruder, Margaret Bryant, and the whole team from editing to marketing, for their enthusiastic assistance and support. In particular, a special thanks to my editor, Dominic Farrell, and my publicist, Jim Hatch.

A writer's life is solitary, and without friends and family, it's possible to go days without human contact beyond the characters in our head. Thanks to my sister, my children, my mother, and my friends, for everything!

FROM THE SAME SERIES

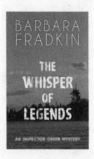

The Whisper of Legends
An Inspector Green Mystery
Barbara Fradkin

When Inspector Michael Green's teenage daughter goes missing on a wilderness canoe trip, he enlists the help of his long-time friend, Staff Sergeant Brian Sullivan, to accompany him to the Northwest Territories to look for her. Green soon discovers his daughter lied to him. The trip was organized not by a reputable tour company but by her new boyfriend, Scott. When clues about Scott's past begin to drift in, Green, Sullivan, and two guides head into the wilderness. After the body of one of the group turns up at the bottom of a cliff, they begin to realize just what is at stake.

Beautiful Lie the Dead

An Inspector Green Mystery

Barbara Fradkin

Inspector Green explores a web of betrayal and deceit. In the dead of night, the phone rings in the missing persons unit of the Ottawa Police. A brutal blizzard is howling, and a wealthy social activist has not heard from his fiancée in over twenty-four hours. Friends, family, and police are mobilized to search the snowbound city. He comes to believe that his partner is fleeing for her life, possibly from his own family. When a frozen body is found in the snow, just blocks from the man's home, Green knows that someone is conspiring to keep the truth hidden.

Available at your favourite bookseller

Visit us at

Dundurn.com | @dundurnpress | Facebook.com/dundurnpress
Pinterest.com/dundurnpress